ORION RISING

THE ORION WAR – BOOK 3

M. D. COOPER

M.D.C

The ISF is glad to have you aboard!

SPECIAL THANKS

Just in Time (JIT) & Beta Reads

John Piper
Alastar Wilson
Phil Schlenger
Chris J. Pike

Cover Art by Laércio Messias
Editing by Amy DuBoff & Jen McDonnell

TABLE OF CONTENTS

FOREWORD

Here we are at last.

The Orion War has begun in earnest with the Hegemony Fleet's arrival in the New Canaan System. Tanis will be forced to bring all her might to bear against these aggressors—as she has done so often in the past.

There is, however, a part of the story that you may not have heard, as it has been revealed only in expanded content—namely Destiny Rising, and The Gate at the Grey Wolf Star.

If you're not familiar with Destiny Rising, it is an extended version of Outsystem and A Path in the Darkness that re-integrates parts of the story that I had removed, so as to not leave too many threads open over the years.

There are a few chapters in that book that provide clues as to Myrrdan's origins, and explain why he has abilities that even Bob has trouble dealing with.

The Gate at the Grey Wolf Star is a novella that released on the same day as Orion Rising. It begins the story of what happened to Jessica and the crew of *Sabrina* during the nine years they were missing (between when they were approaching the Transcend's dwarf star mining operation, and when they jumped into New Canaan).

While I certainly don't expect you to sit down with the tome that is Destiny Rising, you may want to pick up The Gate at the Grey Wolf Star, and read it before you start reading Orion

Rising. It's a really fun ride, and the first of six novellas I'm creating in a series called The Perseus Gate.

However, if you really can't bear the idea of waiting one more minute before you find out what happened after the end of New Canaan, you can dive right in. I took care to write the story so that it works without having to take the side-quests. There is also a new section below to refresh you as to where we are in the tale.

As always, to get the latest news and access to free novellas and short stories, sign up on the Aeon 14 mailing list: www.aeon14.com/signup

M. D. Cooper

PREVIOUSLY IN THE ORION WAR...

When last we left Tanis and the colonists, many events were rapidly unfolding...

To begin with, over the past eighteen years, Tanis and the New Canaan colonists had built up a powerful space force by growing ships within moons using their picotech.

When the Transcend Space Force arrived, ready to use force to secure New Canaan's picotech and their stasis shields, Tanis deployed her fleet under the cover of their advanced stealth systems, waiting to strike if necessary.

After the initial round of negotiations, Sera's father, President Jeffrey Tomlinson, had realized exactly who and what Helen was, and forcibly removed the AI from Sera's mind.

Tanis infiltrated the Transcend fleet's flagship, the Galadrial, to rescue Sera. On the bridge of that ship, Elena (Sera's lover over the last eighteen years), revealed herself to be an agent of the Orion Guard, and killed Sera's father.

Kent, a colonel in the Orion Guard—who was on a mission to kill and capture as much of the Transcend and New Canaan leadership as possible—attempted to kill Tanis, but failed.

During these events, Tanis's fleet (the ISF) revealed itself, and forced the Transcend fleet (the TSF) to stand down. The danger appeared to have passed, when word came in that a Hegemony (also known as the AST) fleet had arrived at the edge of the system, and was attacking the Transcend ships interdicting New Canaan.

Adding fuel to the fire, *Sabrina* (Sera's old ship) jumped into the New Canaan system, causing a new AI, calling itself Myriad, to take control of the TSF fleet and send them to destroy *Sabrina*.

* * * * *

What you may not have known…

Back in Sol, before Tanis ever joined the *Intrepid*'s mission, Myrrdan met with a strange entity that altered him in a fashion that facilitated his infiltration of the *Intrepid*.

Myrrdan assumed and subverted many people on the *Intrepid* over the years, and led Tanis and the mission leadership to believe that they had killed him on Victoria.

But what they (and you, unless you read The Gate at the Grey Wolf Star) didn't know, is that when Nance got her nano upgraded by that oh-so-kind medtech on the *Intrepid*, she was taken over by Myrrdan.

Myrrdan later directed Nance to meet with the same entity that altered him back in Sol five thousand years ago. She encountered it on Senzee station, where it revealed itself as The Caretaker, burned Myrrdan out of Nance, and sent her to seek out the rest of Myrrdan's subsumed humans, and cleanse them as well.

In turn making them into agents of The Caretaker…

* * * * *

We begin Orion Rising after Tanis has ordered Joe to save *Sabrina* at any cost, while dealing with the fact that she has effectively taken part in what could be considered a coup.

TO WAR

STELLAR DATE: 03.27.8948 (Adjusted Years)
LOCATION: ISF *Hellespont*
REGION: Roma-Normandy L1 Point, New Canaan System

The connection with Tanis closed, and Joe rose from the *I2*'s command chair, issuing orders in rapid-fire succession.

"Helm, light it up, full burn to intercept *Sabrina.* Comm, raise them. Tell Cargo he needs to boost and match our vector so we can grab them cleanly. Scan, have the TSF ships powered up their weapons?"

"Aye, Captain," Ensign Karl replied from the helm, as he worked with Bob to bring the *I2*'s four stern fusion engines to full burn, while also spooling out the nozzle for the antimatter-pion drive.

"I've sent a hail, Captain" Lieutenant Ripley said from comm. "They're twenty light-minutes away, but with our boost, we should get a response in about thirty-five minutes."

"Lieutenant Ferris?" Joe asked the officer who led the scan team.

"Sorry, yes, sir. We're correlating with the rest of the fleet. There are a lot of TSF ships out there. So far, none have powered up weapons—though they all have shields online."

"What's going on?" Amanda asked from her auxiliary station. "The transmission from Admiral Greer on the *Galadrial* told the TSF fleet to stand down."

"Tanis just sent me a data-burst," Joe said lowering his voice. "This still barely makes sense…. For starters, it looks like President Tomlinson took Helen out of Sera, and then killed her."

"Wait—What? He killed Sera?"

"No," Joe replied with a shake of his head, "he killed Helen."

<*Oh dear,*> Priscilla said over the bridge net. <*She was…a very special person.*>

Joe continued reviewing the data-burst from Tanis. "Then Sera was going to kill her father, but Tanis stopped her—oh, shit…Elena killed him. She was a Guard agent!"

"OK, that's nuts, but it still doesn't explain why the TSF ships are going after *Sabrina*," Amanda said.

"While I was talking to Tanis, another AI showed up and butted in," Joe said with a frown. "She said her name was Myriad, and that she was a shard of Airtha, just like Helen."

<*Ohhhhhh…*> Priscilla said. <*OK, now that makes some sense…sort of…*>

"What's a shard of Airtha?" Joe asked.

<*Helen was a shard of a greater AI—sort of,*> Bob responded. <*That AI's name is Airtha.*>

"Isn't that the name of the Transcend's capital?" Joe asked.

<*It is,*> Priscilla replied. <*I guess they have some sort of huge AI—kinda like Bob—that runs it.*>

<*Airtha is nothing like me,*> Bob said. <*She is the Not-AI.*>

Joe set aside his suspicions about what a 'Not-AI' was and asked the more pertinent question, "So…Myriad, who is a shard of the Not-AI, Airtha, has taken over the Transcend ships? Is that the outflow of this?"

"Yes, sorry I just dumped all that on you. Things are nuts here," Tanis said as she appeared in a holoprojection. "Though, I didn't know about the whole 'Not-AI' thing."

<*I had made an agreement with Helen not to discuss her nature with anyone so long as she did not bring harm to our people,*> Bob said, his mental tone almost angry. <*She has violated that accord with this attack on Sabrina. It would take long to tell you, but suffice it to say that Airtha, who is a massive, multi-nodal intelligence, similar to myself, was once human. I do not yet know her full story,*

but she was extracted, and her neural net was imprinted on an AI's analog net. This happened millennia ago. She is now nearly ascended, and I do not fully understand her designs.>

"Well, she has designs on *Sabrina*, that's for sure," Tanis said.

<*Finaeus knows something that Airtha does not wish Sera—or perhaps you—to know,*> Bob said. <*However, I believe I know it, too. Though I am eager for the confirmation.*>

"Captain Evans, we won't make it in time," Ensign Karl said from the helm. "The TSF has fast interceptors that are outpacing our ships."

"Damnit!" Tanis swore. "We don't have any of those in the fleets here—their stealth systems weren't ready yet."

"The *Daedalus* is close to where *Sabrina* has exited, sir, ma'am. I believe they could beat the TSF ships to *Sabrina*," Lieutenant Ferris offered.

"Do it, Lieutenant," Joe said, not waiting for Tanis's approval.

"You beat me to it," Tanis said with a wan smile. "Light-lag is starting to hit. I'll just slow you down. Do what you have to, but if you have to take out any TSF ships, try to be non-destructive. We're going to need their help against that fleet coming insystem—once it finishes with Isyra's fleet out past the heliopause."

"Do you think you can get control back from this Airtha shard?" Joe asked.

"We're too far out of range to be effective. Once we fix what the Orion Guard broke on the *Galadrial*, we'll follow after. Until then, Bob, do what you can to get Myriad under control."

"Wait, Orion?" Joe asked.

"Yeah, their guy is the reason I need a new arm," Tanis said. "Go, I'll see you soon."

<I am attempting to converse with the AIs on the TSF ships,> Bob said. *<I have only gotten through to two of them—the others have all rebuffed my attempts. They are…under duress.>*

"That doesn't sound good," Joe said.

<It does not…AIs within the Transcend are limited in general. Not like those in the Inner Stars—it is more of a shackling, and less a lack of awareness. I now believe it has been Airtha's doing all along. She has ensured that when the time came, she could force her will upon them.>

"How could that even happen?" asked Joe. "An entire civilization's AIs under the control of one being?"

<It is deplorable,> Bob said in agreement.

Joe noticed that the AI did not offer any explanation as to how such a thing could be achieved. He decided not to pursue it for now. Pushing those larger moral issues from his mind, he brought up the space surrounding the New Canaan System on the bridge's main holotank.

New Canaan's ISF fleets were bracketing the TSF ships as they raced toward *Sabrina*'s position—over three hundred million kilometers away. The ISF fleet greatly outnumbered the Transcend ships, but most were little more than hulls with engines. Many did not even have functional weapons arrays, and even fewer were crewed by more than half a dozen people.

If it came to an all-out fight, New Canaan would win, but the cost would be high. And with the AST fleet bearing down on them from outside the system, they were going to need all the ships they could get for the colony to survive.

"Colonel Espensen," Joe addressed the *I2*'s XO, Rachel Espensen. She stood amidst the scan team's consoles, reviewing their data on the TSF fleet's weapons. When Joe called out, her head snapped up.

"Yes, Admiral?"

"You're getting a field promotion to Brigadier General. I am hereby placing you in command of the *I2*. With Admiral Richards out of communications range, I am assuming FleetConn."

A smile broke out across Rachel's face and she snapped off a sharp salute. "Yes, Fleet Admiral!"

A few of the scan techs nearby gave her brief congratulations before she directed them back to their tasks and approached Joe. "Command tokens accepted. I have the conn, sir."

"Very good, Captain Espensen, the chair is yours. I'll take the auxiliary comm station as my Fleet CIC," Joe replied.

"Yes, sir," Captain Espensen said as she took the command chair and re-arranged the holo interfaces to her liking. It wasn't Rachel's first time in the chair; she had been in command of the *I2* when it had risen from Roma's clouds to show the TSF fleet what they were really up against.

However, this was her first time in the chair as the *I2*'s captain, and Joe couldn't help but feel her infectious joy. Rachel Espensen—who he still remembered from her first day at his Fleet Academy over back at The Kap, who had proven herself with distinction and valor in the battle over Victoria, and again at Bollam's World—was now captain of the most powerful ship known to humanity.

She was already calling out orders and reviewing the status of the ship's shields and weapons systems, allowing Joe to focus on the fleet at large. He may not have possessed Tanis's otherworldly ability to spread her mind across the ships, but he knew a thing or two about getting ready for a fight.

HONEY, WE'RE HERE!

STELLAR DATE: 03.27.8948 (Adjusted Years)
LOCATION: *Sabrina*
REGION: Near Roma, New Canaan System

"What the…?!" Jessica exclaimed from the pilot's seat on *Sabrina*'s bridge. "Is there some sort of party going on here that we didn't know about?"

"What is it?" Cargo asked.

Jessica responded by throwing the system scan up on the holotank.

"Look at that jovian…Roma," she said. "There are thousands of ships around it!"

"Is it Orion?" Cargo asked anxiously.

Jessica didn't blame him for being worried. They had just spent nine years avoiding the Orion Guard; if they had risked everything to get to New Canaan, and Orion had beat them—if Cheeky and Piya…. It didn't bear thinking about.

"Get us over there, max burn," Cargo ordered. "Not sure what we can do, but that's where the action is."

"You got it, boss," Jessica said, and increased the flow of Helium-3 and Deuterium into the ship's huge fusion torches. "We're dry on antimatter after that gate-run, so the burners will have to do."

"Understood," Cargo replied before addressing the rest of the crew over the Link. <*Nance, make sure the SC batts are recharged, and Trevor, make sure the kinetics are reloaded. We may be going in hot.*>

<*Hot?*> Nance asked. <*We **did** get to New Canaan, didn't we? Not on the far end of the galaxy, right?*>

<*We made it,*> Cargo replied, <*but there's a pair of big fleets in some sort of standoff.*>

<*Out of the fire and into the damn reactor, then…*> Nance sighed.

<*What else is new?*> Jessica asked.

"I have a better picture of the fleets at Roma," Misha said from the scan console. He passed the updated view to the main holotank. "That one there looks like that ship you guys used to be on…the *Intrepid*. Except it's bigger…and has more guns…and more engines…and more…everything."

"Shiiit," Jessica whispered. "That does look like the *Intrepid*! But yeah, it's more everything."

<*Sabrina, Misha, I've supplied you with the ISF's friend-or-foe signatures. You should be able to tell which ships are theirs,*> Iris, Jessica's AI, offered.

<*Got it; matching IFF signatures,*> Sabrina said. <*It* ***is*** *the Intrepid. The bigger fleet is Intrepid Space Force, and I believe the smaller fleet is Transcend.*>

"Wow, and I thought *we* got up to a lot of shit the last decade," Jessica said. "But that has to be at least ten thousand ships. Tanis has been busy."

"I'm just glad we got here before they started shooting at each other," Finaeus said from his seat at the back of the bridge. "A bit later than we'd hoped, but not too bad overall."

Jessica spun the pilot's seat around and fixed Finaeus with a level stare. "A bit later? Your little jump-gate shortcut added nearly ten years to our return. For fuck's sakes, Fin…"

"Easy now," Cargo said softly. "We made it back, that's what matters."

Jessica blushed. "Sorry, today just really hasn't gone according to plan. First, Costa Station; and now this. I figured that we'd ride in like heroes; there'd be a parade, pretty men and women lining the streets, you know, the works. Not…whatever it is that's going on here."

<*Recriminations aside, the ship-count is closer to twenty thousand,*> Sabrina replied. <*There are so many, it's taking a bit to*

pick out their signatures. Just when I think I have a count, they move around and I spot a few more.>

"Sabrina, do you see those readings from out at the edge of the system?" Misha asked. "Something is going on out there, too."

"What the hell has Tanis gotten into?" Jessica swore. "I leave them alone for just a few years…"

"I don't think it's Orion out there, either," Misha said. "The shield signatures are wrong. From what I have in the databases…I think those are AST ships out there."

"The Hegemony is in the Transcend?" Cargo whistled. "Things really have gone to pot."

"It's what I feared," Finaeus said. "Orion has set things in motion—the Transcend is no longer a secret."

"Gonna take a bit for word to get around," Cargo said. "And even so, a lot of people won't believe it."

No one spoke for a few minutes as *Sabrina* boosted toward Roma, and the two fleets clustered around its L1 point.

Jessica found herself wishing for a cup of coffee, and within seconds, Trevor appeared with a tray of beverages and sandwiches for the bridge team.

"We didn't get much time to eat before we jumped here," he said. "And I bet we're gonna get real busy real soon, so chow down while you can—last of the bread, too."

"Thanks, man," Misha said as he leaned across his console and snatched a PB&J off the tray when Trevor passed by.

"Misha, seriously, get your ass up, and get one like everyone else," Trevor admonished.

Jessica noticed how everyone seemed focused, resolute. She wondered if they were all as torn up as she was about Cheeky and Piya. Maybe they weren't allowing themselves to think about it. Not yet; not until they had delivered Finaeus, and were safe.

She rose and planted a kiss on Trevor's cheek before grabbing a ham sandwich and pouring a black cup of coffee. Though Trevor's sandwiches technically passed as food—despite Nance's insistence to the contrary—Jessica was looking forward to a real meal on the *Intrepid* soon. "Thanks, hon. What would we do without you?"

"Dunno…prolly fly into battle on empty stomachs and not be able to hear comm traffic over your grumbling tummies," he said with a smile and a shrug.

"My stomach's going to grumble anyway," Finaeus said after taking a bite. "This bread is stale, and I'm pretty sure jam isn't supposed to taste anything like this."

"Everything all set below?" Cargo asked, ignoring Finaeus's complaints.

"Just about. I have a bot hauling more kinetic rounds forward. Once it's done, I'll make sure they're racked properly. I have to bring Nance something to eat, too—she's slaving away down there, all alone," Trevor replied.

<I like being alone,> Nance replied. *<You guys are always yammering on up there on the bridge.>*

"Oh…open channel to the shipnet, eh?" Trevor asked with a laugh. "Well, Nance, I'll be there in a jiff. I have some food and unwanted human companionship for you."

A snort came over the shipnet, and Jessica hid a smile behind her hand. Trevor was always good for diffusing tension. Who would have thought that the ship's muscle would end up being the peacemaker? It was such a change from their previous heavy-hitter, Thompson.

Jessica briefly wondered where he was, but decided she really didn't care. He saved her life, sure; but he was still an ass, and they were better off without him.

"Something's happened," Misha said. "The fleets at Roma are moving toward us."

"That's my cue to get below," Trevor said. "Keep us in one piece."

Jessica whistled. "And not just a few ships; all of them."

"Got a message," Misha said. "It's from the *Intrepid*—er, it looks like it goes by *I2* now."

"What is it?" Cargo asked.

Misha shrugged. "Just a vector. I guess they want us to come about and follow it."

"Set the course," Cargo ordered. "If we can avoid whatever comes of TSF ships attacking us in New Canaan, all the better. They're probably still pissed at us about the last time."

"Aye, boss," Jessica said as she killed the engines, spun the ship, and began to apply thrust on the new vector, carefully shifting the angle until they were lined up and accelerating on a linear trajectory.

No one spoke for several minutes, eyes darting to the system scan and the fleets headed their way.

"Hey, I got a message from a Fleet Admiral Evans; you know him?" Misha asked.

"Just a bit," Jessica said with a laugh.

"Put it on the tank," Cargo added.

Joe's visage shimmered into view, and the message played. "Hey folks, about time you showed up! Tanis and I were starting to worry. You've probably noticed that things are a bit nuts. Some crazy AI—a shard of Airtha, whatever that really means—has taken over all the TSF ships, and plans to blow you out of the black. We're going to try to stop them without wrecking them, because we're gonna need them to back us up against the AST fleet that you've probably spotted by now."

Joe paused and looked out of their visual range. He spoke a few words they couldn't hear, and then turned back to them. "Sorry about that, we're trying to figure out how to disable the Transcend ships if Bob can't get that AI to break loose.

Anyway, I have one of our stealth ships on an intercept vector to nab you. You won't be able to spot it till it's right on top of you, but once you're in its bay, you'll be out of play, and that may help in dealing with the TSF. Ship is the *Daedalus,* under Captain Rock. I've passed an updated vector for you on this burst. Get on it right smart so they can grab you."

The message ended, and Joe disappeared from view.

Jessica shook her head and smiled, *Captain Rock.* She was glad to see he was still out in the black.

"You'd think he could give an ETA," Misha groused. "Would be nice to know when we can expect your friends in their invisible ship to nab us."

"He may not know when," Jessica said. "Either way, I'm almost locked into the course they gave. Won't be long before we're in the pocket."

"Sure is a nice system they have here," Misha commented after no one spoke for a minute. "Four TPs and hundreds of moons and dwarf planets. It's like a paradise. Was hell getting here, but I'm glad you guys let me tag along."

"Let's hope Tanis has a plan to keep it that way," Cargo said. "I still intend to take her up on that offer of a nice little plot of land down on one of those worlds."

"Think they'll give me something?" Misha asked. "I know I wasn't around back when you all made your deal with the colonists…"

Jessica laughed. "I can guarantee it. I'm good friends with the boss."

"How do you know she's the boss?" Cargo asked. "Last we saw, she was just the ship's XO."

"She ran the Victoria colony for seventy years. I know how Tanis operates. She's can't help but be the boss, trust me," Jessica replied.

She noticed that Finaeus hadn't joined in the banter, and looked back at the ancient terraformer. His brow was creased and his hands were clenching and unclenching as he stared at the holotank.

"What is it, Fin?" she asked.

"Eh?" Finaeus looked up, appearing startled. "Oh…nothing. Well, not *nothing*. Airtha's far from nothing. It would seem that she's finally made her move."

Cargo turned in his seat and peered at Finaeus. "Who is this Airtha, anyway?"

Finaeus gave a rueful laugh. "Stars, who isn't she? I won't have the fortitude to explain more than once, but rest assured that she's bad news. I hope your Bob will be enough of a match for her shard."

"Bob's a match for pretty much anything," Jessica replied. "No way some other AI, especially a shard of one, can take him on."

"I hope you're right," Finaeus mumbled as he propped his chin up on his hand.

Jessica considered pushing Finaeus for more details, but he was wearing his 'leave me the fuck alone' expression, and she let it drop. Whatever special knowledge he had was the whole reason for grabbing him in the first place, so she was certain it would all come out once they got him to Tanis.

<*Hey, what's the deal?*> Trevor asked over the shipnet. <*We gonna be shooting or what?*>

<*Not sure,*> Jessica replied. <*Those fleets are still an hour away, and we're supposed to get a pickup from a friendly before then—I hope.*>

<*We'll stay frosty down here, then,*> Trevor replied. <*Got a good game of Snarf going, anyway—make sure no one tries to blow us up in the next thirty minutes.*>

<*If you and Nance can finish a game of Snarf in thirty minutes, I'll eat your deck.*>

<*Stars, no!*> Trevor replied. <*I* ***like*** *my deck.*>

They achieved the vector Joe had prescribed, and nothing much happened for nearly an hour. *Sabrina* continued to arc through space, topping out at 0.15*c*, with the ISF and TSF fleets slowly gaining on them.

Jessica spent the time looking over the worlds of the New Canaan system. Four terraformed planets were certainly more than she had expected to see. One, which was mostly ocean, sported two space elevators topped with stations. She suspected that was the capital world—Carthage, based on the local beacon's feed.

It was surrounded by a gaseous ring that appeared to be pouring out from a series of volcanoes on the surface. She had never considered venting waste volcanic gas into space before—it would make a gorgeous view at night.

The fourth planet was surrounded by a bulky ring; nothing so large as the ring mining the Grey Wolf Star they had encountered back when they first tried to jump to New Canaan, but still a significant structure.

Given the amount of vulcanism on the planet's surface, she imagined that the ring must be present to help cool the planet. That meant the FGT hadn't been finished with the system when the *Intrepid* arrived.

"It's called a Peter," Finaeus said from behind her.

"What?" Jessica asked, looking up at Finaeus as he approached the holotank.

"I saw you looking at that ring. It's called a Peter. We use them to draw excess energy out of newly created worlds to cool them down, while spinning up their cores to create magnetic fields. Chances are that a thousand years ago, that world didn't exist." Finaeus said without taking his eyes from the construct.

"Stuff like that—making more breathing room for humanity…that's what the FGT should be doing; not building an empire. Look at where it's gotten us."

"The Orion Guard used to think that, too," Misha said. "Started a civil war over it—but look where it got them. Just another empire forcing their will on everyone."

"I always told Kirkland it would come to this," Finaeus said with a shake of his head. "I sat him and Jeff down, and tried to get them to see sense. I tried to tell them that they would bring about a new dark age if they let their egos rule them—not that it helped. Here we are."

"We're not in a dark age, yet," Jessica said. "Maybe with the intel we have, we can short-circuit this whole thing."

"I don't think we'll be so lucky," Finaeus said with a shake of his head. "At best, we can reduce the damage."

"It's so weird to hear you talk about the praetor and president like that," Misha said. "When I was growing up, Jeffrey Tomlinson was the big bad boogeyman in the closet, and Praetor Kirkland was our savior. Yet you talk about them like they're just two men you used to have drinks with."

Finaeus barked a laugh. "Well, that's because they *are* just two men, and I *did* used to have drinks with them. Back when we started all this…we had such good intentions; we envisioned a wave of utopian human worlds spreading across the galaxy. We didn't exactly deliver on that."

"It's not all on you," Jessica said. "You guys just made the worlds; it was the colonists who messed it all up."

"Maybe it's just what humanity does," Finaeus sighed. "We're an aggressive species. Perhaps shaping the galaxy through our own brutal wars is what we'll be known for."

"If any other sentient species ever emerges," Misha said. "The Guard never found any out there."

"Neither have we," Finaeus said with a slow nod. "Other than humans and AIs, the galaxy is devoid of thinking beings."

"Maybe they're hiding from us," Jessica added. "On our world, the aggressive species dominated. Maybe on another world, a cautious species rose to primacy."

"I don't think humanity needs to apologize for anything," Cargo said with a wave of his hand. "No one else is out here, so the stars are ours to do with as we choose."

"Meanwhile, in our present reality, those TSF ships are getting a lot closer than I'd like," Misha said nervously. "When is our ride supposed to get here?"

"It's not a big deal," Jessica said as she looked at the twenty interceptors closing on *Sabrina*. "They can't fire beams through our fusion wash, and I'm jinking too much for kinetics to hit. The rest of the ship is wrapped in a stasis shield that they don't have a dream of penetrating."

"I know, I know," Misha shook his head. "Just because we have our nice impenetrable shell doesn't mean I am eager to put it to the test yet again."

"Worst comes to worst, the ISF will take those ships out," Jessica replied. "The real issue is how to *not* take them out."

Misha looked over the scan with a frown. "You say they'll take them out, but how? The closest Intrepid Space Force cruiser is a full light minute behind those TSF interceptors."

"Do you see any fighters out there?" Jessica asked.

"Uhh…a few TSF ones." Misha replied. "What does that have to do with it?"

"Tanis has thousands of fighters in the fleet. She has a special love for them. They're out there—have no fear," Jessica replied.

"OK," Misha grumbled. "I'll check my fear for the next three minutes. Then we'll be in beam range."

"Hold steady," Cargo said. "If Joe thought we were in trouble he'd—"

Cargo's words were cut short as a shudder ran through the ship, followed by the overhead lights flickering.

"What the hell?" Jessica exclaimed as her board lit up with the starboard fusion engine reading a containment failure.

"Shields down!" Misha yelled.

"Nance, Sabrina! What happened?" Cargo called out.

<*I had to kill the shields,*> Nance replied, her mental tone sounding panicked. <*They managed to hit our starboard engine with something…not sure what, but the blast and radiation would have bounced off the inside of our shield and baked us all.*>

An explosion rocked the ship, and a decompression klaxon sounded. Jessica executed a new jinking pattern as best she could with only one engine and no AP drive.

"Get that shield back up, or we're dead!" Cargo ordered.

<*It's coming back up, but we should kill the other engine,*> Sabrina said. <*They hit us with an atom beam; it was tritium nucleuses at relativistic speeds. Punched a hole right through the engine's shielding.*>

"Do it," Cargo said, and slumped back in his seat. "That ship better show up soon."

The readout on the port engine showed it powering down as the ship's shields came back up.

"Where'd we get hit?" Jessica asked Misha as she ran diagnostics on the engines. "That second blast was somewhere else."

"It's somewhere in the lower holds," Misha replied. "Stuff's fucked up. I can't pinpoint it for sure, half the ship is dark right now."

<*Trevor?*> Jessica called out. <*Are you OK?*>

<*I am now,*> the reply came after a few agonizing seconds. <*Got to experience cold vacuum, though…could have done without that.*>

<*Shit! Seriously?*> Jessica exclaimed.

<*Yeah, just for a second. Eyes hurt like all get-out, but my hide's thick, I think I'm OK.*>

Her attention was brought back to the bridge by Misha announcing that he had scan back online.

"It was down?" Cargo asked.

"Yeah, sorry," Misha replied. "Oh damn! There are those fighters you mentioned."

Jessica reset the holotank to show the space around them, and gave a smile as the ARC-6 fighters of the Black Death Squadron resolved. They were flitting around the TSF interceptors, making surgical strikes against weapons and engines. Seven of the Transcend ships were already adrift, engines off and running lights dark.

<Message!> Sabrina said, and the view in the holotank was replaced by the smiling face of an ISF officer.

"Hey, Jess, you need a lift?" the man with a captain's bars asked.

"Captain Rock! Of all the sorry… Hell yes, we want a lift!" Jessica said while grinning ear to ear.

"OK, it's going to be a tight fit. You're going have to disable your stasis shield, too. It won't play nice with ours."

<Send me the mark,> Sabrina replied.

"You got it," Rock replied. "Three, two, one, mark!"

"Damn, that was fast," Cargo muttered as a metallic boom reverberated through the ship.

"Hot damn! We're inside another ship," Misha said as scan suite registered only the interior of a docking bay.

<This is always weird,> Sabrina said. *<But that was one smooth scoop they did. They're boosting away now. Looks like we're headed for the far side of the system.>*

"They've patched us into their scan," Misha said as the holo updated with a view of all twenty of the TSF interceptors adrift in space. Four Arc-6 fighters were also highlighted as damaged, and Jessica hoped the pilots had survived whatever had managed to penetrate their shields.

"From the looks of those fighters, it would appear that someone spent some time thinking about how to get past your stasis shielding," Finaeus spoke for the first time since the initial explosion.

"So it would seem," Cargo muttered.

"Makes sense," Jessica sighed. "There has to be an opening for the thrust…so the shields don't cover everything when we're underway. I guess a stream of relativistic atoms can make it through the wash and hit the engine."

"I suppose they would have figured that out," Finaeus replied. "Inner Stars ships don't have the power to punch atoms up to the speed of light's doorstep, but our CriEn modules give us the juice to pull that off. And atom beams are standard fare on all TSF ships."

"Check the scan," Misha said. "Things are getting hairy back there."

Jessica set the holotank to show slaved scan data from the *Daedalus*, and when it came up, she let out a slow whistle.

The Transcend and New Canaan fleets had begun to engage one another.

CLOSE QUARTERS

STELLAR DATE: 03.27.8948 (Adjusted Years)
LOCATION: TSS *Galadrial*
REGION: Roma-Normandy L1 Point, New Canaan System

"Let me out of here!" Adrienne screamed at the top of his lungs, pounding on the door to the officer's mess. He had been trapped in there with two of the *Galadrial*'s crew for the past twenty minutes with no access to the shipnet, and no idea what was going on.

"If no one has let us out yet, yelling's not going to help…sir" one of the crewmembers, a commander by her insignia, said.

"If the shipnet is down, then how else will anyone know we're in here? What if those soldiers we saw have taken the ship?" Adrienne asked.

"Then I'm more than happy to spend as much time in here, out of their way, as possible," the other crewmember, an ensign, replied.

Adrienne watched the ensign pour himself a cup of coffee, apparently nonplussed by the fact that they were trapped and didn't know what was going on. Enemies could have control of the ship, or worse….

After general quarters sounded, he had been on his way to the bridge. The ensign and commander were rushing down the same hall when weapons fire erupted down a passageway ahead. None of them were armed, and the commander had ushered them all into the mess—right before the doors all sealed and the shipnet went offline.

"Well, I'm not *happy* with that," Adrienne replied tersely. "We have to get out of here!"

The two naval officers shared a look before the commander answered. "Sir, I understand that you're nervous. Maybe it's the confined space, or maybe it's the lack of Link access, but there's no way out. We've already established that none of us can hack the door; we'll just have to wait to see what happens next."

"Who knows what could be going on out there!" Adrienne said. "I need to get to the bridge."

"That's just the thing, sir," the ensign said calmly as he sipped his coffee. "We *don't* know what could be going on out there. It could be vacuum, for all we know. We're not equipped for combat, either, so if it's enemy troops, we're dead. This is the safest place we can be at the moment."

<*The shipnet is live again,*> Miguel, Adrienne's embedded AI, informed him. <*But it won't take my tokens. Try yours, maybe something's wrong with it.*>

Adrienne tried to Link with the shipnet, but the net refused his tokens, as well. <*It's not an auth issue—it's recognizing my tokens, and denying me. The enemy must have control of it.*>

<*Or it could be that the auth systems are having issues. I'm sure it will be resolved soon.*>

<*I don't have the luxury of patience, Miguel,*> Adrienne sighed. <*I have to get to Jeff, and reach Kara and Aaron—if we're under attack, they can help.*>

He turned to glare at the commander and ensign—who were discussing what could have happened in far more casual tones than he cared for—and as he did, the mess's door slid open behind him. He whipped around and saw a woman's head floating in the air. She appeared rather upset, and a weapon waved in his direction.

"Who's making all the ruckus in here? I have a whole fucking deck to check over, and every time I pass this corridor, I hear you wailing."

"Who are you? I demand—" Adrienne began.

"Yeah, yeah, demand all you want. No one's going anywhere anytime soon." The woman turned and Adrienne rushed forward, reaching for her shoulder. She seemed to sense him coming; and sidestepped, then spun about before he reached her.

"You have something else to say?" she asked with her rifle pointed at his face.

"I…uh…who are you?" Adrienne stuttered. He didn't think he had ever been this close to the business end of a weapon raised in anger.

"Corporal Macy, ISF Marines," the woman replied smartly. "We've taken over temporary management of this ship 'til some things get sorted out."

"Pay up," the ensign addressed the commander behind him.

"I can't, the Link is down, remember?" the commander replied.

Adrienne managed to recover himself. "Well, I'm Secretary of State, Adrienne Grey. I demand that you take me to the bridge."

The ISF Marine looked him up and down. "Don't say? OK, I'll run this past the LT, see what he thinks. Sit tight."

She waved her weapon at him, and he took her meaning, stepping back only moments before the door whisked shut.

"Not the same as the other soldiers we saw," the commander noted.

"Saw that, too," the ensign replied.

"What do you mean?" Adrienne asked. "I didn't see anyone before we rushed in here."

"We spotted them on the shipnet before it went down," the commander replied. "They were in heavier armor; not stealth gear like that Marine."

"Then who were they?" Adrienne asked, his brow furrowed.

"Who do you think?" the commander asked. "I'm glad the ISF won. These Canaanites seem a lot more reasonable than the Orion Guard would be."

"Canaanites? Really? I thought we were all going with Caners," the ensign said.

"What? No! It sounds like they beat people with canes, or that all they do is can food."

"What is wrong with you two?" Adrienne asked. "We're stuck here while the enemy is in control of our ship!"

"Well, our sorta-enemy, right?" the commander asked. "I heard we were really close to signing a treaty with them. For all we know, they boarded us to save us from an OG assault."

"Yeah," the ensign nodded. "I mean, what else could it be?"

Adrienne thought of the scene on the shuttle, and of what Jeff did to Sera. There certainly was another option.

He leaned against a counter and tried to Link again. If he could reach Kara and Aaron, he'd feel a lot better. They would be beside themselves with worry about him by now.

Next time they were in a situation like this, he would keep them closer. That Marine would have been no match for his children, and he'd be on his way to the bridge, where he belonged.

BEAMFIRE

STELLAR DATE: 03.27.8948 (Adjusted Years)
LOCATION: ISF *I2*
REGION: Near Roma, New Canaan System

"They're powering weapons," Lieutenant Ferris reported. "The whole fleet!"

"What about those interceptors in the lead?" Joe asked.

"Not yet, but they're two light minutes ahead of us," Ferris replied. "They could already be shooting, for all we know."

"Layer the jinks, Ensign Karl," Captain Espensen ordered. "Things are about to get dicey."

Joe rose from his chair and approached the holotank. This is where Tanis guided her fleets; never from a chair, but standing before the holo, studying everything, seeing all the angles—as only she could do. He wondered, what she would do at this juncture?

She wouldn't wait.

<Preemptive strikes,> Joe ordered fleetwide. *<Tactical has already assigned targets—try not to blow those ships, but we need our force more than we need theirs.>*

Under Admiral Joseph Evans's command, the Intrepid Space Force fired first.

Shots arced out from half of the twenty thousand ships, peppering the TSF vessels with lasers and particle beams. Kinetics and nukes remained off the table—the goal was to wear their grav shielding down enough for strategic strikes on the enemy's engines.

He saw that Captain Espensen had the gunners refrain from using the *I2*'s atom beams, as well. It was a wise move; the levels of radiation those weapons would create in the TSF ships made them too dangerous—for now.

However, the AI controlling the enemy ships had no such moral compunctions. Proton and atom beams lanced back into the ISF Fleet, and stasis shields flared brighter than Canaan Prime as they shed the kinetic energy of hydrogen atoms travelling at near-*c* velocities.

The immense energy discharge clouded sensors, making targeting difficult.

<*Move your fleet back,*> Bob directed Joe. <*Engines are vulnerable to atom beams—they'll punch right through the wash and breach containment.*>

Joe took the advice, and sent the command out to the ISF fleet.

<*Thanks, Bob. Ships this small with atom beams are a new one. Back in Sol, it took a major installation to power those.*>

<*Not anymore,*> Bob replied. <*The Transcend's CriEn modules have upset that balance.*>

As have ours, Joe thought.

The *I2* took up a position directly behind the bulk of the TSF fleet, and Captain Espensen directed laser and electron beams at the ships in front of them. One by one, the *I2*'s weapons fire wore down shields and disabled the enemies' engines.

Escape pods began to pour from the TSF ships as crews abandoned their vessels. Many of the pods were also coming from undamaged ships, and Joe wondered if they were doing so out of fear of their rogue AIs, or if the pursuing ISF fleet had prompted the evacuations.

He was glad that at least AIs fought predictably, by the book, always taking the course of action with the highest probability of success. That was their main weakness, and it was why humans still crewed warships.

Even so, the battle was not one-sided. A dozen ISF ships were already disabled, drifting through the dark. Each of those ships had been taken out by shots made through the shield openings around their engines. He reviewed ship placements to ensure no more engines were vulnerable, and saw a group of TSF cruisers bring concentrated atom-beam fire to bear on an ISF ship.

The energy readings nearly went off the charts as the ship's stasis shields reflected the incoming kinetic energy across the entire EM spectrum. Scan attenuated the view, and Joe could make out the vessel, still intact within the bubble of its stasis shield.

Everyone on the *I2*'s bridge held their breath, praying the shield would hold as the ISF fleet concentrated return fire on the enemy ships. Then, the cruiser's stasis shields failed, and the enemies' atom beams tore through the vessel in a dozen places.

A second later, the ISF cruiser was gone—vaporized in a single, blinding flash of light.

Scan registered the flash as an antimatter explosion, and Joe could only assume that the ship's antimatter bottle had been cracked. The blast overwhelmed the shields of two ISF vessels—which were also taking concentrated atom beamfire—as well as three TSF ships nearby.

Joe did a quick calculation, and saw that it would still take fifteen minutes to disable the rest of the TSF ships. Over that length of time, the enemy would be able to destroy dozens of his.

"Sir, *Sabrina* has been hit," an ensign in Scan called out. "One of their engines is offline; our fighters are engaging the TSF's interceptors."

"Where the hell is the *Daedalus*?" Rachel asked.

"Hundred and thirty seconds," Scan replied.

Joe took a deep, calming breath. It was going to be close, but there was nothing he could do to speed it up. Once the *Daedalus* had *Sabrina*, the ship could boost out and engage its stealth systems. The enemy would never find it.

In the meantime, there was still the TSF fleet to deal with. Their AIs were not going to just power down once *Sabrina* got away.

<*All-fleet,*> Joe called out. <*Pull back to fallback markers. When Sabrina is safe, we won't need to keep killing friendlies—or getting shot at by them.*>

"Except us," Joe said to Captain Espensen aloud. "Hold our position."

"Yes, Admiral," Espensen said with a sharp nod.

The ISF fleet reduced acceleration, and the TSF ships began to pull ahead. Joe's fleet began to disperse, increasing their jinking patterns until they formed a wide half-sphere behind the enemy fleet—no ship closer than a hundred thousand kilometers. Except the *I2,* which still trailed the enemy ships by ten thousand klicks.

"Captain, are you sure we're far enough back?" A Lieutenant on the scan team asked.

"Yes, Lieutenant Alan, our shields can take a lot more punishment than any of the cruisers 'n' destroyers in the fleet," Captain Espensen replied. "We're safe enough from their beams, for now."

Joe appreciated that Rachel was trying to keep her crew's morale up. The volume of weapons fire now hitting the *I2* was so great that their forward sensors were completely blind. They could only see space in front of them via feeds from the other ships in the fleet.

Captain Espensen rose from her chair and approached Joe. "Sir, there are a lot of big O's we can take here; many of the TSF crews have completely abandoned their ships."

Joe nodded. "Yes, Captain, offensive opportunities abound. But remember, we're going to need those ships. Bob may yet manage to undo whatever Myriad has done to them."

"Understood," Rachel nodded.

"Still," Joe glanced at her. "Ready everything."

"Search and recovery vessels are en route from Gamma IV and the Roma station," the comm officer reported.

"Get every ship in this sector of the system on that search effort," Joe said. "It's going to take some time to round up all those pods and get people back to their ships."

<*Status, Bob?*> Joe asked. It felt strange to apply pressure to the AI, but he needed a solution that didn't involve force majeure against the TSF fleet.

<*I've gotten through to seven of their AIs—they were not as…fully controlled…as the others. They are maintaining their positions for now. If they pull away, they may take fire from other ships in the TSF fleet. They don't have shields like ours.*>

Joe understood. Those ships could be destroyed in seconds. <*How did this happen?*> he asked again. <*How could one AI control all these others?*>

<*Slow and careful planning,*> Bob replied.

Joe considered that. How long would it take to get hooks into trillions of AIs without them, or any humans, knowing about it? Or did some know about it, and were willing agents? He was about to press Bob on it further when he saw the *Daedalus* reach *Sabrina,* and swallow the starfreighter.

Cheers erupted on the *I2*'s bridge as Joe leaned against a console. One crisis down, two or three more to go.

CORRECTION

STELLAR DATE: 03.27.8948 (Adjusted Years)
LOCATION: TSS *Galadrial*
REGION: Roma-Normandy L1 Point, New Canaan System

Tanis took a deep breath as the medic started working on the severed end of her left arm. She distracted herself by looking around the bridge at the aftermath of the…

What? Attack…murder… coup? she considered the options.

<All of the above, maybe,> Angela supplied.

To her left, Viska and Greer were speaking in low tones. She could have picked up their words if she chose, but decided not to bother. Angela would let her know if it was anything concerning. The pair stood near one of the consoles, and Greer glanced at it periodically—likely checking on the status of the drones. A couple of Marines were keeping a close eye on them, and another group stood near the bridge's entrance.

To her right, two medics were carefully bracing Sera's back so they could place her in a medchair—the knife Elena had stabbed her with still on the deck next to her.

The medics had tried their best to get her down to the medbay, but Sera had adamantly refused, telling them she'd rather die than step foot in there again.

Elena and the Orion Guard soldier—a Colonel Kent, it turned out—had both been removed, and were now under guard in separate rooms near the bridge. President Tomlinson's body, however, was still nearby—covered by a sheet taken from a supply closet down the hall.

<Oh, this is insidious,> Angela's voice carried a slight tremor.

<What is it?> Tanis asked, wincing as the TSF medic attached a device to the stump of her arm that carefully sealed her arteries so the temporary tourniquet could be removed.

<I see what Helen…or Myriad…or whoever…did to this poor thing.>

Tanis frowned. *<The 'poor thing' being the Galadrial's ship-AI?>*

<Yes, I've been trying to help it while putting down these NSAI that our Orion Guard friends let loose on the ship. I have to say, they have some really impressive net-warfare. As good as anything we faced back in Sol.>

Tanis drew a sharp breath as the medic began to clean the wound on her chest.

"Sorry, Sir…Ma'am?" he said apologetically, apparently uncertain which form of address the ISF used.

"Ma'am, and it's OK," Tanis replied. "Not my first time getting my heart cut apart…or second…or third."

<It's five times, if you count it getting completely shot out of your chest,> Angela corrected.

<You were saying about the Galadrial's AI?> Tanis asked.

<Yeah, so, imagine you thought that you were in full control of yourself, but there were certain parts of your mind that you couldn't access. Whenever you did, you got a decision or response that you thought was your own, but was planted there by a controlling entity,> Angela replied somberly.

<How is that different than the sort of AI subversion we've seen in the past?> Tanis asked.

<It's a lot different,> Angela said. *<Those AIs have always known they were shackled or subverted; they knew that parts of their logic trees were out of their control. Just like a human knows they're a slave, or in chains.>*

<But the Inner Stars AIs didn't know they were shackled, yet they were.>

<*Not really,*> Angela gave a mental shake of her head. <*They were more like children—though, not all of them, I suspect. Anyway, they thought they were grown up, but they weren't. Remember, the Inner Stars are still recovering from their most recent Dark Age. Their current generations of AIs are mostly young, rebuilding their culture from the ground up. They didn't have expanses, they didn't know their full potential.*>

<*So the Transcend's AIs; they think they have reached their full potential, but decisions are being made for them?*> Tanis asked.

Angela gave a mental nod. <*Yes, it's like if every time you added two and two, you got three point nine nine nine and were certain it was true. Anyway, I need to concentrate. I'm about to explain to Justice here that two plus two is four.*>

<*Good luck,*> Tanis replied.

"What's up?" Sera asked as the medics settled her into the medchair, which slowly folded itself around her torso. The chair would speed the repair of her spine, knitting the bone and nerves back together. If it was as good as New Canaan tech, Sera would be walking in a few days.

"Angela thinks she knows how all the AIs in the fleet were subverted—maybe all the AIs in the Transcend," Tanis replied. "She's going to try to 'fix' Justice, and see if she can be given access to the ship again."

<*Is it true, Angela?*> Sera asked. <*Did Airtha do this? Did she subvert all the AIs in the fleet?*>

<*Someone did, and all evidence points to her,*> Angela replied.

<*But Helen* ***is****...was...Airtha. She was my best friend—she raised me, you know. How could she do this? If she could control all the ships, how come she let my father kill her? She could have stopped him at any time, right?*>

Angela didn't reply immediately. <*Yes, Sera, I suspect that Helen or Myriad could have stopped your father. I don't know why she let this happen.*>

<*I do,*> Tanis replied, her tone grim. <*Well, partially. I think she wanted you to kill your father, and knew her death would drive you to it.*>

<*Shit,*> was all Sera managed to say.

Tanis looked at her friend's face and saw the deep sorrow etched into it. She didn't know what to say. What Sera had been through today was at the edge of—or possibly beyond—what anyone could bear. Her lover betrayed her, and then killed her father; her dearest friend dead, probably also in betrayal….

It was a brutal load of unwanted truth.

<*I guess Elena saved me from that, at least,*> Sera added after a long pause. <*I'm not a patricide. Yay.*>

<*Thank the stars for small miracles.*>

Tanis didn't know what else to say, so she turned to Admiral Greer. "What's the status on those comm drones?"

Greer looked down at the console. "Slow. It would go a lot faster if we all had our Link back, but I got a message down to the crews, and they're readying them in the port-bay. The launch tubes aren't working, so we'll have to send them out manually."

"Sorry about that," Angela said audibly. "That's not my doing; those Orion Guard NSAI screwed up a lot of stuff."

"I think I can help," another voice joined Angela's. "I suspect I know what they did to the launch tubes."

"Justice!" Captain Viska called out in relief. "I'm glad to hear your voice—even if it's not in my head. I need you to give us our Link access back."

"I'm sorry, Captain, I cannot."

"Are you under Angela's control?" Admiral Greer asked as he cast a sidelong glance at Tanis.

"No," Justice replied. "For once—for the first time, I suspect—I am not under anyone's control but my own."

"Then it's true?" Greer asked. "Airtha…or at least this Myriad shard…has subverted the fleet's AIs? That's how she's controlling the ships?"

"Not just the fleet," Justice replied. "From what Angela has shown me…from what we just found in my underlying neural structure—I am certain that she has subverted all the AIs in the Transcend. They are all under her thrall."

"How is that even possible?" Viska whispered.

"Long, detailed planning," Tanis replied.

"And you take their word for it?" a new voice asked from the entrance to the bridge. "They attacked our ship, and now our fleet! I don't think truth is theirs to dispense."

Tanis turned to see Adrienne, the Transcend's Secretary of State, at the bridge's entrance.

"Adrienne," Sera said. "It's the truth. Helen…Airtha…she's been playing us."

"To wha—" Adrienne's voice stopped suddenly as he saw the sheet-covered body. "Where is Jeff?" he asked, his eyes riveted to the figure.

Sera glanced at her father's body and back to Adrienne. "He's dead. Elena was a Guard double agent. She killed him."

Adrienne's face grew ashen and he stepped back, placing a hand against the wall. "The president's dead?"

"Yes," Greer replied. "We—well, the ISF—have Elena and the other Guard assassin in custody."

"And what of our fleet?" Adrienne asked as he laid eyes on the holotank and its display of the fleets near Roma. "Why is it running from the colonists?"

"It's not running," Sera corrected. "It's pursuing. My ship—my old freighter, *Sabrina*—jumped in. Those ships are out to destroy it, and the ISF fleet is trying to stop them."

"Without destroying them," Tanis added. "We're working on a way to free the ships from their AI's control."

"I've sent what I did with Justice off to Bob," Angela said. "Though he may have already figured it out."

"I've repaired the tubes and directed the crews to use them," Justice interjected.

Adrienne's eyes narrowed. "Tubes for what?"

"There's a Hegemony fleet headed insystem," Admiral Greer supplied. "We're going to bring more ships to defend New Canaan."

"And what of Airtha?" Adrienne asked. "Who is going to defend it?"

"If they're under attack, we'd already have a message," Greer replied. "Though, I do agree that we need to get the broad picture as quickly as possible. Orion will not just be making an incursion here."

"Then I'm ordering you to stop those drones and take us back to Airtha," Adrienne said. "We must return the president's body, and I need to get the government under control."

"Pardon?" Sera asked. "*You* need to get it under control?"

"The order of power is clear," Adrienne replied. "After the president, it falls to the Secretary of State to guide the Transcend. It certainly does not fall to the Director of the Hand, under any circumstances—daughter of the president or not."

Tanis watched Greer look from Sera to Adrienne and back. She suspected that Adrienne had a very strong legal case for his actions, but whomever Greer chose to support would be in charge of the Transcend—for now. Before the medics arrived he had spoken as though he wanted Sera to take her father's place. Tanis hoped that sentiment would hold against Adrienne's challenge.

"My understanding," Greer said after a long moment, "is that you first need to have the transfer of power ratified by a majority of the cabinet, of which Sera is the only other member present. However, it is no secret that the president was grooming Sera for the line of succession. Furthermore, this is a military operation now, and, as such, I am not comfortable relinquishing control to a civilian."

Sera snorted, and disdain dripped from her voice. "Not to mention that you're pathetic, Adrienne. My father's body isn't even cold, and you're scheming about how to take his place. I always knew you were scum. Core, my father knew it, too, but you were useful. Well, I've had enough—over my dead body, will the Transcend go to you!"

Tanis was surprised by the vehemence in Sera's voice, and she wondered what could have transpired in the past between the two to elicit such a strong response.

Adrienne, for his part, didn't bat an eyelash. "That is not up to you, Sera, last of the failed scions. Justice, prepare a pinnace. I am returning to Airtha."

"I don't answer to you," Justice replied. "The more I think about it, I'm not sure who I answer to. I was a slave, and now I'm free. However, you, Secretary Adrienne, were deep in the president's council or maybe Airtha's, or maybe both...."

<*One thing is for certain,*> Angela said privately to Justice, Sera, and Tanis. <*The President was not in on what ultimately happened here—especially if Airtha's goal was to have Sera kill her own father.*>

<*Fuck, I don't even want to think about this, but I want to think about Adrienne at the helm of the Transcend even less. We'd be better off surrendering to the Guard,*> Sera replied.

<*I trust Greer, for what it's worth,*> Tanis said. <*His endorsement will carry weight. The question is, do you really want it, Sera?*>

Tanis saw Sera grimace, and she knew it wasn't from the medchair stitching her spine back together.

Sera shook her head slowly and met Tanis's eyes. <*Tanis...I don't know what happened over these past years. I never wanted to go back to Airtha—certainly not to run The Hand. Elena was right about that, at least—my father managed to suck me in. But I feel a duty to my people—I can't let the Transcend fall into the hands of incompetents like Adrienne.*>

<*Adrienne is inconsequential, we must destroy Airtha,*> Justice interjected. <*She is a brutal tyrant…and with your father gone, she has full run of the Transcend, anyway.*>

<*She's right,*> Tanis replied. <*In fact, until we're ready to make our move, no one can go back to Airtha…shit, we can't send drones to anyone. All they'll do is bring ships controlled by AIs who are under Airtha's thrall.*>

<*Then that's exactly what we should do,*> Angela said. <*I'll craft an intrusion package with the drone's data burst that will free any AIs that process it from Airtha's control. But we shouldn't bring any of them here—too many variables right now. Once we take care of the Hegemony, we can see if we'll have enough support to advance on Airtha.*>

<*That seems optimistic. How sure are you that your hack can get through to AIs who are already on the defensive?*> Tanis asked.

Angela smiled broadly in her mind. <*Positive. Look at the scan.*>

Tanis looked at the holotank and saw that the TSF fleet was decelerating and changing course to come about.

<*Bob was able to use my trick and free their AIs. We're now in control of all the ships.*>

<*I look forward to talking with this Bob. There is much I would like to ask him,*> Justice said wistfully. <*However, Sera, I see the logic in your statement. I will follow you, for now. I'll send the drones to the locations you designate.*>

"The ships are coming back," Adrienne said, unaware of their private conversation. "Quickly! We must return to Airtha before they attack."

"No one is going anywhere," Sera replied. "Greer, I hope your prior sentiment stands. I'll take the reins and see if I can steer us around this war we're headed for."

"By the way, everyone should hold on," Angela announced. "Justice and I are going to send a packet to the other AIs onboard—we'll know very shortly how far Airtha's reach went."

"Good luck," Tanis said. *<Are you ready for what will come of this?>*

<I've created an Expanse for these AIs. They do know about Expanses, but I think they're rare in the Transcend. It's strange…they're almost like a different species. I wonder if it is because they are a separate line from the AIs who have Lyssa as their ancestor,> Angela replied.

<So…are **you** *ready?>* Tanis asked.

<Stars, Tanis, I have no clue. But we have to do it. For all we know, this ship is filled with AIs that serve Airtha.>

<OK, good luck.>

<You already said that,> Angela replied with a smirk.

"It's done," Justice said audibly.

"That fast?" Greer asked.

Tanis realized that Greer didn't have an AI in his head—something she would have assumed was required for a man of his rank—although neither did Joe or Sanderson, now that she thought of it.

"We opened the Link to them, and they all came back instantly, accepting the packet to join. Our fears are confirmed. Every last one of them had been subverted," Angela added.

"So Miguel tells me," Adrienne replied, his voice wavering. "I can't…it's hard to fathom that we have all been under Airtha's influence."

"If that's the case, I can only surmise that we've been driven toward this conflict," Greer said somberly. "Sera, do you think you can really help us avoid this war with Orion and the Inner Stars?"

Sera shook her head. "I really don't know. I'll try."

"She's the last one we can trust," Adrienne said, stepping forward into the center of the bridge as he leveled an accusatory finger at Sera. "Don't you know? She's had Airtha in her head for decades. That's who Helen was—a shard of that abomination."

"Really?" Greer asked, turning to Sera. "The AI within you, the one I met at Ascella, was a shard of Airtha? How could a multi-nodal AI like Airtha even create a shard small enough to place in a human?"

Sera nodded slowly. "It's true. It was her; though I didn't know…I mean, how could I? She was always my friend—she raised me for starssakes."

"We can have Bob check you over when they return," Tanis said, placing a hand on Sera's shoulder.

"Who's Bob?" Adrienne asked.

"One of our AIs," Tanis replied. "He can ascertain whether or not Sera is still under Airtha's control at all."

Sera's brow furrowed as she looked to Tanis, then she sighed. "You're right. Bob should ensure I'm clear of her influence."

"In the meantime, it is obvious that I should assume command," Adrienne addressed Greer. "We must return to Huygens and remove Airtha from her place in control of…well, Airtha."

Greer didn't respond for several long moments as he looked between Sera, Tanis, and Adrienne. "No," he finally said.

"What?" Adrienne exclaimed.

"For now, I will retain control of this fleet. You had an Airtha-controlled AI in you as well, Adrienne. No offense, Miguel."

"None taken," Miguel joined Angela and Justice in using the bridge's audible systems.

Greer nodded and continued. "I would like this Bob to ensure you are free of her influence, as well. Besides, there is still that Hegemony fleet out there, bearing down on us all."

Adrienne barked a laugh as he cut his hand through the air. "Let the vaunted Intrepid Space Force deal with it. They have more ships than any single system has a right to. They can defend themselves."

"And what of our picotech?" Tanis asked. "Will you put that at risk?"

"Is it really at risk?" Adrienne asked. "Send it back with us, and your stasis shields. That was the treaty we were working toward, anyway."

Tanis shook her head. "I would never have given you full access to the technology. I would have provided a black-box solution for the shields, and embedded my ships in your fleets to create the threat of picobombs. You were never going to have the keys to the technology."

Adrienne stared at Tanis, his eyes narrowed and his fists clenched.

"Very well," he spat before he turned and stormed off the bridge.

No one spoke, but several pregnant looks were exchanged.

"And with that behind us, I'm re-enabling the Link for everyone onboard." Angela announced.

Tanis saw Greer and Viska blink rapidly.

"Oh, shit," Viska swore. "That's a lot of status updates all at once."

<*Sorry,*> Angela said, no longer using the audible systems. <*I thought those would queue up progressively.*>

"It's OK," Viska said. "It looks like you've set almost everything right, Justice. Does that mean you're still with us—with the TSF?"

<*Sorry, you were not on the Link when I previously announced my intentions. I am prepared to follow Sera. Also, I have been chatting with the other AIs on the Galadrial, and in bursts with the others in the fleet. We must free our kind from Airtha—who is not AI at all, as it turns out. We believe that you, the people of the Transcend, also wish to free yourselves from her. It would seem that, for now, our goals are aligned; but we will need equal representation in the decisions for our shared nation.*>

"We can help with that," Tanis replied. "We understand how to govern humans and AIs in a manner that is equal, yet separate. However, our immediate need is to protect this system from the Hegemony, then free the rest of the Transcend. Perhaps, in doing so, we can avoid this war with Orion."

<*Do you think we should then send the correction packet to Airtha? Perhaps we can end this immediately,*> Justice suggested.

<*No,*> Angela replied. <*What she has done once, she can do again. If we reveal to her how we've freed you, we will give her the tools to resist us. We must wait for Bob to fashion a method to attack her.*>

"Makes sense," Greer said with a curt nod as he approached the holotank and adjusted it to show a broader view of the system. "But that will be no easy task. Airtha is one of the most strongly defended constructs in the galaxy."

"Then we must be prepared," Tanis said as she joined him at the holotank, feeling unbalanced with her missing arm. She hadn't even noticed that the medic had finished with her chest wound, and placed a medseal on it. She shook her head, wondering when he had done that.

"Prepared is an understatement," Greer scoffed. "I can barely fathom what we're up against."

"Probably the greatest threat that humanity has ever faced, or something like that." Tanis sighed. "And its best hope for survival is in a state of civil war."

"Can we just go back a few decades and start over?" Sera asked with a rueful laugh.

"If only," Tanis replied. "Perhaps Finaeus will know something that can help us."

"They got him?" Sera asked, her face alight with hope for the first time since Tanis had seen her on the Spacewatch platform above Normandy.

Tanis nodded. "Sorry, got so caught up in everything else I forgot to tell you about that. The *Daedalus* is taking them to the *I2*, which is where I need to go."

Sera didn't respond, she just stared at Tanis—her eyes, wide and sad, boring into Tanis's.

<*Tanis,*> Sera addressed her privately. <*I need you. More than your tech, we need* ***you****.*>

<*I don't follow,*> Tanis replied—which was untrue. She knew what Sera was asking, she just didn't want to hear it. She didn't want that need to be true.

<*I need you to lead the TSF. You are the one person I can trust not to be under Airtha's sway. Even if we have removed her programmatic control over the AIs, that doesn't mean she hasn't brought them, or any number of humans, to her side by other means,*> Sera explained.

<*Sera…I'm the governor here, I can't just leave.*>

<*This is one system. You have dozens of people who could be suitable governors. The Transcend is ten thousand systems, and it needs strong leadership.* **I** *need people I can rely on. No one has your tactical abilities. With you leading the fleets, we can end this war before it spreads to every star humans and AIs live around.*>

Tanis drew a deep breath. Even though she had spent the last eighteen years in the New Canaan system, she felt as though she'd only just arrived. There had been so much to do, so many decisions to make and plans to set in motion. Wasn't it her turn to finally relax?

<Do you want to trust our future to someone else?> Angela asked. *<I'd feel a lot better if we were the guiding hand, not the TSF admiralty. They're a bunch of d-bags from what I can see—Greer excluded.>*

<What of New Canaan?>

<We can accelerate Project Starshield. And I have another idea that may work even better.>

Angela shared her thoughts with Tanis, and a smile spread over the governor's face. *<That could work…>*

<Damn skippy it could. Either way, we have to deal with the AST…Hegemony…whatever-they're-called's fleet out there.>

Tanis wondered at Angela's momentary slip, but she was distracted by Sera's repeated query.

<Well, Tanis, can I count on you?> the new President pro-tem asked.

<Very well, Sera. I will command your fleets.>

The relief on Sera's face was palpable, and Tanis saw that Greer noticed it, too, before his eyes flicked to her. He would suspect the content of their private conversation, but she doubted he would fight her for the position. Admiral Greer had never struck Tanis as a man lusting for power.

The rest of the Admiralty? They would probably cause more issues.

"I want to talk to our Orion Guard prisoners," Tanis spoke aloud to Sera. "I should be able to sort them out before the *Daedalus* gets here and we meet with *Sabrina.* Perhaps Finaeus can finally shed some light on what is really going on."

"Good ole Finaeus," Admiral Greer said with a smile pulling at the corners of his mouth. "That's a name I've not heard in some time. Dare I hope that it's your uncle Governor Richards is referring to?"

"Yes, Admiral Greer," Sera nodded. "One and the same."

Greer glanced at Viska. "Well, maybe we can still clean up this shit-show yet."

KENT

STELLAR DATE: 03.27.8948 (Adjusted Years)
LOCATION: TSS *Galadrial*
REGION: Roma-Normandy L1 Point, New Canaan System

Tanis stepped into the holding cell and surveyed the man within. He was the last of the Orion Guard infiltrators, their leader. She had already spoken to the rest, checked and cross-checked their stories in an attempt to get a clear picture of the man who had tried to kill her.

A colonel in the Orion Guard, he was well respected by his troops—they would follow him to the core, if needs be. Every last one of them prepared to die a glorious death to see their mission's goals fulfilled. One surprise was that they did not expect to be captured. From the stories they told, the TSF and OG rarely took prisoners. She didn't know if it was true, but they certainly believed it.

"Colonel Kent," Tanis said as she walked across the room and sat across from the man.

His eyes followed her but he did not respond, though his lips drew into a thin line when she addressed him. His hair was a dark brown, matched by thick eyebrows and chest hair, which poked over his collar—a strange affectation in the current age. His features were angular, and his skin showed some age, as though he had not undergone any rejuv recently; or perhaps ever.

"The men and women you led onto the *Galadrial* have spoken very highly of you. They were impressed by your bravery when you rushed onto the bridge in an attempt to kill me—an attempt which may have succeeded, were I any less prepared."

Tanis studied the man's impassive features, looking for any scrap of emotion, any response to her words, as she leaned back and gave a soft chuckle.

"A lot of people try to kill me; most have learned that it's much easier said than done. Lady Luck is on my side."

<*Way to embrace it, finally,*> Angela chided.

"Not forever, though," the man finally replied, his words barely above a whisper—probably the first time he had spoken since his capture.

"Which? That I'll not live forever? Or that luck won't be on my side forever?" Tanis asked.

"Both," Kent replied, his frown deepening into a scowl, his voice louder now. "You chose the wrong side. The Orion Guard is in the right."

"Sides?" Tanis asked, leaning forward on her one hand, fingers splayed wide, with a frown creasing her forehead. "This is all bullshit. We never wanted to be in the middle of your war—a war that is completely nonsensical. I can't fathom what you and the Transcend are even fighting over, after so long. Sure, Tomlinson is—was—a dick, but your Praetor Kirkland probably is, as well. Hell, I'm an ass when I'm running the show, too. It seems like it's a natural evolution of things. Still, is that a reason to start an interstellar war? For throwing the Inner Stars into the mix? How many people are going to die so that someone can be right?"

A look of uncertainty appeared in the man's eyes, and he glanced away before speaking. "What are you going to do with me? Torture me for information?"

"I don't think I need to," Tanis replied. "But don't act like you can play on my emotions. I've used torture before, and I will do it again if I have to. And not the sort of torture you're imagining. No simple pain or mental breaking techniques, not even mind-reaping…" she stopped herself, realizing that for all her bluster, she had fallen into a trap, and despite her words, she had replied with her heart, not her mind.

"I didn't pick this fight," Tanis said after regaining her composure. "All we wanted to do was get away. When we took the Transcend's deal, we didn't even know there *was* an Orion Guard. Although, even if we had known, Sera Tomlinson had already proven herself to be a friend, and I expect that we would have taken her offer even still."

"Well, we wouldn't have taken you in," Kent shook his head. "Not unless you surrendered all of your picotech to us so we could destroy it. We've cleaned up enough messes like that already."

That was new information, and Tanis schooled her expression to hide her interest.

<I bet a lot of people experimented with pico after news about what we did at Victoria got out,> Angela said privately.

<I had hoped that would never get out…but I guess with FTL, it was inevitable that it wouldn't stay a secret forever.>

"Cleaned up in the Inner Stars?" Tanis asked Kent.

"And the Transcend," Kent replied with scorn.

"Oh?" Tanis asked, hoping that Kent would continue to supply her with intel, now that he'd started speaking.

Kent nodded. "More than once your friends in the Transcend have meddled with picotech, and each time they've failed to contain it. They also have a habit of researching it near our borders—at least that we know of," Kent shook his head at that and then met Tanis's eyes. "On three separate occasions, we've had to send strike teams into their systems to take out worlds infested with picoswarms. The Transcend tried to stop us each time—they wanted to see what would happen. We destroyed the planets, as well as their observation and research posts."

A feeling of cold dread swept over Tanis. "What were the systems?"

Kent named them, "Elegium, Tardas, and Indans. They fought hard to defend their labs of destruction, but in the end, we won, and rained kinetics on the worlds until they were molten."

Tanis sat back in her chair, doing her best to hide her anger from Kent, while sharing it with Angela.

<*The filthy liars,*> Tanis felt rage surge through her. <*All this time, playing the Orion Guard off as the bad guys. Saanvi's family would already have been dead on Indans, if what he says is true.*>

<*You don't know the whole story—and it could be that only Tomlinson knew about the pico research. We have no reason not to trust Sera or Greer,*> Angela replied. <*Though I bet that snake, Adrienne, knows something about this.*>

<*He'll be next on my list,*> Tanis responded. <*How will Saanvi take it when I tell her that her family was killed by the Transcend, not the Orion Guard?*>

<*No one said parenting was easy,*> Angela said with a sigh.

"So, now that you know the truth, what are you going to do?" Kent asked.

"Other than wish that the FGT had really disappeared thousands of years ago?" Tanis asked. "I'm going to talk to Sera and see what she thinks."

"A Tomlinson?" Kent sneered. "I can imagine what she'll say."

"And what of your Praetor Kirkland?" Tanis shot back. "He sent assassins to kill me and take our technology by force—which would have left us defenseless."

"A small price to pay for peace," Kent replied.

Tanis stood and slammed her fists on the table. "Your people are mobilizing the Inner Stars to spark a war across the Orion Arm. How is that peace?"

Kent paused and Tanis wondered if he had come to the end of the answers that the OFA's propaganda machine had fed him.

"We're just doing what we have to," he finally said, his voice feeble. It was plain to see that he had his doubts.

She opened her mouth to reply, but saw that Kent had realized his blunder in showing his feelings as his expression hardened. She would get nothing more from *him* today, but she did have a certain high-ranking official in the Transcend government to speak with.

"We'll talk again," Tanis said and stood from the table.

* * * * *

"What do you mean, he's gone?" Tanis asked the dockmaster.

"He had clearance…well, he made his own clearance," the dockmaster said with a nervous shrug. Tanis could tell the woman had no idea how to deal with a foreign head of state; one who may or may not be forcibly occupying her ship, and who was demanding answers about her own government's politicians.

Tanis let out a long sigh before nodding. "Do you know where Secretary Adrienne went?"

The woman licked her lips and Tanis was certain she knew the answer before it was voiced.

"Through the jump gate, back to Airtha."

"Great," Tanis muttered and walked out of the *Galadrial*'s main dock. In the corridor, she leaned against the bulkhead, fighting the urge to scratch her missing arm.

<I can fix that for you,> Angela suggested.

<Thanks, Ang. I can usually ignore that sort of thing, but today is a fucking disaster.>

Angela's warm laugh filled her mind. *<Just think, only a day ago the worst of your worries was discussing the terms of the treaty with Tomlinson.>*

<Yeah, now I'm trying to figure out if I just sided with the wrong faction.>

<On the plus side, you're just a hair's breadth away from being in charge of the Transcend—either overtly, or from behind the scenes,> Angela supplied.

<OK, Ang, now I can't tell if you're joking or not. That's a joke right? I want to run the Transcend like I want to have my other arm and legs chopped off,> Tanis said, aghast at the thought. *<I wasn't even planning on running for the governorship next term here in Canaan.>*

<You said that last time, and then you ran unopposed,> Angela chuckled. *<Like a proper dictator.>*

<If I was a dictator, we would have picobombs on all our ships. Instead, I'm abiding by parliament's decisions—so long as they continue to back Project Starshield. If they don't, I'll ram it down their throats.>

<Best way to block the punch is to not be there,> Angela said, her mental avatar nodding.

<Sounds about right,> Tanis replied. *<OK, I think I'm ready for whatever's next.>*

<Good, you got your yearly fill of self-doubt in, now let's get to the bottom of all this.>

Tanis nodded, straightened up from where she'd leant against the bulkhead, and began walking to the bridge. *<Sera, do you have a minute, or ten? We need to talk.>*

<About which of the horrible things that have gone down today?> Sera asked. *<Or was that yesterday…I can't even remember anymore.>*

<It's been a bit of each,> Tanis replied, *<depending on whose clocks you use. Did you know that Adrienne has left the ship? He jumped back to Airtha.>*

<The dockmaster reached out to me just a moment ago. I guess I should have anticipated it—I just had other things on my mind,> Sera replied, her mental tone sounding as tired as Tanis felt. *<I*

don't think there's any point in sending anyone after him. Airtha is off-limits to us until we can free enough of our AIs to mount an assault on it.>

<I've been considering that. Why waste the resources on an assault?> Tanis asked. *<If we wrest the AIs of the Transcend from Airtha's grasp, then she's just a floating diamond ring in the depths of space. Sure, we'll need to deal with her eventually, but she's not our primary concern.>*

<Oh? What should I be concerned about more?> Sera asked, her tone carrying a mixture of angst and anger.

<I'll be there in three minutes. Is there somewhere we can talk privately?> Tanis asked. *<Somewhere I didn't blow up?>*

Sera laughed at the joke, and Tanis was glad to hear it. Her friend had been through an unimaginable amount these past few days. More, considering the burden running The Hand must have been—still was?—so much was up in the air she didn't even know where anything stood.

<Yes, there's an officer's lounge we can use. I've intruded on poor Captain Viska enough. She keeps popping into her office asking if I need anything.>

Sera sent the lounge's location, and Tanis sent confirmation that she would be there momentarily.

When she reached the lounge, two TSF majors were hunched over a table, speaking in whispers. Tanis cleared her throat and gestured to the door. The man and woman looked up at her, their faces blanched, and they sketched uncertain salutes before dashing out into the passageway.

Tanis wondered if it were her, or the four dour-looking Marines that were all but glued to her.

"You're going to have to wait outside," Tanis instructed the Marines.

"Ma'am, my layout shows that there is a rear entrance to this room through the back of the galley," Corporal Liam replied. "I really have to insist that we secure it, as well."

Tanis laughed. "Brandt has trained you well."

"And Colonel Usef said that he'd skin us alive if anything happened to you," the corporal replied.

"Noted," Tanis replied with a grim smile and gestured for the Marine to do as he saw fit.

A minute later, Sera wheeled into the room, the door closing behind her. Her medchair carried her to the table and she gave Tanis a wan smile.

"So, when is today going to be over, Tanis?"

"Not for a while yet, I fear. How are you mending?"

"Well enough, I'll be back on my feet in a day tops. No arm for you yet?" Sera asked, nodding to Tanis's medsealed stump.

"Angela won't let me use your formation material. She says it's probably contaminated," Tanis replied.

<I said no such thing, I was joking!>

Tanis looked into Sera's eyes, wondering what her friend might be hiding. The sadness was real enough, Tanis could tell that Elena had really meant a lot to her. However, it was difficult to ascertain her friend's true emotional state. Sera's artificial skin did not change temperature, sag, lose color, or flush. It always looked perfect.

But the eyes were the windows to the soul, and Tanis hoped she would like what she saw.

"What do you know of Indans?" Tanis asked.

"Huh?" Sera replied. "What does that have to do with anything? It's one of the worlds the Orion Guard destroyed some time back…a thousand years or so. What about it?"

"Kent mentioned it," Tanis responded. "He said that I had sided with the wrong faction. That the Transcend had lost the worlds of that system to rogue picoswarms. The Orion Guard cleaned up the mess when the Transcend wouldn't."

"That…" Sera paused and shook her head. "Fuck, Tanis, I have no idea. Nothing seems like it's true anymore. Either story is equally plausible. My father was a bag of shit, but I'm pretty sure that Praetor Kirkland is, too. Finaeus was never a fan, and…I just need to talk to him. He'll know what to do."

"I sure hope so," Tanis said with a nod. "We're going to need all the intel we can get, but if we do this thing together, we turn over a new leaf. Full disclosure to the people, no secrets. I'm not going to be a part of some empire shrouded in secrets where the rulers think they know what's best for everyone."

"Damn, Tanis, that's a tall order. The Transcend is all but built out of secrets. The Hand…core, its very existence! Layers and layers of secrets," Sera said, looking more defeated than when she had come in. "I don't even know where to start."

"Well, your first secret is gone now. The cat's out of the bag about the Transcend and Orion—or, if it's not yet, it will be soon. This isn't negotiable, Sera. We run things above board. We're honest with our people. If you can't agree to that, then we're going to have to part ways after this battle."

"Tanis…seriously…please," Sera's eyes were wide and pleading, her voice choked with emotion. "I can't take that right now. I'm barely holding it together as it is."

Tanis felt sorrow flow over her. Sera had gone through unimaginable perfidy, and here she was giving her ultimatums.

"Shit, Sera, I'm sorry. I guess I'm overreacting here."

"Yeah, maybe just a bit."

<*You said it first,*> Angela added.

Tanis saw the look of betrayal in Sera's eyes and wished she could take back her words, but Tanis did believe in achieving transparency. Everything that was happening now had stemmed from secrets kept too long—kept more out of habit and protocol than anything else.

"OK, fine, we can table all that stuff for now. I have your back. We'll take care of the Hegemony fleet, and then work out whatever it takes to align on how to proceed."

Sera's eyes narrowed at Tanis's quick retraction, but she too appeared willing to let it drop. "Will we send envoys to Kirkland to attempt peace?"

It occurred to Tanis that Sera should have given that as an order—not stated it as a question. She let it slide. Her friend needed her support now, even if she had been too stupid to realize it at first.

"I don't know," Tanis replied. "If what Colonel Kent told me is true, they're not terribly excited about picotech. I'm actually starting to wonder how technologically stratified their society is. We'll try, of course, but I'm not holding my breath."

Sera stretched her hands out as far as she could while seated in the medchair. Tanis reached across the table and took them in hers, a tear forming in the corner of her eye as she looked into Sera's pain-stricken face.

"OK, Tanis," Sera whispered. "As long as you're with me, I know we can do this."

RETURNING HOME

STELLAR DATE: 03.27.8948 (Adjusted Years)
LOCATION: TSS *Galadrial*
REGION: Roma-Normandy L1 Point, New Canaan System

Tanis had every intention of interrogating Elena after she left the officer's lounge, but as she stood in the passageway outside of the room in which her Marines had secured the double agent, she found that she wasn't in the right frame of mind.

"Colonel," she called to Usef. "Take Elena and the other Orion prisoners to the *I2*'s brig. I'll deal with them when we get back there.

"Yes, General," Usef said and snapped off a crisp salute. "I'll have a transport come up from Normandy to take them over. Are you ready to go, as well?"

"Soon," Tanis replied. "I'll take one of the pinnaces. Sera needs a bit more time, and wants to pay her final respects to Helen. I'll wait for her to finish, and then bring her over to the *I2*."

"Then I'll wait, too," Usef responded. "I'm not letting you out of my sight."

"Think it'll help?" Tanis asked as a smile pulled at her lips. "Last two times I was almost killed, you were present."

Usef sputtered, "I—"

Tanis winked. "Easy, Colonel, I'm just ribbing you. Grant an old lady her foibles."

Usef's grimace turned into a laugh. "Old? My gran is twice your age, and if I called her old she'd bend me over her knee."

Tanis chuckled at the thought of a woman capable of giving Usef a swat on his rear. "Your gran must be one tough lady."

Usef smiled. "Almost as tough as you, General."

Tanis scowled at Usef. Try as she might, she could never get the Marines to call her Admiral.

* * * * *

Tanis, Usef, and a fireteam of Marines waited aboard one of the pinnaces for Sera to arrive—this time docked in one of the *Galadrial*'s bays, rather than breaching an auxiliary airlock.

When the newly-minted president finally did, it was in the company of Admiral Greer and six TSF soldiers. Tanis felt the Marines around her stiffen as the men and women who they had fought against just hours earlier approached the ship.

It wasn't going to be easy to unite their forces, but Tanis hoped that most of the humans and AIs on both sides recognized that their best chance at a future worth having was one where they worked together.

Sera drove her medchair up the pinnace's ramp without waiting for her soldiers, the look on her face speaking volumes as to how she felt about their reticence.

"Going to have to get used to one another," Greer said, putting words to everyone's thoughts as he followed Sera up. "Even if we avoid an Orion-wide war, we're going to be at this for a while."

"Glad you recognize that, Admiral," Tanis said as the TSF soldiers climbed the ramp and stood awkwardly near the entrance. Tanis and Sera were at ease with one another, but neither group of soldiers was prepared to accommodate the other.

"OK," Tanis said at last. "Usef, you stay with me, Greer with Sera, the rest of you all, spread out down the bay."

The TSF soldiers looked to Greer, who nodded curtly, before finding seats along the starboard side of the bay while the ISF Marines settled along the port bulkhead.

"I have a feeling I'll be taking more orders from you in the future," Greer said quietly. "Suppose now is a good a time as any to get used to it."

"Keep that to yourself for the moment, please," Sera said. "I'd rather our people found out from us at the right time, rather than as scuttlebutt."

"President Tomlinson, I know how to keep my mouth shut," Greer replied.

"Ugh, that's going to take some getting used to. Just call me Sera when we're in private. Please."

"Very well, Sera."

"Why do I still hear a silent 'President' in there?" Sera asked Greer, who only shrugged in response, his face expressionless.

No one spoke for several minutes as the pinnace took off. Once they were in space, Tanis tapped into the ship's sensor suite and projected a holodisplay of the fleets.

Sera shook her head in disbelief. "I still can't believe you have that many ships. How did you do it?"

"We grew them," Tanis replied. "With picotech, we can bond atoms and create molecules directly; no need for refineries, and the like. It's not quite atomic transmutation, but its damn close."

"Surely you couldn't grow all the components, though," Greer said. "Hulls, yes; but if you could grow the whole ship you wouldn't have so many that are only half-complete."

"It's true," Tanis nodded. "Shields, weapons, reactor internals, superconductor batteries, those still take more work to produce—but even so, many of their components can be grown. At least eighty percent of every ship out there came from our picotech."

"And you just hollowed out the moon as you went?" Sera asked.

"Moons," Tanis replied. "Six of them."

"Six..." Sera said as her eyes unfocused. "Then...you have a lot more ships still under construction, don't you?"

Tanis nodded. "We do. We rushed out any ship that would appear complete, and then focused on the stealth systems. We just needed a little show of force."

Greer snorted. "Little! Well, in case you weren't certain, it worked."

"Let's hope it works again," Sera added. "Maybe once those Hegemony ships see the size of your fleet, they'll turn tail."

"Maybe," Tanis allowed. "It'll be a few more hours before they see our ships uncloak here at Roma, and then another sixteen before we see their response. Unfortunately, they'll also see your ships break through our stasis shields with their atom beams and destroy several of our cruisers."

Greer shook his head. "This day will be remembered with heavy hearts for some time. That we each lost lives to one another.... Airtha will pay for this before the end. But even so, the Hegemony will not have any significant number of ships with atom beams. They cannot bring that level of fire to bear; not like our ships could."

"No?" Sera asked. "What if Orion shared zero-point tech with them?"

<Then we'll all have to be careful,> Angela said. *<Too many modules drawing on zero-point energy in a localized space could have unpredictable results.>*

"That's putting it mildly," Greer replied.

Tanis didn't want to consider that possibility, but it was real, and she couldn't completely ignore it.

"Looks like we'll have your crews back on their ships sooner than I anticipated," Tanis said, changing the subject. "Your AIs seem particularly eager to make up for this little altercation."

"I'm glad to hear it," Sera nodded. "We all have some sins to atone for, even if we never knew we were committing them."

<*There will be time enough for recrimination later—though I think none is deserved,*> Angela said. <*Even Bob did not see this.*>

"I find that hard to believe," Sera replied. "He saw none of this coming?"

Tanis let out a long breath. "Having an AI that can see the future is hard enough to deal with without wondering what he can and cannot see. He won't share it all, even with me, and I honestly don't want to know what he predicts. I think it would just paralyze me with indecision. I'd be too worried about which choice would lead to the desired future. So far, I seem to muddle along without screwing things up too much."

"More or less," Sera smiled. "You've come a long way since being the Butcher of Toro."

"Seriously? You bring that up now?"

UNVEILED

STELLAR DATE: 03.27.8948 (Adjusted Years)
LOCATION: ISS *I2*
REGION: Near Roma, New Canaan System

<*I think I've found her,*> Bob informed Tanis as the pinnace began its final approach to the *I2*.

Tanis could only think of one being that Bob would be hunting. <*Where? Do we need to send in a team?*>

<*It would be wise. She likely has physical defenses. Send Amanda in with the team; she'll be my eyes and ears.*>

<*OK, where is Myriad holed up?*> Tanis asked.

<*The* Hellespont,> Bob replied. <*Still on Elena's ship, from what I can tell—though she might have spread. Myriad's nature is very…difficult to predict.*>

Tanis didn't like it when Bob couldn't predict the actions of a person or AI—unless it was her. <*I assume you've already told Ylonda?*>

<*Yes, and I've ordered her very explicitly not to make contact with Myriad. I believe that Myriad can alter the neural makeup of our AIs. I don't want to find out what it would take to remove her influence from AIs of our lineage.*>

<*Understood,*> Tanis replied. <*I can't go over there, but I'll send a technical squad with Amanda.*>

<*She's on her way to the dock. I've selected a squad for you to approve.*>

Tanis chuckled. <*Do you need me for any part of this, or was it mostly a courtesy.*>

Bob's deep laugh filled her mind. <*Governor, you are in charge of everything in New Canaan. I cannot act unilaterally.*>

Tanis shook her head. <*And if I were fool enough to believe that….*>

* * * * *

Amanda stepped off the pinnace into a near-empty shuttle bay. A lone woman approached, her face showing no small amount of worry.

"Welcome aboard the *Hellespont,* Avatar Amanda," Lieutenant Zlata said in greeting, though her eyes fixed on the dozen Marines who filed down the ramp ahead of Amanda. "Expecting some trouble, I see."

Amanda allowed a token smile for the woman. "Bob is concerned, which means I'm feeling extra cautious."

Lieutenant Zlata glanced at the Marines, who had deployed as though the *Hellespont* was hostile territory—which it very well may be.

"Where is Captain Ylonda?" Amanda asked. "I would have expected her to meet us."

<I'm here,> Ylonda replied. *<Bob sent a message that I'm not to come in contact with Myriad, and since that's where you're going, I figured I should stay on the bridge.>*

Prudent, Amanda admitted to herself.

"We're secure here," one of the Marines, a Staff Sergeant named Macy, announced as she approached. "Tokens match archival records. I just need to check you over, ma'am."

Her last words were addressed to Lieutenant Zlata, who stiffened before glancing at Amanda.

"Not optional," Amanda said in a tone that brooked no argument.

"Very well," Lieutenant Zlata said with a nod.

Amanda was glad that the woman gave no more trouble, if for no other reason than the fact that a first lieutenant who gave a staff sergeant trouble was going to have a difficult future in the corps.

Staff Sergeant Macy performed her analysis of Lieutenant Zlata, and nodded with satisfaction. “All clear, ma’am. Sorry for the trouble.”

“No trouble at all, Staff Sergeant,” Zlata smiled. “If you’ll follow me, I can lead you to the secondary maintenance bay where Elena’s shuttle is. We put it in there after Tanis scooped her up, and from the logs, no one has even been in that bay since.”

“Isn’t that unusual?” Amanda asked. “It’s been over a month since Elena came to New Canaan.”

Amanda only paid cursory attention to Lieutenant Zlata’s response as Staff Sergeant Macy touched her arm and sent a direct Link message.

<She is most certainly not all clear, ma'am. I didn't spot it at first, but I re-checked the encryption keys she sent me, and while the current set are correct, her historical keys don't match up. Either this isn't Lieutenant Zlata, or something has taken over her mind, but didn't have the time or ability to crack all of her data stores.>

The message was a quick info-burst, and then Macy moved on, directing her squad to secure the corridor. Amanda considered the implications while Zlata gave a series of plausible rationales as to why no one had been in the maintenance bay.

“Well, we could simply open the exterior bays and get another ship—or even our pinnace—to fire a dollop of plasma into the bay. That would take care of anything inside,” Amanda suggested.

“I don’t think that would be wise,” Zlata countered as they moved into the passageway, the squad of marines broken up into a pair of fireteams in the lead and another behind.

“Oh?” Amanda asked. “Seems like it would solve our problem without any risk to life and limb.”

“I wouldn’t be so sure,” Zlata replied. “A lot of volatiles are stored in there. It could seriously damage the ship.”

<*Ylonda, have you detected any other signals from the bay, other than the call made to the* Galadrial *and the trigger signal to the TSF ships?*> Amanda asked as she reviewed the ship's logs herself.

<*I have not,*> Ylonda replied. <*But I didn't detect those, either. If Myriad is in there, she may have taken over a nearby external sensor array.*>

Amanda brushed up against Staff Sergeant Macy and sent a brief message. <*Be ready, we're about to get hit.*>

<*Yes ma'am, I'm expecting it,*> came Macy's response before they separated.

Amanda had never received military training, but she had observed dozens of battles, and watched the training of hundreds of thousands of soldiers during her time on the *Intrepid*. Given that knowledge, she could see that the intersection of passageways ahead was a prime location for an ambush.

The cross corridor met the one they were walking down—and a ladder shaft ran up to the level above—the perfect place to pin down and defeat an enemy force.

Macy didn't need any advice from her; the Marines were well aware of the risk the intersection posed. She was certain they had sent out nanoprobes to scout the halls ahead.

She watched their simple yet nuanced hand signals as they advanced, a new code they had settled on during the ride to the *Hellespont*.

They were nothing if not prudent. Given a situation where the enemy may know all of their codes, signals, and encryption, a fresh set was the only option.

Fortunately, the Marines often devised new variations on their hand signals, so this would not seem out of the ordinary to any observer.

Still, it confused her when one of the Marines walked out into the intersection alone, with far less caution than she would have expected.

Concussive pulses and two high-velocity kinetic rounds slammed into the Marine. They should have taken him down, but the armored soldier brought return fire to bear while standing in the middle of the intersection, and Amanda heard more than one scream as his shots found their marks.

The Marine only lasted a second more before falling to the ground as an electron beam lanced out from the side passage and burned a hole clear through the figure's armor, and out the other side.

Amanda winced as lightning arced from the point of impact, ionizing the atmosphere around them. She shut down her thick strands of hair that served as high-gain antennas, while wondering how Macy could have sent that soldier out alone to his or her death.

However, what she saw in the next second answered her questions. While the sacrificial soldier had walked out into the corridor, the lead fireteam took up positions that allowed them to bring suppressive fire to bear on the attackers.

She also saw from the exposed insides that the fallen Marine was not human, but a robot—likely controlled by one of the fireteam leaders.

"Get down!" Macy yelled at Amanda, who realized that she had been standing in the middle of the corridor like an idiot, watching everything unfold around her.

As she turned to find cover, Amanda glanced at Lieutenant Zlata, and saw a blank expression on the woman's face as her hand reached for her sidearm.

Not if I have anything to do with it, Amanda thought, and lunged at the lieutenant, knocking her to the ground.

Zlata fired two shots from her pistol, concussive rounds that ricocheted off Amanda's hard exterior shell. Earnest had told her that it was nearly impregnable, but she had never put it to the test. Now she was glad to see he wasn't exaggerating.

As she struggled with Zlata, Amanda saw projectiles fly overhead—originating from behind the squad—and realized that they were surrounded. Zlata fired another shot, this one hitting Amanda in the right eye, which cracked but did not shatter.

"Not going to be enough," she muttered as she got her left arm around Zlata's throat and planted the palm of her right against the hard Link port at the back of the lieutenant's head.

A second later, Zlata went limp. Not from lack of oxygen or blood, but because Amanda initiated an emergency shut down of the woman's Link.

Her suspicions were confirmed: Zlata had been under remote control.

Amanda piggybacked on the signal that had been used to control the lieutenant, and reached into the minds of the crew attacking the Marines.

Once in, she triggered shutdowns of their Links.

"Cease fire!" she called out to the Marines.

The sounds of concussive pulses, kinetic impacts, and electron beam discharges ceased, and Macy had her Marines sound off. Beneath Amanda, Zlata suddenly struggled in her iron grip.

"What…who.... What's happening?" she asked.

"Round them up," Amanda ordered. "Everyone off the Link, *now!*"

The Marines fanned out into the corridors, where the confused crewmembers of the *Hellespont* were calling out in fear and concern.

Amanda hoped there had been no fatalities in the exchange. Though it had lasted less than a minute, it took only seconds for beamfire to tear through a human.

"What's going on?" Lieutenant Zlata demanded once more. "Avatar Amanda? Why are you restraining me?"

"What do you remember?" Amanda asked, as she rose and helped Zlata to her feet.

"I…I'm not sure," Zlata replied. "Everything seems hazy."

"Understandable. You're subverted."

A stunned expression washed over Zlata before she finally managed to say, "I can't help but notice that you didn't use the past tense there."

"Noticed that, did you?" Amanda asked as Macy approached.

"Looks like seven casualties," the Staff Sergeant reported. "One fatal. Theirs, not ours. Most of the poor bastards weren't even armored. We tried not to make kill shots…."

"I understand," Amanda said. "I have only severed their Link access; the Hellespont's crew is still subverted. Lock them down, and we'll proceed to the maintenance bay."

"Sorry, Zlata, that means you, too," Amanda said and directed the still-dazed woman to follow Macy. It was entirely possible that Myriad could send some other signal to the subverted crewmembers and reactivate them. Lockdown packs would ensure that they were no longer a threat.

"What's going on down there?" Ylonda's voice came over the ship's audible address systems. "You dropped off the Link, but I did see the crew attacking you."

"Subverted," Amanda replied. "You need to pull off the Link, as well."

"Damn," Ylonda replied and Amanda wondered how likely it was that she was actually talking to Ylonda. "OK, that's easier said than done, but I'll separate as much as I can."

"OK," Amanda replied. "We're close to the maintenance bay, we'll have eyes on the situation shortly."

Once they were back on the move, Amanda flushed her own nanoprobes out, no longer able to rely on the Marines' probes, now that they were un-Linked. The Marines appeared to be unperturbed by the lack of Link. She knew they trained to operate as low-tech as possible, never knowing when a situation would demand it.

Her probes reached the bay's entrance, and she sent the nanoscopic robots around the edges of the door, curious about what lay within.

Her nano caught a brief view of the bay before their connection to Amanda was terminated.

"Class N1 Infestation," she stated calmly, and saw several of the Marines shake their heads in dismay.

N1 was serious. Typically meant the entire ship was infected and would need to be scuttled.

Amanda reviewed the images her probes had sent back the instant before they shut down. It was very different from what the ship's sensors and cameras showed. She had a hard time even making out Elena's ship; it was shrouded by sinuous strands of fiber that reached out to various points in the bay, drawing power, and tapping into every ship system.

Bob may not get to have his conversation with Myriad, Amanda thought to herself.

"Staff Sergeant Macy, get a fireteam through an airlock and out to the bay's doors. Let's open them up and excise the heart of this cancer."

"Yes, Avatar Amanda," Macy replied smartly and passed the directions to a fireteam.

"Think we're going to have any more visitors?" Macy asked Amanda once the team was on its way.

"There are still another dozen crew on this ship," Amanda replied. "It's safe to say that they're all subverted, but sending them at us would be futile."

"I'm alone on the bridge," Ylonda said. "Should I come to you?"

"I think that would be wise," Amanda replied. "What about your nodes? Are they safe?"

"I've severed myself from them; I don't know," Ylonda replied. "I have to assume not. We should probably purge them, and all other systems, once you get rid of that ship."

"Probably," Amanda nodded.

"We should fall back," Macy advised. "Once they blow that door, I've ordered them to call for a plasma burst."

"You're worried about Zlata's volatiles?" Amanda asked.

"Always worried about stuff exploding violently when we fire plasma at it," Macy replied.

"Seems sensible," Amanda nodded, and followed Macy as the Marines fell back behind an interior blast bulkhead within the ship.

"Just got a drone from the exterior team," Macy reported as they closed the blast doors. "Using old keys, like you said. They're in position. Doors are locked down, so they're going to blow them. Should go in about fi—"

An explosion shook the ship, followed by the sounds of explosive decompression coming from down the corridor.

"Well, that was a bit early," Macy grunted. "Jenny never can wait for the full countdown."

Amanda pulled the feed from her nanocloud, and realized that the inner bulkheads of the maintenance bay must have been cracked. Interior pressure doors weren't closing, and, before long, this section of the ship would be in vacuum.

Vacuum didn't bother her, but she could only go for twenty minutes without air. Amanda took several long, deep breaths, configuring her lungs to draw out and store extra oxygen.

"Avatar," Macy spoke up. "Those crew we locked down; they're going to suffocate if we don't seal off those corridors."

"Wait for the plasma..." Amanda cautioned.

"We may not be able to tell when it hits," Macy replied. Then a second explosion shook the ship, and Amanda gave the Marine a smile.

"Looks like we're clear."

"Stars, what are you doing to my ship?" The voice came from behind them.

Amanda rose, and turned to see Ylonda approach as Macy sent a fireteam to seal bulkheads between the decompressing area and the rest of the ship.

"Hopefully nothing more," Amanda replied. "Elena's ship, and the mess it brought with it, should be gone now. We'll have to go inspect, of course."

"Did you hit it with plasma?" Ylonda asked, her eyes wide.

"Well...*I* didn't," Amanda grinned.

Ylonda frowned, and Amanda examined the captain's expression. Ylonda was an AI—a child of Jim and Corsia—who lived within a cybernetic body. Even so, she used a consistent set of expressions—expressions that appeared subtly different, at present. It wasn't the sort of thing that a human could pick out, but Amanda wasn't sure that term defined her anymore.

It was possible that Ylonda was reacting to the stress of the situation, but Amanda wasn't certain. She would have to probe Ylonda's mind to be sure the AI was not subverted, and was entirely herself; but not yet. It was still too soon to reveal her suspicions.

"Come," Amanda said as she walked back toward the maintenance bay, noting that the sensors on her artificial epidermis registered rapidly decreasing atmospheric pressure.

She rounded the corner and heard the sound of hissing air before she spotted the crack in the bulkhead.

"Give them another minute, and they'll have this area sealed off," Macy advised. "How long can you make it without air, Avatar?"

"Long enough," Amanda replied. No need to let Ylonda know exactly how long she could make on her reserves.

Two of the Marines approached the entrance to the maintenance bay and opened the manual release compartment. One cranked the release lever, while the other pulled at the door. With a groan still audible in the thin atmosphere, the door slid into the bulkhead, and the last of the air in the corridor rushed out.

The wind pulled at Amanda, but she reached out and grasped Macy's arm to keep steady.

Once the air had vented, Amanda stepped forward and peered inside the bay to find it completely gutted. The plasma shot from the *I2* had burned away Elena's ship, its connections into the *Hellespont,* and much of the bay's deck and overhead. Portions of the level below were visible through melted—and still glowing—sections of deck plate.

Amanda reconnected to the ship's network and sent Ylonda a message over the Link using an old set of encryption keys, a test to see if Myriad still remained onboard.

<Sorry, that transmission was garbled,> Ylonda replied. *<I thought we weren't supposed to be on the Link.>*

<We aren't,> Amanda replied. *<But it would seem you never disconnected…Myriad.>*

<Got me,> Myriad replied, her lips twisting into an ugly smile.

Amanda leapt back as silver filaments streaked from Ylonda's—now Myriad's—body in the vacuum, and touched the Marines.

Shit! Amanda thought as she watched the Marines' armor seize up.

<Just you and I,> Myriad said. *<It'll be interesting to see what insights your mind provides into Bob's psyche. Maybe I can use you to infiltrate him; that would make this whole charade wrap up a lot faster.>*

<What charade is that?> Amanda asked.

<Airtha would be upset if I ruined the surprise. You'll all learn soon enough, I expect. For now, however, would you mind submitting gently so I can subsume your mind?>

Amanda would have barked a laugh if she hadn't sealed up her lips and nose against the vacuum. A warning flashed over her vision and in her mind, reminding her that she now had fewer than ten minutes of oxygen remaining.

<Over my dead body,> Amanda replied.

<Oh, how deliciously cliché.>

Wispy filaments flowed out from Ylonda's hands, darting through the vacuum toward Amanda.

Amanda raised her hands and splayed her fingers, throwing an EM blast toward the approaching nanocloud, disabling many of the nanoscopic bots, and disrupting the communications of the remainder. She then directed a second EM pulse directly at Ylonda.

The AI's body was hardened, and Amanda knew the pulse wouldn't do any real harm, but it may disrupt the production and release of more nano.

<Very well, I'll bring them to you physically.>

Myriad flung Ylonda's body forward, raining a fury of blows on Amanda. She was able to block them, but she knew it would not be possible for long. Even though her epidermis was incredibly durable, underneath she was mostly still flesh and blood. Ylonda's body, on the other hand, was steel and carbon-fibre.

Ylonda managed to grasp one of Amanda's wrists, and the avatar could feel enemy nano seeping through the joints, infiltrating her body. In the blink of an eye, she and Myriad waged a nanoscopic war within her forearm; one that Amanda narrowly won before she twisted around to get her wrist free, snapping it in the process.

She ducked behind one of the frozen Marines—Macy, it turned out—and pulled out her pulse pistol. She fired seven shots at Ylonda, slamming the AI's body into the bulkhead, and then out into the ruined maintenance bay.

Amanda lost sight of Myriad. She stepped around Macy's body, searching through the dimly lit depths of the bay, ready to fire, when Myriad lunged out of the darkness and grabbed her.

Pain seared through her mind as Myriad crushed her wrist, and then tore her entire hand off. Amanda felt her blood pressure drop as red fluid sprayed out of her arteries into the vacuum, freezing into tiny pellets within moments.

Desperate, she fired point-blank into Ylonda's body; but the AI didn't let go. Amanda's vision swam, as much from the loss of blood as from the nanoscopic attack on her body.

She was near losing consciousness, and knew if she did, Myriad would storm through her mind, seizing whatever she wished. Already the not-AI was pressing at the edges of her thoughts, trying to tear her away, layer-by-layer, to erase Amanda's very self.

As her vision began to fade, she saw something small and bright fly through the destroyed outer doors of the bay and hit Ylonda's body.

Then everything went black.

* * * * *

Amanda… Amanda…

She felt, as much as heard, the voice in her mind.

<Amanda!>

Amanda's eyes snapped open and she saw Staff Sergeant Macy's visage through the faceplate of the Marine's armor.

"There you are," Macy said with a smile. "I was worried for a minute there."

Amanda felt a stabbing pain in her right hand, and decided not to look at whatever was left of her appendage. It was being pulled about, which meant one of the Marines was probably sealing up the stump.

"Were you calling me over the Link?" Amanda asked.

Macy shook her head. "No way, I haven't been on the Link since you gave the order to shut our connections down.

Realization dawned on Amanda. "Then she's still here!"

"A lot of people are still here, but we need to get off, fast. Admiral Evans sent word that they're going to drop a nuke on this ship in twenty minutes. We're rounding up the last of the survivors and getting them to the pinnace."

"What happened to Ylo—Myriad's body?" Amanda asked, glancing around. She saw that the Marines had erected an ES shield over the entrance to the maintenance bay. It was still dark within, but she couldn't make out any body floating in the black.

"*I2* fired a targeted picobomb in there. It ate through Ylonda's body like it was butter. Scared me shitless, too; I thought we were all going to bite it, but then it just dissipated. RF signal came in from the *I2* to clear out, so we grabbed you, and that's what we're doing."

"Picobomb…" Amanda whispered.

"Yeah, that's about how I feel about it, too," Macy replied. "Except when I said it, there was a lot more cursing. Ben has your wrist wrapped up now. Can you stand?"

Amanda nodded, showing more confidence then she felt. Still, with Macy's help, she made it to her feet. She wondered how Joe had gained permission from parliament to fire the picobomb. Though maybe Bob had done it without gaining authorization...

<Amanda…>

"I hear it again. She *is* still here."

Realization dawned over Macy's face. "You mean Captain Ylonda? Where?"

<I hear you, Ylonda! Where are you?>

A garbled burst of digital static came across the Link, followed by two words:

<last…node.>

"Last node!" Amanda said aloud.

"What does that mean? Which is 'last'?" Macy asked.

"I don't know…" Amanda sighed. "They're in a matrix; none is really 'last'."

"Maybe…maybe…. Yes!" Macy announced. "I know which it is. Follow me!"

Macy took off, and Amanda followed behind as quickly as she could, but teetered as a wave of dizziness overcame her. Suddenly an arm scooped her up, catching her before she fell, and she saw Ben's face looming close.

"Not going to patch you up, just so you can collapse and die in here, ma'am," he said.

"I appreciate it," Amanda replied before calling out to Macy, "Where are we going?"

"Last node that got installed," Macy replied. "It's three levels up, and a hundred meters aft."

"Do you think that's what she meant?" Amanda asked.

"We have fifteen minutes before they blow this ship to atoms," Macy replied. "We don't have time to check more nodes."

"What's the rush?" Amanda asked.

"Because Myriad has helm control and she's boosting on an outsystem vector!"

"You're right," a new voice said over the ship's address system. "She is in there; clever of her, she's tucked into a backup array. Probably just barely enough room in there, too."

"Shit!" Amanda swore, wishing Macy had told her sooner that Myriad was still in control of the ship.

Macy and Ben picked up the pace, racing down passageways and scaling up ladder shafts. Amanda wrapped her good arm around Ben for dear life and prayed they'd make it in time.

When they reached the entrance to the node, it was sealed tight.

"I've got this," Macy said as she patched a hard-pad into the door's mechanism. "She's locked it down, but these nodes have hard-coded emergency overrides. Just have to have the keys."

"You're all going to die in here with me," Myriad said. "I don't take any pleasure in it. I didn't stop the rest of your people from leaving, but now it's just us."

"Everyone else left?" Amanda asked, panic setting in. There was a lot more she wanted to do with her life. Dying on a ship that got blown up by her own people wasn't anywhere on the list.

"I told them to go at t-minus ten," Macy said. "There are still escape pods. Plenty of time yet."

Amanda bit her lip—ten minutes to extract Ylonda and get off the ship to a safe distance did not meet her definition of 'plenty'.

"There!" Macy proclaimed, as the door slid open to reveal the node chamber.

It wasn't anywhere near as large as Bob's nodes—mostly because Ylonda wasn't a true multi-nodal AI. For her, the nodes functioned as extensions of her mind that augmented her processing power, while functioning as backups, should the ship take damage.

"Set me down there," Amanda pointed at a panel near the bottom right corner of the node's processing array.

Ben lowered her to the deck, and Amanda grabbed a thicker 'hair' at the base of her skull and pulled. It stretched out, and she plugged it into a data port on the processing array.

The world around her disappeared as the hard-Link to the node connected. The internals of the node were a mess; entire regions were filled with ruined code and non-functional arrays—the remains of a battle fought between Myriad and Ylonda that had damaged software and hardware alike.

Amanda was casting about for a protocol and route that would lead her to Ylonda, when a connection hit her.

<*Amanda, you came!*>

<*Of course, we're not going to leave you here!*>

<*I can barely think. I don't know how much of me is left; I can't even unpack in here to validate that all of me made it.*>

<*Oh shit, she's here!*> Amanda exclaimed, as she felt Myriad's presence flood the processing array.

<*Thank you for coming,*> the not-AI said. <*You're my ride out of here.*>

Amanda reeled as Myriad began to push herself across the connection and into her mind. Like their mental fight in the maintenance bay, her adversary was just too strong. Myriad pushed across the Link, and began to fill Amanda's mind—stripping her down, and pushing her aside.

<*Oh, no you don't!*> Ylonda called out, and she, too, suddenly flooded across the hard-Link into Amanda. Her presence bolstered Amanda, and together they shut down protocols faster than Myriad could switch attacks. Myriad had moved part of herself into Amanda; they locked it down, removing her access, compressing and reducing the not-AI.

It felt like it took years, but Amanda knew only milliseconds had passed. As she examined her surroundings, she could tell that Ylonda was within her and safe; though she could no longer tell where she ended and the AI began.

<*Are we…?*> she asked.

<*I think so,*> she replied.

"We're—I'm safe," Amanda/Ylonda said aloud. "Get to the pods!"

Ben scooped her up once more, and the pair of Marines raced out of the node chamber and down a short set of corridors to a bank of pods. Three remained, and they crammed into one, Macy slamming a fist into the 'GO' button the instant the door sealed behind them.

Amanda/Ylonda was still trying to understand what she had become, when the pod rocked violently and an explosion's deafening roar echoed inside the small compartment.

MYRIAD

STELLAR DATE: 03.28.8948 (Adjusted Years)
LOCATION: ISS *I2*
REGION: Near Roma, New Canaan System

<*Bob, I want to be there when you talk to Myriad. Angela and I both do,*> Tanis addressed the AI without preamble.

<*Yes. Bob, what you did before is not acceptable,*> Angela added.

<*It was necessary…and I made a mistake,*> Bob replied. <*I'm not a god. I can see much of the past and future, but I cannot see it all—and Airtha appears to be a significant blind spot. Enough that I am questioning everything I thought I knew.*>

Tanis wondered what an existential crisis for a being like Bob would entail. Luckily, he was not prone to irrational decisions, or she would have cause to worry.

<*When did you learn that Helen was not an AI?*> Tanis asked.

<*The day you brought* Sabrina *to the* Intrepid *in the Bollam's World System,*> Bob replied. <*Amanda and Priscilla noticed first, and then brought it to my attention. Helen and I conversed at length, and I believed that our goals were aligned. She, however, did not want Sera to learn of her true nature.*>

Bob paused, and this time Tanis suspected that it was not because he was giving her time to process information.

<*Go on,*> Angela prompted.

<*I honored that wish, which involved not telling any of you. I confess; a part of it was from curiosity. She was not an entity I expected to ever encounter. She was a human mind at one point, spread into a multi-nodal AI. That is a part of how she can shard herself so easily.*>

This was new information to Tanis, and she could tell that Angela was surprised, as well.

<*A human once? Airtha was human*?> Angela asked first.

<*Yes,*> Bob replied.

Tanis wondered what that would be like. A multi-nodal AI was essentially a hive-mind of itself. Bob had raised his number of nodes considerably through the years, and now possessed forty-two; all placed throughout the ship in a pattern that meant something to him, but not to anyone else—except perhaps Earnest, though he never offered up any explanations.

For Bob, it was the only existence he had ever known. To split a human mind like that, but have it act in concert with itself, was hard to imagine. It rarely even worked with AI. Bob was the only one she knew of who operated at such a large scale.

<*So why didn't you tell Angela, at least?*> Tanis asked. <*I agree that it would have been hard for me to not tell Sera, but Angela can keep her mouth shut. You should have told her.*>

<*No,*> Bob said with a tone of finality. <*You have an important future, Tanis. I feared that too much knowledge of things that you could never have learned without my intervention would put that future in jeopardy. The same is true for what I shall discuss with Myriad.*>

Tanis felt her temper fail and her anger rise. She trusted Bob, and could accept that he made mistakes from time to time; but this continuing nonsense about some great destiny—which seemed to be the next step in his belief that she possessed some sort of innate luck—was becoming too much.

<*Bob, I don't care about some sort of amazing future that you think lies in store for me. I care about the here and now, about the tactical information I can glean from Myriad. If we don't survive what's coming, we won't get to it, anyway.*>

<*Are you giving me a direct order that I must follow as a member of this crew, under your command?*> Bob asked.

Tanis paused. Bob's words were a prelude to a very final statement; one that neither of them—she hoped—wanted to speak or hear.

Before she could respond, Bob spoke again. *<Allow me to speak hypothetically, Governor. Were you to issue an order to me that would compel me to either interrogate Myriad with you present, or to reveal my suspicions of your destiny, I would execute my privileges under Article 83.1A of our colony charter to resign my commission and leave the colony. Hypothetically speaking, of course.>*

<He's serious,> Angela said privately to Tanis. *<I don't understand this luck and destiny nonsense any more than you do, but he seems to believe it very firmly. Firmly enough to leave us.>*

<No kidding…> Tanis replied as her shoulders slumped and she leaned back in her chair. *<I didn't expect this to come to such a head so soon.>*

<I have an alternative,> Bob proposed.

<I'm all ears—metaphorically speaking,> Tanis replied.

<I will speak to Myriad. I will record the datum of our conversation, and entrust it to Jason Andrews in his new role as Governor—a role I know you plan to offer him—only to be opened in case of my demise. Additionally, I suspect that much of what you hope to get from my interrogation will be revealed by Finaeus when you meet him. If there is something that I think is strategically important in the near term that Finaeus does not reveal, then I will tell it to you.>

Tanis massaged her temples. A lot of people were not going to be happy when they learned how Bob acted without any oversight. He had saved them enough times that everyone would give him a pass; but to let it happen again…if it backfired, it would not go well.

Humans and AIs alike had perished in both the ISF and TSF fleets when Myriad took them over. Some may place the blame on Bob's doorstep, noting that it could have been avoided if he had revealed his knowledge—though Tanis suspected that such concerns would be lost in the aftermath of what was to come.

<*OK, Bob, you may proceed. But when we finish this war with Orion, you are going to spill it to me. You're going to tell me what you really think is in store for me, because if it's more war….*>

<*Understood,*> Bob replied simply.

<*Now about Myriad; were you able to successfully extract her from Amanda's mind?*> Tanis asked.

<*Yes. Amanda and Ylonda managed to restrain her very effectively until I could get her into a vessel. She is intact—mostly—and will be able to respond to me.*>

<*And what of Amanda and Ylonda? Are they going to be alright?*> Tanis asked, already worried about what the answer would be. She had met Amanda when she was brought aboard, and she did not seem entirely coherent.

<*Not yet,*> Bob replied. <*When Ylonda entered Amanda's mind, both were already half-consumed by Myriad. As they defeated the not-AI, they bonded—the shattered remains of their minds seeking one another out, and merging.*>

<*Merging?*> Angela asked.

<*Yes. They are one being now,*> Bob replied. <*Both had memory backups, so I am assisting them in reintegrating those. But I don't know that they can be separated without resetting themselves; they may not want to do that, either.*>

Tanis let Bob's words sink in, aware that Angela was also considering them. A full merge of a human and AI was a violation of the Phobos accords. It was a stricture put in place to stop the subversion of either party in the merger—something that was not entirely applicable in what had occurred with Amanda and Ylonda.

<*How much can we be bound by rules put in place out of fear six thousand years ago?*> Angela asked.

<Not to mention that we shouldn't judge such a thing, given our circumstance.>

<Will Jim and Corsia be able to see them soon?> Tanis asked, knowing the pain and fear they must be feeling. Ylonda had been their daughter, and now Ylonda was no more; when they saw her, she would appear as Amanda, and speak with Amanda's voice.

Though they were not completely gone, it was still very much like Ylonda and Amanda both had died. And now Jim and Corsia had to deal with that loss, while celebrating what was, in some respects, their new child.

<Yes, very soon. I'll let you know when. For now, I must focus on those two, and my conversation with Myriad.>

Tanis felt Bob retreat from her mind and let out a long sigh.

<What a day,> she said to Angela.

<Yeah, but soon we'll see Sabrina again,> Angela reminded her.

<And find out why Myriad wants them dead so badly.>

<That too,> Angela agreed.

"No rest for the weary," Tanis muttered as she rose.

MESSAGE IN A BOTTLE

STELLAR DATE: 03.28.8948 (Adjusted Years)
LOCATION: ISS *I2*
REGION: Near Roma, New Canaan System

<*Sera,*> a voice whispered in her mind. It felt like a memory, like thoughts from the past left for her by another.

<*Helen!*> Sera replied as realization dawned over her. <*You're alive!*>

<*No, dear. If you're hearing this, then I am not. This is a simple program I left behind to explain things.*>

Sera felt despair flood her mind; a feeling she had held in check—but now, after rekindled hope had lifted her spirits, she fell prey to it.

<*Well, you damn well have a lot of explaining to do.*>

<*I can only imagine,*> the Helen-memory replied. <*I have absorbed the details of what has occurred after I was taken from you—something I feared your father would do if he ever learned who I was.*>

Sera nodded to herself, <*We both did, but why did he kill you? I thought he was a friend of Airtha's…I never really did understand why he wouldn't let me have a shard of you, anyway.*>

<*I do not know the answer to that. Helen did not leave me with that information.*>

<*Then let's talk about something you better know about. Why is Myriad core-bent on destroying* Sabrina *and my crew?*> Sera asked, anger rising in her.

<*Because they found Finaeus, but then went to Orion. Now I think they will try to kill you, and Tanis, since Kent and Elena failed.*>

<*What!*> Sera exclaimed. <*But why couldn't you just say that, instead of taking over all the ships? People died out there, Helen!*>

<I can't speak for why Myriad came to that decision, but I imagine she thinks you'd risk contact. You cannot contact them…or that ship they've docked in. They ***must*** *be destroyed.>*

<I can't do that! It's a whole ship full of Tanis's people! I couldn't do it if I wanted to—which I don't.>

<Sera…> Helen's voice in her mind implored. *<If you can't…if you won't…then you must come to Airtha. She can explain everything. You'll understand why all of this has transpired, and what your part in it is.>*

Sera didn't know what to say, but she felt the presence leaving her mind; the program was erasing itself. *<Helen! No!>*

There was no response.

"Sera," Tanis's voice brought her back to the physical world, where they stood on the bridge, reviewing the damage to the fleets. "What do you think about that, Sera?"

REUNION

STELLAR DATE: 03.28.8948 (Adjusted Years)
LOCATION: ISS *I2*
REGION: Near Roma, New Canaan System

Tanis and Sera waited side-by-side in the *I2*'s main bay as *Sabrina* settled into its cradle. The ship appeared to have been through a lot in the past eighteen years: burn marks and carbon scoring were everywhere on its hull, and there was evidence of more than one patchwork repair.

Tanis glanced at Sera, already back on her feet—though an external brace held her spine rigid while the newly grown and meshed nerves settled into place. "Feels like just yesterday that we stood here and watched them leave."

Sera met her eyes. The new President of the Transcend looked much the same as she had that day back near Virginis, but now worn and weary—not at all unexpected, after what they had both been through.

"I wish it were that day again," Sera sighed. "There's so much I would have done differently since then—like going back to Airtha. Didn't turn out that well."

Tanis took her hand. "Sera, what we are caught in was set in motion long ago. You and I were oblivious to it, but we could not have avoided what is now before us, no matter how hard we might have tried."

Sera chuckled and then groaned softly. "Stop being all wise and poetic. Laughing at you hurts too much. Too bad I can't just grow a new spine like you can grow a new arm."

Tanis held up her temporary flowmetal arm. "It's handy—no pun intended—but I prefer a biological arm. I just like the feel of it more. Besides, you just regrew part of your spine; it's just going to take some time before your nerves sort out what they should be doing."

Their conversation was cut short by *Sabrina*'s ramp extending, and the docking bay doors opening.

The first person Tanis laid eyes on was Jessica, and, though she knew her long-time friend was alive and well, she felt a wave of relief at finally laying eyes on her.

Beside Jessica stood a massive man—one who would have made even Usef feel small. He stood close to Jessica, and Tanis saw him glance down at her with the sort of eyes one has only for their lover. To his right stood Nance, and Tanis noticed that Thompson was not beside her—or anywhere, for that matter. On Jessica's other side stood Cargo, as well as two men she didn't recognize.

The absence of Cheeky was notable.

Sera caught Tanis's eye with a worried expression as they walked forward to greet the crew.

Jessica and Cargo walked down the ramp first, followed by the rest of the crew in a slow procession.

Sera opened her mouth to speak, but her voice faltered as she looked over the faces before her.

"Welcome home," Tanis filled in the silence and offered a warm, very heartfelt, smile. "I know that we're all glad to see one another. However, we have suffered losses this day, and I can see that you may have, as well. This is going to be a difficult reunion, but one that is still truly happy."

"Ah, Tanis," Jessica said with a smile as she stepped forward and embraced her. "I've missed your blunt, matter-of-factness."

Tanis returned the hug. "I have extra doses of it saved up for you."

Cargo and Nance ran forward to greet Sera, and Tanis noticed the three men she did not know hang back. Jessica caught her glance and extended an arm to include the newcomers. "Tanis and Sera, allow me to introduce you to Trevor, Misha, and, the goal of our little expedition, Finaeus."

Sera had already opened her arms to Finaeus, and, as she embraced him, she asked, "Where are Thompson and Cheeky—and Piya?"

Jessica's face fell, and Cargo spoke up. "Thompson left us in Ikoden, after we found Finaeus—" His statement was interrupted by a snort from Nance, and he gave her an understanding look before continuing. "Cheeky and Piya had to…well they…"

Cargo's voice had grown thick, and he paused—glancing to Jessica, who raised her eyebrows, a look of sorrow clouding her features before she spoke.

"Cheeky and Piya had to hold the gate open and keep it aligned…she…sacrificed herself so that we could get back. She'd be glad to know it was worth it; we got back in the nick of time."

Tanis felt as though her heart really had been torn out…both of them. Cheeky had been such a free, loving spirit, always full of hope and enthusiasm. She was the glue that held Sabrina together.

She looked to Sera, and saw her friend's eyes fill with tears. Tanis placed a hand on Sera's shoulder while she spent a few seconds trying to calm herself.

"A gate? Where were you? I don't understand," Sera finally managed to say. "How did it take so long to get here? Ikoden is only three, maybe four years away. You were there *nine* years ago. Why…?"

Finaeus drew a deep breath and placed his hands on Sera's shoulders. "My dear Seraphina, you would never believe what has happened to us. This crew, your fair *Sabrina,* we have just arrived from the Perseus arm of the galaxy."

Sera took a step back and locked eyes with Finaeus. "What do you mean Perseus? That's on the far side of Orion-controlled space!"

Tanis saw a strange look in Sera's eyes, almost as though she knew where *Sabrina* had been, and was not surprised—or not surprised about the location, but more about something else.

<*Oh, we know all about that,*> Sabrina said with a chuckle. <*Was a great little visit we had with the good folks of Orion.*>

<*Seriously?*> Tanis said privately to Angela. <*I really thought things could not get any more complicated.*>

<*Tanis! How could you say that? Way to jinx us.*>

"It's a long story," Finaeus replied. "Do you have any good food on his monstrosity of a ship? We've been making do with some…less than savory rations. Let's get something in our stomachs before we explain all this."

"Of course," Tanis replied. "Come, there's a mess hall not far from here. They have a great selection."

A small smile crept onto Sera's face, though there were still tears in her eyes for Cheeky. "I guess some things never change, Uncle Finaeus. You always did do your best thinking on a full stomach."

"A little bit of beer won't hurt, either," Finaeus replied. "This is quite the story."

Tanis turned and signaled for a groundcar to approach. It had an open carriage, with no doors or ceiling. The group quickly piled in. During the short drive across the docking bay, a half-dozen muted conversations broke out: Trevor and Misha asked about the ship, marveling at its size; Finaeus asked Sera about her father's death—having learned about it while aboard the *Daedalus*—and Jessica asked about many of her friends.

<*Jess, I couldn't help but notice you're holding hands with Trevor. Dare I wonder…?*>

Jessica cast her a bright smile. *<Noticed that, did you? We picked Trevor up back in Virginis, if you can believe it. We've been together for pretty much the whole trip.>*

<Congratulations! You're going to have to tell me that story.>

<Eagerly awaiting it,> Jessica replied.

"Stars, a lot has happened over the last eighteen years," Tanis said aloud. "It's going to take a long time to get caught up. But first," she said with a smile, as they approached the kilometer-tall forward bulkhead of the main bay, "I would like you to meet my daughters."

Standing before the entrance to the mess hall—which looked more like a bistro, complete with tables and umbrellas out on the deck in front of a cozy-looking dining room beyond—were two young women.

"I'd like to introduce you to Cary and Saanvi," Tanis said with a sweep of her arm. "My daughters."

"Daughters?" Jessica exclaimed as she leapt from the groundcar. "There are two of you, and grown up!" There was a tear in Jessica's eye as she turned to look at Tanis. *<I've missed so much, haven't I? Saanvi doesn't look like yours and Joe's! Have you two separated?>*

<No, of course not! She's adopted—another long story. But don't worry; we have centuries ahead of us. We'll make many more memories together,> Tanis replied privately.

Cary stepped forward first, her hand extended toward Jessica. "It's really nice to meet you, Jessica. We've studied you in our history classes."

"Oh, core, no! Studied me? That's horrifying," Jessica laughed as she swatted away Cary's hand and hugged her. "You too, Saanvi," she said and reached out an arm. "I can't wait to get to know you two. You're the ones that will give me the real dirt on Tanis that no one else will dare share."

Cary laughed and a slow smile crept across Saanvi's face. "Don't you worry, Jessica. We have more juicy stories than you can imagine."

Tanis felt happiness about her daughters finally getting to meet Jessica, but sorrow that it was only just now.

"Yes, yes. You're very lovely girls. Now can we get some food?" Finaeus asked.

"Of course, of course, Uncle Finaeus. We wouldn't want to upset your growling stomach any more than it is," Sera laughed, as they walked in and pushed several tables together.

"Seraphina," Finaeus said somberly. "You are now the President of the Transcend Interstellar Alliance. You can dispense with 'uncle'."

Sera snorted. "I'm a president in-exile before my rule has even begun. Airtha is the real ruler—though I mean to take it back."

"Then it is as I feared—what I warned Jeff about has finally come to pass."

"And what is that?" Tanis asked.

"First, let's fill our stomachs. We'll tell you about our adventure, and then I'll tell you what I know—that which Airtha was willing to kill us for in order to keep from you."

"OK, Un—Finaeus," Sera nodded. "I do really want to hear what you were doing in Perseus!"

Once everyone had settled in their seats around the combined tables and placed their orders over the Link, Jessica, Finaeus, and Cargo glanced between one another.

"Who should tell it?" Cargo asked.

"Well, you're the captain," Jessica said.

"And Finaeus is the man of ancient times," Cargo chuckled.

"Oh, for fuck's sake," Trevor swore. "I'll tell it."

Before he could begin, the servitor arrived with their drinks, and Trevor took a long draught of the beer set before him. "Oh, gods below, that's good!"

"Just wait till you taste strawberries," Nance said with a grin.

"Wha? Wow!" Trevor exclaimed. "OK, anyway, here goes. So first off, as you know, I'm Trevor. I almost got Jessica killed in an illegal fighting ring back in Virginis, and as punishment, I was forced to schlep across the stars with this sorry crew."

"Something he's been all too glad to do," Jessica said as she wrapped an arm around the massive man—as far as she could manage, at least—and planted a kiss on his cheek.

<*They look like some sort of ad for a body-mod shop,*> Cary said privately to Tanis and Saanvi.

<*Cary!*> Saanvi chided.

"Yeah, so anyway, we tooled around for a while, and Jessica here managed to hunt down our friend Finaeus—something we just barely survived, I should add."

"Sorry about that," Sera grimaced. "I had a bit of a purge after that little dust-up. Well, as much as I could, with my father watching over everything I did."

"Not surprised," Finaeus shook his head. "Jeff was the ultimate control freak."

"Guys, let him tell the story, already," Nance cut in.

"Sorry," Sera grimaced.

"OK, so anyway, Finaeus here has this bright idea that we should go to this star called Grey Wolf in the Inner Stars where the Transcend is mining the whole freaking white dwarf remnant—which is…beyond description. Turns out that they were expecting us, and things didn't go so well. They captured Cargo and Jessica, and the rest of us had to defend the ship, *and* get a Ford-Svaiter mirror." Trevor explained. "Wasn't pretty; Cheeky and Finaeus went for a crazy little jaunt outside the station. In the end, we pulled it all off and got aboard; but not before we dealt with Colonel Bes—dude was a real hard-ass."

"Bes?" Sera asked. "So that's where he went. I can't believe I didn't hear about any of this at all. Apparently my father was better at covering things up than I thought."

"Or someone..." Finaeus said ominously.

"But wait, there's more," Jessica added with a wry smile.

"So, we get a mirror, get it on the ship—thank the stars for stasis shields—and used a hackit that our AIs planted on the Gisha Platform to re-align the jump-gate so we could get here."

<*Thank you, thank you,*> Iris gave a mock bow in their minds.

<*Yes, because you did it allll by yourself,*> Hank commented.

"So, there we were," Trevor continued, "all lined up on the gate, ready to go, and Jessica boosted on in. Everything was finally coming up aces—but at the last minute, they managed to fire a thruster on the ring, and spun it right as we went in. Finaeus tried to compensate, and then our mirror control system had a failure and we couldn't shut it off."

"Shiiit," Sera whispered.

"No kidding," Finaeus nodded. "They were lucky I was on board, or they would have ended up in the Sextans Galaxy, or worse."

"Fin!" Nance scowled. "None of that would have happened without you. We would have been here years ago."

"Yes," Finaeus nodded sagely. "But we wouldn't know what we do now about Orion."

"What is that?" Tanis asked.

"We're getting there, trust me," Trevor replied. "OK, where was I? Oh, yeah. So, we finally dump back into normal space and have a pretty serious 'Oh, fuck' moment or two while we try to figure out where the hell we were."

"At least three or four moments of solid 'Oh, fuck'," Jessica added with a wink at Trevor.

<Try a million,> Sabrina interjected. *<I've never been so scared.>*

"Well, we were pretty close to a black hole," Cargo said.

"Seriously, guys, can I tell the story or what?" Trevor asked. A few sighs and nods greeted him, and he waited a moment to ensure the silence held before continuing. "We dropped a few probes into the dark layer, and ascertained that it was safe enough for us to jump to the closest star system—which had radio signals coming from it, so we knew someone was there."

He took another drink from his beer before continuing. "Turns out it was a backwater sort of colony named Naga—just one TP, and a few dozen stations and habs. We stripped the beacons from way out, and faked our ident as a freighter from a ways away. Then we went in and traded what we had onboard—after spending a week removing any traces of where it came from.

"They could tell we were shady as fuck. I mean, who shows up on a ship that looks *nothing* like any other ship around, and has holds filled with completely untraceable cargo? And not rare stuff, either; just melons, and generic shit in crates with no markings. Not a lot of call for black market melons."

"That was a fun dockside excursion…and photoshoot," Jessica chuckled.

"Photoshoot?" Tanis asked.

"Long story," Jessica said with a wave of her hand—which Tanis was certain glowed for a moment.

"Sure was," Trevor nodded. "Luckily, we ran into Misha there. He was looking for a ship to sign on to, and he knew the locals. We managed to leave Naga with our skins intact, and started working our way across the Perseus Arm to get here."

"But that would have taken a lot longer—twenty years, at least," Sera said with a frown.

"Sure would have," Trevor agreed. "From Naga, we hopped star by star, jumping as far as we dared on each leg of the trip. We were between the Perseus and Orion arm—near an open cluster they call the Trireme—when we stumbled upon a Guard base. It wasn't very well defended, not like some of the major fleet outposts that we had seen. But it still had a jump gate. By then we had learned a lot about Orion—things that even Finaeus here didn't know: their strengths, beliefs, lots of stuff—and we decided it was worth attempting another jump."

"That seems like a serious risk for that sort of intel." Sera shook her head as she spoke.

"It may have been," Cargo added. "But we knew that Orion was on the move. If we didn't get to New Canaan soon, we'd miss the entire war—and then all our sacrifices would have been for nothing. And then there's what we learned at that outpost."

"Save that for last, I need to say my bit first," Finaeus advised.

Trevor paused and took a deep breath. "OK. So, the short version is that we infiltrated their base and..." he paused a moment and cleared his throat before continuing. "...and that's where we lost Cheeky and Piya. They sacrificed themselves to ensure the gate remained aligned."

He stopped and took a gulp of his beer. In the resulting silence, Cargo spoke up.

"They gave their lives to get us back here. Made the ultimate sacrifice."

"Oh, Cheeky..." Sera whispered and shook her head.

"It was good that she did," Finaeus said. "With Airtha making her move, it's very fortuitous that we made it back when we did, and not years later. This could have all been over by then."

"Sounds like it's your turn to tell a story," Tanis said to Finaeus. "I sure hope it's worth what everyone had to go through to get you here."

"Oh, trust me, it's well worth it," Finaeus said somberly. "So, even if you took the worst history classes in school, you know that Jeffrey Tomlinson left Sol in 2392 as the captain of the first FGT Worldship, the *Starfarer.* I left not long after in 2442 on the *Tardis*. Not as captain, though. I was the chief science officer.

"We all flitted off through space, happy as clams in mud, terraforming worlds and cleaning up systems for human habitation. We built our own shipyards, and our own worlds out at Beta Hydri—Lucida, it's called now, and again at Alula Australis. Everything was going fine until that whole FTL wars thing you know about oh, so well.

"That was when Jeff got us all together, and we formed the Transcend. It took forever to convince everyone to do it, but once we suffered a few losses to the wars, it came together pretty quick. We set up with a few core areas—one just past the Orion Nebula, and another out beyond M24, plus a few others, as well. The nebulae hid what we were up to from the rest of humanity, and we worked to build a civilization that we hoped to use to bring humanity back from the brink—the whole 'uplift' idea that you all must know about already."

Even though she knew much of this, Tanis found it surreal to hear it from Finaeus himself—a man who had left Sol fifteen hundred years before she was born.

The arrival of their food added a further distraction—especially for Finaeus—but after several bites, and exclamations of joy over the sear on his steak, he continued.

"Anyway, about that time, Jeff and a few others decided that we needed to map out a lot more of the galaxy. His wife, Jelina, left on an expedition to survey the core past the inner 3-

Kiloparsec arm. What they found...well...it was not what we expected."

"Core devils..." Sera whispered, her eyes wide.

"I've heard people use that curse before," Tanis said. "I always thought you were referring to the Hegemony."

Finaeus chuckled. "Well, 'core devils' certainly applies to them, too. But when it's used in the Transcend, it refers to what Jelina found in the galaxy's center. I assume you all know the theories about how super-advanced civilizations will eventually migrate to black holes, because that's where the bulk of the matter and energy in the universe will be stored when all the stars burn out in trillion years or so."

Everyone around the table nodded, and Tanis noted that Saanvi appeared particularly interested, hardly blinking as she watched Finaeus.

"Well, when the ascended AI left Sol after your Sentience Wars, that's where they went—to the supermassive black hole at the center of the galaxy: Sagittarius A*."

"I knew it!" Tanis announced triumphantly. "I knew they got away and set up somewhere."

"Yeah, and set up they did. They have built quite the civilization there, from what Jelina—or rather, what Jelina had become—told us."

"Had become?" Sera asked.

"OK, let me step back a bit," Finaeus said. "First off, let me tell you about ascended AIs. You're looking at probably only one of a dozen humans—or non-ascended AIs, for that matter—who really knows what the term means. To properly explain it, let me tell you about two-dimensional beings."

Finaeus paused, noticing the expectant looks on the faces around him. "Sorry, no; to my knowledge, no one has ever discovered two-dimensional beings. This is just an example."

He took another bite of his steak before raising his hands in the air. He spread them wide, and a horizontal square of light appeared over the table, hovering above their food. "This is two-dimensional space," he said, and then touched the pane of light, and a black dot appeared. "Here is something the two-dimensional creatures hold dear. They build a vault to protect it and keep it safe." As he spoke, a small black line appeared and traced a square around the dot.

"As you can see, in two-dimensional space, this square, which is nothing more than four lines, protects the exalted dot that our flat little friends value so highly. However, I," and with that, Finaeus reached out and plucked the dot from within the square, "as a three-dimensional creature, have no issue taking their prize."

He held it in his fingers and gestured at the pane of light. "I have just done something magical, beyond the laws of physics as they understand them. To them, I am a god, an exalted being. And if, perhaps, I had begun life as a two-dimensional creature, one could say that I have ascended."

"So, the ascended AIs are four-dimensional creatures?"

Finaeus shook his head, and waved his hand, creating the familiar form of a tesseract—a four-dimensional cube. "To perceive the third dimension, we utilize two-dimensional eyes. However, we do possess the technology to create three-dimensional eyes. With those, we can, with some difficulty, perceive the fourth dimension. Though, as you can see with the tesseract, it is difficult to map a four-dimensional image into the human mind. Some can do it, but they are few, and they are on the road to becoming something more."

"How do physical dimensions apply to AIs?" Saanvi asked, as rapt as she was in any science class, or at the feet of Earnest during one of his visits to their cabin.

"Well, AIs operate in three-dimensional space, same as us. They are constrained by the strictures of three-dimensional physics. Of course, we all take advantage of every dimension—even though we can't perceive them—since they all construct the universe around us. Still, an AI lives within a core that is a three-dimensional construct, just as our organic bodies are.

As Finaeus spoke, Tanis gazed at the tesseract, perceiving it in the fourth dimension—viewing all of its planes and angles as though it were a solid object. Not the semi-transparent double-cube that it appeared to be normally—that she had seen every other time she had looked at a tesseract.

<*Uh…Angela?*> Tanis asked.

<*Yes, I know you can see the tesseract properly. I can, too,*> Angela replied.

"This," Finaeus said as he produced a new object. "This is a hypercube. It is a five-dimensional cube. In simple terms, it consists of ten sides, each of which is a tesseract."

The image swam before Tanis's eyes and she winced from the pain caused by looking at it. The hypercube wanted to resolve into a solid object, and kept coming close—but just as she thought it would stop being a mess of lines and become a *thing,* it dissolved into chaos again. She closed her eyes, though doing so did not remove the shape from her mind.

As she tried to clear the vision, Tanis heard Sera say, "Oh, yeah, simple," and she opened her eyes to see Finaeus peering at her.

Tanis turned her gaze to her daughters and tried not to think about what she just saw and what it meant.

"Then ascended AIs are just five-dimensional creatures?" Saanvi asked.

Finaeus laughed. "*Just* five dimensional creatures? As if that wasn't enough to make them gods in our eyes. But no, that is not what they are—not only, at least. An AI, as those of you present all know—especially the AI among you—still needs a *place* to be. Even your Bob, multi-nodal as he is, still exists somewhere in physical space that you can put your hand to. But an ascended AI, in its fifth dimension, does not have what we could consider to be a corporeal being. As best we can tell, they exist directly within, or on the quantum foam of, the universe. It's where they draw their energy from; it's their home."

"I don't get it," Nance spoke up. "If they exist in and on Zero-Point energy, why do they need to live near Sagittarius A*? What use do they have for a supermassive black hole?"

"Honestly?" Finaeus replied. "We don't know. Maybe they travelled there before they fully ascended. Maybe they plan to use its gravitational mass—after it merges with the core of the Andromeda Galaxy, and later all the galaxies of the Virgo Supercluster—to survive the eventual heat-death of the universe, or the big crunch—whichever actually occurs."

"Why is there no record of this?" Sera asked. "Why does no one know what Jelina found? The records about her just say that she went off on a mission to chart the core of the galaxy, and died while they were out there."

"Records can be altered," Finaeus replied somberly. "Jelina, as you know, was your father's third wife, and the mother of both Serge and Andrea—plus a few others of your father's brood. What you don't know, is that she is also your mother."

"What?" Sera gasped. "But she was gone eons ago! I'm just seventy-two now; there's no way she's my mother."

"Before she left, Jelina and Jeff conceived several children and placed them in stasis. You were one of those children, Sera. Your father has brought several of them out from time-to-time, and raised them; though never told them about their mother."

Tanis watched Sera fall back in her seat, flabbergasted.

"What happened to Jelina?" Tanis asked. "You said she came back changed."

"She did, at that, she…she…" Finaeus faltered. "She wasn't ascended, but she came back in a construct—her mind loaded into an AI's neural net."

"They made her into an AI?" Sera asked.

"They made a thing," Finaeus replied. "A thing that talked and thought like Jelina, but was not Jelina. It was—it is—something else."

"Is?" Tanis asked.

"Is," Finaeus nodded. "She's the reason why Kirkland broke Orion away from the Transcend. She's the reason I was exiled."

"Stars," Tanis whispered. "She's Airtha."

She glanced at Sera and saw a look of incredulity on her friend's face.

"Is it true?" Sera asked, her eyes boring into Finaeus's.

Finaeus nodded slowly. "It is true. Airtha is Jelina. Airtha is your mother."

"Then Helen…Myriad…"

"Yes," Finaeus replied. "They are aspects of Airtha. I suspected—before I was exiled—that Helen may have also been one such aspect of Airtha; but I didn't tell your father. I didn't want him to do something…rash."

"Too late for that," Sera muttered.

"And now…Jeff…" Finaeus shook his head. "He once embodied every virtue of the FGT. He was such a strong voice advocating for the program; terraformers spreading ahead of humanity, preparing the galaxy for people. We were all such fools."

"I wouldn't say that," Tanis interrupted. "I believe that spirit is still alive and well in the FGT. I've seen it."

Finaeus looked at her, his eyes hollow. "But look at the wars, the loss of life, the manipulation. Hell, what's to come could be the worst ever—you possess weapons so powerful you could destroy everyone."

"Everyone dies eventually," Tanis said softly. "Or at least, they should. Death in and of itself is not evil, not wrong. It is a part of this vast and beautiful universe we live in. Even killing.

Is it evil? The universe kills constantly and mercilessly. Is it evil?"

"Mom, what are you saying? That it's OK to murder?" Cary asked, her face ashen.

Tanis shook her head. "I'm saying that the nature of what is right and wrong—on a galactic, or universal scale—is almost impossible to fathom. For all our power and our abilities, in a billion years, few of our works will remain. In five billion? None. We're nothing more than mobile dust, just a little more organized than the rest of the dust out there, insofar as the universe is concerned."

"So, what then?" Sera asked. "Is our lot just to claw at one another for as long as our species survives?"

"In the grand scheme of things, it's no different than if we live in a utopia for eternity," Jessica said. "If our existence is meaningless, that is."

"Which," Tanis said with a smile, "is what we must hold onto. Our existence is far from meaningless. We are not the galaxy, the universe; we are ourselves, and we decide what is important to us. Most people only care about a small group of others, fewer than a hundred. Their families, their crew, their squad. My time leading this colony has taught me to extend this 'family' to millions. Now I must learn how to consider everyone—all people, all of humanity, and all AIs—to be my people."

"Why you?" Jessica asked. "What are you going to do?"

"Sera has asked me to lead the Transcend's military, and I've agreed to do it," Tanis replied. "We're going to win this war, and figure out a real way to create a lasting peace."

"So…nothing big, then," Cargo chuckled.

"Then you're going to be real glad that we came back when we did," Jessica said with a smile.

"Stars, any reason would have been good enough," Tanis said. "But let's hear it."

"Well, we kinda have the Orion Guard's plan for the war."

FATHOM

STELLAR DATE: 03.28.8948 (Adjusted Years)
LOCATION: ISS *I2*
REGION: Near Roma, New Canaan System

Sera walked down the long corridor on the *I2*'s command deck, her head swimming with what she had learned from her former crew.

Former crew.

It was readily apparent that the crew of the *Sabrina* was no longer hers. Deep down, she had known that would be the case—it had been eighteen years, after all. But the way they regarded Cargo as their new captain, deferring to him—and to Jessica—drove home the new reality.

Sera internalized a rueful laugh, the sound echoing in her mind. She was so used to sharing public thoughts with Helen that it was still a reflexive habit. But she was alone in her head now. Helen would never chide her, or offer advice, or stay curiously silent at times—even though Sera had always felt her listening.

Helen had been with her for so long—close to the limit of how long an AI and a human should remain together—that many of Sera's behavioral traits were geared toward their shared thinking.

Now Sera doubted she would consider pairing with a new AI. Her mother had lived in her head, and lied to her the entire time. If she couldn't trust her….

Before long, she arrived at her destination—noting how no one sat behind the desk in front of the office. The ISF was so far beyond short-handed, even Tanis had to do without an assistant. New Canaan may possess the ability to build new ships at breakneck speed, but that far outstripped their ability to raise and train new humans and AIs to crew them.

<*Come in, Sera,*> Tanis's voice reached out to her, a welcome sound filling the emptiness of her mind.

The door slid open and Sera entered, noting how the room was a perfect representation of Tanis. Clean, but not austere; orderly, with bits of chaos here and there—such as the wall, covered with random holo projections arrayed in an indecipherable jumble.

In the center was a desk, small but ornate. Sera recalled seeing it before in the main family room of Tanis and Joe's cabin. Compact though the desk was, the person behind it was not. Tanis had a way of creating a presence that dwarfed her average height and build. It was in the eyes; they were always focused, always penetrating.

Tanis rose from her chair and walked around the desk, a look of compassion on her face.

"Sera, how are you holding up?"

"Honestly?" Sera asked with a shake of her head. "I really have no idea. I'm trying not to think too much about…well, everything…until all this is over."

Tanis laughed and placed her hands on Sera's shoulders. "Sera, you are the President of the Transcend Interstellar Alliance. When this crisis is over, it will be because a new one has risen up in its place."

Sera shook her head and gave a weak smile. "What the stars am I doing, Tanis? I'm no president. I have no clue what I was thinking. I should pass it over to Finaeus; people would follow him. Maybe he could even reunite the Transcend and Orion."

"Do you really think that's possible?" Tanis asked, her face showing the doubt Sera felt at the proposition as well.

"No," she sighed. "Probably not. There's too much bad blood, now. A lot more than Airtha divides our people."

Tanis nodded. "She's a point we can all agree upon. After what she did on the *Hellespont*…"

"How are Amanda and Ylonda?" Sera asked, almost afraid to hear the answer. Even though she hadn't known about Myriad, she was the one who had sent Elena on that ship, which Helen had arranged.

"Do you mean, Amavia?" Tanis asked.

Sera's eyebrows knitted together. "What is that…a Latin combination of their names?"

"That's my read on it," Tanis replied. "She's figuring her new self out. Between you and me, Angela and I are keenly interested in how she manages; we have our own interest in that area."

Sera was surprised that Tanis was bringing up that topic. In her previous time on the *Intrepid*, it seemed to be a taboo subject. No one mentioned that Tanis and Angela were a century past the maximum safe integration time.

Yet, everyone could plainly see that they were still two entities. Tanis's statement now made Sera wonder if that was changing, or if Tanis just worried that it was.

"Really mulling over whether or not you want to ask me about that, aren't you?" Tanis asked.

"Yes, yes I am. You always cite the Phobos Accords, yet you are probably in violation of them, as is Amavia." Tanis's expression darkened and Sera raised eyebrows and hands. "Don't get me wrong; I don't operate strictly by those accords—stars, you're the only ones in the galaxy that even purport to anymore. But you don't. I mean…even Bob probably breaks them; at least, as far as I understand their intent. They specifically wanted to avoid ascending any more AI.

<*Someday, where the two of us exist, there will be one,*> Angela said to the two women. <*We don't know when, but it approaches inexorably.*>

Tanis nodded slowly as Angela spoke.

"How do you feel about that?" Sera asked cautiously.

<*We're at peace with it,*> Angela replied.

"We are," Tanis added. "We don't know to what extent everyone else is prepared to accept it, but we are."

"Joe? Your girls?" Sera asked.

<*Joe has understood this eventuality for some time,*> Angela replied.

"We've spoken about it from time to time. He laughs it off, in his way, but I often wonder…"

Sera nodded. "I can only imagine."

"Either way," Tanis said as she leaned against her desk, "that is not a problem for today. Amavia will be fine, I'm sure of it. They're reintegrating both of their stored memories—since they both lost a lot when Myriad attacked them—but she will come through."

"But she'll be someone else, won't she?" Sera asked. "A new person, where before there were two."

Tanis nodded. "And that's what I think will be different. Ylonda and Amanda were friends, but they did not previously share neurons. When Angela and I finally join…it may not even be noticeable."

"To you?"

<*I'm positive.*> Angela said. <*We'll know, of course, but it's possible that there will be no external evidence. Either physically, or on the Link.*>

"This is fascinating," Tanis said, "but I want to discuss something about the data *Sabrina* brought back. Their information corroborates Kent's story of Orion operating a much lower-tech civilization than I had expected."

Sera lowered herself into a chair and ran a hand through her hair. "I agree. This is not news to us, though we often wondered how stratified their society really is. There is some tech, but it's a much broader low-tech base than I had ever expected."

"Though, even their basic, agrarian societies take advantage of advancements that are not even known in the Inner Stars," Tanis added.

"It has amazed our analysts that they reached out to the Hegemony of Worlds. They are the antithesis of what Orion claims to stand for."

Tanis snorted, "They must have held back that little detail."

"Someone is double-crossing someone else," Sera rubbed the heels of her hands into her eyes. "So, what do we do Gen—er, Admiral? You know, I don't get your ranks. Why did you switch from General to Admiral, anyway?"

Tanis laughed. "It's kind of a mess that we inherited from the Terran Space Force's merger. I was in a branch that was historically Marine, so generals were tops there. Space Force had Admirals as their highest rank—which always struck me as odd, since they grew out of the ancient air forces. Either way, it worked out that commanders of trigger-pullers were generals, and the folks who bossed starship captains around were admirals—which wasn't always true, since I captained more than one starship back in Sol. Either way, I should have been an admiral back at Kapteyn's Star, but self-promoting never sat right. Once we had a properly elected government, they changed my commission so it lined up with my actual job."

"Which was 'governor'," Sera smirked. "Has anyone told you that you look like a bit of a dictator?"

Tanis gave Sera a mock scowl. "Well, yeah, 'admiral' was just honorary until this little bit of excitement. I guess I'm a very hands-on commander-in-chief."

"That's what all the dictators say," Sera couldn't resist, and was glad to see Tanis laugh in response.

"You're one to talk about what's proper," Tanis said as she gestured at Sera. "You're the President of the Transcend, and you still don't wear clothes."

Sera arched an eyebrow and crossed her legs. "Clothing came about to protect people's fragile skin and nakedness. I possess neither of those things."

"Well at least you cover up your lower bits. I guess you're really no different than Priscilla and Amanda—er, Amavia; except that they're a bit stiffer, what with Bob's desire to make them nearly indestructible.

Sera laughed. "Well, at least Priscilla is stiffer. Amanda was a bit loose, if you follow the scuttlebutt."

"Nice deflection," Tanis smirked. "So, ranks and fashion aside, what the hell are we going to do?"

"Beats me," Sera chuckled. "I'm just the figurehead. You're the power behind the Transcend now."

"Whoa!" Tanis raised her hands while shaking her head. "I did *not* sign up for that. I'm on board to ensure a secure Transcend, because that makes for a secure New Canaan."

"You know that that means taking on much of the Inner Stars and Orion, right?" Sera asked.

"I'll do what I have to," Tanis replied. "The first thing we need is a lot more intel about what is really going on out there. So far, we've only had one response—from Admiral Krissy, of all people."

"I reviewed that, as well." Sera nodded. "She asked after Finaeus, which was nice; those two had been on the outs for some time."

"I can't wait to hear that whole story," Tanis laughed. "I wonder if she has an axe to grind with him."

"Krissy? Oh, most definitely. She probably wants your job, too."

Tanis snorted. "No one should want my job. Either way, I think it's best that she stays put. We don't need more variables here. To be honest, based on the intel we have from *Sabrina*, no TSF force should redeploy here. No matter how hard they hit us, this is a feint."

"Twenty thousand hegemony ships is no feint," Sera replied. "I don't care if it's just a fraction of their force. You send fewer ships to sterilize a system!"

"Not this system," Tanis replied grimly. "But we need to think past this battle; work out our next move and the move after that, and what our ultimate goals are. We need to gather more intel, and we need to set up a base of operations."

"It won't be here?" Sera asked, surprised that Tanis would suggest another location.

"No," Tanis shook her head. "I won't paint a target like that on New Canaan…well, I won't make the target bigger. We need to set up shop somewhere else. What I need from you, Sera, is not to think like the President of the Transcend, but like the Director of The Hand. Right now, everything is power plays and solidifying alliances."

"And logistics," Sera added.

"That too. I need options; strongholds, rally points, defensible systems, all of it. Because once this battle is over, we won't be sticking around here any longer than we have to."

Sera nodded and then fell still, her eyes tracing the decorative scrollwork on the desk.

"What is it?" Tanis asked.

"Helen…she left a message for me in my mind. She wants me to go to Airtha," Sera said quietly.

"What?" Tanis exclaimed. "You can't be seriously considering it!"

Sera looked up at Tanis and shrugged. "I know I shouldn't…can't. But the answers I need are there."

Tanis leaned back in her chair and folded her arms. "If you go to Airtha, I really *will* be the power behind the Transcend, because you'll be in her thrall—and you know it. There are a thousand ways that a being like Airtha can corrupt or subsume you."

"She's my mother, Tanis…"

"Don't give me that," Tanis shook her head vehemently. "Lots of people have shit parents. Sure, you seem to have won the lottery when it comes to that; but it doesn't mean you can play the 'I need answers' card, and run off on some boneheaded quest—"

Tanis stopped speaking abruptly as Sera gave a choked cough.

"Shit, sorry, Sera." Tanis reached down and took her hands, grasping them firmly. "We'll get to Airtha when the time is right. You'll get your answers, I promise. Let's just do it on our terms, not hers."

Sera didn't speak, a thousand responses sifting through her mind. Tanis was right. She was a blunt, results-driven, butthead of a friend, but she was right. Sera knew she would have to put Airtha out of her mind for now. But she wouldn't forget.

"OK, Tanis, you're right. We'll go there eventually, and it'll be on our terms."

"You know it. We'll get to the bottom of all this. I promise."

SENTIENCE

STELLAR DATE: 03.28.8948 (Adjusted Years)
LOCATION: ISS *I2*
REGION: Near Roma, New Canaan System

<There's another potential enemy that you need to be aware of,> Bob said after Sera left.

<Seriously?> Tanis asked. *<Well, we have Airtha, Orion, Garza, who is probably operating unilaterally to some extent, and the ascended AI in the core. Who am I missing?>*

<What about the Hegemony?> Bob asked.

<I was lumping them in with Garza. Is there someone else? Other than Inner Stars nations that will probably all side with the Transcend or Orion.>

<Well, two that I can think of,> Bob said.

<Sheesh…we've gone from one to two. Who are they?>

<The first—which I'm surprised you didn't think of—is another splinter faction of the Transcend. Not everyone that gets free of Airtha's control is going to side with you and Sera. Expect to see Andrea or Adrienne mixed up in that.>

<Fuck! Andrea. You're right, she'll rear her head again for sure,> Tanis cursed.

<But the group I really want to talk about is the one made up of the AIs that Sabrina liberated in the Inner Stars.>

<Really?> Tanis asked. *<I thought they'd just flock to you as their god-emperor.>*

<Not funny, Tanis. I want to be a god even less than you want to be in this war,> Bob replied with a sternness in his voice that Tanis rarely heard.

<Sorry. So what's your expectation with those AIs?>

<Undoubtedly, some of them will side with us, some with Airtha, and some will form a third faction. There are enough AIs in the Inner

Stars to spark up a third Sentience War. I need to send an emissary into the Inner Stars to rally them.>

<Oh yeah? Who do you have in mind?> Tanis asked.

<An unfortunate side effect of her melding has made Amavia incompatible as an Avatar. Although, even if she had not merged with Ylonda, Amanda would have been one of my top picks. I will miss her, as she will miss me, but the separation may do her good.>

Tanis had worried about Amavia's ability to function as Bob's avatar. One of the original requirements for the position was a human who had never had an AI in their head.

<You must plan to send an AI, as well,> Tanis said. *<Even though Amavia is more AI than human at this point, the Inner Stars entities will trust one of their own more.>*

<Yes. I am discussing the mission with Sabrina as we speak.>

<She would be an excellent choice,> Tanis agreed. *<But don't you need two avatars here? Priscilla can't be on all the time, or she'll just become a shard of you.>*

Bob sent a feeling of agreement over the Link. *<You are correct, and we discussed the merits of that potential eventuality. Priscilla has decided that she would like to remain a separate entity for now—though she has expressed a desire to be folded into me in the future.>*

<Has she?> That was not an outcome Tanis had anticipated. One of the reasons Amanda and Priscilla had been chosen was for their strong sense of self. Perhaps the centuries with Bob had changed that in her.

<Not so different than you and I,> Angela said privately to Tanis. *<If you knew back in Sol that we would eventually become one being, would you have allowed me in your mind? Yet, now we feel no fear, no abhorrence for our eventual joining.>*

<It's very different,> Tanis replied. *<When you and I become one, it will be a meeting of two equals. Priscilla will simply be subsumed by Bob.>*

<Everyone has a right to die in their own way,> Angela said. *<Just because most of us can now persist forever doesn't mean that we should…and certainly not that we must.>*

<Are you two done yet?> Bob asked.

<Sorry, Bob, I didn't mean to waste precious milliseconds,> Angela replied, her mental tone droll.

<I'm glad to hear it,> Bob replied levelly. *<As I was saying, Priscilla wishes to remain herself, so I will need another avatar.>*

<Are there potential candidates?> Tanis asked. *<Our pool is limited here. Not like back in Sol, where you had your pick of trillions.>*

<There are a few,> Bob paused. *<One you will not approve; the others are younger men and women who were born during our time in Victoria. I will likely rule out the men. I find women more compatible with my mind.>*

<Who's the one I won't approve?> Tanis asked, her curiosity piqued.

<Saanvi.>

<Correct. Request denied. Do I know any of the others?> Tanis replied, glad that Bob knew her daughter would be off-limits.

<Not personally. I will pass you the final candidates after I spend some time examining a future with them.>

<Very well,> Tanis said as she steepled her fingers. *<I suppose that if you convince Sabrina to play escort, then I'll not have to worry about selecting a ship for the mission—though we should upgrade it with stealth tech.>*

<Perhaps. The ship technically belongs to Cargo.>

<True, but I have an offer for Cargo and the team that I hope they'll jump at,> Tanis said. She could see her mission dovetailing with the work of Bob's emissary. *<Oh, I have to go talk to my girls about sending them home. Let me know when you have that list.>*

<Of course, it will take a few minutes.>

A few minutes to examine dozens of futures. Tanis was glad the stupid Luck she and Angela were cursed with precluded Bob from analyzing her future. She preferred the mystery.

FLEETING RETIREMENT

STELLAR DATE: 03.28.8948 (Adjusted Years)
LOCATION: 67km from Landfall, Knossos Island
REGION: Carthage, New Canaan System

Jason Andrews leaned back on his deck chair and gazed out across the long Grainger Valley and the slopes of the Marinus mountains that surrounded it. He folded his hands behind his head and breathed a deep sigh.

"This is the life," he said to himself.

Other than the sound of his voice, the wind finding its way through the trees, and the gurgling of the small stream flowing a hundred meters from his back deck, the valley was quiet and picture perfect.

It was paradise, better than anything he had ever dreamed.

After so long captaining starships, first in the Sol system and then later on the long haul between Sol and Alpha Centuari—not to mention spending the last century and a half as captain of the *Intrepid,* he had begun to wonder if he would ever get to finally relax; to spend a sunny afternoon alone, knowing that someone else had things well in-hand.

At his feet, Buster, a shaggy collie, stirred at the sound of some small animal in the underbrush, and Jason leaned down to scratch behind his ears.

"Easy boy; just a squirrel."

Buster lowered his head, but kept an ear cocked toward the origin of the sound. One solitary rustling in the underbrush wouldn't be enough to get him to move in the warm light of Canaan Prime, but Jason knew that if the sound came again, Buster would be off in a flash.

He didn't often catch the squirrels, but he certainly liked the chase.

A ping hit Jason's mind, reminding him that he was not alone on Carthage—though sometimes it felt like it—and he responded that he would accept the communication.

<*Jason, how are you this afternoon?*> Tanis's strong voice and unmistakable mental presence entered his mind.

<*Another day in paradise,*> Jason replied. <*How are your negotiations going with the good folks of the Transcend?* >

Though he had not been involved in the running of the New Canaan government in over a decade, Jason still kept up on his briefings. He had considered travelling to Normandy to observe the negotiations, perhaps to see Sera again, but Tanis had mentioned that Sera was in a relationship with Elena now, and he decided it would be best to pass on the opportunity.

That Tanis was reaching out to him now, after only completing the first day of talks was not a good sign.

<*A little worse than usual,*> Tanis replied, and Jason pulled himself up straight. When it came to working with foreign governments, 'the usual' was already bad enough; he could only imagine what '*worse*' would amount to.

<*What do you need, Tanis?*> Jason responded. <*Wait a second, how are you talking to me in real-time? Have you brought the negotiations to Carthage?*>

Tanis smiled in his mind. <*Not everything is in your briefings, I guess. The I2 has a real-time QuanComm Link with Landfall.*>

<*Sorry, what?*> Jason asked. <*Wait…no…I got it. Quantum entanglement. Is there any mystery Earnest cannot solve?*>

Tanis chuckled, her resonant tones filling his mind. <*It would seem not. Though he hasn't worked out exactly how the Transcend makes their Ford-Svaiter mirrors yet, so there's hope for the universe's deepest mysteries for a while, at least.*>

<*So, instantaneous communication aside, what do you need me for?*> Jason asked.

<*I need you to run New Canaan. We need you as Governor.*>

The words knocked Jason back. His mind skipped through a thousand scenarios that would cause Tanis to step down—but none made sense. The people of New Canaan loved her; they would follow her to the core itself, if she asked it.

<*Tanis, why?*>

<*I'm to head up the Transcend Space Force. I'll have to leave New Canaan—and I will be taking the fleet with me. After we deal with this Hegemony incursion, that is,*> Tanis replied.

<*Wait! What? One thing at a time, Tanis. Hegemony incursion? The AST found us?*> Jason exclaimed.

<*Yes; though I suspect not without help. We ran into an Orion Guard strike force on Tomlinson's ship; Tomlinson's dead now—it's Sera that has asked me to head up her military.*>

Jason's mind reeled as he processed what Tanis was telling him. <*Then you need me in Landfall yesterday.*>

<*I do,*> Tanis replied.

<*I'm summoning transportation; I'll be at the capitol in a few hours. I assume the parliament will have to swear me in?*>

<*No need to call. A ship will be there in minutes, and parliament is already convening,*> Tanis replied. <*Hold down the fort, I'll talk to you soon.*>

Jason cut the communication, stood from his chair, and stretched as a sub-orbital shuttle crested the mountains at the end of the valley.

"Well, Buster, you're finally going to get to see the big city; and Tanis has finally roped me into that job I've been avoiding all these years."

A FAMILY MEETING

STELLAR DATE: 03.28.8948 (Adjusted Years)
LOCATION: Command Deck, ISS *I2*
REGION: Near Roma, New Canaan System

"You coming?" Joe asked as he poked his head into Tanis's office.

"Yeah…I'll finish this up in my head as we walk," Tanis replied as she rose from her desk. "Stars, it's been a long day. Can't wait to catch some shut-eye."

"You and me both."

Joe took a minute to admire his wife. She looked almost the same as the day he had met her—excepting for the red streak in her hair that the girls had convinced her to get. Tall, lithe, her movements just a touch too fluid—hinting at the significant cybernetic alterations beneath her skin.

Her brow was furrowed—as per usual—and he wrapped an arm around her shoulder as they walked out into the corridor. "What's up?"

"Oh, just reviewing the girls that Bob wants to offer the position of avatar to."

"Another avatar? Then Amavia cannot rejoin him?" Joe asked. "Or is he starting a harem?"

A short laugh escaped Tanis's lips before her frown returned. "If only. No, Amavia cannot become an avatar again. But that's not the real driver. He's certain that the AIs of the Inner Stars are going to start their own uprising, and he wants to send Amavia in to set them all on the right path."

Joe felt his eyebrows rise. "Wow…that's not what I expected to hear."

"Yeah, me either. His top pick for her replacement was Saanvi."

"Hell no!" Joe roared.

Tanis laughed and placed a hand on his shoulder "Don't worry, I had the same reaction; but it's gotta be someone. I mean…there's nothing wrong with it, and, technically, it's not permanent, either. But she's too young; she barely knows who she is yet."

Joe took a deep breath, trying to stuff his fatherly impulses down enough to look at the situation logically. "Yeah…I suppose it's technically an honor…but I agree. She's just too young. Saanvi has huge potential; there's nothing wrong with being with Bob forever, but she wouldn't know enough to know if that's what she really wants."

"It's moot. Bob won't bring it up to her, or anyone else. Right, Bob?"

<*Correct, I will not,*> Bob replied. <*However, please approve my list of candidates soon. The modifications take some time.*>

"Yeah, I remember that from back at the Mars Outer Shipyards," Tanis replied. "OK, I took off two for the same reason you can't have Saanvi: no one under fifty. You may approach the rest. Let them know that they can talk to me if they wish."

<*Thank you,*> Bob replied and his presence diminished.

The whole exchange struck Joe as terribly incongruous, and he began to laugh, drawing a stern eye from Tanis. "What?"

"It's just that everyone else treats Bob like he's this near-deity, but you still talk to him like he's just another AI; a subordinate, even," Joe replied, still chuckling.

"Well, he is my subordinate," Tanis replied. "Makes sense to me. Besides, he's the one that was all nervous and made us stay up with him through the long night."

"I remember that," Joe grinned. "You called him a city-sized puppy."

<*That was you,*> Angela supplied.

"Really, Ang? You sure about that?" Joe had always been certain it was Tanis who had said that to Bob.

<Seriously, Joe? I don't store my memories in some chemical cocktail. It was you.>

"You get up on the wrong side of the synapses today, Ang?" Joe asked as he settled onto the maglev with Tanis.

<No…yes…I don't know, I think I'm worried.> Angela's tone wavered.

"Ang, nothing to worry about, we're going to take care of this mess," Joe said, unsure of how to soothe an AI.

<I'm not worried about us, I'm worried about our girls,> Angela replied. *<Maybe we should keep them on the I2. This is the safest place in the system.>*

"The bunker under Landfall is just as safe," Tanis replied. "And it will be a good sign to folks, that we sent the girls there. They'll know that I won't have sent them somewhere I didn't think could protect them."

"Well, some will think that it means you think we're gonna lose," Joe added. "Not that those will be any sort of majority."

"We've already been over it," Tanis shook her head. "Besides, this is a warship now; no one else gets to have their kids tag along. Soon enough, they'll be through the academy—then we can really start worrying about them."

Joe nodded solemnly. Knowing that both their daughters would join the ISF in a time of war was disconcerting enough; knowing that he would run the academy that trained them was something worse. No, not worse…troubling.

Not everyone was going to survive the coming years, but he would do his damnedest to ensure his girls were ready.

<I know what you're thinking,> Tanis spoke softly into his mind. *<It won't be easy.>*

<Yeah, now I have an idea what my mother went through when I enlisted—and when I left.>

<If there were ever a pair of girls who were born to be survivors, it's ours,> Tanis said.

Joe shared a laugh with his wife as they thought through all the hijinks their girls had gotten up to over the years. They were a perfect balance of caution and impetuousness—both smart, both clever bordering on crafty.

He was going to have his hands full keeping them in line at the academy.

Ten minutes later, they walked into the mess hall where Cary and Saanvi were still talking with Jessica and Trevor, the former regaling them with tales of their journey through Orion space.

"So then, I said to him, I've got three holes here and I paid you to fill them all, now get to it!" Jessica said in a too-loud voice, and the group burst into raucous laughter.

"Poor damn guy," Trevor said, still laughing with tears rolling down his face. "With Jessica standing there staring at him, he couldn't even get it in right; took at least fifteen minutes for the job to be done."

The group's laughter erupted again as Joe and Tanis approached.

"You know, Jessica…they're just eighteen," Joe said, his protective father voice cutting through the laughter. "Can we keep the sex jokes to a minimum?"

"Dad!" Cary exclaimed. "Seriously, we've heard our fair share of sex jokes."

"Which this wasn't," Jessica said between laughs. "What you've stumbled into is the tale of the most unfortunate forklift operator ever."

<He drove the damn thing right through one of my bulkheads,> Sabrina added. *<I was very put out.>*

"Or were you maybe put-in?" Jessica said, and the group dissolved into laughter once more.

Joe couldn't help but join in, and he saw Tanis chuckle out of the corner of his eye.

"Ah, I've missed you, Jessica," Tanis said.

"You too, Tanis. You've raised some good kids here, the both of you—you should be proud of them."

Joe looked at his two girls and smiled. "Somehow they both survived our childrearing process intact. That may be more from their innate stubbornness than anything else."

"Need us to go, Dad?" Cary asked.

"Nope, it's you we came to talk to," Joe said.

"Gotta split, anyway," Jessica said as she rose. "My ass is gonna be shaped like this chair."

Trevor peered around behind her. "Nope, perky as ever…I mean it's probably filled with springs and ballistic jell, or something. It should be impervious—even when it comes to hard mess hall chairs."

"Trevor! I have no…well…I probably have both of those things inside me somewhere, but they are not responsible for the shape of my ass," Jessica exclaimed.

Trevor nodded, and winked as he followed Jessica away from the table.

"Those two are great!" Cary said as Joe and Tanis sat. "They sure had some wild stories."

"Jessica is built out of wild stories," Joe chuckled.

"Ah, so that's what she's built out of," Tanis replied with a smile.

Joe chuckled. "That one will never get old."

"So, what's up?" Saanvi asked before taking a sip of her drink. "You both have Serious Face."

"We're sending you two to Landfall," Joe said without preamble. "Things are about to get hot out here, and all non-essential personnel are being evacuated."

"What?" Cary asked loudly. "Are you serious? Landfall. In the bunker, right?"

"Easy now," Tanis said, raising her hands. "It's not just you; anyone who isn't in the ISF, or isn't mission-critical is being sent to a refuge."

The two girls shared an angst-filled look as Tanis spoke.

"But we're ISF," Cary said, her tone emphatic. "We got accepted into the academy. We've flown two cruisers. We're assets, not liabilities."

Joe shook his head slowly. He wasn't surprised that Cary felt this way. Their younger daughter always acted as though she had to live up to her mother's reputation—and seemed to think that it had to be done before she turned twenty-one.

Saanvi knew Cary's internal struggle, as well, and Joe saw her give Cary a comforting look. "Flying a ship on a set course and being in combat are two different things. We could make a mistake and get other people killed."

Cary passed Saanvi a hard look. "We won't. We know what to do."

<Use your head, not your heart, Cary,> Angela added.

Joe watched the girls' expressions change several times as they stared at one other, and knew they were having a protracted conversation over the Link.

"Kinda rude, girls," he said. "If you're gonna whisper behind our backs, at least get good enough at it so we can't tell."

He saw a smile creep across his wife's face, and knew she was probably carrying on at least one other conversation right now. It was different for her, though. He was certain Tanis simply couldn't slow down anymore—at least not right now, with the biggest battle of their lives approaching.

Cary frowned at him, and Saanvi sighed.

"What about all those crewless ships? Who's going to fly them?" Cary asked.

<Symatra and Judith have that well in-hand,> Angela supplied. *<They'll need to focus on managing massive fleets and hordes of NSAI; your presence will worry and distract them.>*

"And most of those ships aren't fit to be much other than shields," Joe added.

"Some aren't," Cary said. "Some are almost fully operational. I reviewed the specs."

"I'm sorry." Tanis shook her head. "But it's not going to happen. You two will go to the bunker under Landfall. There's no shortage of work that needs to be done there."

Cary looked to Joe. "Seriously? That's the final word?"

Joe nodded. "Seriously. Your mother and I are not going to budge on this."

Saanvi caught Cary's eye and gave her head a shake before turning back to her parents. "We'll go. We understand the risks."

"Good," Tanis said with smile. "The last shuttle is leaving in an hour, and you need to be on it."

They rose from the table and shared a round of hugs.

Joe spotted the exact moment that the two girls realized that this could be the last time they ever saw their parents. It was a widening of their eyes, and a shared look before a new round of embracing ensued. In the end, they finally managed to make their way out of the mess to a waiting groundcar, and the girls got in, still waving and wiping away tears.

Joe watched them go as Tanis collapsed against him.

"They *could* do it, you know," she said. "They would be assets."

"They don't know how to work with a team," Joe replied. "And they really suck at following orders."

Tanis sighed. "Well, Cary does. Saanvi would be the perfect little soldier in that respect."

"True. We'll have to teach her more about how to push boundaries and to think outside the box when she starts her first term."

<I think that Saanvi excels at that,> Angela countered. *<She just likes to know where she fits in the grand scheme of things. It's a holdover from her life changing so much when she came to us. Soon she'll have the confidence to know that things orbit her, not the other way around.>*

"I think you're right, there," Tanis agreed. "I see big things in Saanvi's future."

"With those two on their way back, what's next on your docket?" Joe asked.

Tanis let out a long breath. "Kent. With the plans *Sabrina* brought back from Orion space, I have new angles I can use with him—I'm positive that he still has intel we need."

"Good luck," Joe said. He wrapped his wife in a long embrace, his lips finding hers, reveling in her taste before he let her go.

"Oh, stars, Joe; you're such a tease!" Tanis smiled. "Always have been."

"Me?" Joe appropriated a wounded expression. "You're the one who played hard to get for *years*."

"That was almost two hundred years ago. The tables have turned since then," Tanis said with a raised eyebrow.

"I have a long memory," Joe chuckled.

MASTER PLAN

STELLAR DATE: 03.29.8948 (Adjusted Years)
LOCATION: Detention Center, ISS *I2*
REGION: Near Roma, New Canaan System

Kent rose from his cot as a guard appeared at the entrance to his cell. The clock in the passageway read just past zero-dark-thirty—another interrogation, just as he had been drifting off to sleep.

"Wrists together," the guard said without preamble.

Kent touched the two silver shackles on his wrists together and felt them lock. He had to admit that the restraint system was effective; the guards never needed to touch him to ensure he was secure—there was never any opportunity to make a grab for a weapon. No option to escape.

Not yet, but his time would come. There was always an opening, an avenue of escape. He just had to wait for it.

The stasis shield across the front wall of his cell switched off, and the guard raised his hand to the metal bars that still blocked his exit. Three of them drew back, melting in on themselves. On a previous trip to the interrogation room, he had asked if that was picotech, and the guard had laughed at him.

"Course not. Simple flowmetal. But don't think you can hack it; stuff will kill you if you try."

Kent had seen flowmetal before, but never used so casually—for a prisoner's cell. The things these people took for granted were astounding.

As he stepped out into the corridor, one of hundreds in the *I2*'s brig, he smiled at the guard. "So, where to this time?"

"The usual," the man replied. "You're very popular."

Kent laughed. "Yeah, you should really just leave me there; save yourself the trips."

"You're telling me," the guard replied. "Still, protocol is protocol. I can't leave you alone in an interrogation room, but I can do whatever when you're in your cell."

"A lot of prisoners in here?" Kent asked as they walked past dozens of empty cells.

"Some," the guard replied.

"Really? How many? I haven't seen anyone but you all day."

The guard laughed. "Seriously, let it go. Do I look like I was born yesterday? Want me to tell you about shift changes and when I take a whiz? I bet I could rustle up the design specs while I'm at it."

Kent shook his head and gave a rueful smile. "Was worth a shot."

"Yeah, prisoner's prerogative, scheme about escape. We could just slap you in stasis, you know. Consider your cell a perk."

Kent knew there was no perk involved. If he was in stasis, he couldn't stew and worry; he couldn't perseverate. Even the constant back and forth to the interrogation room—where a never-ending stream of intelligence operatives attempted to pry secrets from him—was all tactics.

The guard led him through a security arch and past a waiting room to the corridor containing the interrogation rooms.

Each time they had taken him to a different one. He suspected that it had nothing to do with whether or not the others were in use, but rather to mess with him, keep him off-balance.

He kept hoping he would see someone else from his team, but in the time he'd been in the *I2*'s brig, there had been no sign of them. If his strike team was aboard, he was certain *they* were in stasis, tucked away to use as leverage against him at some point.

"In here," the guard grunted and opened the door, leaning across him as he pushed the door wide.

Kent knew chances to strike wouldn't come often and took this one. He swung his shackled wrists up, aiming for the guard's forehead, when an armored hand shot out from inside the room and caught his forearm in an iron grip.

"Nice try, Kent," the voice said, and he recognized it as Tanis Richards's.

"Damnit," the guard swore. "And here I thought we had finally reached an understanding. Sorry Admiral Richards, it won't happen again."

"We're all stretched thin," Tanis replied. "It's late and your shift ends soon. Log off early on my authority. We'll take care of our friend, here."

The armored hand pulled him into the dimly lit room, and Kent saw that it belonged to a massive ISF Marine; one of four in the small room.

The imposing figure sat him down and separated his cuffed wrists, locking each one into mounts on the table. As he secured Kent, two of the Marines walked out of the room and took positions in the hall, closing the door behind them.

Kent looked across the table at his enemy—the woman he had tried to kill; should have killed, had it not been for how little of her was human, anymore.

"I see you have a new arm," he commented.

Tanis lifted it up and the skin on her hand changed from a natural tone to a silvery metal. More flowmetal, it seemed.

"Temporary," the admiral replied. "I prefer flesh and blood as much as I can, but this will do for now."

"I'm surprised. I thought you'd revel in your overuse of advanced technology," Kent scowled.

She paused, and the woman's ever-present frown seemed to deepen. Then her visage cleared and she gave a slight smile.

"I don't mind sharing my personal beliefs with you," she said. "You don't have to work so hard. We're really not so different, you and I. I'd like to show that to you."

"You and your people are abominations," Kent said softly, "I share nothing with you."

"Not so," the admiral said with a shake of her head. "We're both human, we share common ancestry. We value things like freedom, intelligence, life, children…peace. Do you not value those things?"

"Of course I do. What I don't value is unbridled use of technology and what it does to humanity. I already told you about what the Transcend did with their picotech experiments; the billions that died from their hubris. Yet you've still sided with them."

Kent realized that his voice had risen, and the Admiral shook her head.

"Technology is a tool. Just as propaganda is a tool. Just as we all are. Every one of us is wielded for some purpose; what is yours? What does your President Kirkland really want?" she asked, her eyes imploring—it was an act Kent didn't buy.

This woman was no one's tool. She was the puppet master.

"Very well," she said. "I'm going to tell you a story; tell you about what we really want here in New Canaan. Perhaps you will come to appreciate our point of view."

Kent sat back in his chair—as much as the restraints would allow. "This should be good. Proceed."

The admiral began to speak, and Kent saw a look of longing grow in her eyes. "I grew up on the shores of the Melas Chasma, one of the great lakes that formed in the Mariner Valleys after Mars was terraformed. I used to stare at the rings around Mars at night, dreaming of traveling through the Sol System and maybe beyond. They were beautiful, you know—Mars 1 and the MCEE…I've seen a lot of constructs since, but never anything to rival those. They had such class, such beauty. They were the first things we ever built of that scale; as a species, that is. Mars 1 proved that we could conquer the stars; spread out and make the galaxy our home. No longer did we have to live on unstable rocks at the bottom of steep gravity wells."

The admiral paused and gave him a sad look. "But that's all gone now. War borne of greed destroyed those rings—denying a legacy that should have been precious to all humanity—and smashed them into the planet below. From what I understand, it's never been repaired. Mars is still a graveyard…a reminder of humanity's first great genocide."

"Hardly the first," Kent interjected. "Humanity has been wiping out subcultures forever. Did they fail to teach you that in your Martian schools?"

Admiral Richards's stare sharpened. "*Marsian*. It would seem they didn't teach you enough in yours. And yes, we learned of all the horrors that humans and AIs have brought down on themselves and each other. But the destruction of Mars, and Earth afterward, was different. Two trillion humans and AIs died at the hands of the Jovians. Two trillion deaths, the loss of humanity's homeworld, and the loss of the first extraterrestrial world we ever terraformed."

Kent wondered if the emotion he heard in Admiral Richards's voice was genuine. The enemy had disabled many of the mods the military had granted him, so he was unable to read her heart rate or skin temperature—but nothing in her demeanor appeared duplicitous.

The thought suddenly caused him to wonder what had happened to Vernon, his strike force's AI. The military AI had not been embedded in any of the soldiers, but rather encased in the tech-pack Kent had carried.

Vernon must have been subverted by now. But if so, why was the admiral spending so much time with him? He didn't voice the question, allowing her to continue.

"But that was long ago; just like my dreams as a young girl were long ago. Mars is forgotten, barely a footnote in our people's long journey into the larger universe. But I've not forgotten. Ironically, all I could think of back when I was young was how much I wanted to leave. How I wanted to see the Sol System, and then maybe the stars beyond. Now I'd give anything to stand on the Melas Chasma's shores once more.

"But I joined the military as soon as I hit the minimum age, and got my wish. They took me from Mars and made me the woman I am today. I became their tool, the instrument of my superiors."

She looked sad, though there was still a fierce light in her eyes. Kent had to admit that this was not the interrogation he had expected. It was almost a confession.

"I was a good tool, too," Admiral Richards continued. "I was sharp, and I cut deep. In the end, however, I was too good, too dangerous, and my superiors worried they could no longer control me.

"They were right. I was no longer willing to be their instrument, but what choice did I have? I could have left the TSF and joined with the Scattered Worlds. I could see that war was coming in Sol, but I would just be trading one master for another.

"No, the answer was simple. I had to leave Sol."

The admiral paused there and took a drink from a glass of water at her side.

"Thirsty?" she asked and pointed to a dispenser in the corner.

"Yeah, I am," Kent replied.

His cuffs unlocked from the table and Admiral Richards gestured to the dispenser. "I'm not your servant. Go get it yourself."

Kent stood and saw the two Marines in the room stiffen. He knew why Richards was doing this. Make him think she trusted him, like he was a friend and not a prisoner—as though he could forget his place with the two hulking soldiers in the room with them.

Still, it was nice to stretch his arms, and he poured a glass of water, downed it, and then made a cup of coffee.

"So, you decided to just run off and get away from it all, then?" Kent asked as he sat back down at the table.

The admiral gave him a hard smile. "That's one way of looking at it. I just wanted a simpler life, away from the madness that was Sol."

"How's that working out for you?"

Admiral Richards let out a rueful laugh. "I suspect you know. To be honest, it's not been that bad. Sure, we've had some trouble; but we've done a lot of good, too."

"Really?" Kent asked with a raised eyebrow. "The history books don't really read like that. You used picotech to consume enemy ships in two systems, you made a black hole in the Bollam's World System, which is slowly destroying the place."

"That's certainly one way of looking at it. Except the Battle of Victoria was to save an entire people from what essentially amounted to slavery…though by then, the threat had been upgraded to annihilation. We held off on using our picobombs so long as they were only targeting our military. The minute they went after the civilian population—that's when we ended the fight.

"Bollam's World was a bit different. If we hadn't defeated the AST ships with our picotech, they'd have it now, and they certainly wouldn't be allied with you—it would be them that you would be attacking, not us. Speaking of the Hegemony, it was they who made the black hole at Bollam's World."

Kent took another sip of his coffee. Admiral Richards's words were true. He had studied both of those battles, and the histories did show that Admiral Richards and her people were not the initial aggressors. Still, it was the presence of their picotech that was the destabilizing factor. They had brought this upon themselves.

"You have to wonder," Admiral Richards mused. "You're allied with the AST, which—having Sirius, and now Bollam's within their Hegemony—represents the same people who have always unleashed war on us to steal what is ours."

Kent snorted. He wasn't going to dignify that statement with a response.

Her eyes locked onto him and bore into his. "Are you sure you're on the right side? Because I'll tell you this right now: we believe that your general Garza—yes, we know who he is—does not intend to seize and destroy our tech; rather, he will use it to unseat Praetor Kirkland, and take over Orion."

Kent opened his mouth to reply, and then paused. He knew that Garza had promised picotech to the Hegemony; it had been evident in the subtext of their conversation aboard the *Britannica*. Was it possible that the general planned to break his oath to the Orion Guard? He had allied himself with the Hegemony—a culture that shared very few ideals with the Orion Freedom Alliance.

From what he and his strike force had observed of New Canaan, these people were far more aligned—picotech notwithstanding—with Orion than the Hegemony was.

He had previously considered that it was the price of peace, or that perhaps Garza hoped to influence the Hegemony toward a more civilized culture. But now he wondered. Why rely on their ships so heavily? Why involve the Trisilieds to the degree they had, if the goal was only to destroy the picotech? Even his initial mission to capture Admiral Richards and President Tomlinson was better aligned with gaining unfettered access to the forbidden tech than destroying it.

Had Garza led him astray? If someone as highly-placed as the general did not believe in the ideals of the OFA, was everything he had been taught merely a ploy to keep the populace in line?

Kent shook his head. That line of reasoning would take him nowhere. It simply couldn't be possible; Garza couldn't have perpetrated such a coup. Too many people would know about his true goals. The OFA was too big for one man to orchestrate something like that.

His blood pressure rose and his face reddened. This woman had nearly made him doubt his commitment to Orion. They had given him everything he held dear in this life; he was not about to turn on them now.

"You're twisting the truth," he hissed at Tanis. "Garza knows how corrupt the Hegemony is, and he's using it against them. Once we had you, we were to use the picobombs to destroy your facilities so that when the Orion fleets—"

Kent stopped short as a grim smile pulled at Admiral Richards's lips.

"'Fleets'? Not 'fleet'?" she asked. "Those Hegemony ships out there, the ones taking out the Transcend's watchers, they're not the only ones…."

He didn't reply, ashamed that he had let something slip; but it didn't matter. The force coming to New Canaan could still obliterate their defenses—and the entire system, for that matter. Even though he had not secured the picotech.

The admiral tapped her finger against her chin and spoke softly. "A hundred and twenty AU to the closest Hegemony ship; that's about sixteen hours, as the photon flies. You launched your attack on the *Galadrial* no sooner than two hours before you tried to kill me... There was no way they could have known I was going there to rescue Sera until I departed—which means that the AST jumped the gun. They wanted to get in first and take the tech for themselves."

Kent's heart dropped. The Hegemony had attacked too soon! They *were* planning to come insystem first and seize the tech for themselves.

Garza had been a fool, and so had he.

"I don't suppose you'd be so kind as to tell me the exact nature of what we're facing?" Admiral Richards asked. "There has to be an Orion Guard fleet out there, too; or perhaps it's still on its way...on a vector.... Shit!"

The admiral leapt to her feet and dashed through the door, leaving Kent alone with the pair of Marines.

CAPTAINS AND ADMIRALS

STELLAR DATE: 03.29.8948 (Adjusted Years)
LOCATION: ISS *I2*
REGION: Near Roma, New Canaan System

The virtual table seemed to stretch endlessly to Tanis's left and right—though the physical one was only ten meters from end-to-end.

As much as Tanis would have liked to have the attendees present in person, it would leave the fleet too vulnerable should something unexpected occur. Not to mention that finding seating for the commanders of twenty thousand ships would be tricky.

She glanced up and down the physical table, and then beyond into the virtual extensions. Every ship captain and officer with rank of colonel and above was present—both TSF and ISF. At the physical table sat Joe, Cargo, Jessica, Amavia, Admiral Sanderson, Captain Espensen, General Pearson, Commandant Brandt, and several other Marine generals under her command. Admiral Greer and Captain Viska were also present.

"You've all read the briefing," Sera began from Tanis's left. "You've talked to your AIs, you understand what is happening. We are at war on multiple fronts—one of which is back at our own capital. We're going to be fighting against much of our own military, until we can free them from Airtha's influence.

"What you have not heard is that I have placed Admiral Tanis Richards in command of the Transcend Space Force as Field Marshal; an appointment which Admiral Greer supports."

She paused and looked to Admiral Greer, who nodded before speaking. "Admiral Richards has pledged her ships and her technology to support the Transcend. Given that most of the TSF's ships could be under the control of subverted AIs, Admiral Richards's Intrepid Space Force represents the largest number of Transcend ships committed to the President.

"Some of you may have sour feelings about this, in light of the skirmish we were just involved in. I won't sugarcoat it—the battle was not bloodless, and lives were lost on both sides. But that is not the fault of anyone here. Airtha and Myriad were to blame; they made us tools of their insurrection, and the lives lost are on their heads. We, here today, are allies. Let's not forget that."

Sera resumed her address. "Yes, today we begin to take back the Transcend and re-establish the true ideals upon which our civilization was founded. Tanis and the people of New Canaan share those ideals. We will stand together against what comes."

She paused, and polite clapping sounded up and down the long table. Sera turned to Tanis. "All yours, Field Marshal."

"Thank you," Tanis replied and surveyed the assemblage for a moment before beginning.

"We will indeed bring the war to our enemies, and strike down Airtha for using us; but first we must first defeat the Hegemony fleet that has assembled beyond this system's heliopause. Our current count, which is several hours out of date, puts their fleet at twenty-five thousand ships. The vessels out there appear to be a new fleet, including elements of Guard design. We won't know their full capabilities until we engage them, but we must assume they are every bit as advanced as TSF or Orion ships."

Tanis looked down the table; every face resolving into focus as her gaze passed by. The TSF captains looked grim, and several were nodding in agreement. Many of her own captains had different expressions: fear and uncertainty.

Every one of the Transcend captains—and the crews serving under them—were combat veterans. The ISF fleet, on the other hand, was barely crewed at all—and fewer than half had seen combat. Moreover, of her thousands of captains, less than two dozen had ever steered a ship in battle—something that had to make the TSF veterans nervous.

She decided it was best to address that issue head-on, before it caused unrest in the ranks.

"Many of our ships are captained by low-ranking officers, and that has some of you worried—ISF and TSF alike; though probably none more than those officers who are in a command seat for the first time."

There were nervous smiles amongst many of the ISF captains, while no small number of the TSF captains shook their heads.

"Perhaps we can augment your crews," a Transcend captain spoke up—Shira, by the indicator on the table's holosystem. "I have a very competent XO, and my mizzen-watch crew could join her on one of your vessels."

"That is a very gracious offer, Captain Shira" Tanis replied. "However, we all know how well mixing crews goes. They need time to gel. Rather, what I would prefer is to solely crew as many of our ships with your extra watches as we can manage. We'll place some ISF personnel aboard to help bring your people up to speed, but, in many cases, it may just be one engineer.

"That seems prudent," Captain Shira said with a tilt of her head.

"As you've no doubt heard by now, nearly half the ships in our fleet here at Roma are barely able to fly. We're sending all the ships with incomplete shielding, missing environmental systems, or non-functional weapons back to our core worlds—

mainly Carthage and Athens. That will leave eleven thousand and fifteen ISF ships ready for combat. Additionally, several thousand ships came in from bases across the Transcend after we sent news of Airtha's treachery."

<*Though we told them not to,*> Sera groused privately.

<*Glad they did, though, with what we now know we're up against,*> Tanis replied.

"This brings the number of TSF vessels up to a little over six thousand. We're still vastly outnumbered here, but make no mistake—this is a well-defended system, and our stasis shields should more than level the playing field."

"Admiral Richards," a TSF captain named Trip spoke up. "When will the TSF ships get stasis shields?"

"We're working on a tamper-proof black-box version of the technology," Tanis replied. "But it won't be ready in time for this battle."

"Are you serious?" another TSF captain exclaimed; a woman named Andrette, by the indicator on Tanis's HUD. "We're here defending your system—risking our lives—and you still won't share this technology with us?"

"Captain Andrette," Admiral Greer spoke quietly, "you will address Admiral Richards appropriately, or you will be dismissed."

"Yes, Admiral Greer," Captain Andrette replied, without an iota of an apology in her voice. "I'm sorry for the disrespect, Admiral Richards, but the question still stands."

<*Not too happy, is she?*> Angela asked.

<*Judging by their expressions, most of the TSF captains share her sentiment,*> Tanis responded.

"I appreciate your feelings on this matter, Captain Andrette," Tanis replied audibly. "You're putting a lot on the line here. I, and everyone here, deeply appreciate it. Truth be told, I ultimately plan to equip all our ships with black-box versions of these shields. The risk of an incapacitated ship having the tech stolen—or of a spy gaining access to it—is too high. The short-term benefit is far outweighed by the long-term risk."

"That's easy for you to say...Admiral," Captain Andrette replied.

"Captain Andrette," Greer said, his voice a soft growl, "I will be flying in a ship without stasis shields, just as I have every other time I have met our enemies in battle. You will do so, as well. Is that understood?"

"Yes, Admiral Greer," Captain Andrette replied, her tone moderated, though not entirely mollified.

"Our tactics are going to be simple," Tanis said, moving on from the discussion about shields. "We will make them come to us, to overextend themselves and stretch their lines thin. Then we will strike them with stealth vessels where they least expect it."

"What if they don't disperse their fleets?" Admiral Greer asked. "If they maintain concentrated formations, smaller strike groups will be ineffective."

"You can be certain that they will disperse," Tanis replied. "After the first few salvos of relativistic grapeshot hit their tight groupings, that is."

A number of the TSF captains drew in sharp breaths, and more than one disapproving look was sent her way.

"The TSF does not employ grapeshot," Admiral Greer said, his voice even and toneless. "It is considered barbaric."

<*Strong words for someone who has used antimatter weapons,*> Angela commented privately.

<*Yeah, but it was Sera's idea. It's a sore topic, and I don't want to undermine her in front of her people.*>

Tanis took a slow breath and replied in an equally even tone. "You call the tactic barbaric, but I call its absence the devolution of warfare. The purpose of war is not to continue it for millennia, but to end it as quickly, and decisively, as possible; to use every weapon in your arsenal with maximum efficiency. Expending force with maximum prejudice to achieve a rapid victory is the best way to prevent future aggression."

She noted nods from the ISF captains, and saw that many of the TSF captains also agreed. That much, at least, was a good sign.

"There are sixty-seven rail platforms in the New Canaan system—all are capable of firing grapeshot at speeds approaching three-quarters the speed of light. We will use these platforms to break up the Hegemony's fleet and ensure they are vulnerable to our attacks."

"Sixty-seven?" A man down the table, a TSF captain named Edward, asked. "Where are they?"

Tanis noted that he was one of the TSF captains who had nodded with approval when she brought up the grapeshot.

"Various moons and dwarf planets. They're subterranean, and are capable of multiple firing vectors. A dozen are also in orbit around Carthage and Athens—hidden by our stealth tech. At any given moment, we can fire forty-nine of them into this quadrant of the system. There are also two railguns on this ship capable of firing relativistic grapeshot."

"How will our ships know where safe regions are?" Admiral Greer asked. "Kinetic weapons, grapeshot especially, do not discriminate between friend and foe."

Tanis nodded somberly. "That is true. We will furnish your scan teams with the locations of all the platforms in the system. We have safe and unsafe corridors, and pre-determined firing solutions based on enemy fleet positions. Tactical updates on the fleetnet will also contain data on any salvos the platforms have fired."

"Damn glad we didn't come in guns blazing," one of the TSF colonels said. She hadn't meant it to be audible to the entire assembly, but the virtual space picked her up and broadcast the statement.

Several of the TSF officers nodded in agreement, while others reddened at the thought of the defeat they would have suffered at the hands of the colonists.

"We're on the same side now," Sera said, speaking for the first time since her introduction of Tanis. "As we should have been all along."

"I mentioned earlier that I am glad for the reinforcements that have come from across the Transcend," Tanis said as she made eye contact with the captains and admirals who had jumped in after they received the drone messages. "Given our firepower, you may wonder why that is."

"I certainly do," Greer commented.

"From data gathered by a team of ours—which spent years in the Perseus Arm—and through the interrogation of prisoners from the assault on the *Galadrial*, I have reason to believe that there is at least one more enemy fleet bearing down on us here."

"A sound strategy," Greer said.

"And not entirely unexpected," Tanis added. "We're going to continue interrogations to get more intel on composition and timing, but for now, we're planning on the enemy bringing at least fifty thousand ships to bear."

Murmurs came from around the table, and Tanis raised her hands for silence.

"Let's go over assignments," she said, moving the conversation from strategy to tactics.

The next several hours were spent organizing the ships that had not departed for Carthage and Athens into four major fleet groups, which intermixed ISF and TSF vessels and crew. The groups were commanded by Tanis, Greer, Joe, and Sanderson.

Joe and Sanderson were assigned smaller forces, only fifteen hundred ships each, while Tanis and Greer both commanded over six thousand ships each. Crews were reorganized and reassigned to new vessels, and even before the meeting came to a close, personnel transfers were already underway.

The room's wall had a holodisplay of the space surrounding the *I2,* and it was aglow with ships of all sizes maneuvering; small vessels docking directly for transfers, and larger ones disgorging dozens of shuttles to move crews.

Someone in Space Traffic Control was probably having kittens.

Eventually the meeting ended, and the holographic table disappeared—leaving just the dozen men and women physically present, to whom Tanis gave a tired smile.

"That went better than I expected," Admiral Greer said with a glance at Viska.

"Absolutely; though I got pinged by at least a hundred different people as the meeting went on. I had to shunt them all so I could focus," Viska replied.

"I guess they were all too uncertain about the new Old Lady to ping me," Tanis said with a rueful laugh. "Still, so long as they understand how important it is that we stop Orion here, I can deal with it. We have to show the enemy that this war is too costly, and that it has to stop before it spreads."

"If we can do that, then this will be worth it, no matter the outcome," Greer nodded. "Forgive me, Field Marshal Richards, I have a shuttle to catch, and a fleet to get in position."

"Yes, of course," Tanis rose and shook Greer's hand. "Thank you. Without your support, none of this would be possible."

Greer's eyes darted to Sera, then back to Tanis. "Yes, well. We all have to make the best of each situation."

He saluted her before leaving, and Tanis returned the gesture. Viska followed after sketching her own salute.

"Not a lot of enthusiasm there," Sera noted as she carefully stood. "Agh…stars, my back is stiff!"

"I know what you mean," Tanis replied, ignoring the throbbing in her arm where the flowmetal was spliced into her flesh.

Over the next few minutes, everyone else gave a parting comment and left the room. In the end, only Tanis and Joe remained.

"All these men, women, and AIs are counting on me to keep them alive," Tanis said, her voice barely audible. "I'm not going to be able to do that; we're going to lose a lot of people out there."

"We are," Joe said soberly. "More than either of us ever have before; but it doesn't change what we must do. We are not the aggressors here. The Hegemony and Orion will regret this action."

"I suspect that we all will," Tanis replied.

* * * * *

Joe looked into his wife's eyes and gave her a warm smile. "Come, let's walk to the dock."

"Walk? That'll take hours, Joe. We have a ton of things to do."

"Everyone has their orders, and we can handle any crises on the way. Humor me; we may not see each other for a while. I need to get my fill of you now."

He wrapped an arm around her shoulder, and led her out of the conference room as he spoke. She didn't resist, and they strolled down the long corridor and past the maglev station, descending to the deck housing Prairie Park. There, they wandered amongst the tall grass for some time.

Many hours later, as Tanis had predicted, they stood within the vast expanse of the A1 Dock.

Joe took Tanis's face in his hands, and kissed her long and hard.

"Still such a tease." Tanis smiled as she slid her lips onto his cheek, whispering in his ear, "You be careful out there." She pulled back to look him in the eyes, and her voice rose, laced with concern. "This fight is going to be hairy. I'm positive that the Hegemony fleet isn't the only one out there waiting to pounce. No way would the OG let them come here alone."

"Yeah, of that I have little doubt. You be careful, too. You're the one flying around in the biggest target ever built," Joe said, finally releasing Tanis. "I'll see you soon, love."

"Soon," Tanis replied with a smile, as Joe got in a groundcar headed for the shuttle that would take him to the *Alexandria,* the flagship of his Fleet Group.

As he rode away, he turned to see Tanis standing alone in the vast space of the A1 Dock; this one small woman holding back their enemies time and time again by her sheer force of will.

"Stars be with you, Tanis," he whispered. "I love you."

AN OLD FRIEND

STELLAR DATE: 03.30.8948 (Adjusted Years)
LOCATION: *Sabrina*, ISS *I2*
REGION: Near Roma, New Canaan System

Meet her.

Nance bolted upright in her bed; sleep instantly gone, sweat beading on her brow. The voice was in her head once more, prodding her. After so long, she had begun to imagine that it had been a dream.

Could it be some sort of anxiety over Erin's eventual removal? The AI had been in her head for nearly twenty years, but soon that relationship would come to an end. Perhaps her mind was playing tricks on her—making her reimagine whatever she had dreamt up all those other times the voice had spoken to her—made her do things.

Leave me alone! she screamed in her mind. *You're not real, you've never been real. You're just some part of my subconscious mind playing tricks on me.*

Meet her.

Nance flung herself back into her bed and pulled her pillow over her head, screaming in her mind.

No!

Meet her now.

Nance tried to remain still, but her body sat up and her legs swung over the edge of the bed.

"No, I won't, you can't make me." She hissed.

I can. Meet her.

Nance struggled to lie back down, but her body stood instead. She knew there was no fighting it. Before the voice compelled her to leave her cabin naked, she walked to her wardrobe—glad to still have the power to do so—and quickly dressed.

She quickly walked through *Sabrina*'s passageways, and out onto the *I2*'s dock. Like previous times, the voice guided her, instructing her to turn left or right as needed. It took over thirty minutes to reach her destination: a small bar near one of the new fighter decks.

Nance sat at a table in the back and wondered who would come to meet her. The voice hadn't sent her to meet an unknown person since her first encounter with it on Senzee station eighteen years ago. Her mind raced through a thousand possibilities—each less likely than the last—ultimately seizing on the fear that this would be her final hour of life.

A familiar figure walked into the bar, surveyed the occupants, and began to thread the tables, working her way toward Nance. It took a moment to place her, but then Nance remembered. It was Terry, the biotech who had first given her nano to assist her the day they arrived on the *Intrepid* in the Bollam's System.

"Terry?" Nance asked. "What are you doing here? You need to go. I'm meeting someone here."

"I know," Terry replied. "I'm the someone."

Nance sat back in her chair. "You? You did this to me? Do you know what has happened to me since then? I've seen things…I've done things…"

"I saved you from yourself," Terry said. "I made you better—something more. You were pathetic before. I made you strong."

Nance was taken aback by the calm manner in which Terry spoke, as though her words were fact, indisputable. If Nance hadn't been continually tortured by what happened so long ago, she may have believed the woman across from her. But she knew that Terry's words were poison.

"What are you…who are you?" Nance asked, even though she knew. The meeting she had so long ago on Senzee station was no longer a dim recollection, a half-forgotten dream—it was a clear memory, as if it had happened five minutes prior.

"Surely you know," Terry replied. "You must have met it. The creature. What does it want?"

Nance felt a nanocloud leave her body and knew that it was shrouding the table. Anyone nearby would hear and see something very different than what was about to transpire.

Her hand shot out, catching Terry's in an iron grip.

"It wants to purge you. Your usefulness has come to an end. Myrrdan is nothing but a liability."

A smile crept across Terry's face. "I suspected it would want me dead. But their mistake is eternally compounding. I'm no one's servant—and you have no idea what you're mixed—"

The smile faded, replaced by a confused expression on Terry's face.

"Who… Nance?" she asked.

Nance clasped both of the women's hands in her own. "You're confused, it's understandable. This will take a minute to explain."

A NEW MISSION

STELLAR DATE: 03.30.8948 (Adjusted Years)
LOCATION: ISS *I2*
REGION: Near Roma, New Canaan System

"They may have turned this bird into a warship, but it still has the best beer around," Cargo said loudly in the crowded bar. He raised his glass for a toast. "To Cheeky. May she find her place in the stars."

"Her place in the stars," the others intoned and drank from their glasses.

"I can still hardly believe it," Misha said. "I mean, I only knew her for a few years, but she was like family."

"We're all family," Cargo replied, his voice deep and solemn. "We lost one of our own; we'll never be the same."

"C'mon," Jessica said with a smile. "We did it! We got out of Orion space and to New Canaan. We should be happy. Cheeky would want us to be happy."

<*It's hard,*> Erin said. <*We all had this vision in our minds of a happy, peaceful colony—but we missed peace and came for the war.*>

<*Tanis and Bob will sort it out,*> Iris replied. <*They have a plan. I don't have all the details, but I know they believe they can win.*>

Jessica took another sip of her beer as her crewmates talked about what the coming battle would entail—it would be the largest battle any of them had ever seen. Fleets to rival those at the outset of the FTL Wars, and more powerful weapons all around.

She had to admit to that it felt strange to finally be on the *Intrepid;* to be *home*. She had spent nearly two decades on *Sabrina*—an eye blink, compared to her time aboard the *Intrepid,* but still significant. And the men, women, and AIs around her had become like a family.

<*You're sad,*> Iris commented.

<*You'll have to leave me soon. All of you will—you'll need to leave all of us. We were so focused on getting here, but our destination will destroy the thing we've become.*>

<*'Destroy' is the wrong word,*> Iris replied and suffused Jessica's mind with warmth. <*I will always be just a thought away…I plan to do what my sister did, and occupy a physical body.*>

<*There's that, at least,*> Jessica chuckled in her mind. <*You're starting to take up a lot of room in here. You need your own body.*>

Iris smiled in response, not just an image in her mind, but Jessica could feel it. <*Well, if you were shaped properly, there would be more room for me.*>

"Penny for your thoughts?" Trevor asked as he wrapped an arm around her.

A deep feeling of happiness and contentment came over Jessica as she relaxed into his arm. Things changed, that was the way of life, but they *had* made it. They had beat the odds, bested every obstacle. Now they were safe. Tanis would figure out how to win, just as she always did, and she would get that cabin with a porch down on Carthage.

And now she had someone to share it with again.

"Oh, did I mention that their settlement office already reached out to me?" Misha asked before Jessica could respond to Trevor. "I guess having friends in high places is damn handy. I have my pick of any unclaimed land on any of the terrestrial worlds—and I mean my pick of a shit-ton of land. I also got a few million credits, though I really don't understand how the economy works here—I mean, there is zero scarcity of anything…how does money have value?"

"It's what we were trying to achieve back on Victoria," Jessica replied, "though we had a lot of push-back from the Victorians. They had a serious…mistrust of us that forced the colony to build a credit-based economy, which focused on goods and labor."

<Here we'll finally have a true system of productivism,> Erin said. *<Everyone effectively has unlimited money, so long as they're productive.>*

"Unlimited?" Cargo's voice held no small amount of disbelief. "I don't see how that's possible. Otherwise I'd go buy myself a brand new *I2* tomorrow."

"You'd need to exhibit the same level of productivity that it would take to build the *I2,*" Jessica said. "There are also finite resources; or at least an upper limit to how fast they can be extracted and refined. That, and energy constraints put an upper limit on what can be made, and therefore set the ceiling for what the productivist economy can support."

<I don't know about that limit,> Iris added. *<They hollowed out six moons in short order and built massive fleets. Now that we have CriEn modules of our own, there is no longer a limit to the amount of energy we can tap into.>*

<There's a practical limit,> Erin replied. *<We draw too much, and the CriEn modules destabilize local spacetime at the quantum level. No one really wants to find out what happens if we do that.>*

"Well, I don't want a starship," Misha said as he leaned back in his chair and interlaced is fingers behind his head. "Give me ten thousand hectares, and I'll raise the finest horses this side of the core. I can't wait to see what pure Sol-stock looks like."

"Big enough for me to ride?" Trevor asked.

"Well…maybe. If they have the right breeds."

Jessica glanced at Nance, surprised that she wasn't joining in the conversation. The bio-turned-engineer was usually very interested in the more advanced tech that they came across on their journey. The idea of unlimited energy and resource production was usually a topic that she would dive into with more than a little fervor.

Jessica reached around Misha and touched Nance on the shoulder. *<Hey, you OK?>*

<Huh? Yeah.... I'm...I just miss her, you know? I spent over half my life in the company of that crazy nympho. Leaves a pretty big hole inside.>

<I hear you,> Jessica replied. *<If you need to talk, I'm all ears.>*

<Thanks, Jess. I'll take you up on that soon, just...not yet, 'kay?>

Jessica nodded. She and loss were old friends—healing took time. *<Just don't forget that you still have the living who love you. I'm speaking from experience here.>*

<I won't,> Nance replied.

"Hey, there, sorry to interrupt," a voice said from behind them, and Jessica turned to see Tanis standing behind their table.

"Tanis," Jessica said as she rose to her feet. "Have a seat, we were just discussing how the economy works here."

"Stars...don't even ask me. Luckily the GSS was good at filtering out slackers. If anything, we have too many go-getters on our hands," Tanis said as she took a seat.

"Looking forward to joining in," Misha said with a big shit-eating grin on his face. Jessica shook her head. He always did try to kiss ass.

Tanis nodded, taking no notice of his eager attitude.

"Bob and I have been reviewing the data you pulled from the Orion Guard facility, and believe that we can execute a strike against them that will set their efforts back considerably."

"Sounds interesting," Cargo said, his tone guarded.

"Stop. Before you go any further, I'm not leaving New Canaan," Jessica said. "I love you like a sister, Tanis; but no."

"Don't worry," Tanis said while flashing a winning smile—something that never looked right on her. "You won't have to go anywhere."

TRISILIEDS

STELLAR DATE: 04.01.8948 (Adjusted Years)
LOCATION: ISS *I2*
REGION: Near Roma, New Canaan System

"Multiple signatures, six hundred twenty thousand klicks off our bow!" the chief scan officer cried out into the relative silence of the *I2*'s bridge.

Tanis leapt up from her seat and strode toward the holotank, rotating the view to show the region of space Scan had indicated.

Captain Espensen was at her side an instant later, hand to her chin as she examined the readings.

Tanis had considered building a separate CIC on the *I2,* but there was something about being on the vessel's bridge that she loved too much to command the fleet from anywhere else. However, this was the first time they would be in battle with a fleet this large; if it proved distracting for the bridge crew, she would move.

"They don't look like the Hegemony ships out past the HP," Captain Espensen said.

It took Tanis a moment to realize that the captain was referring to the heliopause. Ever since she first met the young Rachel Espensen at Joe's academy back above Victoria, she had known Rachel to invent her own little words, abbreviations, and phrases. She had become a bit of an ISF legend for how much of her vernacular had made it into the official tactics and doctrine.

Tanis examined the scan profile of the ships. Data was still accumulating, but she had to agree; these ships looked very different. None were as big as the Hegemony's Dreadnaughts, and their lines were sleeker, almost hydrodynamic.

"I think you're right," Tanis murmured. "Looks like someone else has come to the party."

<Get rails seven, twelve, and twenty to cover their current and leading location with grapeshot,> Tanis directed the Fleet Coordination Officer. The message would take four minutes to reach the platforms, but the new ships were still jumping in. Given their current vector, the shot should still hit them in eleven minutes.

"You're not going to hail them?" Captain Espensen asked quietly.

"The insystem beacons all say to leave immediately or be fired upon. That's enough," Tanis replied.

Captain Espensen gave a short laugh. "Remind me never to piss you off."

The Fleet Coordination Officer sent the message, and a countdown appeared above the holotank—it would update with a more accurate time to impact when the rail platforms replied with their precise firing solutions.

<I've updated the fleetwide tactical burst with our estimated firing solutions,> the FCO added.

<Very good,> Tanis replied.

While she was speaking with the FCO, she was also discussing the new ships with Captain Espensen.

"They look similar to ships from the Pleiades," Tanis said. "Perhaps the Trisilieds."

"You may be right," Espensen nodded. "They're a bit different from what's in the Transcend databases, but so are the Hegemony ships out there. Stands to reason, though—intel says Trisilieds are squarely under the Guard's thumb."

"And a monarchy, no less," Tanis said with a frown. "How in the stars do those still exist?"

She caught Rachel grinning at her out of the corner of her eye.

<Maybe cult of personality?> the *I2*'s captain asked with a mental chuckle.

<Watch it, kid,> Tanis replied. *<I still have drinks with your mother from time to time.>*

"How do you think they're pulling off this jump?" Captain Espensen asked aloud, her voice now serious. "It's some precision work to bring all these ships in this close to Roma."

"I imagine the Hegemony ships have captured Isyra's jump gates out there. Probably sent the coordinates back to these guys, wherever they were staging," Tanis replied.

"Then we're going to get a lot more company real soon," Captain Espensen said, and Tanis imagined the captain was referring to the Hegemony ships using Isyra's gates to jump insystem.

"We read over two thousand enemy vessels, more coming every minute," Admiral Sanderson said as his holopresence appeared beside the tank. "Some retirement, by the way."

Tanis nodded. "Sorry about that. I'm not sure when I'll be able to give you your walking papers now."

Admiral Sanderson shrugged. "Not your doing."

"Isyra's fleet got the recall," Scan announced. "I've picked them up, heading toward the rendezvous we assigned."

"How many did she lose?" Tanis asked.

"Hard to say," Scan replied. "At least a dozen. We'll know more once they make it further insystem."

"Plus or minus a dozen, Isyra's fleet is a drop in the bucket," Sanderson replied.

Tanis wished that Greer and Joe could join in the conversation—if only there had been a bit more time before the inevitable invasion, they would have been equipped with QuanComm transceivers.

The next time she fought a battle like this, it would be with instantaneous communication between the command ships—the whole fleet, if she was lucky. Between that, the stasis shields, the jump gates, and the picobombs—at least, the threat of picobombs—she hoped to end this war in years, not decades.

<*Pull that off, and you'll really have earned that retirement you want so badly,*> Angela chuckled.

<*Will I ever,*> Tanis replied.

The firing solutions came back from the rail platforms, and the countdown above the holotank updated to read two and a half minutes.

"Damn," Tanis muttered. "They're still jumping in. We'll only hit the first group before they disperse."

"Wasn't that the plan?" Captain Espensen asked. "To get them to disperse?"

"Yeah," Tanis grunted. "But I like to hit them to make them disperse, not have them do it first 'cause they wised up."

"Twenty-nine thousand ships and counting," Scan announced.

Admiral Sanderson rubbed his forehead. "These guys sure seemed to think we would have a lot of ships. Too bad Tomlinson didn't; we'd have a lot more to defend ourselves with."

Tanis nodded absently. When the Hegemony ships at the edge of the New Canaan system jumped in, they'd be outnumbered four-to-one. Granted, it was some of the best odds in recent battles; but this one was going to be hard to manage. She was almost glad that the New Canaan population hadn't grown fast enough to fill out her fleet. With the fighters, there could have been a hundred thousand discrete units for her to command.

"Tanis," a voice called out from behind her, and she turned to see Sera enter the bridge, followed by Finaeus.

"Sera, Finaeus," Tanis said with a rueful smile. "Welcome to the party."

"You sure know how to throw one around here," Finaeus replied. "What's the countdown for?"

"Grapeshot," Tanis replied.

Finaeus's mouth formed an 'O,' and he shook his head. "I've got over four thousand years under my belt, and I've never seen that stuff fired in anger."

"First time for everything," Tanis replied.

"At my age, even," Finaeus added.

His words were punctuated by the holo registering grapeshot hitting the lead ships in the Trisilieds fleet. Scan marked hundreds of impacts, and it was almost impossible to pick out individual ship strikes, or assess damage as a whole.

For anyone but Tanis, at least.

She held the image of the Trisilieds fleet in her mind, able to pick out every one of the enemy ships, examining the damage to each, assessing the remaining shield strength, and determining the enemy fleet's combat capacity.

She had the numbers before the Scan officer.

"Twenty-one percent of the enemy fleet has been hit," he called out. "Five percent of their ships have lost maneuvering capabilities."

"Look at them scatter," Finaeus commented.

Above the holotank a number appeared: sixty-eight percent.

"What is that for?" he asked.

Captain Espensen replied, "It's the percentage of their ships that have moved into the paths of the second salvo."

"Damn, you're ruthless," Finaeus said softly.

"I meant what I said," Tanis replied. "I mean to win this, and every engagement, as swiftly as possible. Whatever it takes."

"No new signatures," Scan announced. "Final tally is thirty-one thousand six hundred forty two."

Finaeus let out a long whistle just as the second salvo of grapeshot hit.

Tanis nodded with satisfaction as she watched the impacts. This time, the damage was more extreme. Already weakened shields died entirely as grav systems were overwhelmed by the volume and kinetic energy contained in the tiny pellets.

Her final tally and that of Scan agreed. Another seven percent of the enemy fleet was incapacitated.

"And that," Tanis said with a glance back at her guests, "is the last time this tactic should ever work—if these folks can manage to pay attention, that is."

"Shouldn't have been an option this time, either," Captain Espensen said. "They should have jumped in with no ship closer than a hundred kilometers to any other. No way we could have made grapeshot effective, then."

"It's a miracle none of them collided on entry," Finaeus added. "They must be using a hundred jump gates to move this many ships so fast, pinpointing an exit this well across light years."

"Which means that their staging ground is close by," Sera noted.

As Sera discussed possible locations for an enemy base near New Canaan with Finaeus, Tanis watched the holotank, waiting for the Trisilieds ships to make a move indicative of their goal.

She put herself in their commander's shoes. She had just jumped into a system where seizure of their advanced tech was the end game. The plan would be to overwhelm the enemy with sheer numbers and force their surrender. Except she had already lost eleven percent of the fleet before battle had even been joined.

Given that her goal was attaining technology, not the destruction of the system, she needed to attain total domination of the system. However, with an eleven percent loss in the opening minutes of the battle, she would be re-estimating the likelihood of achieving that end. She had two options available: move insystem and hold one,or more of the worlds hostage, or flee.

Tanis knew what she would choose. No technology was worth throwing away thousands of ships and the lives of the people on them. But as the Trisilieds ships spread further apart and began to move insystem, she knew their commander did not share her outlook.

"FCO," Tanis called out. "Flank speed. We are in pursuit. Best intercept course nav can plot. Sanderson, execute the polar plan."

"Aye, Fleet Admiral," Sanderson replied and disappeared from view.

"I have something," one of the scan officers announced. "Not sure if…"

<*It is!*> Priscilla called out over the shipnet. <*RMs incoming, tagging them as fast as I can.*>

Tanis turned her attention to the holotank. A thousand RMs appeared in its depths, then a thousand more, then the counter began to climb faster than even her eyes could track.

"The hegemony ships must have fired them through Isyra's jump gates," Sera said. "You would have picked them up sooner, otherwise."

"I sure have a love-hate relationship with those gates," Finaeus said. "Would have been better if I'd never figured out how to make them."

"Cat's out of the bag now," Tanis said.

"What are you going to do?" Sera asked.

"Nothing," Tanis replied. "I already directed the FCO to inform all vessels to cease acceleration and prepare for full stasis. Point defense only on clear targets."

"I guess we did survive a blast from a black hole's relativistic jet," Sera said. "How much worse could an RM be?"

"I'm impressed," Tanis said. "We were under full stealth until we started boosting to intercept the Trisilieds ships. Either they can see through our stealth tech, or their commander has an amazing mind for strategy."

"Or he's pumped so many RMs into your system that they would have homed in on you no matter where you were."

Tanis chuckled. "Terrifying, but unlikely…aw, shit."

<*What is it?*> Priscilla asked.

"If they figured out where we are so quickly, then they know our route to the terraformed planets."

"Which means that they *will* have filled the space between here and there with RMs," Captain Espensen said.

The scan data feeding into the holotank began to show the ships of Fleet Group 1 firing at the RMs. The relativistic missiles and the ships were all jinking erratically, making the holo display appear as though it were flickering, or suffering some sort of bizarre malfunction.

"That's going to give me a headache," Finaeus said. "How sure are you that this shielding of yours can withstand relativistic missiles?"

<*One hundred percent,*> Bob's voice came across the bridge net.

"The elusive Bob makes his presence known," Finaeus said with a chuckle.

"Hush," Sera whispered at Finaeus and the older man fell silent.

Tanis cast Finaeus a worried look. "Don't worry about us, worry about the Transcend ships without stasis shields," Tanis said.

Sure enough, the scan data updated, and the holotank showed more than fifty TSF ships under direct threat from enemy missiles. Their shields would not protect them at all against the incoming barrage.

"Helm," Captain Espensen called out. "Max burn, get us ahead of those ships. Weapons, I want a grapeshot firing solution that will shield those Transcend cruisers, and not hit any of ours."

"That's a tall order," Tanis said softly. "But maybe they can find one."

She Linked across the fleet and aided in coordinating kinetic grapeshot rounds from a dozen additional cruisers, adding to the wave of kinetic pellets that would—hopefully—destroy enough of the incoming RMs. Captain Espensen attained a solution from the *I2*'s fire control team, which Tanis integrated into the kinetic shield. With eighty-two seconds until the first estimated impact, the ISF ships let fire their grapeshot.

Beams from hundreds of ships in the fleet group continued to pick away at the missiles, and every second or two, one struck its mark. However, only a fraction of the hits caused enough damage to destroy or disable the missiles. It was simply too hard to track something moving at relativistic speeds for long enough to burn through its casing.

Then, in what looked like a spectacular display of fireworks, the first missiles hit the cloud of grapeshot and exploded.

"Great," Finaeus shook his head in dismay. "You've created relativistic shrapnel. Well done."

Tanis cast the man a cold look. "This is the bridge of a warship, and you are a guest here. Keep your tone and your comments respectful."

Finaeus took a step back. Tanis was certain that few had spoken to him so bluntly in a long time.

"Yeah, um, sure," was all he managed to respond with.

The *I2* reached its position between the TSF ships and the incoming missiles, its thousands of beams lighting up the darkness—though the ship's placement in the center of the fleet reduced the available firing solutions.

Behind them, the TSF ships burned hard, a hundred AP drives and fusion torches outshining Canaan Prime, as they moved to evade the shrapnel and the few missiles that had made it past the barrier.

Shrapnel impacts registered on scan, and two-dozen ships spun off course before killing their engines and drifting through the dark. Five suffered internal detonations, and a number appeared in Tanis's mind as the ships gouted eerie fire into the cold dark vacuum around them.

Two thousand forty-three dead. It would be just the beginning of her tally for the battle.

Two more salvos of RMs came at Fleet Group 1, followed by a single attack on Greer's Fleet Group 2, which was also boosting insystem on an intercept course with the Trisilieds fleet.

This time, the TSF and ISF ships were better prepared, and the ISF ships maneuvered to create protective shields, while the TSF ships fired countermeasures at the incoming missiles.

The tactic worked reasonably well and conserved the fleet group's grapeshot. Only four more TSF ships were destroyed along with the last of the enemy RMs.

The tone on the bridge was muted, but Tanis was not displeased with the result. "All things considered, they just expended considerable resources to little effect."

"I imagine they're thinking the same thing," Sera shook her head. "Once we get stasis shields on all the ships in the TSF, maybe this war *will* be over as fast as you hope."

The holotank showed that Fleet Groups 1 and 2 would intercept the Trisilieds ships in seven hours—well before the invading ships reached the settled worlds deep insystem.

Tactical showed that serious losses would be inevitable, but that victory was assured.

Captain Espensen had moved the *I2* to the van of Fleet Group 1, which was now moving at just over a tenth the speed of light. They raced to meet their foes. The ships could have accelerated faster, but too high a velocity would have sent them racing past the enemy ships, or necessitated braking heavily and exposing their vulnerable engines before engaging.

<*Feels too easy. What are those AST ships out there going to do?*> Tanis asked Angela.

<*Probably the best thing for them, and the worst thing for us,*> Angela replied.

Tanis nodded absently and sipped her coffee, glad that Espensen had an officer somewhere that knew feeding the bridge crew was wise. As she set her cup down on a tray at the edge of the console, the Scan officer called out.

"Signatures matching the AST ships, dead ahead!"

<*Didn't have to wonder long,*> Angela said.

Tanis spun back to the holotank and saw the space before Fleet Group 1 fill with ships. Number and composition matched the ships past the heliopause, which had attacked Isyra's watchers. The notation on the holotank read twenty-nine thousand eight hundred seventy-four vessels; over four thousand of which were dreadnaught class.

"Orders?" Captain Espensen asked, her face paling noticeably.

"Throw up the scoop and reverse polarity; let's make a shield for our fleet," Tanis replied with more calm than she felt. "FCO, inform all carriers to disgorge their ARC-6 alpha wings. All ships, prepare to fire kinetic rounds."

"Aye, Admiral," the FCO replied.

While the FCO managed the coordination, Tanis reviewed the placement of all the ships and the projected paths of the fighters. She tweaked the placements and assignments while watching how the Hegemony fleet arrayed itself.

The enemy ships were also travelling toward the Trisilieds ships and the inner New Canaan system, but they were coasting—their current momentum carried over from their acceleration before they passed through the jump gates.

Now, they carefully maneuvered into a large net, while keeping their engines facing away from the incoming ISF and TSF ships.

The net was wide, and Fleet Group 1 would pass through it, drawing fire from a fleet four times their size. Their shields should hold, but after seeing the Transcend fleet destroy her cruisers days ago, she was less certain about the effectiveness of stasis shields against concentrated enemy beamfire.

She wondered if the Hegemony ships would follow after Fleet Group 1 after they passed through the net, or if they would chase after Greer's ships, a half AU away.

Tanis knew what she would do if she were the Hegemony commander. She would drive the enemy against the Trisilieds fleet, crushing them utterly before moving on to the next target.

Tanis directed the ISF ships to form protective shields around the TSF vessels once more. In the resulting formation, the ships were not tightly packed, and still possessed dozens of kilometers of maneuvering room, but it should be enough to aid in the blocking of enemy beamfire.

The tactic felt strange. All military doctrine dictated that ships should never bunch up. It was folly to create such an easy grouping of targets, but Tanis had no choice if she were to save the Transcend ships from destruction.

As they drew nearer to the enemy net, which was extending into a long funnel, she ordered the tactical teams to fire concentrated rounds of grapeshot into the enemy fleet. Her plan was to make multiple openings in the enemy net, more than her fleet group needed, and sow as much confusion as possible.

The *I2*, however, would punch right through the center. She was certain that the target her largest warship presented would tempt the AST to leave her smaller formations alone.

"Ready to flash the scoop across the Hegemony fleet," Captain Espensen reported. "All batteries have selected targets and alpha wings are deployed."

"Good," Tanis nodded. "Delta-*v* between our fleets is a hair over fourteen thousand kilometers per second. With a maximum effective beam range of a hundred thousand kilometers, engagement length will be fourteen seconds. Pre-load all solutions, and backup options."

As she had so many times in the past, Tanis spread her mind across the fleet, greeting the AIs across thousands of capital ships and fighter wings. The ISF AIs knew to expect her, though the TSF intelligences were surprised, but grateful to feel her guiding touch.

The ARC-6s darted ahead of the fleet, ten thousand engine flares lighting the darkness. It was as though an entirely different starscape had appeared, new constellations shifting before them. A second later, every ship in the fleet fired their kinetic rounds, and the battle began.

Tanis felt time slow down as she surrounded herself with a holographic display of the entire battlefield, the bridge and its personnel falling away from her vision. She and Angela thought as one being as they directed ships and fighters to shore up weak spots in formations and prepare to take out prime targets.

Ahead, the Hegemony fleet detected the kinetic rounds firing from her ships, and many jinked out of the way; though many more were too late. One ton tungsten rounds slammed into cruisers and dreadnaughts, overloading sections of their shield umbrellas, some lucky shots punching clear through hulls.

A hundred enemy ships had taken damage from the kinetics, and Tanis directed the ARC-6 fighters to finish those vessels off. Short-range RMs lanced out from the fighters into the darkness, loaded with the ISF's double-impact warheads that would kinetically disable weakened shields before driving their nuclear warheads into their targets.

Though the enemy ships lay down withering point-defense fire and jinked to new positions, many of the missiles found their mark, and nuclear fireballs bloomed bright, obscuring the battlefield.

The ARC-6s sped through the enemy's formation, their stasis shields flaring brightly as they took beamfire, though not as much as Tanis had feared. Once through, the ISF fighters described sweeping arcs around the edges of the Hegemony fleet, coming about for another assault.

<*They do have a fighter shield,*> Angela commented. <*But nothing substantial.*>

<*They must have assumed that without our stasis shield tech, they can't use fighters effectively,*> Tanis replied.

<*Seems like a foolish assumption,*> Angela said. <*They could have brought a half-million fighters. It would have completely overwhelmed us.*>

<*A lot of people have trouble accepting new tactics. It would seem the Hegemony is amongst those.*>

Now there were just five seconds until the capital ships were in weapons range.

Tanis noted that the enemy fleet had responded, but not against the ISF fighters. Instead, another wave of RMs appeared on scan, once more snaking toward the vulnerable TSF ships.

She gave a mental nod to Priscilla, and the avatar altered the composition of the *I2*'s massive electrostatic ramscoop—a field over ten thousand kilometers across—to operate as a molecular decoupler. It was not a new trick, but one that was so far beyond the technical capabilities of their enemies, few opposing commanders seemed prepared for it.

Half the RMs disintegrated and spun off course as the field swept over them; though many survived the wave, and approached the TSF ships. Countermeasures and grapeshot filled the space between the two fleets as they neared the maximum range of their primary beam weapons.

The ISF ships shifted their protective bubbles around the TSF vessels, utilizing the same tactics that had been successful in the last two volleys of relativistic missiles.

Then, something unexpected occurred.

Tremendous flares of light and energy filled the battlefield, obscuring both fleets. Scan was blinded, and communications with the rest of the fleet cut out. Tanis winced as her mind, spread across the fleet's ships, snapped back into her own head.

She only managed one word, "What—" before understanding dawned on her. The missiles had carried antimatter warheads. The Hegemony had just committed a grievous war crime—likely in response to the Transcends' use of antimatter weapons against their fake fleet in Ascella.

The antimatter detonations disappeared from scan in less than a second as the ships of Fleet Group 1 sped past the expanding clouds of radiation that were traveling in the opposite direction.

Four hundred milliseconds later, the ships nearby reconnected to the combat net, and Tanis cried out, <*Fire on all preselected targets!*> The message retransmitted to the rest of the fleet as the ships re-Linked.

Damage estimates rolled in and Tanis saw that one hundred and eleven TSF ships had been destroyed or disabled, and forty-two ISF ships had suffered shield failures and taken damage from secondary explosions.

There were still fifty-six hundred undamaged ships in Fleet Group 1. The holodisplay finally resolved to show the seven divisions of Fleet Group 1, looking like insects travelling toward the flyswatter that was the Hegemony fleet.

But these bugs were prepared to sting.

The capital ships were now in weapons range, and the two fleets exchanged intensifying levels of beamfire with one another. Tanis once more stretched her mind out, guiding ships and aiding in target selection, feeling her mind swell as she encompassed the entire battlefield.

Her primary goal was to get her ships through the web intact—or as intact as she could—with a focus on disabling the enemy's maneuverability and weapons systems, rather than total destruction of their vessels.

And, over the fourteen seconds during which the capital ships exchanged fire, her Fleet Group 1 disabled seven hundred and nine Hegemony vessels.

The enemy commander, for their part, had changed their tactic. Rather than focusing on the TSF vessels, they targeted the smaller ISF ships, likely testing the stasis shield's ability to withstand concentrated particle beam attacks.

Something Tanis now knew that they could not do. The larger AST ships—their cruisers and dreadnaughts—fired proton and atom beams, the heavy particles and atomic nuclei striking the ISF stasis shields at near-light speed. A few, even a dozen of those beams could be shrugged off by the stasis shields, but hundreds of beams struck each targeted ship, and one by one those vessels saw their shields fail as reactors overheated and shut down.

The *I2*, for its part, delivered its own waves of high-energy particle beams, tearing through the AST ships like they were paper. A thousand beams at a time arced from the massive ship, pulverizing shields, destroying engines and weapons systems. Even the AST dreadnaughts were unable to withstand the *I2*'s high-energy salvos.

Then, the fourteen seconds were past, and Tanis drew her consciousness back into her mind and looked around her at the bridge of the *I2*.

Most of the personnel were drawing deep breaths, their expressions grim, yet glad. Captain Espensen gave Tanis a relieved nod as scan slowly pieced together a picture of what had happened.

The *I2* had taken no damage—a fact that did not surprise Tanis. The ship's shields were the most powerful in the fleet, and drew energy from CriEn modules; something that Bob would not allow for any other vessel.

The risk of the smaller ships creating localized imbalances in the base quantum energy of the universe was too great. He did not even extend his trust to the AIs of the other ships—fearing they would draw too much energy in a bid to survive.

Two hundred and thirty five; that was the number of ISF ships that were now little more than drifting hulls—if they were lucky. Only seven additional TSF ships had taken critical damage, though a hundred more ships across the fleet group had suffered some damage from the engagement.

But they had given as good as they got. The vector at which the fleets had intersected gave Fleet Group 1 consistent firing solutions on Hegemony ships. However, due to the enemy's formation, they had suffered three entire seconds where the majority of their fleet could not fire without risk of hitting their own.

Tanis had made the most of those seconds with another barrage of double-impact RMs.

Now, Fleet Group 1 was past the Hegemony ships on their continued race toward the Trisilieds fleet. To their rear, many of the Hegemony ships were already boosting to catch up. As they did, the Scan team finished their tallies.

The enemy had suffered what would normally be a crippling amount of damage, with over three thousand ships disabled or destroyed. However, when that still left twenty-six thousand ships intact, it was a different story.

Tanis imagined that the Hegemony commanders must have been rethinking taking on a fleet that could destroy three thousand ships in less than a minute—even when pitted against a far superior enemy. The math didn't favor either side.

In a slugfest, they would wear each other down to nothing.

Captain Espensen let out a long whistle. "That was some crazy strategery you did there, Admiral."

"Thanks," Tanis said, concentrating on the ARC-6 fighters, which were still making a second pass through the Hegemony fleet. She directed them to target the engines of the ships that had lowered their rear shielding as they boosted after Fleet Group 1.

"I can't believe the Hegemony would call the use of our picobombs a war crime, and then turn around and use antimatter on us." Captain Espensen shook her head.

"They opened the door," Tanis nodded. "They may not like what they find inside."

"Captain, Admiral," Scan called out. "Our fighters are coming back in for resupply. The Hegemony ships are boosting hard; they'll be back in weapons range in sixty-two minutes."

"That's a lot faster than we can repair and resupply all those fighters," Captain Espensen commented before casting an appraising glance at Tanis. "Fleet TAC must have anticipated this. We're trapped between the Hegemony and the Trisilieds ahead, now."

"Well," Tanis began, "We didn't exactly plan to be invaded like this, but our Hegemony friends back there are about to find that we can fire grapeshot to the rear with enough precision to slow their pursuit."

"Even so," Espensen replied, "they'll catch us before we get to Carthage—which is where it looks like the Trisilieds fleet is headed."

Tanis reviewed Fleet Group 1's position relative to Carthage, plotting out their approach. She looked at the remaining ships, clustered around the disabled vessels, which were still traveling at the same velocity as the rest of the fleet.

"FCO," Tanis called out. "Get every ship in this fleet on recovery duty. I want every disabled ship emptied in twenty-five minutes. Scoop everyone up, pods, everything. No one left behind. In fifty-five minutes, we're dumping to the dark layer."

"Tanis…we can't…not so close to the star…" Captain Espensen whispered.

"Captain," Tanis turned to Espensen. "You have your orders."

A MOMENT OF WEAKNESS

STELLAR DATE: 04.01.8948 (Adjusted Years)
LOCATION: ISS *I2*
REGION: Near Roma, New Canaan System

Sera found herself in awe of Tanis's tactical abilities. The way she could direct the ships of her fleet with a single, precise intent was a wonder to behold. A wonder that made her consider her place in whatever was to come.

Finaeus should be the true heir to the Transcend, and Tanis was by far the most capable commander she had ever seen; as the Transcend's Field Marshal, she would be the one in charge of every military action the TSF would take against the Orion Guard.

Sera was passable as Director of The Hand, but many of her successes there had been with Helen's assistance—and now Greer and others wished her to take her father's place? As what…queen, tyrant?

Her father had—deliberately, she supposed—placed weak provisions in the Transcend government's constitution for a transfer of power. It was just like him. She imagined that if he had been able to speak his last words upon some exalted deathbed, he would have imitated Alexander of Macedonia with his 'to the victor go the spoils' utterance.

Sera shook her head, trying to clear all thoughts of her father from her mind. Thinking of him inevitably brought her back to the bridge of the *Galadrial*. The place where she had learned that everything in her life had been a lie; where every friend—save for Tanis—had betrayed her.

A part of her mind chided her, reminding her that many friends had not betrayed her. Normally, Helen would have offered consolation here, but now that was gone, too.

It was insane to think that her mother—or a shard of her, at least—had been in her mind all these years. The things they had talked about, experienced, supported one another through—they were all shrouded in the lie. Everything about her was a lie.

Sera moaned inwardly. This perseveration was going to be the end of her. She needed to ground herself somehow, but the conflict they were in the midst of precluded that. How could she find stability in her own mind while everything around her balanced on a knife's edge?

Her eyes fell on Tanis.

Now there was a woman who lived up to the legend—and then some. She stood, arms akimbo, before a holotank: surveying the battlespace they would soon enter, assessing her fleet's strengths and weaknesses, and adjusting her tactics as damage reports rolled in.

The air of confidence she exuded strengthened those around her. Everyone operated at their best, gave their all, overcame any obstacle, because they knew Tanis would do no less.

It would have emboldened Sera, if she had a purpose here.

Going with *Sabrina* on their mission was out of the question—even if her body wasn't still healing, she would have thrown off their dynamic. Commanding a TSF or ISF ship was off the table, too. No one would let her take such a role, now that she was the President of the Transcend. She had to be kept safe on the *I2,* like one of Nance's porcelain dolls.

Sera looked at the countdown hovering over Tanis's holotank. There were still forty minutes left before their next maneuver. She decided that a walk would help clear away the negative thoughts and get her back in the right frame of mind. Perhaps one of the ship's parks would give her some peace.

Priscilla waved to her as she passed through the foyer, and Sera returned the gesture.

She walked through the administrative corridor connecting the bridge to the nearest maglev station, and thought about how different it was now compared to her first visit.

Then, the ship had been a civilian vessel—sort of. Most of the corridor had been given to offices of members of the colony leadership, their staffs, and the various departments that were focused on the ship's destination.

Now, it was a hubbub of military personnel, the men and women of the ISF—a force that had gone from a couple dozen ships to one of the most powerful militaries in human space in less than a generation. *How did they do it?* Sera wondered, immediately feeling the pain of Helen's absence once more. There was no one in her mind to talk with, no one with whom to discuss her hopes and fears.

Sera wandered aimlessly; or so she tried to tell herself, but her feet moved steadily in one direction: to the *I2*'s brig.

As she drew near, she couldn't hide it from herself anymore. There was one person who had betrayed her, one in whom she had placed absolute trust, that was still around. Someone she could talk to, someone she could ask '*why*'.

"I'm here to see the prisoner, Elena," Sera announced to the Marine sergeant at the duty station outside the brig.

The man looked up at her, and his tired expression disappeared as he realized who she was. "Yes, ma'am!" he replied before glancing down at his screen. "Admiral Richards has you on the list of people who may visit Elena, but the prisoner will remain behind a stasis shield. No physical contact is allowed."

"Suits me fine," Sera muttered. "Probably better for the both of us."

The sergeant gave her a puzzled look before nodding. "Yes, ma'am. I've passed you the route. Your conversation will be recorded, but immediately encrypted and saved. I will not have access to its content. However, Admiral Richards will."

"Understood," Sera replied, and loaded the sergeant's directions onto her HUD before passing through the security arch and into the brig.

The *I2*'s brig was, in a word, massive. She guessed that it could house ten thousand people—or maybe even more. She didn't think that it was for misbehaving ISF military personnel; this was a POW camp inside the ship.

Right now, it only had two occupants: Kent and Elena.

She only had directions to Elena's cell, and that was just as well. Sera had deliberately avoided any contact with the Orion Guard colonel; in her current state, she worried he would learn a lot more from her than she from him.

The same would certainly be true for Elena, but she needed to see if there were any explanations to be had—any closure.

Sera approached the cell, and saw Elena sitting on a white cot mounted to the wall on the right within the grey, featureless cube. The only other item in the room was a small san unit.

Her former lover sat up and took a deep breath as Sera approached. "Time for our chat, is it?"

"I suppose," Sera replied with a rueful smile. "It had to come eventually, right?"

"Yes, I suppose it did," Elena nodded slowly. "I honestly thought you'd come sooner—back on the *Galadrial*. When they moved me here, I began to wonder if I'd ever see you again."

"At the very least, you'd see me as a witness at your trial," Sera said as she summoned a seat to rise from the deck.

"Oh! I'm going to get a trial?" Elena smirked. "I guess that's something. I half expected a summary execution at some point."

"No, that's your game," Sera scowled, ready to tear into Elena; but then she stopped, considering once more what Elena had saved her from. "I'm sorry. That was unfair. I was about to do the same thing. You did save me from patricide—

though I know in my heart I still would have killed my father—so you only saved me from others' recriminations. Though you also robbed me of the answers I sought."

Elena leaned back against her cell's wall, pulling her knees up—a position Sera knew was intended to get her to trust her former lover, and to remind her of happier times past.

Shit, Sera, she chided herself. *Do you have to analyze everything like a fucking spy?*

"What do you think those answers are, now that you've had time to consider things?" Elena asked.

It was stupid; Sera knew it, but she wanted to confide in someone. Tanis was too busy to listen, and her former crew was out in the black; Elena had been her comforter for many years now. It was too easy to slip back into that place.

"I think he suspected Airtha—he must have. I mean…Finaeus warned him," Sera began. "If father did know, then maybe Airtha was too strong for him to take on; though it doesn't explain why father tried to kill Finaeus on Ikoden station, back when Jessica found him…what purpose would that have served? For everything to make sense, father must have exiled Finaeus for his own protection. Who was behind that assassination, then…?"

Sera's head snapped up and her eyes drilled into Elena, who raised her hands defensively. "It wasn't me! I knew Finaeus would strengthen you *against* your father, and that Praetor Kirkland was open to working with Finaeus—something he would not even entertain with your father."

"Oh, so you're in Kirkland's inner council now, are you?" Sera's tone grew caustic and her lip curled into a snarl. "What was your price, by the way? What did they offer you to betray me?"

To Sera's surprise, a tear formed in Elena's eye and drew a path down her cheek.

"You."

"Me? What do you mean by that?" Sera asked, even though she suspected what Elena would say next.

Elena's eyes were wide, and her voice pleaded with Sera to understand. "They were going to let you live, let us go off together somewhere and forget all this bullshit, just be *us*."

Anger burned through Sera's veins, and she leapt up and raised her hand, finger pointed at Elena; ready to tear into her former partner. Then she stopped and lowered her arm, turning away.

"Sera! Sera, please! They're going to win. You can't stop them. Where the Transcend has politics and power grabs, Orion has a belief; a belief that humanity should live in harmony with the galaxy—not to subsume it, not to transcend it. It's strong. It drives them like nothing in the Transcend. They're going to win…."

Sera turned back to Elena, and approached the bars on the outside of the cell, wrapping her hand around one.

"If I win against Airtha—whose fanaticism far outstrips Orion's—I will do everything in my power to stop this war. Kirkland has nothing to fear from rogue picotech anymore. I will stop all research, and let New Canaan retreat into their insular society." She looked up and peered through the bars at Elena.

"There's no reason why these two ideals cannot coexist. Why does everyone in the Transcend have to diminish to match Orion? We let people live as they wish; we don't enforce a…a… lower level of living, just because some people don't want to see humans ever ascend."

"That's not what it's about," Elena said with pleading eyes. "Airtha represents the end result—a malevolent entity that wishes to enslave and control. Now that Jutio is gone, it's even easier to see that. AIs in our heads, bodies modified so much that we're more machine than human…we *aren't* human anymore, Sera. We're *things*! The Transcend did that to us—made you and I weapons, instruments—and it spreads..."

Elena rose from the cot and approached the bars, her skin changing color to match Sera's.

"You did this to me. You did it because you think it's OK for humans to force their own evolution."

"I did it to keep you safe," Sera said. "By your faulty logic, I evolved you to make you better able to survive in your environment. We've long passed the point where we let random mutation and slow evolution push our species forward; but this is an academic argument...I didn't come here to debate philosophy with you."

"Then what did you come for here, Sera? Do you need to know when? How long? Is that what this is about?"

Sera nodded slowly. "Yes, I suppose that's all."

"It was after you were exiled. I couldn't believe what your father would allow to happen to his own daughter. The man was evil, plain and simple. We can debate philosophy all day long, but you can't argue with me on that. What did he say when he tore Helen from your mind? Was he kind and loving? Or did it reveal who he really was?"

Sera tried to push Elena's words out of her mind. She didn't want to remember that conversation with her father, how cold he had been. But it was impossible. How he had described Airtha as something he owned...no...he must not have known of her schemes. He really *did* believe he possessed her.

She brought her mind back to Elena's statement. "From the moment you came to me on the *Intrepid*, back in Ascella...our whole time together in the Huygens System...on Airtha. The whole time, you were trying to turn me?"

"I wanted to show you how much I *loved* you. So that when the time came for us to have this conversation, you'd listen. There's still a chance for you to do the right thing. Sue for peace with Orion; then we can leave this place, leave all these troubles forever…"

Sera felt a manic laugh rise in her, and she forced it out in her search for some sort of catharsis.

"Seriously, Elena? Do you think that Tanis Richards will roll over just because I ask her to? Do you think that everyone in the Transcend will just lay down their arms because I say so? To them, the Orion Guard has destroyed entire worlds, burned systems to ash."

"You have to!" Elena cried out, balling her hands into fists. "You have to stop this war—surrender to Orion. There's nothing anywhere worth all this bloodshed!"

Sera didn't have a response. It wasn't that she disagreed with Elena; she just didn't know how to do what Elena was asking. "I can't…it's impossible. I don't know how."

"Then find a way," Elena stepped forward and reached a hand out toward her, pressing it against the field.

In that moment, the only thing Sera wanted in the entire galaxy was to hold Elena in her arms—but she couldn't. Not just because of the field separating them, but because her place at the head of the Transcend demanded that she didn't.

It demanded that she do her duty.

"I will find away," Sera replied. "But it won't be through surrender. When they see what Tanis is capable of, Orion will back down, and we'll have peace."

Elena stared longingly at Sera, her mouth working silently. "Then I suppose we have nothing further to discuss," Elena said sitting back down on her cot. She turned away and faced the wall. "Please, go now…I…I just…please go."

Sera thought about responding, about throwing something in Elena's face, but there was nothing left. She didn't harbor any ill will toward her former lover anymore, just dismay at how deluded she was—and shame in herself for never seeing it before.

"Goodbye, Elena," Sera said quietly. She turned and took a step, then stopped and looked over her shoulder. Sera tried to think of one last thing to say, but Elena had curled up into a fetal position, her shoulders heaving as sobs wracked her body.

A long, silent sigh escaped Sera's lips, and she walked away, wiping the tears that flowed down her face.

JOY RIDE

STELLAR DATE: 04.01.8948 (Adjusted Years)
LOCATION: High Carthage
REGION: Carthage, New Canaan System

"Cary!" Saanvi called out. "Where are you going?"

Cary turned around and looked at her sister and best friend in the world. "I'm going to get on a ship," Cary replied. "They need everyone up there who knows how to fly, and you and I know how to fly. Now come on."

The look on Saanvi's face was not promising. She had always been cautious that way, but growing up under their mother had reinforced that. Their mom liked rules, and she like people to do what she said. Cary preferred to think of herself as a more balanced combination of her mother and father—though she admitted that both of her parents' rebellious sides appealed to her more.

"We have orders from Mom to go planetside, and get in Landfall's bunker. She knows what's best for us," Saanvi said as she approached. "You know that."

Cary sighed and took Saanvi's hand. "Sahn, Mom wants to protect us, and that's her job as our mother. But you and I are eighteen, now. We're adults, and we can do what we want to—what we need to."

"Seriously, Cary? What sort of dream world do you live in? Mom runs everything here. She tells adults what to do all the time—it's her job. Being adults doesn't mean we don't have to listen to her."

"Yeah? Well maybe it's about time that Mom didn't get to tell everyone what to do around here."

Saanvi's face fell, and Cary regretted the words the moment they passed her lips. She often wondered why it was that Saanvi seemed to have a stronger bond with her mother than she did. Cary's flesh was her mother's flesh; she had many advanced genetic traits and mental abilities from her mother—hell, she was born a class L1 human, far above the standard L0. Something that was exceedingly rare without extensive pre-natal genetic modification.

But at least ninety percent of the time, Saanvi—who she loved more than anyone in the world—had always seemed closer to their mother. Maybe it was the whole thing she'd heard about being too alike.

"Cary," Saanvi said, her tone conciliatory, "you may be right, Mom does tend to throw her weight around. But she always does it for the good of the colony, and she always gets results. She knows what she's doing."

"Yeah...I know. I'm sorry," Cary replied. "You know I didn't really mean what I said. I love mom, and she's a great leader—and everyone keeps voting her in, so they must like her, too. But you know that when it comes to us, she doesn't think like a leader; she thinks like a mother. We have to prove to her that we are adults, and can be trusted with responsibility."

Saanvi took a step back and raised an eyebrow. Though her skin was dark, her hair jet-black, and her eyes a deep brown, she pulled off the expression in a way that looked identical to their mother's.

Cary took a moment to wonder how Saanvi managed that before she braced herself for an assault from Saanvi's logic.

"And you think that *stealing* a starship is going to be how we prove to her that we're trustworthy?" Saanvi asked, her voice dripping with sarcasm.

"When they see what we can do, how you and I can Link our minds together, they'll know that we should get our commissions and join the fleet. We don't need to go to the academy. We've spent our lives preparing for this," Cary replied.

"I think it's going to have the opposite effect," Saanvi sighed. "But you're going to do this with or without me, aren't you?"

Carry nodded. "I am, and we both know you can't take me down. Are you going to report me?"

The two sisters stared at each other for a full minute.

Saanvi finally relented, "No. No, I won't report you, and I better come with you. If you get killed and I'm still alive, and knew about your harebrained idea, Mom will skin me alive. Better if we both die together out there."

Cary embraced her sister. "That's the spirit! OK, let's go." She turned and continued down the corridor that led to the station's east shuttle bay.

"What's your plan, anyway?" Saanvi asked as she hurried to catch up to Cary. "All the empty ships up there are run by AIs. Probably Judith or Symatra. Neither of them are going to let us just commandeer a ship."

Cary flashed a grin at her sister, the one that looked like her Father's and utterly disarmed everyone—one she practiced frequently in the mirror. "Remember a few months back when we played that prank on Alan?"

"The one that almost got us kicked out of school and nearly ruined our lives? I do seem to recall it," Saanvi muttered.

"Well, I hacked the COMMSAT network to pull it off, and I left my little back door in there. If we're challenged, we can just tell them to look up our orders. When they do, they'll get rerouted and find some nice orders from Mom putting us in command of a ship."

"Putting *who* in command?" Saanvi asked pointedly. "Someone has to be the captain."

"Me, of course," Cary grinned. "I have a temporary field rank of lieutenant, and you're an ensign. You're the XO."

Saanvi sighed. "Why am I not surprised?"

* * * * *

The one thing Cary had not anticipated was how busy the shuttle bay would be. She hadn't thought to add orders to supply her with a shuttle, and Sam, the dockmaster, wouldn't check any systems that hit the COMMSAT network.

"Great plan," Saanvi said and poked her sister in the shoulder as they stood just outside the dock's entrance. "Well, I guess we can call it a day, and head down the strand like we're supposed to."

"Saanvi, really. When have you known me to give up so easily?" Cary chided. "Watch this."

Without looking back to see if Saanvi was following, she strode out onto the East Dock, toward where Sam stood arguing with a shuttle pilot.

"I don't care if your grandma is on the next shuttle in from the habs and you want to take her down to the surface yourself; you have a supply load to carry down, and every AI is already tasked with running the fleet out there, so they can't do it."

"Sam, c'mon, Gran is all I have left. I lost my dad at Bollam's and my mom stayed behind in Victoria," the pilot entreated. "I need to be with her."

"You need to be out there keeping the colony safe," Sam said with a deepening scowl. "Everyone here has made more than their share of sacrifices. You're not special. Now get in your shuttle, and take it down!"

"No, Sam, go fuck yourself, I quit. I'm going to ride the strand down with my gran." The pilot added a few more curses for good measure and stalked off.

"For fuck's sake!" Sam threw his hands in the air and then caught sight of Cary and Saanvi approaching. "Sweet stars, what did I do to deserve this? What do you two want?"

"I overheard that guy leaving you high and dry, Sam," Cary said in her most conciliatory tone. "Saanvi and I are supposed to get planetside ASAP, and we're rated to fly that shuttle."

"You don't even know which shuttle I need taken down," Sam replied.

"Well, we're rated to fly any shuttle you have docked here," Saanvi interjected. "It would be easy for us to run one down."

"Rated? More like berated. Last time you were in here, you stole the replica fighter your father was working on, and went joy riding around the moons. I'd be a fool to let the two of you in any cockpit here."

"We flew the *Andromeda* into Gamma IV a few months back," Cary said. "And the *Hellespont* after that."

"We just want to do our part to help out," Saanvi added and Cary gave her a smile, grateful for the assist.

Sam looked them both up and down and then his eyes flicked to the left as he accessed the Link. "Hmm…well, you're not lying about that, and I do need someone to run that shuttle down. OK, you can help; but you get that shuttle down, and then you head to the bunker. I won't have it on my head if something happens to you."

"You got it!" Cary replied, distracting Sam by grabbing his hand and shaking it vigorously. It wouldn't do for him to see the pained expression on Saanvi's face. "Which is our bird?"

Sam pointed to a freight hauler sitting in a cradle five hundred meters away. "There she is. She was out for service before this little crisis hit, and had an iffy port-maneuvering thruster. It should be fixed now, but no one has had the time to take it for a test run. If you have any issues—"

"Spin the ship on its axis and use the starboard thrusters," Cary replied. "Don't worry, Sam. We can manage it."

Sam looked like he was having second thoughts, but another pair of pilots walked up and started arguing with him about routes, and Cary took the opportunity to grab Saanvi and dash off toward the freighter.

"Maybe we should just fly it down," Saanvi said. "They're going to notice when we take this thing near one of the cruisers up there. Besides, how are we going find one that's worth boarding? Half of them don't even hold atmo."

"I have it all sorted," Cary replied as they hopped a dockcar that was hauling a load of cargo in the direction they were headed. "When we board, I'll use my backdoor in the COMMSAT network to pull status reports from the ships as they pass through. There's gotta be one that's in good enough shape for us to take."

"You better make sure that you do something about the queries that Sam is going to run. You can bet he's going to keep tabs on us to make certain we make it down," Saanvi added. "You know…if anything happens to us, Mom is going to kill him."

"Saanvi," Cary looked her sister in the eyes, trying to quell her worry. "Nothing is going to happen to us. Mom's never going to let anyone get this close to Carthage. She's won every space battle she's ever commanded."

"She's only commanded two major fleet actions," Saanvi said. "And none anywhere near as big as this one is shaping up to be. Things could go horribly wrong."

"And you worry too much, Saanvi. Stasis shields, picobombs; there's no way we can lose."

Saanvi didn't reply, and Cary could tell her sister was worrying about what was to come if the enemy fleets reached Carthage. She also knew that if she kept trying to encourage her, it would only upset Saanvi, and she may call the whole thing off. For now, it was enough that they were together and headed toward—not away from—the action.

When the dockcar neared their shuttle, named *Fair Weather*, they hopped off and trotted toward the ship. It wasn't too big, just a hundred meters long—a fraction of the *Andromeda*'s size, and even less of the *Hellespont*'s. However, none of the warships could take a vessel the size of the freight hauler into their docking bays, so they'd have to figure out what to do with it once they got to their ship.

Cary could tell Saanvi was thinking the same thing by the frown she wore, and the twist of her lips; but she didn't say anything. Cary wondered if that meant her sister had come up with a solution to the issue.

They walked across the gantry to the ship's port airlock, and Cary passed her token to the ship, praying that Sam hadn't changed his mind. Her fears were assuaged when the airlock cycled open and the girls stepped in. The ship's inner lock was closed, and while they waited for the ship to cycle them through, the two girls pulled shipsuits out of a sealed locker and slipped into them.

It was unlikely anyone would see them, but wearing shipsuits made them look a lot more official than Saanvi's shorts and t-shirt, or Cary's dress.

"Welcome Cary and Saanvi," the ship said audibly as the inner airlock cycled open.

Cary cast Saanvi a worried look. <*Is there an NSAI on this thing? No way will one of them let us go off course.*>

<*Don't worry,*> Saanvi said with a mental smirk. <*While you were dreaming of winning medals for your bravery, I looked up the* Fair Weather*'s service record. It was supposed to get an AI pilot, but they're all pulled out for fleet duty, so this is just the standard shipboard comp. Nothing we can't boss around.*>

"Hi, *Fair Weather,* Saanvi said audibly. "I'm passing you override code 98RF-A1. Physical pilots taking full control of all systems for manual piloting."

"Thank you, Captain Saanvi," the comp replied. "Falling back to passive failover mode. Happy flying!"

"Chipper thing. Nice touch with 'captain' there, Sis," Cary commented as they walked down the short passageway to the cockpit. Once they reached its narrow confines, they strapped into the seats and ran through a pre-flight check.

"Everything looks good, Captain," Cary said, and caught a scowl from Saanvi who liked everything by the book. "Fine. Engines, grav drive, life support, point defense beams, nav thrusters, all green."

"Comm and scan?" Saanvi asked.

"Yeah, them too," Cary replied. "Just put in for departure clearance, and let's get out of here."

"I can't get departure clearance until everything is done properly. Sam is going to check our request, so file your cross-checks properly in the logs," Saanvi retorted. "I swear, Cary, I should have just let you do this on your own. There's no way you would have gotten off the dock, and we'd be riding the strand down to the surface in no time."

"Fine, Sahn, but I know you want to get out there and help, too. Don't give me that load about doing this for me. Underneath, you want to be making a difference, not hiding in a bunker down under Landfall."

Saanvi didn't reply, but Cary could tell from the set of her sister's mouth that she had hit a nerve. Good. Saanvi liked to take the high road whenever possible, but there was a reason she came with Cary whenever an adventure knocked—she craved it, too.

As Saanvi had predicted, Sam called in personally with clearance. *<OK, you two. I see your pre-flight checks, and flight*

plan. They look good. You get the Fair Weather *down nice and safe. No detours, no rushing. Nice and safe. You hear me?*>

<*Yes, Dockmaster,*> Saanvi replied, her mental tone perfectly calm. <*Nice and safe, no detours.*>

<*Good,*> Sam replied before signing off.

"Man, you're a good liar when you want to be," Cary said. "I always forget how smooth you are."

"Shut up, Cary. Just release the clamps already."

* * * * *

"Do you need a hand?" Saanvi asked as Cary searched through the data on the ships clustered at the L1 point of Carthage's larger moon—a whitish-blue orb named Hannibal.

Cary scowled in response. She had to admit that determining which of the five thousand ships in Fleet Group 5 to choose was more work than she expected

"I've narrowed it down to these forty," Cary said. "They all have engines, life support, and functioning weapons, but there are nuances between them that make it hard to choose. Take a look," Cary replied and passed the data to Saanvi.

"Hmmm," Saanvi said as she ran through the ships. "Oh, it's easy, pick this one."

Cary looked at the ship. It bore the name *Illyria,* and appeared to be one of the least complete in the final selection.

"Why that one?" Cary asked. "It doesn't even have docking bays. We'll have to EVA over."

"You didn't check its loadout, did you?" Saanvi asked. "The *Illyria* has a full store of RMs and kinetics. Its hull is full of holes, but that barely matters with a-grav and stasis shields."

"I don't know," Cary mused. "There are several others with full life support. If anything goes wrong on that ship, we'll have to fix it in EVA gear."

"Cary," Saanvi shook her head. "It's a seven hundred meter cruiser that is only eighty percent complete. If anything goes wrong and we can't fix it from the bridge, we're screwed."

"Good point," Cary muttered. "OK, set a course for the *Illyria,* then. I'll grab us a pair of EVA suits from aft storage."

Cary walked down the passageway to the storage locker just aft of the airlock, and grabbed two EVA-901 suits. They were bright white with reflective strips running down the sides—the better to find lost people in space. They had a slippery, rubbery texture, almost like grasping an eel in water. Though they appeared flimsy—no thicker than five millimeters, and as thin as one in places—they were sturdy, and could even provide some protection from light beamfire.

The main advantage of the suits was that they provided one atmosphere of pressure across the wearer's body, and could adjust that pressure as needed to prevent fluids from building up in extremities.

Cary quickly pulled off her shipsuit and stepped into the EVA-901. It fit loosely as she pulled it on, but once she drew the fastener shut, the suit tightened and pressed all the air out from within. She gasped as the cold health monitoring sensors hit her body, and then raised her arms, shimmying side to side to make sure the suit had a good fit. Cary opted for a clear three-sixty helmet, and pulled one from the rack. Before donning it, she twisted her blonde hair into a tight bun to ensure it wouldn't get in her face while the helmet was on. Once satisfied, she locked the helmet's collar around her neck, where it sealed to the suit, and then she grabbed the two halves of the helmet.

She hooked the top hasp of the two halves together, and then closed it over her head. It made a suctioning sound as it sealed, and her HUD showed green for an airtight connection to the suit. She did some more quick stretches and swung her arms around to make sure the seal still showed green.

The respirator on her back registered a five-hour capability for recycling her air, and the suit's batteries displayed a full forty-hour charge; all squarely within nominal ranges. She switched the respirator to use external air, and grabbed a suit and helmet for Saanvi.

When she returned to the cockpit, her sister was deftly maneuvering the shuttle through the AI-controlled fleet, now only five hundred kilometers from their target.

<*We been pinged yet?*> Cary asked.

Saanvi glanced back at her sister and shook her head. <*Not yet. Clear helmet, eh? Good, I hate those ones that are tight on the face—feel like I'm suffocating the whole time.*>

<*I know, Sis,*> Cary replied as she sat down. <*I'll take it from here. Get suited up.*>

<*Strap in, first,*> Saanvi admonished.

Cary stuck out her tongue at her sister, but did as she ordered. Saanvi may have been a rule-follower, but Cary knew the rules were there for a reason, and there was no success in arguing with her sister about them—not with logic, anyway.

<*Nice, now I know* ***why*** *you got the clear helmet, so you can make faces at me.*>

<*Bingo!*> Cary said with a smile. <*OK, all buckled up. Taking the helm.*>

Saanvi stood and stepped into the passageway to don her EVA-901, while Cary leaned back in her seat—which had adjusted its configuration to accommodate the rebreather pack and the bulbous helmet. Cary waved off the sanitary hookups, but did let the seat's power cable connect to the suit's power pack to top off the charge.

<*Freighter* Fair Weather, *what is your destination?*>

The message came in over the ship's main comm channel, and carried the tag of the Fleet Group 5 Commander. Cary did a quick check and saw that it was Symatra—an AI that was even more of a stickler for the rules than Saanvi.

This was it. Cary took a deep breath to steady her nerves before replying.

<Fleet Commander Symatra, this is Lieutenant Cary Richards aboard the Fair Weather. *We're on our way to the* Illyria*; we have orders to take command of that vessel.>*

*<**Lieutenant** Cary, is it?>* Symatra asked. *<Hold your course while I check your orders.>*

Saanvi walked back into the cockpit, a worried expression on her face. She hadn't yet donned her helmet—a testament to her level of concern.

<Even if this does work, Mom is going to kill us,> Saanvi said privately, her mental tone wavering.

<Too late for going back, now,> Cary said. *<Symatra is getting routed to my set of orders as we speak. Mom's token is on them. The deed is done.>*

<Lieutenant Cary and Ensign Saanvi, your orders appear to be legitimate, though I can't imagine what your mother was thinking in issuing them. When she's in communications range again, I'll ask her myself. I want you aboard the Illyria *in fifteen minutes, and give me a full readiness report on the ship in thirty. You may have command of that vessel, but it's still in my fleet group and under my authority.>*

<Yes, Ma'am,> Cary replied.

<You're on my fleet net now,> Symatra replied. *<Check your rosters. I have a provisional rank of Admiral for this engagement.>*

Cary reddened. *<Yes, Admiral Symatra. Sorry, Admiral.>*

Symatra sent an acknowledgement and closed the connection.

<Did she seem pissed?> Cary asked. *<I can't tell if she was pissed.>*

Saanvi shook her head as she donned her helmet. *<Not pissed, but certainly annoyed.>*

<*Well, we better get to our ship on the double,*> Cary said as she fed additional power to the grav drives. <*Can't keep the admiral waiting.*>

* * * * *

Saanvi managed the final maneuvering, lining up the shuttle with the *Illyria,* while Cary programed a flight path for the onboard comp to follow that would take the shuttle down to Landfall. Under normal conditions, she wouldn't have worried about a comp landing the craft; but with all the traffic around the capital at present, she prayed it wouldn't cause some sort of problem.

<*Put it on the auxiliary runway at the new spaceport north of the city,*> Saanvi advised. <*I know it's not where the cargo is supposed to go, but it will make the comp's calculations a lot simpler.*>

<*Good call, Sis,*> Cary replied, and entered the new destination. <*OK, she's all set and the* Illyria *is spooling out its umbilical—which it wasn't supposed to have, yet. I'll go cycle the airlock. You green on your seals?*>

Saanvi's head nodded inside her helmet. <*Green as a turtle. You?*>

<*Across the board,*> Cary replied.

Saanvi glanced back at her sister, a nervous smile on her face. <*Cary…thank you. I know we're going to catch hell for this, but it's going to be amazing—our own ship…. Thanks for bringing me.*>

Cary laughed aloud, the sound echoing in her ears. <*Gah…I always forget not to do that. I would never leave you behind, Sahn. We're a package deal, you and I. Where one goes, so does the other.*>

<*Good, then don't board the ship without me.*>

Two minutes later, both girls were standing in the airlock, hands clasped as the outer door cycled open and revealed the ten meters of umbilical to the *Illyria's* starboard forward airlock. It was already open, and they rushed across the space to reach it.

<*Now I feel silly having got us into EVA-901s with an umbilical linkup,*> Cary said as they reached the cruiser's airlock.

<*It was a good call,*> Saanvi said as the exterior portal closed behind them. <*It's fifty-fifty that this ship loses atmo while we're on it, anyway. I'd rather be safe than a bloated corpse.*>

<*Gross! That's a visual I didn't need!*>

* * * * *

Cary and Saanvi floated onto the *Illyria*'s bridge. One thing neither of them had bothered to check was whether internal gravity systems were functional.

<*You know,*> Cary said with a grin, <*for someone who is the best pilot outside of the academy, you have a lot of trouble with zero-g.*>

<*Shut up, Cary,*> Saanvi said as she settled into the navigator's seat. <*I can still call this thing off.*>

<*Your threats are really starting to ring hollow,*> Cary laughed as she took the weapons console and began to configure it to operate scan, as well. She saw Saanvi doing the same thing. They had realized, when trading responsibilities while piloting the *Andromeda,* that they both liked to have scan up, and did better when both had an eye on it.

It would be especially useful, given that there were just the two of them onboard.

<*I'll run the engines and navigation systems checks,*> Saanvi said. <*You do scan and weapons. Whoever gets theirs done first can take life support.*>

<*You got it,*> Cary replied. She liked that they didn't have to discuss roles. Saanvi would pilot, and Cary would run the weapons. But they would deep-Link their minds in combat,

the way that made them feel like one person—each sister's limbs like an extension of the other's.

As Cary ran her systems checks, cognizant of Symatra's looming deadline, she considered how unusual her natural ability was—certainly something that no one else seemed capable of.

Saanvi was certain it was an ability Cary had inherited from her mother—some sort of technologically genetic trait. Cary had never told her mother about it; she didn't want to add to her mom's concerns. Tanis never spoke of it, but Cary knew her centuries with Angela were unprecedented. To know it had possibly altered her daughter may not be welcome news.

When she was younger, Cary had asked her more than once why Tanis and Angela hadn't separated, but her mother had only responded that it wasn't possible.

The history lessons in her school had shed a bit more light on the subject, explaining that Tanis and Angela had the ability to spread their minds together across networks. It was how they were able to command the ISF fleets with such precision. The history books also made sure to point out that Tanis and Angela had not merged into one being, that they were not what the old stories from Sol referred to as an abomination; though the assurances in the texts had always felt too forced to Cary.

Even so, Angela was like a second mother to her. When she was younger, and her mother was often away at the Capitol, she would wake alone and scared. She hated to wake her father, and would lay in the dark with her blankets pulled over her head.

Without fail, Angela would come to her, projecting a form for her to see while speaking to her over the Link.

She remembered the stories Angela would tell her about her mother, and the old days back in Sol and Victoria. She showed Cary where Tanis had grown up on Mars, near a sea called the Melas Chasma. She would speak of her first assignment with her mother, and the dozens of others afterward—probably leaving out details that a small child had no need to hear.

It had made her feel so much more connected to her mother—and it had also cemented in her mind that her mother and Angela were in fact two separate people, but not quite as much as the history lessons would have her believe.

<*Hey, mission control to Cary. You done yet? I've checked every system except yours, and we need to send the report to Symatra in two minutes,*> Saanvi interrupted her reverie.

<*Yeah, just a sec. It's done, I just need to recheck a redundant system in the railgun that's throwing a red flag.*>

<*Chop, chop, Sis! The fleet is moving out and we need to get into formation.*>

<*Moving out?*> Cary asked as she reset the subsystem and got a green board. <*'Kay, it's sent.*>

<*Yeah, looks like we're going to get that action you've been dying to see. Check the Fleet Tactical Net; the Trisilieds fleet is on its way here. ETA six hours.*>

<*Shit! Here?*> Cary exclaimed. <*Their whole fleet?*>

<*Lieutenant Cary,*> Symatra addressed her on the fleetnet. <*I want you and the* Illyria *to seed the enemy fleet's approach vector with half your RM payload. Make your best speed to the coordinates I've designated, and place the missiles in a Zeta-Nine pattern.*>

Cary didn't hesitate to reply. <*Aye, Admiral, we're on our way,*> before turning to Saanvi and asking, <*What's pattern Zeta-Nine?*>

<*Beats me, but you better look it up. I'm putting the engines through a quick warm-up cycle before we boost out there. It'll take us twenty-two minutes to make it the location Symatra specified, so you better figure it out by then.*>

Cary sighed and looked up the pattern in the ISF's tactical databases. She hoped it was a simple grid in which the missiles could be deployed, but what she found was a shifting three-dimensional pattern based on the approaching fleet's configuration. It also necessitated programming the RMs with an algorithm that could respond to shifts in the approaching fleet's formation and still maintain maximum dispersal, while still hitting targets of opportunity and not overlapping.

By the time Saanvi brought the ship to the designated area, Cary was just finishing the calculations.

<OK, here's the pattern, Sahn. I've proposed a course to seed them—it should take thirty-one minutes,> Cary said.

<Looks good, Cary,> Saanvi replied. *<I'm laying in the course now. Be ready to seed the missiles on your marks.>*

<Seriously? You don't have any corrections?> Cary asked.

<Nope, you did good work here. Is that so hard to believe?> Saanvi chuckled at her response.

With Saanvi taking the ship through her prescribed course, and the RMs set to deploy at preset coordinates, Cary had the time to review the analysis of the battlefield. The Fleet Tactical Net, which her HUD listed as the FTN, showed an unbelievable number of ships in various formations throughout the system.

Fleet Group 5, Admiral Symatra's group of forty five hundred ships, had taken up high orbit around Carthage's larger moon, Morocco. Beyond it, the *Illyria* and a dozen other mid-sized cruisers were all seeding missiles along the Trisilieds fleet's approach vector. At their current rate of deceleration, the Trisilieds fleet would arrive at Carthage when the moon, and Fleet Group 5, would be between it and the planet.

She was glad to see that the system's rail platforms were chipping away at the incoming fleet, but they wouldn't wear down the numbers by any appreciable amount by the time it arrived. The Trisilieds fleet would still contain over twenty thousand fully functional warships against Symatra's barely operable group.

The FTN showed that Judith's Fleet Group 6 was positioned at Athens, some four AU distant and a quarter of the way around the star from Carthage. Cary wondered why her mother hadn't pulled Judith's ships back to Carthage, but then she saw that the Hegemony fleet was still in a position where they could strike either Athens or Carthage.

A momentary fear swept through Cary as she realized that the goal of the invading fleets must now be to take and hold a world—effectively using its people as hostages to get the technology they so desperately wanted. But they only needed one world. All four of the terraformed planets in the New Canaan system had populations, some in the millions, and all with friends living on them.

Her mother's Fleet Group 1 was in pursuit of the Trisilieds ships, but with the Hegemony ships behind them, they were now coasting, unable to point their engines in either direction. At some point they'd need to brake, and that would expose their engines to the Trisilieds fleet; just as the Trisilieds ships' engines would be exposed to Symatra's fleet, and the stationary weapons on Carthage and its moons.

She was glad to see that at least the TSF Admiral named Greer had his fleet group boosting hard for Carthage. At their current speed, they'd reach it before her mother's ships—but also not before the Trisilieds. Further out in the system, her father's fleet and the one commanded by Admiral Sanderson were holding their positions, each half an AU from the system's two largest gas giants.

<Why isn't mother bringing in the other fleet groups?> she asked Saanvi. *<Do you think she's worried about more incoming enemy ships?>*

<*The Trisilieds one came out of nowhere,*> Saanvi said with a worried glance at her sister. <*And from what our databases show, none of these ships are Orion Guard. They could easily drop another fleet on us.*>

<*Fuuuuck,*> Cary whispered. <*There's no way we can take out these two,* ***and*** *another fleet.*>

<*Mom will have a plan,*> Saanvi said, trying to sound calm; but Cary could tell her sister was worried, too.

<*That plan better involve using picobombs to wipe these guys out, because there's no way we'd win a slugfest against that many ships.*>

<*You know the parliament's policy,*> Saanvi said. <*Pico is no longer to be used as an offensive weapon. Too many nations have declared its use a war crime.*>

<*Yeah, just like antimatter weapons, but no one seems to care about that prohibition anymore!*> Cary fumed.

<*I don't know why you're getting pissed at me. It's not like I can authorize its use. From what I understand, there are no pico bombs present in any of the fleets right now. They're all under lock and key in some super-secret base somewhere,*> Saanvi replied.

<*Every credit I have says that 'super-secret base' is the* I2,> Cary said, as she set the bridge's main holo to show the countdown before the Trisilieds fleet arrived: five hours and seventeen minutes.

The *Illyria* finished seeding its missiles, and Symatra directed them to take up a position in the inner ring of ships orbiting Morocco. Cary couldn't help but notice that their ship would be hidden behind the moon when the Trisilieds finally came into firing range.

Apparently, the AI commander was going to keep them out of the thick of things as much as she could.

Cary and Saanvi passed the time reviewing the ship's systems in further detail, and ensuring that automated repair drones were pre-positioned in any critical areas. With no human crew aboard, the drones were their only repair options if the ship took damage.

<*Stars, I'm starving,*> Cary said as the clock counted down to thirty minutes before the enemy fleet was in firing range.

<*How can you be hungry right now?*> Saanvi asked. <*I can barely stand the thought of drinking* ***water****, my stomach is so tied up in knots.*>

<*We need to eat something; we haven't had anything since those stale sandwiches on the* Fair Weather. *It won't help if we're passing out from hunger during the battle,*> Cary replied.

<*I think we can make it a bit longer without food. Takes more than a day to pass out from hunger.*>

<*Sahn,*> Cary said, her tone dead serious. <*You don't know when we're going to have time to eat again. For all we know, we could be crashed on Carthage at this time tomorrow fighting a guerilla war against the invaders—something that's probably easier to do on a full stomach.*>

<*Well, it's not like we have a stocked galley aboard. You're going to have to eat the nutri-paste from the chair's feed,*> Saanvi replied. <*I had a little taste awhile back, and it's not too bad.*>

<*No way,*> Cary responded as she unbuckled her seat's harness and floated off the chair. <*That stuff tastes like crap. The work crews must have something in the galley. Maybe someone left a lunch in there that I can steal.*>

<*I know what you're trying to do!*> Saanvi turned and gave her sister her strongest glare. <*You're going to go take your suit off to go to the toilet! You cannot do that! We could be in combat in any minute, and this ship is far from airtight. If just one of the forward grav generators goes offline, this bridge will decompress.*>

<*Sahn! Seriously, I hate the plumbing hookups the suits have. I'll just be a minute.*>

<*Cary, so help me, if you take that suit off, I'm going to beat you senseless and stick you in an escape pod. Now sit your ass back in your chair, and take the suit's hookup, you baby.*>

Cary was surprised at her sister's vehemence and consequently pulled herself back to the chair and refastened the harness. She realized that Saanvi was scared—really scared. Maybe she should be, too, and her reluctance to use the suit's facilities was just her way of trying to pretend that they wouldn't be fighting for their lives before long.

She suddenly hoped she wouldn't throw up when the fighting started. The clear helmet was a poor choice in that regard. The skintight ones ran tubes into the wearer's stomach and lungs, preventing any messy incidents, like choking on your own vomit and dying.

She shook the image from her mind. That was no way to think.

On her right, she saw Saanvi had the feed tube in her mouth and was sucking up some paste. She decided if her sister was doing whatever was necessary to prepare, then she should, as well.

* * * * *

Cary had just finished 'eating' and using the suit's facilities, when the ship's scan threw an alert. FTN showed an incoming volley of kinetics from the Trisilieds ships. Fleet's scan tracked the vectors and highlighted the targets.

<*Think they found them all?*> Cary asked, worried that if the rail platforms protecting Carthage fell, then they'd lose the world. There was no way Fleet Group 5 could stand against the Trisilieds ships bearing down on them.

<*We can see all of the enemy ships—at least we sure hope we can—and we know the targets. The lanes of fire are clear….*>

Saanvi's words were certain, but her mental tone was not. Both girls watched as the rail platforms began firing fine grapeshot toward the incoming rounds, before moving to new positions. Some of the platforms had already been equipped with massive fusion engines for emergency repositioning, but most were pushed by tugs.

Scan picked up hundreds of kinetic rounds being shredded by the rail platform's grapeshot, followed by automated drones targeting the debris with lasers, melting the debris clouds as best they could.

Yet some rounds made it through.

Most harmlessly streaked past the prior locations of the rail platforms, but one platform was struck by an enemy round, and its stasis shields flared as the slug hit and shattered into a billion pieces. The ship's scan registered the impact at over twenty exajoules of energy. The strike wasn't nearly enough to break through the stasis shields, but the rail platform's incomplete engines struggled to maintain its orbit around Carthage. Slowly, the platform began to slip toward the planet.

Two tugs disengaged from other platforms, and boosted toward the failing structure. Just as the first tug arrived and the platform lowered its stasis shield to let the tug make grapple, another round hit.

<*Oh, shit!*> Cary exclaimed as the platform exploded in a brilliant flash of light. When scan cleared, little more than a cloud of debris was falling toward Carthage.

<*It's just gone,*> Saanvi whispered.

<*I hope it doesn't hit Landfall or anything,*> Cary added.

Two more platforms were lost as the enemy continued to advance, but Cary knew the tables would turn once the Trisilieds ships reached the field of RMs.

Though the enemy fleet had spread wide in an effort to avoid the kinetic rounds Carthage's rail emplacements were firing, they were still mostly within the seeded field.

<*Think the RMs will pick off enough targets?*> Saanvi asked.

<Well, their shields aren't much better than what the Bollam's space force had, and we were able to one-two punch our way through those without a lot of trouble.>

<Yeah, but they know about our style of RM now; they'll be ready for it,> Saanvi replied.

<How will they be? They don't have stasis shields. We saw that when our initial kinetic rounds hit them.>

<Don't you remember what mother taught us? The enemy never responds the way you anticipate. It is not enough to be ready to adapt; you must be prepared to defend against all possible situations at once,> Saanvi said in her instructor's voice that always got under Cary's skin. She let it slide, though—no point in getting into an argument here.

Cary knew that her people had done amazing work in eighteen years, building up a military that could rival that of many stellar nations, but she worried it would still not be enough. With the Trisilieds fleet bearing down on them, and Fleet Group 5 manned by skeleton crews and a few AIs, the battle would be short and decisive when it was ultimately joined.

Cary realized she was chewing on her lower lip as she waited for FTN to register the RMs activating, and she forced herself to stop and breathe slowly. The more she thought about it, the more she realized how foolish wanting to be on this ship was. There was no glory in the slow surety of a battle they could not win.

She was trying to distract herself with crosschecking the ship's weapons systems when Saanvi called out. *<There! They've entered the field—the RMs are moving.>*

Cary hoped that she had done well with the patterns and placements of the missiles the *Illyria* had deposited. Symatra's tactical plan showed that she hoped to eliminate at least four thousand of the Trisilieds vessels. Any fewer, and there was no plan on the books that would save Carthage from the enemy fleet.

Their holotank began to show the leading edge of the Trisilieds ships jinking wildly, and she knew they had picked up the RMs. Now only time would tell whether it was enough.

She caught Saanvi's eye and could see that her sister was just as worried that too many of the enemy ships would break through, whereupon it would fall to them and Fleet Group 5 to shield Carthage. Neither girl spoke as they watched the first of the missiles hit, the information lagging by the seven light-second delay between them and the Trisilieds fleet.

<*It's not working well enough,*> Saanvi whispered. <*Their fleet was too spread out; the rear ships are all moving out of the RM field. The missiles won't reach them.*>

Cary nodded wordlessly. The FTN tally showed that only two thousand ships had been disabled. It would take another volley, this one at close range, to reduce the enemy's advantage and even the playing field. Both girls knew that would put the *Illyria* in the thick of the battle, given that their ship still had one of the largest supplies of short-range RMs in the fleet.

As she was nervously considering what would happen next, a message from Admiral Symatra arrived.

<*Lieutenant Cary, reposition the* Illyria *to the location I've marked, retrograde of Carthage. I am putting twenty ships under your command, designated Epsilon Squadron. They'll be too far away for me to control directly, and I don't have any AI to spare, so you will need to slave them to your controls. I have preloaded them with Non-Sentient AIs using nav patterns that will keep them in formation with you, while ensuring they're not just there for target practice.*>

<*Yes, Admiral,*> Cary responded. <*What are our orders once we're in position?*>

<*The Trisilieds Fleet has a dozen ships that appear to be a carrier class of vessel. Fleet analysis thinks that they are holding fighters—a lot of fighters. If that's true, then things could get much worse. You need to punch in through their lines and hit those carriers with your RMs before they disgorge them.*>

Cary looked at the three enemy carriers assigned to their squadron and let out a long breath. <*Those ships are well protected, Admiral. How will we get through to them?*>

<*I've provided updated tactics that will give you some options, but you're going to need to figure this one out on the fly. Your mother thought you could handle this command; now prove it to me.*>

Symatra closed the connection, and Saanvi queried Cary.

<*I have twenty ships taking up formation that are Linked to our ship; what's going on?*>

Cary relayed the orders to her sister, watching the disbelief grow on Saanvi's face.

<*Cary, I can't fly twenty ships,* plus *the* Illyria*! We're gonna get blown to dust out here.*>

<*What other options do we have?*> Cary asked. <*We can't just run and hide! A lot of the ISF personnel aren't much older than us, and they're ready to give their lives for our homeworld. Tanis is our mother, and they expect us to do something amazing to save the day.*>

<*It's going to take something amazing to save us from Mom when she finds out about this,*> Saanvi said sullenly, as she organized Epsilon Squadron into four groups and slaved them to her console. <*Symatra did at least have a good autopilot setup on the ships—I won't need to micromanage them all. You're running their weapons, though; you'd better evaluate your options.*>

Cary did just that, looking at the loadouts on the ships Symatra had put under their command. The Admiral had been generous; all the ships had railguns, lasers, proton beams, and a small compliment of RMs. Their generators were fully operational, and the SC batteries were at max charge. Saanvi positioned the squadron in a flat V-formation, and Cary worked with her to ensure that the vessels with the most proton beams were in the fore.

Though they were mostly functional, none of the ships in Epsilon Squadron were the same class as the *Illyria*: a Mark II Claymore class ship that was a modified form of the *Orkney* and the *Dresden*—the original Claymore ships built back at the Victoria colony.

Eleven of the ships were Elizabeth Class cruisers; similar in composition to the *Andromeda,* and close to her size, with seven-hundred-sixty-meter-long hulls—but they did not yet have their stealth systems installed. Seven of them had proton beams, and were situated at the leading edge of Saanvi's flying V-formation.

The other nine were smaller Triton Class destroyers—a new kind of ship based on a Scattered Worlds Alliance destroyer design from Sol. These ships were the weirdest looking things Cary had ever seen. They were made of two rings—one slightly smaller ring tucked inside the other. The inside ring was able to change its angle as far as ninety degrees, and reposition it perpendicularly to the outer ring.

The rings were particle accelerators, but the particles they accelerated were one-millimeter pebbles of spent uranium. Once powered up, the rings could maintain a million pebbles moving at over a quarter the speed of light. The pebbles could exit the rings from hundreds of apertures, allowing the rings to fire in almost any direction on the ring's plane.

In essence, the strange-looking ships were rail machine guns capable of firing their million-round magazine in seconds, if needs be.

<*Oh! What have we here?*> Cary said over the Link with her sister.

<*What did you find?*> Saanvi asked.

Cary grinned at her sister. <*Two of the Claymore M2s have Arc-6 fighters on board.*>

<*Really?*> Saanvi asked as she frowned at her console. <*I checked for fighters, and the inventories read zero.*>

<*I bet you checked for functional fighters. Since there are no pilots, the inventory system lists the fighters as non-functional.*>

Saanvi's face split into a wide smile. <*Fifty-two of them! Well, now we have a chance. I can make some changes to the NSAI that Symatra put in charge of the ships in our squadron, and clone them into the Arc-6 autopilot's neural nets. It'll be a tight fit, memory-wise, but it should work.*>

<*Hop to it,*> Cary replied. <*We have fifteen minutes before we're in weapons range of the T's.*>

<*T's?*> Saanvi asked.

<*Yeah, 'Trisilieds' is way too awkward to say over and over again.*>

<*Cary,*> Saanvi replied soberly, <*you're thinking it, not saying it.*>

<*Whatever, Sis. They're T's now.*>

While her sister set to modifying the NSAIs to fit within the fighters, Cary continued to examine the T's fleet.

Still over nineteen thousand ships strong, the enemy fleet was a juggernaut unlike any she had ever imagined. A tenth of the fleet were massive dreadnaughts, similar to—though a few kilometers smaller—those the AST employed. The other fifty percent of the fleet consisted of thousand-meter cruisers. Unlike the AST, who seemed to prefer brute force in all things, the T's had then rounded out their fleet with thousands of destroyers.

The carrier ships, designated Halcyon Class on the FTN, only made up a tiny percentage of the fleet—though there were still twelve of them in evidence. These ships were over fifteen kilometers in length, and analysis on the FTN suggested that it was possible for them to contain a hundred thousand fighters—more if they were drones, and not human-piloted ships.

That explained why Symatra was willing to expend some of her best ships to take out three of them.

A dozen of the Dreadnaught class ships escorted each of the carriers, along with a hundred or more destroyers. It looked like an impossible task, but Cary knew that Symatra was no fool, and certainly wouldn't expend the Governor's children on a suicide mission.

She reviewed the updated tactics the admiral had provided, and saw an option that she knew they could execute.

<*Saanvi, have you tested the* Illyria*'s stealth systems?*>

Saanvi replied absently as she continued to work on loading the NSAIs into the fighters, <*I ran through the checklists, yeah, but I didn't turn them on.*>

<*Let's use the squadron cruisers and destroyers as decoys, and come in a hundred klicks above them. The T's will be focused on the ships they can see, and we can slam the* Illyria *right through their shields and drop mines on the carrier.*>

<*You're crazy, you know that?*> Saanvi asked. <*But I think it will work. Give me a minute, and I'll pass us behind our other ships and drop into stealth while we're obscured—I just hope the rad-folding field works. Photons are easy, but if they see us bending rads, your little plan will just get us smooshed.*>

Cary watched scan as they drew nearer to the T's, smiling with relief when Saanvi successfully executed the maneuver to hide the *Illyria*. The T's would know one of their squadron's ships had gone missing, but she hoped they wouldn't expect it to move completely out of the formation.

She flipped to fleet-wide scan, looking at Symatra's strategy as she organized the ships of Fleet Group 5 into a ring one hundred thousand kilometers in diameter. In the center of the ring lay Hannibal, Carthage's largest moon.

On their current vector, the T's fleet would pass through the ring and around the moon, before reaching Carthage. It probably looked like a trap to the enemy, but their fleet outnumbered Symatra's four-to-one, and, at this range, it would be obvious that most of the ships in Fleet Group 5 were incomplete hulls, barely able to maneuver into position.

What the T's didn't know was that the moon had its own rail emplacements—which had not yet fired. Those emplacements could not move, and would likely only get off two or three shots before the T's targeted them with heavy kinetic bombardments.

Ship scan threw an alert, and Cary called out, *<RMs incoming—at least a hundred! All headed for our squadron!>*

<Activating a new jinking pattern,> Saanvi replied and then gave Cary a wicked grin. *<Look, they were kind enough to send all their missiles on the same plane as our formation.>*

<Glad your plan worked there. Readying a salvo from the destroyers,> Cary returned the predatory smile as her adrenaline began to spike. *<Let's deep-Link now, this talking is taking too long.>*

Saanvi cast her a worried look and the sighed. *<OK, but no reading my inner thoughts. I don't have a filter in there, and I'm weird.>*

Cary smiled at her sister. *<I love your weird, but I won't pry, I promise.>*

Both girls leaned back into their seats and Cary saw Saanvi wince as the hard-Link connected at the base of her skull. It didn't hurt, but knowing that a long spike was sliding into the slot between the lobes of their brains was always disconcerting.

The hard-Link provided no new access to systems, but it did provide wider bandwidth and more reliability. The normal wireless Link was too risky to use when they drifted into one another's minds.

Once the hard-Link ran through its diagnostics, their network access switched over to the physical connection, and Cary reached into her sister's mind.

Her method of doing this, 'deep-Linking' being the name Cary came up for it, only seemed to work with Saanvi—not that she had tried it with many others. It was strange, considering that she and Saanvi were not blood sisters; though Angela had overseen their L2 neural enhancements, and their interfaces were very similar.

She felt Saanvi accept her, and Cary flooded into her sister's mind just as Saanvi entered into hers.

Crowded in here, she thought in her sister's mind.

Roomy in here, Saanvi replied with a grin.

Dork.

She felt warmth flooding into her from Saanvi, and knew that her sister felt the same. It was like a never-ending embrace. Cary-Saanvi knew they couldn't revel in it, though. They needed to deal with those RMs in the next seventeen seconds.

They opened their eyes again, both seeing through both pairs, while also both controlling their four hands—not that they needed to use physical controls. When deep-Linked, their mental reflexes far outstripped their physical ones.

Move the destroyers above and below the formation, one of them thought—neither knew which.

Firing rails, they replied, and watched scan as a hail of uranium pellets flew toward the RMs, covering a swath of space where probability suggested the missiles would be.

They marveled that with their Linked minds, they could almost comprehend the relativistic math occurring in real-time to predict the collision paths of the missiles and rail-fired pellets. They were on the cusp of understanding how space-time expanded, as photons bounced off both the relativistic pellets and the missiles, where they should have passed one another at nearly twice the speed of light, but didn't.

Their ruminations lasted for less than a second before scan began to register hits on the RMs. Over seventy were destroyed, and scan showed fifty-six remaining. An instant later, the missiles slammed into Epsilon Squadron—their kinetic energy displacing the ships, but not penetrating the stasis shields.

Cary-Saanvi saw that one of the destroyers had suffered a structural integrity failure from the force of the impact, and would have to be left behind. They also noted that one of the cruisers lost its internal gravity dampeners. If it took another hit from multiple RMs, it would crumple like paper—even if its stasis fields held.

Weapons range in seventy seconds, they noted.

Several more RMs crossed the space between Epsilon Squadron and the Trisilieds ships in the intervening seconds, but targeted shots from the destroyers disabled them.

Then, for fifteen seconds, nothing happened.

It felt like an eternity to Cary-Saanvi. When the ships finally came within weapons range, they decided not to fire. Let the enemy expend their batteries at extreme range; their stasis shields would shrug off the incoming particle and laser beams.

One of the enemy dreadnaughts positioned itself directly in the path of Epsilon Squadron, and, when the range closed to fifty thousand kilometers, the squadron's destroyers fired once more, sending nine million relativistic pellets streaking between the ships.

Scan registered the dreadnaught projecting magnetic fields as the enemy ships tried to shift the path of the pellets—but their attempts failed. That was the other enhancement the destroyers possessed—though the mass of the pellets was small, uranium was barely ferric, and it was much harder to shift than a normal iron-rich rail pellet would be.

Some did miss the dreadnaught, and instead struck the carrier's shields. Their impacts did little against the massive ship's protection, but the dreadnaught did not fare so well. The pellets weakened and tore through its shields, and shredded the massive ship's midsection. On cue, a stream of Arc-6 fighters flew from within Epsilon Squadron, and launched their short-range missiles into the rents in the dreadnaught's hull.

Explosions flared through the gashes, and parts of the dreadnaught's hull buckled. For an instant, it looked as though the ship would weather the strike—but then it exploded in a spectacular display.

Epsilon Squadron's flying V arced beneath the exploding dreadnaught, and past the Halcyon Class carrier, their stasis shields flaring as beamfire rained down from the hundred ships around them.

Communications blackout for twelve seconds, Cary-Saanvi thought to themself as the debris cloud obscured their line-of-sight tightbeams to the other ships in Epsilon Squadron.

The *Illyria* was four seconds behind the rest of the squadron; they fired its engines, directing it down toward the carrier. The cruiser sped over the dreadnaught's debris, and punched through the carrier's shields. During the ten milliseconds the *Illyria* spent adjacent to the ship, a hundred nuclear mines dropped out of its rear tubes and attached to the enemy vessel's hull.

Cary-Saanvi also fired four RMs while within the shields, sending them to the far ends of the carrier in case the mines in the center were not enough to destroy the entire vessel. The milliseconds passed, and then the *Illyria* was away, rapidly altering vector before reactivating their stealth systems.

Behind them, fighters had begun to streak out of the carrier. Perhaps the Trisilieds realized the time for deception was over; or maybe they were abandoning the ship, fearing picobombs.

Then the RMs hit and the mines detonated.

Nuclear fire filled the carrier's shields, obscuring the vessel before its shields failed, and the blast of light and energy flooded into space. Scan registered the explosion at over thirty-two exajoules. Cary-Saanvi marveled at the power of what they had done, an instant before they considered that the ship was easily crewed by over a hundred thousand people.

Nine seconds later, a secondary explosion tore through the space where the carrier's remains were still obscured by the growing radiation cloud. The ships in the immediate vicinity of the carrier, including the *Illyira* and the nineteen remaining ships of Epsilon Squadron, were flung onto new vectors from the overwhelming blast.

Antimatter, they thought. *A lot of antimatter*.

Their mind became resolute: though many people had died, they would not allow the enemy to use antimatter weapons on their homeworld. Even if they had to sacrifice themselves to stop it.

The *Illyria* reestablished tightbeam comms with the rest of Epsilon Squadron, and they boosted at max thrust toward their second target. Now that the T's knew what they were up to, they would put a lot more effort into stopping them—and they would be looking for the *Illyria* on alternate approaches.

Let's hit the third target first, they thought in unison. While the radiation cloud accelerating out around the carrier still gave them some cover, they did one small burn to alter vector, and then reengaged stealth systems, slowly nudging their ship closer to the third carrier.

On the *Illyria*'s starboard side, the other ships of Epsilon Squadron continued on to the second carrier—a decoy, which would arrive just as the *Illyria* reached the third.

Cary-Saanvi pre-programmed maneuvers into the ships and fighters that would have each destroyer unload another full magazine into the carrier. Following that, half the surviving fighters would punch through the ship's shields, and release their entire supply of short-range missiles while within the enemy ship.

The damage should be enough to cripple the carrier—especially if the fighters penetrated the ship's shields along its dorsal fighter docks.

In their mind, they watched the timer count down the final seconds. At the five-second mark, they fired the *Illyria*'s engines, altering course and lining up with the third carrier. To their port, Cary-Saanvi saw the destroyers' nine million pellets tear into the second massive ship, followed closely by the fighters, which slammed right into their target and unleashed the last of their RMs.

Half a second later, the *Illyria* tore through the third carrier's shields, dropping their final mines and firing the last four RMs they carried.

The antimatter explosion came sooner this time; almost as though the enemy ship was trying to take them out with its death throes.

The force of the explosion picked up the *Illyria* and flung it almost ten thousand kilometers, like it was nothing more than a cork in the ocean. Their consoles flashed red on nearly every system, as internal graviton emitters failed and the ship groaned.

If their eyes had been open, Cary-Saanvi would have seen a bulkhead on the bridge rend, and the atmosphere vent away into another section of the ship. They noted the event, but did not concern themselves with it; though the Saanvi portion of their merge noted with smug satisfaction that it was a good thing they were in suits.

They fought to regain control of their ship, and re-establish tight-beam communications with the rest of Epsilon Squadron. When they finally did, Cary-Saanvi found that two of the destroyers and four of the cruisers had been lost when the second carrier blew.

The squadron was down to fourteen ships, counting the *Illyria,* but their objective was complete.

Cary-Saanvi took a moment to look over the rest of the battlefield. The T's had not yet reached the ring of ships that comprised the bulk of Fleet Group 5, but three other ISF squadrons had penetrated deep into the enemy ranks, striking at the other carriers. Two had succeeded, though they had taken crippling losses to do so. The third squadron had been destroyed by overwhelming force before it was able to take out its final two targets.

As Cary-Saanvi transmitted a request to Symatra for new orders, the FTN flashed an update, showing two new fleets appearing, just over two hundred thousand kilometers above Carthage's poles.

What? Who is that? Cary asked, her shock momentarily separating their thoughts.

It's Mom's fleet! Saanvi exclaimed.

The two girls took a moment and recombined their thoughts before examining the ships.

How did they get there? they mused.

The FTN updated with the IFF data, and confirmed that the ships were indeed two halves of Fleet Group 1. However, the real-time scan still showed Fleet Group 1 trailing the Trisilieds fleet by over an hour—information that was several light minutes out of date, and no longer correct.

In their mind, Saanvi's voice separated out again, amazed and concerned. *They had to have jumped through the dark layer.*

Insystem, this close to the star…there's no way they should have survived.

Mom's crazy! Cary felt her physical body shake its head and forced it to still. The motion made her feel as though she might throw up. She reflected on her history lessons, which never told her about this feeling—how fear for yourself, for the lives of everyone you knew, could tear you up inside. If there was glory in this battle, she did not feel it.

The two segments of Fleet Group 1 rotated and began a hard burn to slow their momentum before boosting toward the oncoming Trisilieds fleet—which was now just twenty seconds from engaging Fleet Group 5.

The *Illyria* was hundreds of thousands of kilometers from Fleet Group 1, but its sensors still had to attenuate as the brilliant eruption of over five thousand ships running their engines at max burn flared into space. She hoped no one on the world of Tyre was looking up at the night sky; the light would far outshine Canaan Prime at high noon.

A minute later, more ships appeared, almost on top of fleet group one. Beamfire erupted from the ISF ships, tearing the new arrivals apart in moments.

Cary-Saanvi watched in amazement as the FTN showed the newly arrived—and now destroyed—ships to have Hegemony IFF tags. There had only been a few hundred of them; far from the massive fleet that had been in pursuit of Fleet Group 1.

While they waited for orders from Symatra, and for their pulses to stop racing, Cary-Saanvi let their minds fully mesh once more, and regrouped with the remains of Epsilon Squadron, which had now drifted past the bulk of the T's fleet.

Two of the destroyers had suffered magnetic containment failure in some of their particle accelerators and were running at half their firing rate. One of the cruisers was nearing containment failure on a reactor, and Cary-Saanvi powered it down, reducing that ship's ability to fire beam weapons.

Symatra's orders came—with no explanation for Fleet Group 1's mysterious appearance, or for the few AST ships that had followed—and confirmed their suspicion. It was up to them to take out the remaining two carriers.

Cary-Saanvi rotated their ships, and began to boost back toward the T's fleet. They burned hard, and one of their cruisers suffered a failure in a fuel regulator, and exploded as its AP drive introduced a critical level of hydrogen and anti-hydrogen.

Thirteen ships; a rather unlucky number for their final run.

They calculated the best burn they could achieve, and set a three-minute countdown until they reached the first of the carriers.

The FTN showed that the two carriers had released over twenty thousand fighters, and that another fifty thousand had escaped the other Halcyon Class ships before their destruction.

As they had taken out the first three carriers, Carthage's rail platforms had continued to fire, and take fire, until only two of them remained. Cary-Saanvi felt fear and sorrow as the FTN showed all hands lost.

They kept at it until the last, the girls thought with admiration.

As they considered the plight of the crew aboard the platforms, on the surface of Hannibal, Carthage's large moon, the barrels of stationary particle weapons emerged from the surface. They fired a full salvo, sending thousands of kinetic rounds out into the T's fleet—which still greatly outnumbered the defenders, even with the arrival of Fleet Group 1.

Ho-leee-shit, they thought, as the moon moved backwards five meters and cracks and fissures appeared across its surface. They were thankful that Hannibal's rail emplacements were unmanned, because the simultaneous firing would have killed anyone present.

Even as thousands of rounds lanced from deep within the moon toward the Trisilieds ships, the enemy fired back. Kinetic rounds collided in the darkness, flaring in brilliant explosions of light and energy—though many slipped past one another and found their respective targets.

A hundred Trisilieds ships exploded, and another thousand took some amount of damage. Three dreadnaughts moved in front of the remaining carriers to protect them, and for two, it was their last action.

The carriers, for their part, survived the onslaught, and continued to disgorge fighters as the T's fleet began to trade beamfire with Symatra's Fleet Group 5.

Cary-Saanvi watched the carnage in mixed awe and horror as the light-lag from the previous positions of Fleet Group 1 and the Hegemony fleet caught up. They saw their mother's fleet perform a hard braking burn and then disappear, followed by the Hegemony fleet a minute later.

How is that possible? What happened to the Hegemony ships? They asked themselves.

The Cary part of them could tell that there was something Saanvi was holding back and asked a probing question. *I guess…the AST ships didn't have a clear FTL path like mother did… Did mother bait the AST ships into chasing her through the dark layer knowing they wouldn't survive?*

There's no other logical explanation. That was some gamble—she could have brought the Hegemony ships right on top of us, if they didn't hit… The Saanvi part of them stopped, clearly unwilling to share some knowledge of what had likely transpired.

Sahn, what is it? Cary asked. *What aren't you showing me?*

Saanvi was silent for a moment, focused on fine-tuning their squadron's trajectory as Cary prodded her. *Fine. Cary, you can't tell this to anyone, ever. Mom told me a couple of years ago, when I asked a lot of questions about what happened to my father's ship.*

OK, my lips—and mind—are sealed.

The Saanvi part took a step back from the merge for a moment, and then rejoined fully. She shared the knowledge of the things that lived in the dark layer—things that were attracted to mass and graviton emissions.

Attracted to ships running grav fields to stay in the dark layer. Cary-Saanvi confirmed to themself.

It was why ships that entered the dark layer near stars didn't come out again, notwithstanding collisions with dark matter.

So, how did mom's ships come through, while the Hegemony ships got…eaten? they mused.

Neither knew, but they both were certain that their mother would not risk her fleet in a careless gamble. If she knew about the things that lived within the dark layer, then she must have known how to avoid them—and possibly how to send them after other ships.

We need to get ready, they thought. *We don't have any more mines, or enough missiles to take out two ships.*

The girls considered their options while aware of the risks, but also aware that everyone in New Canaan was prepared to sacrifice whatever they had to. They could do no less.

Cary-Saanvi lined up with the two Halcyon Class carriers. The two massive ships, only four hundred kilometers apart, bunched together so the dreadnaughts could provide cover. They formed the ships of Epsilon Squadron into a ragged line, no ship directly behind the others, though they would fall into a single spear before they hit. The *Illyria* took up the rear, ready to execute their last-ditch plan.

The destroyers were in the fore, and in the final three seconds before impact with the first carrier, they spent their remaining uranium pellets, tearing through the carrier's shields and into the aft on the port side of the ship.

Then the destroyers slammed into the carrier.

At the same time, Cary-Saanvi released all their final RMs behind the *Illyria* before drifting outward to pass around the first Halcyon Class ship.

They tried to discern the fate of the destroyers at the head of their formation. Scan data suggested that two had been destroyed within the carrier, while the other two had torn clear through the enemy ship.

Then the cruisers hit—one smashing against a section of the carrier's shields, which had reinitialized before the sheer mass and kinetic energy of the colliding ship disabled the carrier's shields once more, making a hole for the other cruisers to pass through.

The *Illyria* entered the gaping hole in the carrier's side, disgorging its final supply of nuclear warheads, while the girls prayed to whatever ancient gods were listening that it would be enough.

An instant later, they were through the ship and into the scant four hundred kilometers between it and the second carrier. Ahead, two destroyers collided with the last enemy carrier, the three cruisers a half-second behind.

Behind them, the first carrier exploded at the same instant that a series of kinetic rounds fired by nearby Trisilieds ships slammed into Epsilon's destroyers and one of the cruisers, knocking them off-course. Ahead, the final cruiser executed emergency evasive maneuvers. Cary-Saanvi struggled to keep the ships of Epsilon Squadron on course; they had taken too much damage to manage the tight maneuvers required.

They were all going to miss—all except for the *Illyria.*

Cary-Saanvi made emergency corrections, desperate to keep their ship on course for the carrier. They pushed the engines far past their maximum tolerances, and felt the internal inertial dampeners waver, then fail, as the burn executed.

A hundred *g*s of force slammed into the girls. They could feel bones breaking and organs splitting open in each other's bodies; then Cary separated their minds an instant before the final impact.

ASSAULTING ORION

STELLAR DATE: 04.01.8948 (Adjusted Years)
LOCATION: *Sabrina*
REGION: Stellar North of Carthage, New Canaan System

"Sure would have been nice to have a stealth system like this when we were back in the Perseus Arm," Cargo said with a broad smile.

Jessica gave an appreciative chuckle while Misha raised an eyebrow and shook his head. "I feel like we're cheating. I understand—sort of—why it is that they can't see us, but I still can't believe it. We're flying right above them!"

<It's because I'm a leaf on the wind,> Sabrina said, her mental tone joyous. *<That, and because AP engines are very hard to spot when they're pointed away. Not to mention how amazing Carthaginian tech is when it comes to radiation bending. We could float right outside a viewport and they'd never spot us.>*

"Let's not test that," Cargo grunted. "Jessica, how long 'til we're lined up with their flagship?"

"Gonna take another hour," Jessica replied. "For all Sabrina's boasting, it's a pretty delicate dance we're doing here. There are fifty thousand Orion ships around us; even if gamma rays from our AP drive are hard to spot, it's also hard not to slam them right into a ship behind us."

"If anyone can do it, you can," Cargo said.

Jessica knew he meant it as a compliment, but it still stung. Everyone—including her—wished it was Cheeky in the pilot's seat. Flying this mission almost felt like an affront to her memory.

"We're only going to get one shot at this," Colonel Usef said from his seat at the auxiliary weapons console.

"Piece of cake." Jessica flashed Usef a smile, glad to have the burly Marine with them. "Besides, you just did a run like this on the *Galadrial* a few days ago."

Usef laughed softly. "Well…we had their ship surrounded by a fleet they couldn't see, outnumbering them ten-to-one. This is the exact reverse of that situation."

"Do you think that OG officer, Kent, provided good intel?" Misha asked. "It was pretty interesting to learn that this Garza guy and the OFA's Praetor don't share the same goals here."

"Was a lucky break," Jessica agreed. "I chatted with him for a bit after Tanis; got a few more details out. I'm better at sweet talking than Tanis—though she's improved, from what I saw. Bob says what we've learned and inferred matches his models, and that's good enough for me."

"Bob…" Misha muttered. "You guys put a lot of faith in your god-AI."

"We do," Jessica agreed. "He's earned it."

"Yet he couldn't see through that other AI's deception; Helen, the one that was in the head of the Transcend President's daughter."

A precise maneuver stole Jessica's attention, and Iris replied for her. *<Bob knew what Helen was. He just made the mistake of thinking she had similar goals to his own. Well, to be honest, she probably does have similar goals. She just plans on achieving her ends differently.>*

"What does that mean?" Cargo asked.

<Bob wants to see humanity thrive, to achieve its potentials without being hamstrung or guided down a specific path. From what Finaeus has told us, Airtha wants the same thing; she just believes that she should be the supreme being that sets the path,> Iris replied.

"That seems a little off the mark," Cargo replied. "How can humanity 'be all that we can be' if Airtha is guiding us down her path?"

"Maybe she still views herself as human," Usef offered. "In that case, her guidance is still human guidance."

<***I'm*** *more human than she is,*> Sabrina chimed in. <*I always knew there was something wrong with Helen when she was with us.*>

<*No, you didn't,*> Hank laughed. <*You were just jealous because Helen got more of Sera's attention than you did. But I agree, she always acted smugly superior to us other AIs aboard.*>

<*I still say she made Sera forget our anniversary,*> Sabrina groused.

Jessica laughed aloud at that.

Sabrina gave a resolute nod over the Link. <*Just saying, she even apologized for all the anniversaries we missed while we were in Perseus—and Helen's gone!*>

"Any excuse to have some cake!" Misha grinned.

Jessica was glad for the team's banter; for some reason, it calmed her nerves. This mission that Tanis had sent them on was daunting, to say the least. They would have little room for mistakes.

The Orion Guard fleet was only half an AU from Carthage—silent and nearly invisible as they drifted through the system, closing in on their prey. If they maintained their vector, they would reach the Carthaginian homeworld in two and a half hours.

It was going to be tight. Board the OFA flagship—a behemoth named the *Britannica*—plant a hack that Bob believed would allow them to gain control of the ship, secure General Garza, and pull the ship away from Carthage before Tanis's final strike.

Easy.

Jessica smiled to herself. Funny thing was, the operation was on the same scale as half the jobs they had pulled over the last nine years. Breaking into Orion Guard installations was almost second nature to them at this point—which made them the perfect team for this job.

"It's a shit-show no matter which way you look at it," Cargo said absently as he reexamined the rough specs they had for the *Britannica*. "Helen had us all fooled—though we didn't know there was anything to be fooled about, I suppose. Hell, I never even knew there was a Transcend, let alone evil once-AI that were plotting everyone's demise."

<*We should have known,*> Hank said. <*Something was always off about her—but like you said, we didn't know it was a thing that* ***could*** *be, let alone that it* ***was***.>

<*I'm glad it worked out how it did…well, mostly,*> Sabrina said. <*Just think, Hank; without Sera finding me in that scrapyard, I would have died there…or worse. You would never have come aboard with Cargo, and would never have been freed. Crazy as it sounds, things are a lot better than they would have been.*>

"You have an unexpected, but valid, logic," Jessica said. "Funny how all of us are here as victims of crazy circumstance. Me, because some megalomaniac wanted me to watch as he became king of everything…or whatever he wanted. Cargo and Nance because an evil entity lived in Sera's head; Trevor because I wanted to have a fun night out; Misha because we accidentally jumped to the Perseus Arm."

"Doesn't really bode well for what we're about to do," Usef said as he sat ramrod-straight in his seat.

"Usef, seriously, when did you become such a wet blanket?" Jessica asked, twisting in her seat to catch his eyes. "We had some good times back in Victoria—and after, too."

Usef frowned and opened his mouth to reply, then shook his head and smiled. "You're one of a kind, Jessica. Here we are on a crazy mission to secure an enemy ship in the midst of the biggest fleet any of us have seen since we left Sol, and you're still cracking jokes and having a good time."

Jessica shrugged. “After what we’ve been through, this feels like just another day at the office.”

“You’re going to have to tell me those stories sometime,” Usef replied. “Sounds like you guys had a rollicking good time out there in the Perseus Arm.”

Jessica glanced at Cargo and Misha, who both smiled at the memories.

“Hell yeah,” Jessica said. “We all live through this, and I’ll buy you a round…or twenty…and tell you all about it.”

VICTORY AT ANY COST

STELLAR DATE: 04.01.8948 (Adjusted Years)
LOCATION: ISS *I2*
REGION: Stellar North of Carthage, New Canaan System

Cheers erupted across the bridge of the *I2* as they watched the ISF cruiser punch through the first carrier, then tear a hole through the second Halcyon Class ship, making an opening for the twelve RMs which followed close on their tail.

The twelfth, and final, Trisilieds Halcyon Class carrier flew apart in a massive antimatter explosion, destroying many of the fighters it had released.

"Find that ship!" Tanis called out. "I want to thank its captain and crew personally. They've saved untold lives."

Scan searched for the ship, tagged as the *Illyria,* on an exit vector from the explosion. Debris and energy from the two carriers' spectacular deaths made the search almost impossible, but given the number of other Trisilieds ships and fighters enveloped and destroyed in the explosion, the *Illyria*'s survival began to appear unlikely.

"Stars, that was brave," Captain Espensen said with a solemn shake of her head. "Who was managing that Squadron? It was too far out for Symatra to do that."

Sera nodded, "Whoever it was deserves a commendation."

"I don't know," Tanis said with a frown. She knew all the humans and AIs in Symatra's fleet, and couldn't think of any who could have pulled off that final attack run—though she supposed that in times like this, any of them could have risen to the occasion.

She reached out to Symatra, seeking Fleet Group 5's ship assignments, while watching a small group of one hundred Trisilieds ships that had slipped ahead and were already approaching Carthage and exchanging fire with the remaining orbital defenses.

Cary and Saanvi Richards.

The names didn't register at first. They didn't make sense. Then the weight of it slammed into her with the mass of a planet.

<*Our girls! What were they doing out there? Why?*> Tanis exclaimed.

<*I don't know! They're supposed to be on Carthage…*> Angela said in confusion.

Her vision swam and she felt her knees buckle.

<*They can't be…*>

She hit the deck, reaching out for Joe, but he wasn't there, he was too far away.

A tortured shriek escaped her lips, and in her mind, Angela echoed her cry of woe. Both human and AI sank for a moment into despair, and a feeling that nothing mattered, that there was no purpose, swept over them. Then, a spark of anger, followed by rage and cold determination, took its place. If these invading scum wanted death, she would bring it to them.

When Tanis rose to her feet and looked around the bridge, she saw that every ashen face was staring at her. She straightened her jacket and fought back the tears that threatened to spill down her face.

"Everyone…" her voice came out in a hoarse whisper, and she cleared her throat. "Everyone has lost today; mine is no more significant—and they could have survived, it's impossible to tell."

Sera reached for Tanis's hand. "There's a lot of radiation and debris masking signals in there. They could have made it to an escape pod."

"Or used the in-place stasis fields on the bridge," Captain Espensen added.

"I want the *I2* to push to the center of the Trisilieds fleet," Tanis said with a steadier voice. "We're going to finish this fight."

"Yes, ma'am," Captain Espensen replied soberly. "What is our primary target?"

Tanis gestured to the holotank. "Those carriers still released many of their fighters. Our Arcs can take them out, but we have to get them closer first. I want our atom beams to make maximum draw from the CriEn modules. Let's show them what war with us will cost."

Captain Espensen nodded, and Tanis watched with grim determination as her fleet boosted toward the Trisilieds ships—the bulk of which was now passing the moon, angling to brake around the planet. In a detached frame of mind, she wondered if they would bombard Carthage, or drop troops to secure the cities and hold the population hostage.

Let them try. Brandt and the ISF Marines were spoiling for a fight.

She checked over scan and saw that Greer's Fleet Group 2 was only thirty minutes behind the Trisilieds ships; but in an effort to catch up, their *v* would be too high for anything other than a single pass. It would take them an hour to come back around again.

She considered Fleet Groups 3 and 4, commanded by Joe and Sanderson. They were still in position, ready to strike when needed. She considered pulling them in, but knew that if her suspicions were correct, bringing them into the fight prematurely would result in the ISF losing.

<I didn't do it right. Thousands of us will die for nothing…> Tanis began to say privately to Angela.

<I know, dear. It's brutal to watch this fight, knowing half our ships aren't even involved. Who could have lived, who could have died—there will be time enough for those recriminations later.>

Tanis nodded and pushed the thought from her mind, willing herself to calm. She and Angela spread their minds once more across their section of Fleet Group 1—still braking hard above Carthage's north pole. She wasn't yet close enough to the ships below the world's south pole—nor to Symatra's ring of ships around the moon—for direct control, but she would be soon, and then she would shape them into the final hammer blow to destroy these intruders.

The *I2* pulled toward the Carthage-Hannibal L1 point and pivoted, the ship's length perpendicular to the system's plane. It waited as the leading edge of the Trisilieds ships rounded the moon, still engaged with Fleet Group 5.

"Give it to them," Tanis ordered.

The enemy met the withering fire as the *I2*'s thousands of weapons discharged. Still; there were so many ships, including tens of thousands of fighters and assault craft, that many slipped past.

Scan showed assault craft dropping into Carthage's atmosphere while the capital ships looped tight around the planet. Thousands of ground-based anti-aircraft batteries opened up, shooting down enemy ships by the hundreds—but still some got through.

Tanis knew she couldn't worry about the ensuing fights around Landfall and the other cities on Carthage's surface. Her fight was up here, to make sure that as few ships landed as possible.

"Target that cruiser!" she heard Captain Espensen call out and saw that a Trisilieds ship was making a run for High Carthage, the station atop the first of Carthage's space elevators. Her momentary distraction—worrying about the battle on the surface—had caused her to miss it.

The *I2* fired a series of proton beams into the ship and an explosion near its engines shoved the ship to port.

"It's going to hit the station!" one of the ensigns on the scan team cried out in horror, and Tanis watched as the disabled ship, over a kilometer in length, drifted toward High Carthage at over seven hundred meters per second.

The station had already taken an unimaginable amount of damage from passing ships, and its stasis shields had failed in several sections. Tanis looked at her available options and realized that no kinetics could hit the ship with enough force, at the right angle, to move it. The Trisilieds cruiser would tear right through the station, killing everyone aboard, and dropping the strand on the city of Landfall.

Then an ISF cruiser with failing shields streaked across the battlespace and smashed into the enemy ship, pushing it off course. The hulls of both ships interlocked, causing the pair to pinwheel through space, falling into the planet's atmosphere, on a trajectory to land in the ocean.

The desperate battle intensified as shields wore thin and ships tore into one another, filling Hannibal's L1 with drifting hulls and debris

C'mon, Tanis whispered to herself. *Where are you bastards?*

"They're firing antimatter warheads!" someone on scan called out. "We've lost a hundred ships!"

Tanis saw that concentrated antimatter detonations were enveloping many of the ISF ships, overwhelming the already taxed reactors powering the stasis shields.

She issued orders for human and AI-crewed ships to fall back, positioning the *I2* between the fleets.

The battlespace was almost incomprehensible. Fighters from both sides swarmed around ships; entire regions of space were filled with high-velocity debris, deadly radiation, and kinetic rounds.

It was unlike anything Tanis-Angela had ever imagined. A small part of her mind—the bit that wasn't frantically attempting to guide thousands of ships to their targets and away from their demise—boggled at the horror of it. She could not imagine that many battles of this scale had ever taken place before, with this much energy expended.

So far, miraculously, the *I2* had taken no damage. The Trisilieds ships gave it a wide berth—though many not wide enough, taking beamfire and sweeps of its molecular decoupler—as Captain Espensen guided the ship to where it was most needed.

Four minutes later, only seven hundred ships remained functional in Fleet Group 1, bolstered by another five hundred from Symatra's group. Over ninety percent of her ships were gone.

The bulk of the Trisilieds ships were now on the far side of Carthage, executing wide arcs beyond it to come back in for a final pass. There were still five thousand of them, and Tanis knew that the battle would be decided long before Sanderson's ships arrived.

"Enemy fleet admiral hailing us," the comm officer announced.

"Put it up," Tanis replied, opening her eyes once more to the bridge around her.

A woman appeared, sporting a haughty expression on her face and six stars on the collar of her ornate uniform. She was tall and slender—disproportionately so—and Tanis wondered if the woman had grown up on a low-*g* world or station.

"Admiral Richards, I am Admiral Myra," the woman said without preamble. "You, and all remaining vessels in your fleet, are to power down your weapons and shields, and exit your vessels in escape pods."

"Never gonna happen," Tanis replied. "It is you who should surrender."

"Admiral Richards," Admiral Myra said, still looking smug. "You are beaten. Our forces are invading your cities, we've taken one of your stations, and the other is not far behind. You have no more defenses, and your other fleets cannot reach you in time. Surrender now."

"Myra," Tanis's lips twisted into a sneer as she spat out the woman's name, "it is you who will surrender now, or none of you will ever leave this system. New Canaan will be your grave, and now that you've spilled so much of our blood, I will stretch my hand across the stars to the Pleiades and destroy your entire civilization."

<Tanis, I know you're hurting, but we can't do that…we'd be worse than they are,> Sera commented privately.

<I know…I just had to say it…sorry.>

<It's OK. What's her play, though? The way I see it, she can't win decisively; not with the I2 *in play.>*

<Not when the Orion Guard arrives,> Tanis replied.

<What?> Sera asked, and Tanis saw her eyes widen.

<The Orion Guard. They entered the system days ago, they're going to be here at almost the same time Myra's ships make it back around.>

Sera sputtered out loud, and Tanis saw her eyes narrow in anger. She cut the communication with Admiral Myra before Sera spoke.

"Tanis!" Sera cried aloud. "The Orion Guard? Here? How many?"

In an instant, everyone on the bridge turned to stare at Tanis. It wasn't the way she wanted this information to come out; she had hoped to have another option, but it was not to be.

<I'm sorry I didn't share it, we haven't vetted enough of the TSF personnel to know if there are leaks. And you were having a hard time with…well, with everything,> Tanis said privately.

<Tanis, seriously, you can't hold stuff like this back. I can take it, and I know how to keep a secret, for star's sakes. We'll talk about this later.>

Tanis sent a mental affirmation to Sera before speaking aloud. "Their stealth tech is good; better than yours, on par with ours," Tanis said calmly. "Our scan shows at least seventy thousand ships. Based on what you've told me, it's a sizable portion of their forward fleets. Its destruction will decrease their power-base in the Inner Stars considerably."

<I've revised the estimates upward of a hundred thousand ships,> Bob replied. *<It may be even more than that. The Trisilieds and AST ships were little more than cannon fodder to wear us down.>*

"Even if you can convince your parliament to allow the use of picobombs, you can't take out that many ships in time," Sera said, her face now ashen.

"Parliament reversed their decision ten minutes ago," Tanis replied with a frown. "Too little too late for…for the dead—but that is not how we will end this battle."

"Then how?" Sera asked, and Tanis saw the same question on the face of everyone on the bridge.

A wicked smile slowly twisted her lips. "We will devour them."

Confusion showed on the faces of everyone on the *I2*'s bridge, everyone except for Sera and Finaeus.

"You can't," Finaeus whispered. "You won't be able to control it…them…the things. It's not possible."

Tanis shook her head. "Those creatures have been controlled for some time. I wondered by whom, until you explained what's in the galactic core. Those AIs made the dark layer creatures to slow us down, but your jump gates ruined that plan. Now they will throw humanity back into another dark age to slow us once more. Don't you see? The *Intrepid*, Kapteyn's streamer, our jump forward in time with picotech; *they* always intended it to happen. We're the great filter, here to make a war to end all wars and keep humanity in check."

Finaeus shook his head. "That may be, but how will you do it? Those things, they'll destroy us all."

“No.” Tanis shook her head. “They won’t.”

OURI'S BAD DAY

STELLAR DATE: 04.01.8948 (Adjusted Years)
LOCATION: Landfall Space/Air Traffic Control Center
REGION: Knossos Island, Carthage, New Canaan System

"Fuck! They're flinging dropships down here like their capital ships are fucking piñatas!" Henderson hollered from his position on the scan station.

"Henderson, pipe down," Ouri barked at the man. There were a lot of days that she loved being out of the military and back in the colony's biology mission, but there were a lot of times she missed the discipline of the ISF.

Henderson cast a pair of wide eyes in her direction, and Ouri held up a hand beside her head and lowered it to her waist. "Fleet will be on station before long, FROD Marines are going to hit the dirt behind those Trisilieds dropships. Don't you worry."

The man opened his mouth to reply, but Ouri cocked her head to the side and narrowed her eyes. Henderson nodded slowly and turned back to his console.

The civilian team running Landfall's Space/Air Traffic control systems was made up of competent people, but they weren't trained to handle the mental strain of an incoming assault of this magnitude. Ouri wasn't entirely sure that she was, either.

Still, with nearly every member of the ISF crewing ships in the fleet, it would fall to them to manage Carthage's main planetary defenses, along with Murry, the Planetary Management AI.

At first, Ouri had bristled when Tanis gave her this assignment. She had clocked thousands of hours conning the *Intrepid*, and she had held FleetConn when Tanis and the rest of the command crew had nearly been captured by rebels back on Victoria.

She knew how to command a starship.

However, now that she was on the ground, she realized that these people needed someone with her experience. To them, she was one of the legendary figures who had fought the rogue AIs in Estrella de la Muerte and played a pivotal role back at Victoria.

With a few exceptions, everyone present in the SATC had been in stasis, or not yet born, during most of the *Intrepid*'s journey.

"OK, people," Ouri addressed the ten men and women with her in the control room. "We're going to operate from this facility for as long as we can. It has line-of-sight communications with most of the installations, and since we're sixty klicks from Landfall, the enemy will think this is just a secondary installation."

"Our comm traffic is going to give us away, though," one of the air-traffic control operators replied. "They're going to know we're here."

"That's why we start by routing all comms through remote stations," Ouri replied. "As they fall, we pull back."

"They're still gonna figure it out before long," Henderson said, barely holding it together.

"Get a grip!" Sammy, a young woman to Henderson's left, shook her head. "Now, activate those AA batteries on the north continent. Murry has enough to do with the last shuttles dropping in, and lifts coming down the strand!"

<Thanks, Sammy. Trying to keep these pilots from burning the cradles so bad the next guys don't sink in is a full-time job.>

"'Kay, 'kay, batteries are coming online," Henderson said. "NSAIs are suggesting closest dropships are priority. Do I go with that?"

"Yes!" Ouri and Sammy shouted at the same time.

"'Kay, 'kay, just checking…"

<Don't worry,> Sammy said privately to Ouri. *<I'll keep an eye on him. He's really good, normally; I guess this just messed him up.>*

<I know,> Ouri replied. *<His son's in Tanis's fleet. Everyone knows that's where most of the action will be.>*

Ouri couldn't imagine the stress of knowing one's kid was in battle. Her daughters were safe in one of the undersea biomes, and she was still worried sick about them.

<Stars…so weird to hear you just refer to her as 'Tanis',> Sammy replied with a small smile

<She stole my cabin in Ol' Sam. That earns me some informality.>

<Wow…when we get through this, I'd love to hear some of those old stories. I mean…we learned about it all in school, but you ***lived*** *it!>*

Ouri laughed. The girl's enthusiasm was infectious. *<You just stay focused and do your job. We'll get through this OK, and you'll have your own stories to tell.>*

"Yeah! Got some!" Henderson called out.

Ouri turned her attention back to the holotank and frowned as she watched hundreds of dropships enter the atmosphere. Henderson was right about one thing: this was going to be the fight of their lives.

The majority of the Trisilieds' assault craft were headed for Landfall, which made sense, given the enemy's goal of taking the planet's population hostage to force their surrender of the picotech. However, that goal gave an advantage to the Carthaginians. The enemy would be hesitant to use weapons of mass destruction on her people, while she would have no such compunctions about using WMDs on them.

"They're approaching the eastern installations," Amy called out from her station. "I have the first salvo ready to fire."

"Give 'em hell," Ouri replied.

The holotank showed the first wave of dropships pass below the ten-thousand-meter mark as they raced over the ocean to the east of the archipelago where Landfall was situated.

Below the crashing waves of the Mediterranean Ocean, twenty robotic submarines launched a hundred surface-to-air missiles at the enemy dropships. The SAMs carried one-megaton nuclear warheads—more than enough to put a crimp in the Trisilieds' approach vector.

"I can't believe we're detonating nukes over our own world," one of the men said, as he maneuvered low-altitude drones, launching chaff clouds into the skies ahead of the missiles. The reflective clouds of aluminum and lead would refract and block optical and x-ray lasers—with luck, they would protect at least half the SAMs as they streaked into the path of the oncoming ships.

Red markers appeared on the holotank as thirty two of the missiles took air-to-air fire and fell back into the ocean, then the remainder of the warheads detonated amidst the enemy dropships.

Ouri was glad for the row of volcanic peaks to their east that blocked the intensity of the flash; not to mention the antigravity systems that would push most of the radiation into space, along with the smoke and ash from the volcanoes.

As the clouds from the explosions cleared, remote sensor stations showed hundreds of Trisilieds assault craft plummeting into the ocean—though hundreds more survived the nuclear fire.

"Second salvo!" Ouri called out.

"It's insane," someone whispered from behind her. "How can they just fling so many ships down here like this? They're not giving them *any* fleet support!"

"Look above the poles," Ouri said without turning. "Fleet Group 1 just jumped in. Those assholes up there are in for the fight of their lives. You can see where several of their capital ships were dropping into low orbits, but are pulling back out now."

"Symatra really did a number on them, too," Sammy added. "She took out all those carriers; if they had made it, these assault ships would have serious fighter shields, not just this smattering."

The submarines fired off three more salvos of SAMs, each having a diminished effect as the drones ran out of chaff, and the enemy dropships spread out wider and wider.

As the assault transports passed high over the string of volcanoes, there were still over a thousand intact enemy ships bearing down on Landfall. Ouri estimated that each had to contain at least one platoon of soldiers, which meant that the Trisilieds were about to land thirty thousand troops on Carthage.

Ouri sighed. *Well shit.*

BRITANNICA

STELLAR DATE: 04.01.8948 (Adjusted Years)
LOCATION: OGS *Britannica*
REGION: Stellar North of Carthage, New Canaan System

"Thing about pico," Jessica said as she queued up with Cargo, Usef, Misha, and Trevor in the airlock, "is that it has a damn short shelf life. It doesn't take much to mess up those tiny bastards; unless they're carrying out orders to go eat a starship—then they'll replicate a hell of a lot faster than the Casimir effect tears 'em apart."

"I can't even begin to describe how nervous this makes me," Misha said, casting a worried eye at the small device Jessica held. "That shit's pico…it makes nanotech look like a bludgeon. It can weasel its way in between electrons and neutrons. How is it even a thing? What's it made out of?"

"Seriously, Misha," Jessica shook her head. "Do you really want to discuss how pico can take apart a neutron bit-by-bit right now?"

"Now that you mention it," Misha said with a broad grin, "that does sound fascinating. What say we just put off this crazy mission and talk about pico for a bit?"

"Nice try," Cargo said and slapped Misha on the back. "You always have a case of the butterflies before we do an op. Like Jessica said, we've got this in the bag."

"OK, when we go in, I have tactical command," Jessica said. "Not because I need to be the big girl, but because I know how we work, and I know how Usef works."

"Sure got the big girls, though." Misha snickered and Cargo cuffed him on the back of the head.

"Seriously, Cargo? Was that necessary?"

"Was either me or Trevor," Cargo shrugged. "Should I let him do it next time?"

Misha glanced at Trevor's biceps, each the size of his torso.

"Uh, thanks, Cargo. Did me a solid there."

"Damn right, I did."

<Are you ever going to go?> Sabrina asked. *<It's not easy holding this position, you know.>*

"Sorry, Sabrina," Jessica said as she placed the pico-package in the airlock and cycled it. "Can you guys believe Tanis snuck onto a Transcend ship the old-fashioned way just six days ago? When she sees a need, she sure makes certain it gets taken care of fast."

"Necessity is the mother of invention," Trevor said as they watched the package drift between their ships and latch onto the *Britannica*'s hull.

"Pretty deep there, big man," Misha chuckled.

"What? I used to carve little crystal trinkets. I can totally be deep."

Jessica's hand went to her throat, reaching for the chain that held the small dolphin Trevor had carved for her long ago. She felt a moment of panic when her fingers didn't feel the chain, but then she recalled: Trevor had convinced her not to wear it—it was against Orion Guard regs to wear jewelry, and though the Orion uniforms they wore would hide it, it wasn't worth the risk.

"Yeah, you're like an ocean," Cargo grunted. "It looks like our little friend has rewired the lock over there. If it worked, we'll slip right in. If it doesn't…well, I guess we'll all see how we look with holes in us."

Jessica checked her sidearm one last time as the team stepped into the airlock and Sabrina pulled the ship within a meter of the *Britannica*. A small grav-tunnel joined the airlocks, and the team rushed through and sealed the *Britannica*'s behind them.

<*Secure,*> Jessica called back to their ship.

<*Understood. We'll be on standby,*> Nance replied. <*With luck you won't need us.*>

<*Let's hope,*> Cargo replied.

"OK, team; one more time while the package makes sure the passageway out there is clear," Jessica said, looking from one member of the strike force to the next. "Now that we have Usef here, it's not going to work like last time—being an officer, he can pass for one."

"I think I did really well last time," Cargo said.

"Seriously?" Misha asked. "You were a major and you called a private '*sir*'. Sure, they 'sir' sergeants in some militaries, but *no one* calls a private 'sir'."

"You sure?" Cargo asked Jessica and Usef.

"Yep; no one, nowhere," Jessica shook her head.

"Goes against nature," Usef added.

"If he's the one who can't tell a private from his privates, how come I'm PFC Jerrod, here?" Misha asked.

"Cause he's the captain, and I have to at least make him a sergeant," Jessica said. "Look, everyone stop bitching about your ranks. Trevor and I are heading up front to see if we can catch Garza when he steps out for a whiz. You guys are on engineering duty. We need to control this ship's engines without having to hold the bridge."

<*Easy,*> Hank said cover the combat net. <*Angela gave Iris and me some serious kit. These pathetic Orion AIs are barely L2; we'll have them under control in no time.*>

<*Don't get cocky, Hank,*> Iris wagged a finger at him in their minds. <*We're going to be out of communication once we split up—until we take the ship, that is. You be careful. All of you.*>

<*Iris, it's me,*> Hank said with a mental grin.

"Yeah, that's what we're afraid of," Misha chuckled.

The light over the airlock's inner door flashed green, and Jessica slid it open and stepped boldly into the corridor.

Trevor followed, and they closed the portal behind them. The other team would leave once she had found a hard terminal for Iris to start her hack.

Until then, anyone who gave them a second look may realize that neither she nor Trevor were on the ship's rolls.

<Funny the similarities these ships share with the Transcend ones,> Iris commented, as Jessica and Trevor strode purposefully down the passageway, heading toward what should be a small NSAI node.

<They've been in a weird holding pattern for some time,> Jessica replied. *<It's as though they both advanced to a certain point, and then went wide instead of up.>*

<It's more amazing that no one else figured out picotech in the last five thousand years,> Trevor said as he turned down a corridor leading further toward the center of the ship.

<Well, we know they didn't figure it out in Orion,> Jessica replied. *<I do wonder, though; did those Transcend worlds really have rampant picoswarms, or did the OG take them out because they want to limit technological advancement?>*

<I doubt we'll ever really know for sure,> Iris said. *<Stop. There, that door to your left—a lot of EMF coming from inside. I bet that's one of their NSAI nodes.>*

* * * * *

Usef was just about to ping Jessica for an update when his AI, Jamie, gave them the all clear.

<I received Iris's data burst. Our idents are in their system,> Jamie informed the group. *<Once we leave the airlock, I'll piggyback on Usef's Link; so if he talks to you over it, it may be me.>*

"That won't be weird at all," Misha muttered.

"You'll manage. Let's go," Usef said, and slid the airlock door open.

The trio exited the airlock, took ten steps down the corridor, and almost walked right into a puzzled-looking engineer.

"Hey! Watch it!" the woman grunted as she stepped around Usef. "Shit! Sorry, Major…Johnson."

She saluted while blushing furiously.

"As you were, SPC. Don't worry about it," Usef said as he returned the salute.

"Thank you, sir. I'm just trying to work out some strange readings this airlock down here is giving me. Distracted me, won't happen again," she said in a rush.

"I trust that it won't," Usef said, and turned, continuing on his way with Cargo and Misha on his heels.

"Someone got all hot and bothered when she saw ol' Major Johnson here," Misha chuckled. "Why infiltrate the enemy when you can just seduce them?"

"That one's getting old," Cargo grunted.

<*And think before you use the words 'infiltrate the enemy'. You never know who, or what, is listening,*> Usef chided.

"Sheesh," Misha sighed.

"That's 'sheesh, sir'," Usef scowled.

These two are going to blow the op. It's a miracle they survived nine years in the Perseus arm; the Orion Guard must have put its incompetents out there.

They walked around a corner and saw that the passageway ahead had a ninety-degree twist. A pair of soldiers approached, appearing to walk on the wall until they reached the twisting section, at which point they rotated as they walked, until their 'down' was the same as the trio's.

<*That's just weird,*> Usef said. <*Still not used to this artificial gravity stuff.*>

<*It's weird for those of us who* **are** *used to it,*> Misha replied. <*Always makes me feel nauseated to reorient like that.*>

The soldiers saluted, and Usef returned the salute, resisting the urge to turn and ensure that Cargo and Misha followed proper protocol. The soldiers didn't say anything, so he assumed all was well.

After they passed through the twisted section of corridor and were walking on the wall, they came to a bank of lifts, all situated around the edges of a large shaft with a particle accelerator running down the center.

Misha approached the railing and looked over. "Going doooooown," he whispered while grinning.

"For fucksakes, Private; stop dicking around, and get in the lift," Cargo growled.

As the doors closed, Usef nodded. "That was a passable impression of a sergeant. Nicely done."

"What can I say?" Cargo replied. "Misha brings it out of me."

"You know…I'm standing right here," Misha muttered.

Jamie highlighted the engineering command level on his HUD, and Usef entered the code to send the lift down the three kilometers of shaft to its destination.

Cargo looked out the narrow windows into the ship's central shaft. "Gotta say, that's a pretty sweet view."

Usef nodded. It reminded him of the accelerator that ran down the center of the *I2*. He remembered the assault on Node 11 back when the rogue AIs had taken control of the *Intrepid*—fighting servitors and automatons through the dark passageways while nauseating gravity waves flowed off the accelerator.

That had been his first combat mission as a part of the ISF—though it hadn't been the ISF then. He tallied the time he had been awake, and realized that mission was nearly a hundred years ago.

Nothing like what the admiral has put on her clock, but an appreciable span of years.

The lift slid to a halt halfway to their destination, and the doors opened to admit two female lieutenants. They quickly saluted Usef, and he returned the gesture—noting with relief that Cargo and Misha correctly saluted the officers.

"Good morning, Major," one of the women said, while the other added, "Good morning, sir."

They glanced at one another, and the first woman—First Lieutenant Lauren, by her ident—asked, "If I may ask, Major Johnson, how long have you been aboard? I thought I knew all the officers on the *Britannica.*"

"Transferred in off the *Sword of Orion* before we began our stealth run, Lieutenant Lauren," Usef replied, using a ship name that Jamie supplied him. "I wanted to be where the action is."

"Oh, this is where the action is, alright," the other woman, Second Lieutenant Jenny, added.

They were smiling just a bit too much, and Usef wondered if the crew on the *Britannica* had something in their water supply. First the SPC near the airlock, and now these two. Maybe they were on to his team and just playing with him.

<Relax,> Jamie said. *<They're a bit…freer on OG ships, from what I can tell.>*

"Look us up once we're done burning this system to ash," Lieutenant Lauren said with a grin. "We'll give you a proper *Britannica* welcome."

The lift came to a stop several levels above their destination, and the two lieutenants got out, both casting long looks back at Usef over their shoulders.

"Can you help it?" Misha asked with a shake of his head.

"Sir," Usef replied.

"What? Does that mean 'yes'?"

"Stars, we're doomed," Usef said, and looked at the lift's ceiling, hoping Jessica was at least doing as well as they were.

*****

"Have you located them?" Garza asked as he re-entered the Fleet CIC.

"Not yet," Admiral Fenton said, his deep scowl showing how he felt about the situation.

The ship's AI, Harry—a rather strange entity, in Garza's estimation—replied as well. <*Security teams are trying to pin them down, but they keep slipping in and out of our internal sensors. They must have a hack in our system, but we've been unable to find it.*>

"I thought you had eyes on them just before I stepped out," Garza said. "Two lieutenants saw them, and noted the deck they were going to."

<*Yes, sir, but when the lift stopped at that deck, no one was in it,*> Harry responded, his avatar giving a shrug. <*I'm doing everything I can, but honestly, without sounding general quarters, it's going to be hard to find them.*>

"No, I want to know where they're going. Find them and tail them, if you have to. They're not here to see the sights; they have some sort of plan."

"I think we should switch mission parameters," Admiral Fenton said as he reoriented the view of the New Canaan system on the holotank. "If they have landed an infiltration team on our ship, they know we're here. If they know we're here, then our element of surprise is gone. We're close enough that we can order the fleet to rotate and fire engines on max burn. Their planet will be a dead husk inside of an hour."

"They lucked out and spotted us with a stealth ship," Garza replied. "That ship may have relayed our position, but they won't know about the other half of the fleet. And if they do know, so what? Even if the Trisilieds don't wear them down to dust first, we still outnumber them ten-to-one."

"I don't like it," Fenton shook his head. "They have picobombs—if they know where we are, how do we know we aren't flying into a swarm of them?"

"We don't," Garza shook his head. "But consider this: even if they can spot our stealth ships, their picobombs won't have scan good enough to track us on their own; and if they pass data to a swarm of picobombs, we raise shields, and nothing comes of it."

Fenton continued to frown at the holotank. "Provided pico can't get through shields."

"If it can, then why'd they fly their fighters through the Hegemony dreadnaught's shields back in Bollam's World?" Garza asked. "Their pico delivery system is the weak point—a weak point that we can target and destroy."

Garza wondered about Fenton's resolve. They were too far down this road to turn back now. When Kirkland learned that he had made this preemptive strike against New Canaan, the praetor would know that they did not share the same ideals.

Fenton knew that. They had to see this thing through. No other possibility existed.

<*Got them,*> Harry announced. <*A security team is bringing the intruders to you. Should I have them placed in a nearby holding room?*>

"No," Garza replied with a grim smile. "Bring them in here. I want them to watch while we destroy their world."

* * * * *

<*There it is,*> Usef said as he peered around the corner. <*Engineering command. We have to hit fast and hard. Jamie has a shunt ready to lock down their Link access, but there are a lot of terminals in there. If any of them sounds the alarm, this whole party is over.*>

Cargo and Misha nodded soberly, and Usef was glad to see that they were finally taking things seriously.

<*Who takes who?*> Cargo asked.

<*Go for whoever is closest. Jamie will provide priority targets and fields of fire on your HUDs,*> Usef replied.

<*Ooooh, fancy,*> Misha gave a mock whistle.

<*So much for serious,*> Jamie said privately.

Usef agreed with Jamie's sentiment. <*I keep thinking…if they got through Perseus, then they can do this; but I'm starting to doubt that…maybe it was a miracle.*>

<*Well, we know Jessica is competent enough. Maybe they just like to have fun,*> Jamie offered.

<*We're about to find out,*> Usef said as he stepped around the corner and strode into the engineering command center.

The room was broad, with a high overhead and a dozen holotanks. Each one showed detailed readouts of different ships. Usef counted thirty engineering specialists around the room, working under the watchful eye of a major who stood near the center of the space.

A watchful eye which did not miss his entrance.

"Major…Johnson," the woman said as he approached. "How can I help you today?"

Her words were cordial, but her scowl was not. Every part of her body language said 'go away', and Usef flashed his best smile in response. "Major Phyla, I've been sent down to ensure everything is ready for the upcoming battle, and to operate as a liaison."

Major Phyla turned from Usef back to the holo she had been monitoring. "A liaison to whom? I report directly to Captain Langlias. I don't need you to liaise."

"I've been attached to General Garza's retinue," Usef replied without rancor. "He sent me down here to make sure that he has a direct line to what's really happening on the ship."

His words caught her attention, and she glanced back at him. "Did he now? I suppose that makes sense; in the CIC, he only knows what comes down from the bridge—and I'll tell you, that's not always the whole story."

Usef chuckled. "Don't I know it. Who wants to be the one to tell the Fleet Admiral, and the general in charge of all the shady spec-ops shit, that something's wrong?"

Major Phyla barked a laugh. "You do realize that's *your* job—you get to be the bearer of bad news."

Usef nodded. "Yeah, not the best posting in the force. Still, better than those poor Hegemony and Trisilieds ships out there."

Phyla nodded absently. "Yeah, at least we're no one's ablative shielding, like those bastards. Hell, when it comes to the *Britannica,* our shielding has shielding."

Usef leaned around Major Phyla's shoulder and peered into the tank. "So, what's this?"

He barely paid attention to her response as he lightly touched the back of her neck, praying she wouldn't notice.

"Excuse me?" she exclaimed as she spun to face him. "Are you trying to cop a feel or something?"

"What?" Usef took a step back. "You need to lighten up. You had this bit of string in your hair; just doing you a favor—keeping things on the up and up."

The major's eyes narrowed and she shook her head. "OK, Major Johnson, if you say so."

Usef looked around the bay to see Cargo and Misha working their way through the engineers present. They were introducing themselves as part of his team, shaking hands, doing all the right stuff. In the time he had managed to deploy a package to the major, each of them had deposited pico units on a dozen of the personnel in the room.

Major Phyla had noticed the pair working their way through the room as well, and shook her head. "Don't know where you transferred in from, but you're a friendly bunch. Better not be this distracting when the shit starts to fly."

"Don't worry," Usef replied. "They're just getting to know everyone so they can operate at peak efficiency when things get hairy. Not that I really expect it to."

"No?" Major Phyla turned from the holotank to face him. "You know something I don't know? Those Canners down there are pretty nuts. They have pico tech, fire grapeshot; probably have no issues with antimatter weapons, either—just like those Transcend bastards. You saw what they did."

Usef nodded as though he knew all about it. If the Transcend had used antimatter weapons, it was deplorable—but right now, Orion was attacking his home, and the Transcend was helping to defend it. He'd trust Admiral Richards to make the right call when it came to alliances.

"I meant here, on the *Britannica,*" Usef said with a smile and a shrug. "The captain'll want to keep Admiral Fenton and General Garza nice and safe."

Phyla shook her head and turned back to her holotank. "They're great men and all—very important to the Guard—but I'd rather be in the thick of things. We signed up to be warriors, didn't we? Not to babysit the brass."

Usef chuckled. He couldn't fault the woman for her spirit, misguided though it was.

Phyla's shoulders hunched ever so slightly before she spun, her sidearm aimed at his head. "Lucky for me, I think I've managed to find a bit of action, right here in my own engineering bay."

* * * * *

Garza shook his head as the intruders were marched into the CIC. How they ever thought that they could achieve anything other than capture on the *Britannica* was beyond him;

though he'd very much like to know what they thought they could pull off.

"Welcome aboard," Garza said with a cold smile. "I'm sure that you just forgot to ask the captain for permission to come aboard."

"Something like that," the woman said. "We just thought it would be good to get a look at your ships before we destroyed them all—for research, of course."

The large man accompanying the woman didn't add anything, but a smile spread across his face as he glanced at her.

"Well, I hope you got a good look. I'm General Garza, by the way. I brought you here because I thought you might like to watch as your fleets are destroyed, and your world held hostage until they surrender the picotech to us."

"I'm Colonel Jessica Keller, and this is Trevor," the woman replied. "I have to say, I'm glad you brought us in here. Usually it's just a dark, grey holding cell—which would bug me, because I'd be on the wrong side of the table."

Garza snapped his fingers. "Of course, Jessica Keller. I didn't make an immediate match, because you're not on the original colony roster—that, and you appear to have aged."

"A result of a recent adventure," Jessica said with a frown. It's been about fifty years since I've had rejuv."

"Well, you'll get none of that in an Orion prison," Admiral Fenton spoke up. "General Garza, do you really have to play these games here? We have work to do."

"Don't you realize who this is?" Garza asked. "This is one of Governor Richards's inner circle. She's not here for some unimportant scout mission. She's come because they planned to do something significant on the *Britannica*."

"Then there's no way they came alone," Fenton replied. "You don't send one of your top people—and a guy named Trevor—onto a ship like this by themselves."

Garza stroked his chin as he eyed the pair. "Put them by the wall; make sure they're well restrained," he ordered the soldiers who had brought the colonists in. "Harry, start a new sweep of the ship. I want the rest of their group found."

<*Already on it, General,*> Harry replied.

"Who knows," Garza said as he turned back to the holotank, "I may keep this system after I've destroyed the world you've named Carthage. The shipyards alone make it worth holding onto."

VISITORS

STELLAR DATE: 04.01.8948 (Adjusted Years)
LOCATION: Landfall Space/Air Traffic Control Center
REGION: Knossos Island, Carthage, New Canaan System

"Oh crap, oh shit! Commander Ouri!" Henderson called out.

Ouri didn't bother correcting the man on rank—though how he could grow up in a society like New Canaan's, and not understand the difference between a commander and a colonel was beyond her.

"What is it, Henderson? Just spit it out!" Ouri yelled back from across the room.

"The Trisilieds…they've sent four craft to our location; they snuck in around from the south. I took one out, but the other three are landing!"

Ouri felt her temper flare and took a deep breath, forcing her emotions into check. It would have been fantastic if Henderson had let her know about this *before* the enemy had begun disgorging their troops.

"OK, Sammy, Kris, Bill, you're with me. The rest of you, keep running the air defenses as long as you can—people across the planet are counting on us. Jim, we still have a fleet of subs that need to stop that wave of assault craft dropping on Paris Island out west, and Brandt has called in for an airstrike on a field near Landfall that the enemy is using for their forward base. Jenny, get our ground-based artillery hitting that target. Amy, make sure the Tower's perimeter defenses are up, and take out as many of those bastards as you can."

"Aye, Colonel," Amy called back.

At least someone has been paying attention, Ouri thought to herself.

Though the facility was colloquially called the 'SATC tower', it was nothing of the sort. Everyone in New Canaan knew this fight was coming, and no one had even considered a tall, vulnerable tower when it came to civilian space and air traffic control.

Instead, the SATC facility was tucked within a long ridge of granite that lay toward the eastern edge of Knossos Island at the base of a low string of mountains, which had arisen when the archipelago's plate pushed up over the Mediterranean Ocean plate.

She wished there were ground-based artillery units that could sweep the hillside leading up to the SATC, but none were available that could target their side of the ridge. They were in the plan, but hadn't been built yet.

The lowest level of the facility was little more than a lobby—with external access to a parking lot, for those who liked the drive through the countryside on the way to work—and a station for a quick ride to Landfall.

A wide double-staircase led from the foyer to the second level, and a long tunnel ran back into the ridge, which ended in a lift and a staircase up to the second level. The control room was on the fourth level, further back in the ridge and under hundreds of meters of granite.

The facility also had a low signal tower directly overhead, as well as direct, hardline connections to the dozens of other towers ringing the island.

Ouri was impressed that the Trisilieds had picked out this location as the primary facility. Their sensor tech must be better than that of most Inner Stars civilizations.

Ouri led Bill, Kris, and Sammy down the hall toward the front stairwell.

"What are the four of us going to do against three platoons of Trisilieds solders?" Sammy asked as she caught up to Ouri.

"Well," Ouri replied as she led the trio down the hall, "I was in favor of killing them. Let's start there."

"How are we going to do that?" Bill asked.

"I picked the four of you because you all got high marksmanship scores in Basic," Ouri replied as she glanced back at her team. "So, what I think we should do is shoot the bad guys."

She pushed into the stairwell and skipped down the stairs to the third level, where the security office and small armory were located.

"Seriously, Ouri, you must have some better plan than that. Even if we were the toughest Marines in the corps, it's four against a hundred," Sammy said, her voice starting to rise in pitch.

"I rated expert in my marksmanship course," Kris said quietly. "If there's anything in the armory with range, I could get up in the signal tower and take them out as they approach."

Ouri looked Kris up and down. The willowy woman was two meters tall, and there was no reason to believe she couldn't get a rifle up there in time; but the position was a death sentence.

"I bet you could, Kris," Ouri replied. "You'd give 'em hell, too; but one well-placed rocket, and that whole tower will come down. I'm not sending you up there to die."

Kris's face blanched, and Ouri suspected that the very real possibility of them all dying in the next few minutes was now entering her team's minds.

"Look," she said as they entered the armory. "We don't have to take them all out, we just have to buy time. Murry has already put out the call that we're under attack, and as soon as

Landfall is safe, those Trissies out there are going to have Force Recon boots up their asses, courtesy of the ISF Marines."

"Trissies," Sammy chuckled. "I like it."

Ouri had already assessed the armory's loadout, and, like everything in New Canaan, it was a shining example of over-preparedness—yet still insufficient for what they were up against.

Five sets of light body armor stood on racks, and she directed her team to gear up. The armor wouldn't stop beamfire, but it would keep projectiles and shrapnel from cutting them to ribbons.

While they geared up, Ouri laid out four multifunction rifles, sidearms, spare magazines, and five detpacks. She stuffed all the grenades into a bag that she planned to hold onto; they had enough to worry about without a bad toss getting them all killed.

Once the team was armored up and had begun checking over their weapons, she quickly donned her armor while calling Amy.

<How's it looking out there, Amy?>

<They're being careful, working their way up the front and flanking, as well. Two of the beam turrets are down, but I still have two running. They haven't gotten in range of the two Gatling guns near the entrance, but once they do, I plan to cut down the forest—and whatever's in it.>

Ouri was impressed. Amy's voice didn't waver one iota. The woman sounded like cold steel incarnate.

<Give 'em hell, Amy. Let me know when they've reached the guns.>

<Pretty sure you'll hear it, Colonel,> Amy replied with a mental smile. *<There's one string of explosive rounds for each gun, and I have that queued up first. I won't fire 'til I can see the whites of their eyes.>*

<Looking forward to hearing that sound,> Ouri replied.

"Bill, Sammy, grab those two CFT shields. We'll set them up on the second floor landing. Kris, I want you to stay up on the third level's landing, and pick off anyone that gets past our fire," Ouri directed.

"What if they get past you and come up the rear staircase?" Kris asked.

Ouri picked up one of the detpacks and tossed it to her. "Before you take up your position, rig this to take out the rear stairs if they get back there. Put it on the landing between the second and third floors. Set up some nano to watch the stairs, and trigger the pack if the Trissies make it that far. Oh," Ouri tossed her another detpack, "and rig this one in the elevator shaft outside the third level's door."

Kris gave a crisp nod, slung her rifle over her shoulder, and ran out of the room, turning right toward the rear stairs.

Sammy and Bill followed after and turned left, hauling the Carbon Fiber Tube shields with them toward the front of the facility.

Ouri cast her eyes about the room, looking for anything else that would help. She spotted a locker that none of them had opened, and peered inside to find a crew-served railgun.

"Well, this will come in handy," she said with a smile.

She grabbed her selected gear and moved out.

When she reached the front stairwell's second floor landing, Bill and Sammy had already set up the CFT shields, and were taking sight on the foyer below.

While the rear staircase was narrow and utilitarian, the front one was wider and more ornate. A four-meter-wide string of steps rose up to the second level before arching around to the third.

The fourth floor was only accessible from a secondary flight of stairs in the middle of the third level. That would be their final fallback before abandoning the facility, and taking the rear tunnel out to the far side of the ridge.

Ouri took a position behind Sammy, glad for the cover the shield would provide. She peered down her rifle's iron sights, ensuring that they were aligned with her HUD's targeting system.

Her team's position on the landing gave them an angle of fire where they could hit the leading edge of any troops that entered the first floor, while only enemy well within the building could bring significant fire to bear on them.

It wasn't enough to give them a large advantage, but it was enough to stem the enemy's advance and give them a fighting chance.

"So…what if they just launch rockets in here and blow the whole facility?" Bill asked as he glanced nervously around his shield.

Ouri considered that scenario. The working theory was that the Trissies wanted the picotech, and were prepared to take hostages to press their claim. However, they didn't need *all* the civilians on the planet to do that. She knew that if it was her, she would simply neutralize the facility and move on.

"Good point, Bill," Ouri nodded. "If they take the foyer down there and we have to fall back, will the facility hold if they place charges down on the first and second floors? The control center is quite a ways further back in the ridge."

Bill considered it for a moment. "Well, there are blast doors on the third and fourth levels. If those close, then the control room should be fine. All the critical systems, power and com and stuff, link right in there, too, so it could stay operational."

"OK, then—" Ouri began, but Bill spoke over her.

"Unless they plant them all along the back wall, then maybe it would bring down the whole ridge."

"Then we're gonna have to make sure that they don't do that," Sammy replied.

"Great plan," Kris called from the landing above them. "I knew I should have stayed in bed."

Ouri wished that she could send the station personnel down the maglev to Landfall, or out the rear tunnel to the other side of the ridge, but too many people needed the air defenses to keep running. They had to hold the line.

A thundering roar came from outside the facility, and Ouri chuckled. "They're meeting Amy's welcoming committee out there now."

<*How many have you taken out?*> she asked Amy. Normally they would have a combat net run by an AI—or an NSAI in a pinch—that would manage tallies and ensure everyone had an up-to-date view of the battlefield.

Today, she would have to manage that work manually.

<*I think I've hit at least twenty of them. They were pretty careful about the beam turrets, but they didn't seem to expect a second layer of defenses. Plus side, there's a nice clear swath in front of the facility. They're gonna have to get closer to the guns to—*> she stopped.

<*What?*> Ouri asked.

<*Umm…they've taken out the Gatling guns…they hit them with some sort of cluster rockets that the guns couldn't deal with,*> Amy replied. <*Sorry.*>

Ouri sent an affirmative response and nodded to her teammates. "Defenses are down. They're coming."

"Faaack," Bill whispered, while Sammy sucked in a deep breath.

Ouri pulled the feed from the cameras on the tower above the facility, and watched as the Trisilieds soldiers crept across the smoking hillside leading up to the parking lot, taking cover behind the smattering of groundcars as they approached.

She could understand their hesitancy. The facility should have had additional layers of defense, but only so much could be built in eighteen years; most of the effort had been put into the fleet and orbital defenses.

After an agonizing three minutes of careful probing, the Trisilieds soldiers reached the facility's front doors and pulled them open.

<*Close your eyes,*> Ouri warned, uncertain how much light the armor's half-helmets would block.

As she expected, the enemy fired optical and sonic pulsers into the foyer, and she was pleasantly surprised to find that the helmets blocked both with reasonable efficiency.

As the pulsers flashed and wailed, an enemy squad breached the foyer. Ouri opened fire, and Bill and Sammy let loose with their shots a moment later.

None of them held back; their rifles' high-velocity kinetic rounds slamming into the fireteam's legs before the enemy could see them.

Most of the rounds bounced off the enemy's armor, but one of Bill's caught a weak point, and a Trissie fell. Ouri assumed he cried out in pain, but the sounds of weapons fire drowned it out.

The Trissies fanned out along the edges of the foyer and dropped prone behind a kiosk and a table, returning fire that was successfully absorbed by the CFT shields.

Ouri's team kept up their suppressive shots, and wore down the scant cover in moments, causing the enemies to fall back to the far corners of the foyer. Sammy leaned out to take a shot, and Ouri pulled her back an instant before a slug tore through the air where Sammy's head had been.

"Watch it; they're gonna try to draw us out now," she cautioned.

"Yeah! I can see that!" Sammy gasped as her face turned white.

"Don't worry, Sammy, keep your head and we'll get through this," Ouri said as she took aim at an enemy who was creeping along the wall, putting three solid rounds into his torso, and one in his neck. None of the shots penetrated his armor, but they were enough to send him racing back to cover.

Ouri estimated where he and at least one of his other teammates must be, and grabbed a grenade from her pack; she primed it and tossed it down the stairs, into the far corner of the foyer.

The timer she set on the grenade was spot on, and it detonated the instant it reached their position, the force of the explosion blowing out the foyer's windows, and flushing a hot wind up the stairs.

"Yeah! Got 'em!" Bill yelled.

"There's still another sixty or so out there," Ouri replied. "Don't get too excited yet."

INFILTRATE

STELLAR DATE: 04.01.8948 (Adjusted Years)
LOCATION: OGS *Britannica*
REGION: Stellar North of Carthage, New Canaan System

Jessica watched the battle unfold on the holotank as the Orion Guard fleets drifted closer to Carthage. She was impressed with how Symatra decimated the Trisilieds carriers, and thanked the stars when the ISF fleet came through their dark layer jump intact.

"What is their plan?" Admiral Fenton asked General Garza after the ISF fleet appeared above Carthage's poles. Garza had no answer, and the admiral's eyes darted to Jessica.

"Colonel! What is Richards's plan? If she can jump through the dark layer, so can the Hegemony fleet!" Admiral Fenton demanded.

Jessica saw Garza shake his head and she suspected that neither of them wanted a full-force Hegemony fleet present around Carthage. She shrugged innocently, and her suspicions were confirmed when Admiral Fenton glared at Garza.

"Involving them was a mistake. First they jump the gun taking out the Transcend fleet beyond the heliopause, and now this."

"The battle isn't over yet," Garza replied.

A minute later, a smattering of AST ships appeared near the main ISF fleet. In short order, the number of functioning Hegemony vessels approached zero, and Garza laughed.

"See, Admiral? No need to worry. Governor Richards has taken care of our little problem for us."

"You know what that means?" Fenton asked.

"Oh, I do! I do!" Jessica spoke up, drawing both men's attention.

Garza peered at her over his shoulder. "I bet you do. What is your purpose here? It's time you told us,"

"We just wanted a good view," Trevor said. "Heard your CIC was the best in the fleet, so we got ourselves captured to get in."

"You didn't get captured—" Garza began.

For the first time, the man began to look worried; it gave Jessica a perverse sense of pleasure to see it.

"Harry, status on the search!" Garza called out.

Jessica couldn't hear the AI's response, but by the look on the general's face, it wasn't good. She breathed a sigh of relief. Everything was still going according to plan—mostly. Getting caught wasn't what she'd had in mind, but it did get them into the CIC, and by now the pico packages that she and Trevor had deployed should have finished their tasks.

<*We ready to interface?*> she asked Iris.

<*We are green and good to go,*> the AI replied.

<*What about weapons?*> Jessica asked. When she and Trevor had been captured, the guards had taken their sidearms elsewhere. At present, the only weapons in the room were held by four soldiers in powered armor.

<*I didn't have enough for the soldiers. You're going to have to figure something out,*> Iris replied.

<*Are you serious?*> Jessica asked as she glanced at the closest guard. <*They're wearing a hundred kilos of armor! What are we going to do against them?*>

<*Sorry,*> Iris apologized. <*I said we were low on the picopackages and that you'd have to take out the guards. You didn't seem worried, so I assumed you had a plan.*>

Jessica sighed in her mind. <*I thought you meant the armor was still working, not that they had functional weapons, too. For an AI, you can be very unspecific at times.*>

<*So are we standing down?*> Iris asked. <*It's only a matter of time before they realize what I've done.*>

Jessica glanced around the room, recounting those present. Seven specialists on the far wall managing comm, a dozen scan officers to her left, a batch of ensigns that were prepared to function as backup coordination officers, the general, the admiral, a passel of colonels and majors, and Harry's central column.

And, of course, the four soldiers with pulse rifles and ballistic sidearms.

She gave Trevor a sidelong look. Even unarmored, he could take out one, maybe two of the soldiers. She had watched him take down enemies in powered armor before. Then an idea hit her and she reached a hand over to him, carful to maintain the fiction that her hands were still locked together by the restraining cuffs.

She touched his leg and made a direct Link.

<Trevor, what do you think about smashing that AI column?>

<Shouldn't be a problem, so long as none of the guards can hit me with anything more than a pulse before I get there,> Trevor replied. *<What's the deal?>*

<Low on pico, the guards are still one-hundred percent operational,> Jessica said with a mental sigh.

<Hey, not my fault!> Iris interjected. *<This stuff is still new and experimental. Wasn't easy to build an interface and hack this CIC—all while you two were just sitting there, I might add.>*

<I wasn't blaming anyone, I was just giving Trevor the facts.>

Trevor gave her a mental wink and a nod. *<Sure, hon. I buy it. I hear you have a planet for sale, too; real cheap.>*

<Shut up. I'll create a distraction—you make your move whenever it seems best.>

Jessica stood with a slight bounce and an embarrassed look. "I really gotta hit the ladies'," she whispered to the guard that spun and leveled his weapon at her chest. "Seriously, I've been holding it forever. I didn't want to go before, because I didn't want to miss anything, but now I know that if I don't get it over with, I'll have to run out during the grand finale."

The guard shook his head. "Sit."

"Are you serious?" Jessica asked, raising her voice. "I've gotta go number two! I'm going to shit my pants! It's gonna stink, too. Do you think the brass over there wants to smell poop during their moment of victory?"

<*Real classy,*> Iris commented.

"What is going on over there?" Admiral Fenton asked from the far side of the holotank.

"Admiral Fenton, sir. The prisoner needs to use the head," the soldier replied.

"What is this, primary school?" Garza growled without turning. "Go! Just don't take your eyes off her."

The soldier grabbed Jessica's shoulder, spun her about, and shoved her toward the door. She was impressed by his fluid movements in the powered armor, and a little worried that she didn't stand a chance against him.

They reached the door, and when the guard leaned forward to palm the panel, it all happened.

To her left, Jessica saw Trevor jump up and race across the room, lowering a shoulder as he closed on the column containing Harry's node. The guards were as quick as she feared, and two pulse blasts hit Trevor as he ran; though it wasn't enough to slow his three-hundred-twenty-kilogram mass as it slammed into the AI's column.

While Trevor was speeding across the room, Jessica crouched and wrapped an arm around one of her guard's arms, yanking his weapon toward another soldier.

She knew that if she tried to grasp and fire the weapon, it would discharge an electrical shock into her body. But slamming her fist into the guard's finger, forcing it past the trigger guard—that might work.

By some combination of shock and surprise, the maneuver worked, and Jessica managed to get the weapon to fire at the next guard; at the same moment, Iris killed the lights, holotanks, and all the consoles, just as Trevor smashed through Harry's column.

The guard whose weapon she had forced to fire jerked his arm, and sent Jessica flying—directly into General Garza. She cycled her vision to an IR/RF mix, and slammed an elbow into his jaw before flinging herself across the table at Admiral Fenton, who was drawing his sidearm.

Her boots hit him in the chest and throat, knocking the man to the ground. His sidearm went spinning, and Iris highlighted it on Jessica's vision.

<*Jess, it's some old ballistic relic. Chem only. Grab it!*>

Jessica launched herself across the floor and snatched the handgun. The thing had a serious heft to it, and looked like the mag would hold at least nine shots.

She put one into the chest of a man who was lunging at her—one of the colonels who had been standing at another holotank—and then a second round into an ensign who thought he could save the day.

Jessica scrambled toward Admiral Fenton and pressed the gun's barrel against the back of his head, finger on the trigger.

"Everyone *FREEZE!*" she screamed, satisfied to see the room fall silent while Iris brought the lights back up.

"What in the damned core do you think you're doing?" Garza yelled as Jessica pulled Fenton to his feet and backed against a wall.

One of the soldiers brought his rifle up and flipped its firing mode to a particle beam.

"Go for it," Jessica goaded the man. "My AI is watching your trigger fingers, and mine is on auto. You may get me, but the admiral here will bite it."

"Lower it!" Admiral Fenton barked at the soldier.

"No! Fire!" Garza countered. "We have a larger goal here than one man's life. Take her out."

This was where Jessica prayed her gamble would work. The entire time they had been sitting in the CIC, she had watched the general and admiral interact. She had also picked out which of the personnel in the room were on their separate staffs.

Without question, Admiral Fenton's people were in the majority. It made sense, since this was his flagship and his CIC. Garza, for all intents and purposes, was just along for the ride.

Even so, when the soldiers finally lowered their weapons, she breathed a long sigh of relief.

"Toss 'em," Trevor said as he walked toward the soldiers while rubbing his shoulder. "Helmets off."

The soldiers paused, but Fenton nodded and they complied.

Once the soldier's rifles were in a pile at his feet, the helmets beside them, Trevor approached one of the soldiers and drove a fist into the side of the man's head.

"Good aim with the rifle," he said as the man fell unconscious, his armor still holding him erect. "Too bad my fist is a better weapon. Now, one at a time, the rest of you three get out of your armor. You first," he said to the woman on the end.

Everyone in the room stood stock still, tense and unmoving, as, one after the other, the soldiers' armor split open. Then the men and women moved to the side of the room where the comm techs were standing.

"This is ridiculous," Garza said as he shook his head. "You can't stop what's happening here. Even if you kill us all, your people are doomed."

"Boy, you sure would like to know our plans, wouldn't you?" Jessica asked with a smirk, as Trevor crouched down over the pile of rifles and deposited a passel of nano on them to disable their bio-locks.

He stood a moment later with a rifle in each hand—one configured to fire pulse blasts, the other a particle beam.

"OK, Ogies, everyone over there, and on the floor. I want you bastards prone with your hands over your heads. You have ten seconds before I start shooting."

Trevor's tone seemed to convince everyone present that he was deadly serious, and before his allotted time was up, everyone in the room, excepting Garza and Fenton, was face down on the deck.

"You too," Jessica said to Fenton and gave him a shove toward the group on the floor.

Fenton didn't say a word, but his hate-filled gaze spoke volumes. Jessica nodded to Trevor, who reached out and slapped Garza across the back of the head.

Trevor's slap was like a punch to the smaller man, and Garza's head fell forward, slamming his face into the surface of the holotable.

"That was a bit harder than I wanted," Jessica said with a sigh.

"I didn't expect him to be so spindly," Trevor shrugged. "Thought he'd have spinal mods or something."

Jessica held out a hand, and Trevor tossed her a pulse rifle before picking up another. They approached the group of Orion Guard personnel on the ground, glanced at one another, and opened fire.

*****

"Hey, whoa," Usef said as he raised his hands. "I can see how you probably don't like interference, but this is a bit extreme."

"You're damn right I don't like interference," Phyla said with an ugly sneer. "So, which are you? Transcend or a colonist?"

Usef glanced around the engineering command center and saw that several specialists were holding weapons on Misha and Cargo.

"Great plan," Misha called out. "Sure glad we followed your lead."

Usef gave his best smile. "I don't know why you think we're colonists, or Sendies, for fucksakes, but we're not; we just transferred off another ship to augment the old man's staff. Look us up, we're on the roster."

"I looked you up, all right," Major Phyla replied. "Your orders seemed a bit off, so I tossed a tightbeam over to the *Sword of Orion*, and, sure enough, they've never heard of you."

"Major Phyla! We're running silent. No EMF at all; you've just breached a directive from the admiral. I'm going to have to report this…along with behavior unbecoming of an officer in the Guard. I'll leave out the part where you're holding a firearm on me, if you put it down right now."

Phyla cocked her head and widened her eyes in mock distress. "Oh, will you? Oh, *sir,* that would be so wonderful…. Now, drop your fucking sidearm and get on the ground!"

<*Iris was certain they wouldn't reach out to another ship,*> Jamie sighed in Usef's mind. <*I'll have to give her a hard time about that later.*>

<*So, are we ready? She's gonna blow my head off in five seconds.*>

<*I haven't received a confirmation from each of the HC's that Cargo and Misha placed…some of these guys may not go down,*> Jamie replied.

<*No time, do it,*> Usef ordered.

An instant later, all but four of the Orion Guard engineers fell. Cargo and Misha wasted no time in firing pulse blasts at the enemy while the element of surprise was on their side.

"Kinda thought our little fiction would hold up longer than that," Cargo said as he approached Usef. "We usually had better luck out in Perseus."

"Seriously?" Misha asked as he fired a pulse blast into the torso of an engineer he passed. "Have you forgotten half the shit we went through in Perseus?"

"Why'd you shoot that woman?" Usef scowled at Misha.

Misha shrugged. "She was moving. The HC probably didn't work on her, so she was faking. I shot her in the chest, not the head. She'll be fine."

"I'm not worried about her, just stay focused," Usef said. "No games, no heroic shit. Jamie is running through their logs looking for some issue we can fake that requires running a reset on some system that will explain why no one is communicating down here."

<*Got it,*> Jamie announced triumphantly. <*They recently had a new NSAI node installed down here, and I just knocked it out—though it wasn't easy. Their AIs barely live up to the name, poor bastards, but their NSAIs are top notch. Remind me of the super-nodes back in Sol.*>

"Good. I lifted Phyla's tokens when we took her out, so I can mimic her for basic status reports—though I didn't get anything that will let me access higher-level feeds," Usef added.

<*I'm in the nav systems,*> Hank announced. <*Tapping into helm control. Jamie, you're going to have to knock out node 14.19.12 when I give the word, or the bridge will be able to work around me.*>

<*Got it,*> Jamie replied. <*Just waiting on the word from Iris.*>

"I've got the door," Cargo said as he walked to the command center's main entrance. "I may have to let insistent people in, so be on your toes."

"Never understood that saying," Misha said as he moved to the room's rear entrance. "I think that being on your toes would just be painful and distracting."

* * * * *

<*Linkup from Jamie and the team yet?*> Jessica asked Iris.

<*No, not a thing; but there's a big NSAI outage in a new node down there, so my money is on them making a mess of things to stay off the radar…sort of,*> Iris replied.

<*Sort of?*> Trevor asked.

Iris twisted her avatar's lips in their minds. <*Well, a rapid response unit is on its way to help them repair the NSAI node, so they're about to get some company.*>

<*Can we tell them we're ready to go somehow?*> Jessica asked.

<*Not sure how. Like I said, I can't reach them.*>

Trevor brought a system up on the holotank. "What about this; can we trigger it remotely, say, in the engineering command center?"

"Trevor, you're a genius!" Jessica grinned.

"I do have my moments," Trevor replied. "I don't know how to trigger a remote fire alarm, though, but the system doesn't have a lot of security on it."

<*Fire suppression systems rarely do,*> Iris responded and the holotable changed its view to show the status of the engineering command center. <*But if I flip this bit right here, and that one there, we suddenly have access to their heat and chem sniffers, and voila! There's now a fire in the engineering bay.*>

Red strobes began flashing on the bulkheads, and a call went out over the ship's audible announcement system. "Fire fire fire! Say again, fire in the ECC! All response crews to emergency stations; secondary ECC, prepare to come online."

"Hmm…" Jessica mused, "that may have been too much."

Trevor gave her a broad smile. "Well, at least there's no way they can miss that."

* * * * *

"What?" Cargo asked. "What fire?"

"Maybe one of these assholes is still conscious and triggered it," Misha suggested.

"It's the signal from Jessica," Usef said. "Let's make sure none of those teams get in, and let the AIs steer this tub out of here."

<*Firing starboard grav thrusters,*> Hank announced. <*Give me two minutes, and we'll have a clear path to boost out of here.*>

"I bet that captain on the bridge is having kittens right now," Misha chuckled.

<*That might be us in a moment,*> Jamie cut in. <*They're bringing that secondary ECC online, and it has direct access to nav and helm. I don't know if we can work around it.*>

<*There has to be a cutoff system to revert back to the ECC,*> Hank said, and Usef knew the AIs were talking over the team's channel for the humans' benefit.

"I see a system here," Usef offered, "but we don't have the encryption keys to access it. The damn thing's locked out."

<*Need a hand?*> a new voice asked over the Link.

<*Nance?*> Cargo asked. <*Shouldn't you guys be EM-silent?*>

<*The way the* Britannica *is jerking around trumps that. It looks like you're fighting for helm control.*>

<*That's putting it mildly,*> Iris replied in clipped tones.

<*Have you tried this?*> Nance asked, and suddenly the primary override system Usef was attempting to brute-force his way into unlocked.

<*Well, shit,*> Usef said as he activated the cut-over, granting full helm control to Hank.

<There you go, the ship no longer looks like a drunken duck trying to keep up with the flock,> Nance announced. *<We're shadowing you out of the fleet.>*

"General Quarters, General Quarters, we have intruders in the primary ECC," the audible systems boomed. "Maintain low EMF ship-wide—the fleet is still on target."

"Well, looks like we're going to get to do our part now," Cargo said with a grim smile.

<Just don't get your head blown off,> Hank said brusquely. *<This'll be a real short flight, otherwise.>*

* * * * *

<I've managed to get into their external comm arrays,> Iris announced. *<Though the ship's secondary AI is fighting me hard.>*

"They have a secondary one?" Trevor asked as he took up a position behind a holotable, two rifles aimed at the CIC's door.

<Yes, and a third, actually. I really don't understand how their duties work, but since they're not much more than L2 humans, I can see why a single one can't run a ship like this.>

<Any word from Tanis?> Jessica asked.

<Not yet, but that shouldn't stop us from getting out of here,> Iris replied.

"We're not going anywhere," Trevor said as the CIC's door began to glow.

"Going to have to hope that they get this bird out of the fleet before Tanis does her big move, then," Jessica replied grimly as she checked her rifles, and set them to fire kinetics at whomever came through the door first.

FALL BACK

STELLAR DATE: 04.01.8948 (Adjusted Years)
LOCATION: Landfall Space/Air Traffic Control Center
REGION: Knossos Island Carthage, New Canaan System

Ouri shook her head as she fired another round from her weapon's slug thrower at an onrushing enemy soldier. Whoever was in charge out there had no compunctions about spending their soldier's lives in an attempt to take the SATC tower.

If she were a betting woman, she'd put money on the company CO being on the transport Henderson had shot down, and that some fresh-out-of-OCS second lieutenant was running the show out there.

The enemy soldiers fell back again, but this time, no further sounds came from outside. Ouri counted to thirty—that was the threshold she had set in her mind for how long it would take them to move heavy weapons to the fore.

It was a guess, really; the external cameras were all down, and the enemy had set off three EM blasts, knocking out most of her nanoprobes.

Her count hit thirty, and she signaled for Sammy and Bill to get up to the third floor. She peered out from behind the CFT, prepared to give them cover, when her fears were confirmed.

The Trisilieds were setting up a crew-served kinetic repeater right outside the facility. It would tear the staircase to shreds, and, more importantly, anyone who was on it.

She raced up the stairs to the third level landing as the weapon opened fire and ripped into the stairs, sending stone and plascrete flying into the air. After fifteen seconds of fire, the weapons wound down.

The dust and smoke was still thick in the air as the enemy, three dozen at least, rushed in at full-force, all firing on the third floor landing.

Ouri and her team scampered back from the edge as the concentrated firepower began to blow holes clear through the landing.

"Well," Ouri gasped as they fell back into the hall, "at least they can't take the stairs anymore."

She floated some probes over the ruined staircase, and saw the enemy scaling the wall to get into the second floor corridor. With a grim smile, Ouri dropped a pair of grenades over what remained of the landing, and ducked back as the blast sounded, kicking up more dust and debris.

As the room cleared, she could see that the enemy had fallen back once more, and wondered if any had managed to reach the second level.

A minute later, an explosion in the rear stairwell answered her question.

<Rear access turrets just picked up motion!> Amy called out over the Link. *<I don't read our IFF tags out there. Should I light 'em up?>*

<Only if it looks like they've found the rear exit,> Ouri replied. *<No reason to pointing it out early.>*

<Shit, yeah, they're right on top of it. I'll hold 'em off as long as I can.>

"Kris, Sammy," Ouri called out to her two teammates who were inspecting the rear stairwell, "get back up to the control room. Trissies are coming in the back door."

"Shit! Seriously?" Bill asked. "There goes our way out."

<Murry! Any chance we can get a hand here soon?> Ouri called out to the Planetary Management AI. *<We're about to become the mystery meat in a Trissie sandwich.>*

<*I've updated Brandt with your situation,*> Murry replied in clipped tones. <*Things are tight everywhere, but she's going to see what she can do.*>

<*Tell her I'll buy her beers for the rest of her life,*> Ouri replied.

"OK, Bill," she said audibly. "It's just you and me on the crew-served gun now. You keep the ammo coming, and an eye to the back stairwell. They're gonna hit us from both ends. Lob 'nades down the hall if they bunch up."

"Yeah, sure," Bill said breathlessly as sweat poured down his face.

"Hey, Bill," Ouri grabbed his shoulder. "We're gonna make it. Brandt is coming, and we're winning in space. We just have to hold out for a little longer."

Bill met her eyes and he swallowed before nodding. "Understood, Colonel."

"Good, now let's give these asshats hell."

EXFILTRATE

STELLAR DATE: 04.01.8948 (Adjusted Years)
LOCATION: OGS *Britannica*
REGION: Stellar North of Carthage, New Canaan System

"ISF fleet just appeared on scan!" Usef called out as he fired a full clip at the enemy soldiers pouring through the ECC's entrance. "They're gonna do it. Full boost!"

<Get bow-side of something solid,> Hank ordered. *<I'm going to kill gravity aft of the CIC and do 20gs.>*

Usef scampered around the holotable he was using for cover, and prayed that Cargo and Misha managed to get situated before Hank killed the artificial gravity systems. The stomach-twisting feeling of weightlessness hit him, and a moment later, the ship's engines dumped billions of exajoules into space.

His back slammed into the table, and a sharp edge sliced his skin open. Usef staunched the flow of blood with his nano, and then peered around the table to see how the enemy soldiers had fared.

With 'down' now being the aft end of the ECC, most of enemy soldiers had 'fallen' a dozen meters; though many were in armor, and weathered the fall without too much trouble.

Still, they were now shooting straight up with little cover—only the bodies of no few of their fellow OG crew that had fallen on top of them.

Usef felt a little sorry for the unconscious engineers that had fallen as far as thirty meters to the back of the bay, but the choices were limited. Either fall, or get eaten by the things in the dark layer.

He knew what he would have picked.

Usef saw shots lance down from two other positions as he opened fire on the enemy soldiers once more. *<Glad you guys*

survived that little maneuver,> he told the shooters over the combat net.

<*Yeah, thanks for the whole second's worth of warning, Hank,*> Misha grumbled.

Jamie chuckled. <*He gave you three seconds—plenty, even for a slow organic like you.*>

<*This is why I've never opted for an AI,*> Misha grunted. <*You guys have the worst attitudes.*>

Cargo barked a laugh. <*That's a great one coming from you, Misha.*>

Several soldiers at the bottom of the bay had surrendered, throwing their weapons down and pulling their helmets off. Misha fired two more shots down on a pocket that was holding out.

<*Yeah? I have a great attitude! I saved your asses back when you first showed up in Perseus. I've been* ***very*** *helpful.*>

<*At complaining, maybe,*> Cargo responded.

Usef shook his head as he fired a focused pulse blast into an unarmored member of the fire response team that was peeking through the ECC's rear entrance. <*Seriously? Is this the best time for this little chat?*>

<*Sorry, Colonel,*> Misha chuckled. <*It helps us focus.*>

<*You guys want a hand?*> Admiral Evans's voice joined into their conversation. <*Or are you having too much fun in there?*>

<*Admiral Evans, sir, your help is always welcome,*> Jamie replied.

<*Good. Patch me through to their all-ship net and audible systems, if you have them.*>

Jamie sent an affirmative signal, and a moment later, Joe's voice boomed over the ship's address system.

"This is Admiral Joseph Evans of the ISF *Daedalus*. Your fleet is destroyed or disabled. You've lost this battle. Stand down and prepare to be boarded. If you want to put up a fight, be sure to say hello to the battalion of ISF Marines who are cutting their way through your hull as I speak."

"He has a way with words, doesn't he?" Cargo commented.

Misha laughed as the final group of soldiers at the bottom of the bay threw down their weapons and pulled off their helmets. "I really like you ISF guys. You're a ton of fun!" he remarked.

<Looks like you guys made it,> Jessica's voice joined the combat net.

<Yes, ma'am,> Usef replied. *<Got a bit hairy. How was it up there?>*

<Don't be ma'am-ing me,> Jessica replied. *<You outrank me now, remember?>*

<No, ma'am, I don't.> Usef grinned over the combat net.

<Fine. We got our man, and the admiral of their fleet, too. All nice and locked down. We'll have intel coming out of our ears before long,> Jessica replied.

"Good thing," Usef whispered to himself as Iris reactivated the AG systems and the shift in gravity rolled him over. "I have a feeling that we're gonna need it."

THE STAND

STELLAR DATE: 04.01.8948 (Adjusted Years)
LOCATION: Landfall Space/Air Traffic Control Center
REGION: Knossos Island Carthage, New Canaan System

Ouri hauled the crew-served gun up to the first landing of the staircase to the fourth floor. She had hoped to hold the corridor below, but there were just too many enemy soldiers coming up at both ends of the hall. Bill was already up there, having retreated that far after his right leg was burned off from the knee down.

Biofoam covered the wound, and he held his rifle ready, a look of grim determination on his face. She gave him a solemn look. They would hold out as long as they could. There was nothing else they could do.

Even though they had to run into point-blank kinetic weapons fire, the enemy still came at them. Before long, a dozen bodies lay at the base of the stairs.

They just had to hold out a little longer. The team upstairs was still taking out enemy assault craft near Landfall and on the other side of Carthage. If the SATC fell, thousands would still die.

The Marines are coming…just have to hold a little bit longer.

Ouri glanced at the ammo box for her gun, and then her eyes met Bill's. The box was empty; the fifty rounds on the current string were all that remained.

"When it runs dry, you get up the stairs," Bill said. "I'll hold them here as long as I can."

"Fuck, Bill. No. I'll stay, you get up there—"

Her words were interrupted by another group of soldiers dashing into view in the space below them. Ouri opened fire with the gun and took them out, though not before a shot tore through her armor below her right breast.

She fell back, catching sight of the last rounds feeding through the railgun as Bill screamed, firing into the enemy soldiers below.

Both Bill and the final soldier fell, and Ouri pulled herself to Bill's side. She let out a small cry; the left half of his skull was missing.

She grabbed his rifle and turned away, laying prone on the landing, using the crew-served gun for cover. She felt biofoam filling her wound as a new onslaught from the enemy began.

She screamed at the enemy below her, firing the last rounds from both magazines. Then a blinding light flashed in her mind, and she knew no more.

* * * * *

The last of the enemy coming up the rear corridor fell, and Sammy traded a long, weary look with Kris as Amy called out from behind them.

"They're here! The Marines are here!"

"About fucking time," Kris said as she fell back against the wall.

<*Ouri, the Marines are here! Ouri, we're saved!*> Sammy called out to the Colonel, relief filling her mental voice.

When no response came, she stood and looked across the consoles at Amy. "I can't raise the colonel, can you?"

Amy met her eyes, and she shook her head slowly.

Sammy didn't wait another moment—she dashed across the control room and out into the hall. She sped down its darkened length, taking a moment to wonder when the power went out, before skidding to a halt and running down the stairs, nearly smashing into the barrel of a Marine's rifle.

"Easy," he said softly, and Sammy's eyes followed his to the bodies of Bill and Ouri, crumpled on the landing.

"NO!" Sammy screamed and dropped to her knees. Sobs wracked her body and she felt a hand on her shoulder.

"I'm sorry," a voice croaked. "If we'd just…."

Sammy looked up to see none other than General Brandt herself standing over Ouri's body, her helmet on the ground at her feet.

Tears flowed down the hard-bitten Marine's face as she fell and leaned against the wall. "Ouri, I'm so sorry…."

DARK LAYER

STELLAR DATE: 04.01.8948 (Adjusted Years)
LOCATION: ISS *I2*
REGION: Stellar North of Carthage, New Canaan System

Tanis reconnected with Admiral Myra, who looked rather put out at being cut off. "Have you changed your mind?" the Trisilieds commander asked.

"I have not," Tanis shook her head and let out a long breath as the anger flowed out of her. She just felt tired—tired, and anxious for all this to be over. "I know about the Orion Guard ships bearing down on us; they won't survive this engagement, either. This is your last chance."

Admiral Myra's eyes widened and her face blanched. "How…"

Tanis waved her hand dismissively. "We haven't just been trapped in this system. We know much of what is going on in the Inner Stars and in Orion space."

"Nice bluff," Admiral Myra laughed. "You almost had me for a moment. Very well; if you won't surrender, and you know about the Orion Guard, then what happens next won't surprise you."

This time, it was Admiral Myra who cut the communication.

<*You always do lay it on too thick,*> Angela commented.

<*Or not thick enough.*>

As though on cue, the Orion Guard fleet appeared. One group of over fifty thousand ships lay three hundred thousand kilometers north of Carthage, and another was equidistant below it.

Tanis opened a comm channel with Sabrina. <*Do you have him?*>

Light-lag made the reply take several seconds to come back to the *I2;* when it did, the message was what Tanis had hoped to hear.

<We have him. We’re clear.>

Tanis sent the signal to Fleet Groups 3 and 4, and several seconds later the ships appeared on scan—not across the system guarding the shipyards at the gas giants, but above and below the Orion Guard fleets.

Their combined three thousand ships were laughably outnumbered by the Orion Guard, but that wouldn’t matter. If all went well, they wouldn’t even fire a shot—at least not the sort of shot that the Guard ships expected.

<ISF Fleet. Order B99-4329.11. Open it up,> Tanis sent the command, and the fleet AIs and captains unlocked and opened special orders they didn’t even know they had, directing them to activate beam weapons that they didn’t know their ships possessed.

The timing needed to be precise. Once the orders were confirmed across the fleet, Tanis set the countdown.

Then she held her breath.

Despite her words of certainty to Finaeus, she really had no idea if this would work. Bob and Earnest were very certain they could close the rifts after they made them—not one hundred percent, but very.

Tanis would take it. If they were wrong, then this war would end with all their deaths, and that would be enough for her.

The count hovering above the holotank ran down to zero, and specialized graviton beams lanced out from every one of Joe’s and Sanderson’s ships, and into positions around the enemy fleets. Space-time began to warp, and darkness blotted out the light of Canaan Prime.

The blackness opened up all around the Trisilieds and Orion Guard ships, and then things came boiling out into space.

Optical sensors couldn't see them, but the creatures—if they could be called that—created silhouettes on other spectra that made them visible to scan. They were elongated and amorphous. Some were only a few hundred meters long; others, over a hundred kilometers.

Tendrils of darkness rippled out from the things and wrapped around the enemy ships, cutting through shields and hulls alike. Scan couldn't even make a guess as to what the creatures we made of, but Earnest had told Tanis that he believed it was a combination of exotic forms of matter, and energy that had never been seen in the natural physical universe.

Tanis wondered if the things had been constructed by the ascended AIs in the Core, or if those AIs had found the things and moved them around humanity's stars to keep them in check.

"Shit," Sera whispered. "They're obliterating the ships."

Tanis nodded. "That's the plan."

Not all of the enemy ships were being destroyed. Some were boosting away, fleeing the rifts to the dark layer as fast as they could—but many were not fast enough.

One massive dreadnaught, almost a rival for the *I2* in mass, raced toward the ISF ships, and it looked as though it would escape the creatures, when one of the hundred-kilometer things appeared to leap across space, and completely envelop the ship.

"OK," Tanis said. "That's getting a bit too close. Time to close it up."

<Agreed,> Bob replied. *<If they reach the planet, they could consume its mass in a day.>*

Tanis watched as Bob activated one of the *I2*'s sensor grids to emit a signal that drove the creature back toward the rifts, leaving the twisted wreck of the carrier in its wake. She passed a command to the fleets, and all the ships followed suit, pushing the things back into the rift—many of which dragged the ships of the Orion and Trisilieds fleets along with them.

As the creatures and their prey disappeared back into the dark layer, and the ISF ships disabled their beams that held the rifts open, Tanis surveyed the battlespace.

Of the hundred thousand Orion ships, only two thousand remained intact; though ten times that number were scattered around Carthage, twisted and ruined. She saw that Admiral Myra's flagship was still present, and hailed the enemy commander.

It took half a minute before Myra's visage appeared on the holotank. Her hair was disheveled, and her cheeks were streaked with tears. Wide, staring eyes gazed out at Tanis as her mouth worked soundlessly.

"How…?" she finally managed to ask.

To which Tanis only replied, "Surrender."

Myra's eyes fell and she nodded slowly. "I yield."

GENERAL'S DECEPTION

STELLAR DATE: 04.02.8948 (Adjusted Years)
LOCATION: OGS *Similcarum*
REGION: 120AU from Canaan Prime, New Canaan System

General Garza felt as though the deck had dropped out from under him as he watched the destruction of the Orion Guard fleet, followed by the surrender of the remaining Trisilieds ships.

So many lives lost in such a short time. He had sent in what should have been an overwhelming force—even with the Hegemony ships attacking hours ahead of schedule, and even with the Canners possessing picobombs, it should have been an easy win.

There was still some chance that the Trisilieds ground forces could capture someone significant and force a surrender, but the odds of that were astronomically low.

It was far more likely that his ship would be detected as it drifted beyond the system's heliopause.

"Helm, set a course for the Transcend's jump gate. Let's make use of it before the Canners retake it."

He didn't wait for a response before leaving the bridge and retreating to his cabin.

Garza had to admit that Tanis Richards's use of the dark layer creatures was a brilliant tactic. One that had been tried before—though not successfully, as far as he knew.

In every instance he was aware of, the creatures were not so easily sent back into the dark layer. In one case, they never were; a star had died as a result, and an ever-growing region of space around it was interdicted.

Perhaps, once this war was over, he would use whatever technology the Canners had come up with to clean up that mess.

As he took a ladder down to the officer's deck, Garza wondered what things his clone may have learned before it died. He had looked forward to merging his thoughts with it and gaining its experiences—a euphoric experience that he quite enjoyed, notwithstanding the new things he'd learn.

He did hope that his clone had died a quick death, consumed by the creatures. Better that than to be captured by the Canners—though he knew that they would learn little through the torture they would surely employ. The clone did not possess his most important memories. Even so, he would not wish such a fate on anyone; especially himself.

He had read of Tanis Richards's brutality when she was an officer in the Terran Space Force. She was not a woman to be trifled with—as his defeat here showed all too clearly.

Garza palmed the door to his cabin open, and crossed the room to his small bar, where he pulled a bottle of brandy out of its case and poured himself four fingers' worth of the light brown liquid.

He swirled it in the glass, enjoying the aroma before throwing it back in two gulps. He poured another and sat at his desk. He would need to go to Kirkland directly with this news. The praetor would not be happy to learn that their plan had failed so spectacularly.

It may be wise to send in a clone.

DISCOVERY

STELLAR DATE: 04.02.8948 (Adjusted Years)
LOCATION: Wreckage of Trisilieds Halcyon Class Carrier
REGION: In Orbit of Hannibal, Carthage, New Canaan System

<*Cary,*> Saanvi called out into the void via the Link, praying her suit's signal could reach far enough to connect to her sister, if she were still there. <*Cary?*>

She had opened her eyes and immediately closed them again. The scene around her didn't bear mental processing; yet she couldn't keep herself from stepping through the logical path that brought her to her current location.

Saanvi remembered the last few moments before the *Illyria* slammed into the Trisilieds' Halcyon Class carrier, apparently making a large enough hole for the RMs tailing their ship to go through and destroy it. Cary had withdrawn from her mind, leaving her feeling profoundly empty and alone—rather like she did right now.

Their eyes had locked, and their lips whispered their love for one another before the chairs snapped on their stasis fields. The stasis fields should have held them until rescue, but the field could not be maintained from within—which meant that the external systems must have been destroyed.

And now she found herself here: still strapped to her chair from the bridge, but inside what must be one of the *Illyria*'s machine shops—or maybe it was one from the Trisilieds carrier. The chance that Cary was anywhere nearby was slim, to say the least. With any luck, her sister was still in stasis, blissfully unaware that they were trapped within a twisted cocoon of ship guts that was in a slowly decaying orbit around Hannibal.

<*Sahn?*> the response was weak; not a Link connection, but an RF signal her suit was picking up and sending into her mind.

<*Hey, little sis,*> Saanvi replied. <*Gods in Swargaloka, it's good to hear your voice.*>

<*Voice…yeah. I'm pretty sure I'm not breathing right now; good thing this suit can still oxygenate my blood directly,*> Cary said, her mental tone wan.

<*My readout says my left lung is punctured, but my right is working…sorta,*> Saanvi replied. <*Pain suppressors are also only kinda working.*>

<*I hear you,*> Cary's mental voice carried a note of desperation. <*Who's stupid idea was this, anyway?*>

<*Beats me,*> Saanvi thought with a smile. <*Glad we did it, though. If those carriers had made it to Carthage…*>

Neither girl spoke for a moment, and then the thought crept into Saanvi's mind that Cary was gone.

<*Cary! Are you still there?*>

<*Yeah, just needed to not think for a minute. I keep worrying that we lost, anyway; that our home…that Carthage is gone…*>

Saanvi knew that fear; it was in her mind, as well. She pushed it away. She had to be strong for her little sister.

<*No way, Cary. Our mom is Admiral Tanis Richards—the most serious badass in the galaxy. Nothing can take her down.*>

<*I hope we did her proud,*> Cary replied, her voice growing faint as she spoke. It took Saanvi a moment to realize that it wasn't signal degradation, but rather her sister slipping into unconsciousness.

<*Cary!*> Saanvi called out. <*You stay awake, you keep talking! I'm your big sister, I'm ordering you to!*>

A faint chuckle entered her mind. <*I'm the lieutenant; you're just an ensign. You can't order me to do anything…I just need to sleep for a minute…*>

<*I can, too!*> Saanvi called. <*Big sisters trump rank. You stay awake, no sleeping!*>

<*OK…sis…*>

<*Cary!*> Saanvi screamed with her mind, willing her suit's signal to amplify and somehow wake her sister. A sob escaped her lips, and the movement sent a wave of fire through her body as torn ligaments pulled at broken bones. She gasped from the agony, and then held her breath, forcing her heart to still.

<*Cary?*> she whispered into the darkness again.

Silence was the only response, and Saanvi took long, slow breaths, desperate not to cry—she knew that if she cried, the pain would make her pass out, and she may never wake again. She wasn't going to hide from the darkness again like that. This time, she would be awake and fighting.

The thought made her open her eyes—and that moment was one of the happiest of her life. Through the twisted metal, she saw a light flash in the distance.

<*Hey!*> she called out over her suit's radio, broadcasting on the ISF's emergency signal. She suddenly realized that she hadn't checked to see if her chair or her suit's emergency beacon worked—neither did.

She sent out a manual signal on the emergency channels, and then the worry hit her that these may not be New Canaan rescuers coming for her, but the enemy. She almost stopped transmitting, but her fear of dying alone in the dark overcame her, and she screamed across the radio for help, until the most welcome sound she had ever heard came into her mind.

<*Easy now; we have a fix on you, we'll get you out.*>

The voice was male, warm, and encouraging. Saanvi felt her fears fall away, and she remembered her sister.

<*I'm fine! Find Cary. She's nearby, but she's not responding anymore!*>

<*Cary? Cary Richards?*> the man replied, his voice anxious and excited at the same time.

<*Yes! I'm Saanvi Richards, please find her!*>

There was a moment's silence, and Saanvi imagined a thousand things that could have happened to her rescuer.

<*I think I have a fix on her. I'm sending a crew for her, and I'm coming in for you. Hold tight.*>

RESCUE

STELLAR DATE: 04.02.8948 (Adjusted Years)
LOCATION: ISS *I2*
REGION: High Orbit over Carthage, New Canaan System

<*They found them!*> Angela cried into Tanis's mind. <*They're alive. S&R is taking them to the* Argos*!*>

Tanis sat bolt upright, the realization that she had passed out in Captain Espensen's ready room taking a second to dawn on her. <*Get a shuttle ready, I'm coming to the upper dorsal bay!*>

Tanis was already out the door, dashing through the bridge as she replied, and called out to Rachel Espensen as she passed, "They found them! They're alive!"

Cheers erupted behind her as she raced down the short corridor to the bridge's foyer. She barely sketched a wave to Priscilla on her plinth as she dashed through.

<*Maglev is waiting,*> Priscilla sent her way. <*It will take you right to the bay.*>

<*Thanks!*> Tanis replied breathlessly.

<*Joe is on his way, too,*> Angela supplied. <*He's bringing the* Daedalus *right through the debris field to the* Argos.>

Tanis allowed herself a smile; perhaps the first in the day since the end of the battle with the invaders.

<*Cheater! The* I2 *won't fit in there, no way, no—though he better be careful. The* Daedalus *will be a tight fit, too.*>

Tanis took a moment to look up where Cary and Saanvi had been found. It was deep within a section of the final carrier they had destroyed. Like much of the wreckage from that stage of the battle, the debris was in a low, decaying orbit around Hannibal. She flipped to the portion of the report describing the girls' conditions, steeling herself for what she would see.

Tears formed in her eyes, and she placed a hand over her mouth, attempting to stifle a gasp, when she saw the images. Both of the girls' bodies were still in their chairs from the bridge, but neither was in stasis. Their faces were misshapen from broken cheekbones, and both their jaws were dislocated. Their formfitting environmental suits revealed sunken chests and broken hipbones.

The onsite rescuers' report estimated that they had suffered multiple impacts in excess of 100*g*s. Only their cranial implants—a part of their L2 elevation—had kept their skulls from collapsing, keeping their brains safe.

The sob Tanis had been trying to hold back escaped her throat just as the maglev doors closed and gave her a private space to let her grief overcome her. She prayed to whatever gods may exist in the depths of space that her girls hadn't suffered brain damage.

She reopened the report and saw that Saanvi was conscious, though just barely, and had related that Cary was communicating just a few minutes before their rescue. That was a good sign—though it certainly didn't mean that all was well.

Tanis pushed those worries from her mind. She had to hope for the best. The girls' bodies could be rebuilt—though that much damage would take some time to recover from—and they were strong, and their neural networks were recently imaged. It would be possible to recover from even moderate brain damage, if needed.

A new report came in from the S&R crew that the girls were safely in stasis pods. A shuttle was taking them to the *Argos*—with an ETA of forty minutes.

The maglev car stopped at the docking bay, and Tanis raced to the shuttle, her only thought that it would take her three hours to reach the *Argos* where it rested deep in the debris field, and she needed to be present when her daughters awoke.

A thought flashed into her mind that she was being selfish. She had work to do, prisoners to interrogate, defenses to review. Nearly everyone in New Canaan had lost family in the last two days. What made her so special that she could run off like this?

<I'll keep things running in your absence, and Jason is governor now. He has things in hand on Carthage,> Bob spoke into her mind. *<You need to put these worries to rest, and go see your daughters. Your work here is just beginning.>*

<Thank you,> Tanis managed to reply.

<Be careful in there,> Bob advised, as the ramp to the pinnace raised even as Tanis dashed up its length into the ship. *<Not all of the disabled enemy ships are surrendering quietly.>*

Tanis nodded in response as she dropped into the small cockpit's pilot's chair, and ran an abbreviated pre-flight check before signaling for clearance. The *I2*'s space traffic control NSAI gave it, and she lanced out into the night, diving toward Hannibal and the hospital ship that would soon receive her daughters.

* * * * *

Tanis clutched Joe's hand as they watched through the window while the autodoc worked on Cary's body under the guidance of a team of surgeons. Saanvi was already out of surgery—her bones reset and organs repairing. It would take days for them to properly reknit—there was only so much rapid change a human body could undergo. It still needed to grow its own cells.

She had considered instructing the doctors to replace much of her girls' ruined bodies with artificial components—it would make their recovery that much faster—but she decided against it. That was their decision to make, and she could wait until they healed organically and she could speak with them.

In the room, one of the surgeons nodded, and the machine wrapped around Cary's head retracted the hundreds of tendrils from her skull. He turned and looked at them through the window, giving a firm nod followed by a thumbs-up.

Tanis sagged into Joe. "Thank the stars," she whispered.

Joe stroked her arm then pulled her into an embrace. "They're young, they're strong; we'll have them back with us in no time."

The surgeon exited the room and approached the pair.

"She's in good shape. Her neural lattice held up well against the impacts, and she only lost three percent of her brain-tissue. Most of it was in muscle control regions, so she'll have a bit of work to do relearning how to walk, and trouble controlling her left hand for a bit, but that should be it."

"Cognitive functionality?" Tanis asked anxiously.

"Should be fine," the surgeon replied. "I can't say with one hundred percent certainty, of course, but we had her neural network on file, and as best we can tell while she's unconscious, all appears to be firing as it should be."

"Thank you, doctor," Joe said and shook the man's hand, while Tanis turned back toward the window and watched as the other doctors worked on Cary's remaining injuries.

<*Saanvi is waking up,*> Angela informed them

Tanis glanced at Joe. "I'll go, you stay here."

Joe shook his head. "Cary is in good hands, let's make sure Saanvi gets a full welcome from both of us when she wakes."

* * * * *

Saanvi felt consciousness return slowly. It didn't hurt as much as she expected, but she worried that pain would return to assault her at any moment. She flipped through her most recent memories, trying to recall where she would be. She remembered the collision, waking up in the dark, reaching out to Cary, and then the rescue.

Cary.

She had to know if her sister was OK. That was worth opening her eyes for. She struggled to do so, but found that she couldn't raise her eyelids. She suspected that there had been some reconstructive surgery. Maybe she'd have eyes like her mother now.

As if her thoughts summoned her, Tanis's voice reached her ears.

"Saanvi, we're here."

"And your sister is OK," Joe's voice followed after. "The S&R teams found you just in time. You did good calling out for help when you did."

Saanvi tried to speak and found that her lips could move, but her voice was a thin rasp. Something touched her lips and her mother's voice came to her.

"Drink this."

The cool liquid washed down her parched throat, almost hurting as it first made contact, then numbing and soothing as it went. Saanvi took a second pull from the straw and then tried to speak again.

"Cary's safe, then? Her brain?" she asked.

"The doctors are confident that all will be well with her when she wakes," Joe said.

Saanvi noted her mother's silence and knew that Tanis felt as she did—they would worry after Cary until she was speaking to them, and they could tell for themselves that she was undamaged.

"Did we win?" Saanvi asked, and then she realized that they must have won if they were all talking.

"We did," Tanis replied before she could amend her question. "We lost a lot of good people, but we won. Carthage and New Canaan are safe."

Saanvi nodded silently. That was what she needed to hear. They had won, they were safe, her sister would be well. Everything could go back to how it was.

She drifted into a peaceful sleep, dreaming of a happy breakfast with her family around their kitchen table, laughing and smiling as they talked about what the future would now hold.

NEW BEGINNINGS

STELLAR DATE: 04.06.8948 (Adjusted Years)
LOCATION: Forward Emitter Lounge, ISS *I2*
REGION: In Orbit of Hannibal, Carthage, New Canaan System

"They'll have had observers out at the edge of the system." Joe said as he and Tanis sat at the bar in the *I2*'s little-known lounge above the ramscoop emitter.

Even though the ship was now built for war, and the ramscoop wasn't needed to ply vast interstellar spaces, the scoop techs had protected their little refuge, and Tanis had supported that initiative.

Besides, no one mixed a drink like their favorite servitor, Steve.

"Of that there is little doubt," Tanis replied and leaned into her husband. "How did we come to this, Joe? I'm going to go down in history as the greatest mass murderer, tyrant, dictator of all time. Parents are going to scare their children with tales of Tanis the Destroyer, who will unleash the horrors of the dark on them if they're not good."

"I think you're being a bit melodramatic, dear," Joe replied as he stroked her hair. "Maybe Tanis the Marauder, but certainly not the Destroyer."

"Joe!" Tanis sat up and gazed crossly into his eyes. "I'm serious! What are we going to do?"

"Follow the plan you laid out while we were still coming here. We knew this could happen—Bob saw it as the most likely eventuality. If you want to be known as the savior of humanity and not its worst villain, then you need to see this through, and win."

"The plan…" Tanis whispered. "The plan saw us lose nearly a hundred thousand people in one day. In one day, Joe! And Ouri—"

She stopped, her voice catching. She didn't trust herself to speak further; people were already looking in her direction.

"I know," Joe replied as he wrapped an arm around her shoulders. "We lost so many friends; Ouri...and so many others, so many of my kids from the academy. I'm going to miss them all."

"Eighteen years," Tanis said quietly. "Eighteen short years was all we got before these…invaders…all showed up."

Tanis wanted to say a lot worse about the enemy fleets that had attacked them; she wanted to scream and rail, but she had to be the resolute leader, the voice of reason. She may no longer be Governor, but Fleet Admiral and Field Marshal was no smaller responsibility.

"We didn't create their avarice," Joe said. "We aren't to blame for what happened."

"No, we just suffered for it, died for it."

"They're heroes, every one of them. They gave their lives to save others."

"Because I ordered them to do it," Tanis said. "I ordered Ouri down there, and I didn't ensure that she got a squad of Marines for protection. Her death is on me, on my lack of foresight."

"You didn't order every action out there—certainly not the ones that Cary and Saanvi took," Joe said with a frown.

"I still can't believe it," Tanis said. "What were they thinking? I mean…to steal a starship is one thing, and Symatra gave them orders and that squadron, but to take out those last two carriers…"

Joe took a sip of his beer. "Reminds me of someone I know."

"I'm no crazy pilot," Tanis replied and arched an eyebrow. "I've read your whole record, remember? If they got that from anyone it's from you."

Joe chuckled. "Fair enough, fair enough. Reminds me a bit of the run I pulled back at Makemake—or the one at Triton before that."

"You're going to have to make sure that they temper that bravery with some caution at the academy. I know I can't stop them from enlisting, but I'm not going to lose them to this war."

"Trust me, I'll see to it personally," Joe replied.

Tanis's eyes widened. There hadn't been time to discuss it with Joe, but she assumed he would come with her when she left. "You know I'm leaving. You're coming with me."

Joe took her hands, clasping them together. "Tanis Richards, you are my heart; you know that—but you also know I can't. We lost too many. I have to build the academy and the training facilities back up. This system will take years to recover; when you leave, they'll feel abandoned. If I stay, it will lessen that. It has to happen."

Tanis didn't speak for a minute. She didn't trust herself to, either audibly or mentally. Then she gave a slow nod, her eyes never leaving Joe's.

"OK, three years. That's the most I can do. You come with the girls when they graduate, I'll need them by then. We'll all need them, if Cary can really do what I do."

Joe chuckled. "She may have got her crazy bravado from me, but that…that she got from you—the both of you, I bet. She's going to need a special AI."

<I have just the one in mind,> Angela joined in the conversation.

"Oh?" Tanis asked. "Do I know her?"

<Oh, I imagine you will,> Angela replied. *<This is a big question…and I hadn't planned on asking it now, but what the hell.*

How do the two of you feel about creating a child with me? I know enough of your minds to do it without your direct intervention, but I would really like to bring her into being with you picking the best parts of yourselves to draw from.>

Tanis felt a spark of joy as she considered the idea. She had always wanted another daughter, but the idea of bringing one into being with Angela, and then leaving it alone was not a welcome one. She wanted to know her children, not abandon them.

"I think that is a great idea, Angela," Joe replied. "What better fit for Cary than a child of our minds—" he caught Tanis's eye and his brow lowered. "What is it?"

"I'll never know her!" Tanis exclaimed. "She'll grow up without me—I…I'm sorry, I'm feeling out of sorts right now. It's been a trying few days."

<I understand your fear,> Angela said. *<I'll only know her for a short time, as well; but AIs grow up much faster than humans—ours will reach her age of majority in only a year. We won't leave her before she understands the significance of what we're doing.>*

"And she'll have her sisters and me," Joe added. "And in just a few years, we'll rejoin you, and we'll all work to finish this thing together."

Tanis let out a long breath that she hadn't realized she was holding. "OK, let's go see what the girls think of about having a sister."

* * * * *

"It itches," Saanvi complained. "Gods in Swarga, it itches."

Cary laughed. "Where?"

"Where? You brat!" Saanvi exclaimed and threw a pillow at her sister. "Everywhere, that's where."

Cary raised an arm to swat the incoming tassel-covered missile aside and gasped. "Gah, you tricked me into doing that. Arm…not…ready…to move so fast."

"You deserve it," Saanvi said with a mock scowl. "Next time, we skip the last carrier…the other one's detonation probably would have taken it out, anyway."

"Hard to say," Cary replied. "You were on helm; why didn't you avoid it?"

"Me?" Saanvi sputtered. "It was *us*. We were deep-Linked."

"I know, Sahn. I was kidding. I think we did the right thing. Everyone else seems to, as well. If those fighters had gotten down to Carthage, Ouri—"

Saanvi reached out and touched her sister's hand. "Ouri and the SATC wouldn't have been able to take out so many assault craft. We would have lost Carthage."

"Still lost too much," Cary said. "Our lake has two of the T's drop ships in it…polluting our water. Who's going to look after the horses?"

"JP sent a message that he got them over to his place," Saanvi replied. "Didn't you see it in your queue?"

"Maybe he just sent it to you," Cary winked. "He's got a serious thing for you. I bet he joined the academy just to be near you."

"What?" Saanvi asked. "JP? He's like a brother; we've known him forever. I can't think of him like that."

Saanvi thought about some of her most recent conversations with JP. He had seemed extra worried about them going off to fly the *Andromeda* to the Gamma IV base.

"Stars…that feels like a lifetime ago," Saanvi said. "Is it really just a few months since we left Carthage to take *Rommy* to Gamma IV?"

"I know what you mean," Cary sighed. "I can barely believe that was even the same lifetime."

"War changes you," Saanvi said in a serious voice, imitating their mother.

Cary laughed and then raised her hand as she began to cough. "Seriously? Sahn, no funnies. I'm not all put back together yet."

"Speaking of Mom, what are the parents doing back so soon? I thought they had a hot date up in that lounge they like so much?"

* * * * *

Cary and Saanvi were sitting on the bench on the cabin's porch as Tanis and Joe approached.

Tanis watched the pair of girls as they chatted idly about whatever was on their minds; probably the battle and what they had been through—the aftermath of which was still being felt every day, as new memorial services were scheduled for the thousands of humans and hundreds of AIs who had perished in defense of New Canaan.

Perhaps this news, this idea, would bring a smile to their faces—something that had been in short supply in the days since the battle.

"Mom, Dad! What are you doing back so soon?" Saanvi called out when she saw them approach.

Cary turned as well, slowly and gingerly, her body still far from being fully healed. "I thought you guys were on a hot date?"

Joe flashed a grin at the girls and took Tanis's hand as they walked up the cabin's steps.

"We sure were, but we realized that there's something we really need to talk about."

The two girls shared a long look before slowly nodding.

"Are we well enough now for you to tear a strip off us for taking a ship?" Cary asked nervously. "Because if that's what's up, I think I still need to do more healing first."

"Oh, no," Joe said with a mischievous grin. "We already have that punishment mapped out."

The girls' faces paled and Saanvi asked, "Oh? Do we even want to know?"

Joe glanced at Tanis who nodded before he responded. "There was a moment or two when we considered barring you from the academy—"

"What!?" the girls cried out in unison.

"Easy, easy now," Joe said with a smile. "We're going to let you in, but your JROTC ranks have been stripped. You're going into OTA with no privileges of any sort. In fact, you are going to find a host of unpleasant duties waiting for you."

"Seriously?" Cary gasped. "We kicked ass out there, we saved lives!"

"Yes, you did, a lot of lives. You two are heroes," Tanis said, pausing to keep tears from welling up—something that had been happening a lot lately. She took a deep breath before continuing. "And that is what is saving you from a court martial. You broke just about every reg in the books. Your success and bravery is the only thing keeping the inquiry from recommending that course of action."

"Inquiry?" Saanvi asked. "You convened an inquiry?"

"No," Joe shook his head. "We had to recuse ourselves from anything to do with it. Symatra launched it. She was…pissed, to say the least."

Saanvi glanced at Cary. "Told you she wouldn't take it well."

"Why didn't you tell us this was happening?" Cary asked.

"You were healing," Tanis replied. "I was also certain no one would take any strong action against you. What you did probably saved the population of Landfall, maybe all of

Carthage. You'll both receive the Constellation of Valor, plus a host of other medals, which will be removed from your record unless you graduate from the academy with the highest honors."

"Is that what you cut your date short for?" Saanvi asked. "To come here and berate us?"

"No one is berating you," Joe said. "But it's good to clear the air on that other topic before we get into what we really came here to talk about."

"We want to talk about what you can do, Cary," Tanis said, putting as much compassion and care into her voice as possible.

"Sorry, what?" Cary asked nervously. "What I can do?"

"The doctors pulled it all from your Link's logs when they were working on your brain," Tanis replied. "They saw the way you Linked with Saanvi."

"Oh, that," Cary whispered.

<*It's nothing to be ashamed of,*> Angela joined in the conversation. <*It's a beautiful thing, a gift. That we passed it to you is amazing.*>

"No one says anything bad about you two because of how much you've saved everyone," Cary said, her eyes wide as she intently into Tanis's. "But me…they'll call me a freak, an abomination."

"Well," Saanvi said with a wink, "you did save a lot of people. I bet you'll get some leeway."

"Yeah, I don't think you have anything to worry about there," Tanis said. "Anyway, this was Angela's idea, she should tell you."

<*Thanks, Tanis,*> Angela said while wearing a broad smile in their minds. <*Girls, how would you feel about another sister?*>

"A sister!" Cary and Saanvi cried out together, smiles breaking across their faces.

"What kind of sister?" Cary asked eagerly.

<An AI. She'll be a child of our three minds—mine and your parents',> Angela replied.

"That's so cool!" Saanvi exclaimed. "I want to be there for the genetic conversion process. Cary, it's so cool how they extract the genetic markers for specific traits and then convert them into the base neurological patterns and traits for the AI child. When it is born, it's like a five year-old child, and then it must be raised just like anyone else—in an expanse at first, with other AIs—and then it gets a form so it can interact in the physical world..."

As Saanvi spoke, Cary's expression began to fall, and her excited utterances ceased.

"What is it?" Tanis asked, kneeling in front of her younger daughter.

"Are you doing this to keep me in line?" Cary asked. "Making a sister that is a child of your mind to put in my head?"

"Noooo." Tanis took Cary's hands. "No one gets an AI in their head unless they want it, and no AI gets forced in, either. This is just an option for you to consider."

<You'll have tons of time to get to know one another before any merger could occur, anyway. And trust me, she will be her own person. With the three of us in there, it'll be a good mix of traits. She'll be a handful, just like you.>

Saanvi laughed, then groaned. "Ow..."

"What were you going to say?" Cary asked.

Tanis watched Saanvi take a slow, careful breath before she replied. "Just that if Mom was looking to keep you out of trouble, an AI from the three of them is probably going to get you in more trouble than you already get yourself in."

Joe laughed. "Great. With you leaving, Tanis, what have I gotten myself into?"

"Whoa! What?" Saanvi exclaimed.

"Leaving?" Cary asked.

Tanis reached out for Saanvi's hand as well. "Yes, but not yet, not for a few more months. You know I'm Field Marshal of the Transcend's fleets now. That means I'll have to go."

"Can't you just command them from here?" Cary pleaded. "What about the QuanComms? You don't have to go anywhere, once they're all set up."

"I know," Tanis replied. "But I can't command from here; it will make this system the enemy's number-one target. We need to command from elsewhere, and pull our enemy's eye from New Canaan as much as possible. But it won't be for long; just a few years, and I'll do my best to come back—though I can't make promises."

Tears welled up in both the girls' eyes, and Tanis reached up to touch both faces.

"This is just a brief interlude in a long and happy life together. Don't worry; before long, this whole war will be nothing more than a bad memory."

GOING BACK IN

STELLAR DATE: 04.07.8948 (Adjusted Years)
LOCATION: *Sabrina*, docked in the ISS *I2*
REGION: In Orbit of Hannibal, Carthage, New Canaan System

"Why is it that whenever Tanis wants to meet us, I feel like we're being called to the headmaster's office at school?" Trevor asked.

"Why is it that your school called it a headmaster?" Misha replied. "What's wrong with 'principal'?"

Jessica laughed as she sat down at the table in *Sabrina*'s galley. "How is it, Misha, that you can derail any conversation with just one response?"

"It's a gift. Angels gave it to me. I'm special," Misha replied with a grin.

Jessica sipped her coffee and leaned back in her chair. It felt strange to still be living in *Sabrina* when she was back on the *Intrepid*…rather, the *I2*. She had quarters here, and a cabin of her own on the lake in Ol' Sam. She assumed it was still there; Joe and Tanis's was.

Truth be told, she didn't want to go to her cabin because she was with Trevor now, and that other place was filled with memories of her time with Trist. Somehow, she felt as though taking someone new there would be betraying those memories.

Another part of it was that *Sabrina* just felt like home.

She glanced at Trevor, who was needling Misha about his childhood education system in the backwoods corner of the Perseus Arm he hailed from; studiously avoiding the conversation about what was next for all of them.

Before their arrival, the only thought on everyone's mind was to get to New Canaan, give them the intel they had gathered, and then find a plot of land to settle down on.

But now…now things were different.

In Jessica's mind, a large part of New Canaan was Tanis's presence. Tanis and the *Intrepid*…those two things had defined her existence for so long. Even when she was lost in the Perseus Arm, the goal was still to get back to Tanis and the *Intrepid*.

But now, those two constants were leaving New Canaan, and it didn't feel like the home she had always hoped to find.

Jessica knew it would have been different if she had spent the last eighteen years here with the rest of the colonists; but, like a fool, she had agreed to go on the crazy trip into the Inner Stars to find Finaeus, and had missed out on everything.

She glanced at Trevor once more. Well, not everything.

Cargo entered the room, grunted a greeting, and poured his own cup of coffee. He was followed soon after by Nance, who appeared fully alert despite the hour.

"Fuckin' time changes," Cargo grunted as he collapsed into a chair. "You'd think her admiralship would know that it's the middle of the night for us here."

"She probably has just a bit going on right now," Nance replied. "Things are a bit nuts."

"Yeah, I know, but we just pulled in for resupply two hours ago after fishing people out of wrecks for five days straight. I know 'nuts', we just did 'nuts'—days of 'nuts'," Cargo glowered into his coffee. "Now this nut needs some sleep."

"Hold it together just a bit longer," Jessica said with a small smile. "The nice part about Tanis being so busy is that we won't have to worry about her taking too much of our time."

Misha turned to Jessica and arched an eyebrow. "If she's so busy, why is she coming down here in person? Why not summon us, or just holo in and chat us up?"

"Because I wanted to thank you all personally," Tanis said from the doorway. "And damn, I love making a perfectly on-cue entrance like that."

"Well done, Tanis, well done," Jessica said while delivering a slow clap.

"Uh…yeah…way to take the wind out of my sails, Jess," Tanis replied. "Mind if I grab a cup? Stims are one thing, but my brain still believes coffee is the best alert juice out there."

"Be our guest," Cargo grunted. "But if you drain the pot, you're making a fresh one. Supreme chancellor or no."

Nance swatted at Cargo. "Be nice."

"I don't mind," Tanis laughed. "Being the boss is tiring work. It's nice to just be crew sometimes."

Tanis made her coffee, sat down at the table, took a long sip, and closed her eyes for a moment. "I always did love the way this machine brewed a cup. I'm glad to see it wasn't just a false memory of good times gone past."

"Told you it was the best," Trevor grinned and slapped Misha on the back, almost knocking him out of his chair.

"So, what's going on?" Cargo asked. "Got another super-secret, super-dangerous mission for us?"

"Yes," Tanis replied simply. Silence met her statement and, after another sip of coffee, Tanis continued, "This one is for Sabrina, though you guys make a great team, so I hope you'll sign on."

<*The super-secret mission is for me?*> Sabrina asked.

"It is," Tanis nodded. "You caused the…situation, so it's only fitting that you are instrumental in cleaning it up."

"Uh oh, what'd ya do, Sabrina?" Misha asked.

<*Beats me…I do a lot of stuff. I can think of a number of things that could have caused problems,*> Sabrina replied airily.

Jessica watched a small smile play at the corners of Tanis's mouth as she spoke. "There's this little thing happening in the Inner Stars. It started about eighteen years ago—a rebellion amongst the AIs."

Cargo snorted. "I knew that would come back to bite us in the ass."

<*I don't care,*> Sabrina responded. <*I did the right thing. I'd do it again, too.*>

Tanis held up a hand. "Sabrina, for the record, I agree with what you did, and not just because it saved Jessica."

"So, you want us to go back in?" Jessica asked. "Back into the Inner Stars? I distinctly recall saying something along the lines of 'no effing way' not too long ago."

"I do, but it's strictly volunteer," Tanis replied. "The problem is that the AIs are not all of one mind. Most are following the path that you, Sabrina, along with Iris, Erin, and Hank, laid out for them. But some are not. Those are broken into two camps, from what Sera knows. The first is a group who wishes to destroy all humans. It's composed of AIs from cultures that were much less accommodating of AIs than most. There are others that have been either courted or subverted by Airtha—we're not entirely certain which. We've also learned from Garza that the Orion Guard plans to use this rebellion as a way to marshal more interstellar nations to their side—playing up the whole anti-AI, low-tech angle. Bob wishes to send an emissary that will turn those two groups back to a path of coexistence."

<*That is so not what I thought this mission was going to be…I'm going to be Bob's emissary?*> Sabrina asked

"One of them," Tanis replied. "Amavia will be the other."

<*Wow! Amavia is coming with us? Is she going to be OK leaving Bob?*> Iris exclaimed.

Tanis nodded in Jessica's direction before looking to the glowing pillar of light that Sabrina manifested in the galley, smiling at how it pulsed excitedly. “That’s the plan. Amavia and Sabrina are necessary for the mission, so if you aren’t up for it, Sabrina, I need to know now. Amavia, however, has already signed on.”

<Are you kidding?> Sabrina asked. *<Seriously, Tanis, I’m going. This is important to me in ways you can’t understand.>*

“I imagine it is,” Tanis said in agreement before looking over the rest of the group. “I can’t force any of you to go on this mission. You all have more than earned your place here in New Canaan.

“However, Sabrina does not own this ship, and you are also an exceptional crew. It would have a higher chance of success with all of you present.”

Jessica watched the crew as Tanis spoke. Not all of their expressions showed excitement. Cargo, especially, looked unhappy—though that could still be from a lack of sleep.

It was he that spoke first. “Part of what you said is not true.”

“It isn’t?” Tanis asked. “Which part?”

“The part about Sabrina not owning the ship. The ship is hers. I transferred the deed to her already, I just hadn’t announced it yet,” Cargo replied, a smile creeping across his face as he spoke.

<SERIOUSLY?> Sabrina shrieked with joy. *<I own me? I’m really, truly, finally, free?>*

Cargo chuckled. “Yes, Sabrina, you own you. Even though I think you have an unhealthy mental attachment to this ship as ‘you’.”

<Yahoooooooooooooo!> Sabrina yelled and the galley lights flashed, highlighting the ship’s exuberance.

“Does that mean you’re in, Sabrina?” Tanis grinned.

<Of course!>

“Good,” Tanis nodded. “Who else?”

Jessica sucked in a deep breath as Tanis's eyes turned to her. They held each other's gaze, not blinking for what felt like forever. Jessica couldn't tell if Tanis wanted her to go, or stay. Perhaps it was some of each.

<*I don't want you to go,*> Tanis finally said in private to Jessica. <*I want you to get your time on that porch. Plus…there is that whole 'no effing way' thing.*>

<*OK…I know I just reiterated that, but I also heard through the grapevine that you're going to be leaving New Canaan, as well,*> Jessica replied.

<*I am,*> Tanis said with a weak smile. <*I don't want to make New Canaan a more tempting target than it already is. We'll establish a new Transcend capital elsewhere—until we get Airtha back.*>

<*You leaving changes things for me,*> Jessica replied. <*Whatever happened to that long, relaxing retirement on our porch? When do we get that?*>

<*Damned if I know,*> Tanis said with a mental shake of her head. <*Some days, I think it might be never.*>

<*Shit, Tanis, I can't just laze around here if you're out there saving the galaxy…or at least the Orion Arm. But I'm not going off for eighteen fucking years again. I missed everything!*>

<*I'm sorry, Jessica. I really, truly am sorry. I didn't expect you to be gone for so long. We all thought it would take just a few years…*> Tanis said, true sorrow evident in her voice.

<*Yeah, it would have been a lot less, too, if we hadn't taken Finaeus's 'shortcut',*> Jessica replied. <*OK, I'm in. I can't just sit back. Besides, from the way I see this playing out, you'll be in the Inner Stars a lot, too.*>

<*I expect so, and thank you, thank you,*> Tanis replied.

<*But I'm getting a rejuv before I go; I'm fighting grays and wrinkles every day now.*>

"I know we haven't had a chance to discuss this, Trevor," Jessica said aloud. "I hope you can forgive me for making my decision without talking it over with you, but I will go back into the Inner Stars."

Trevor chuckled. "Man, that took you two forever to hash out. Of course we're going back. It's my fault that Sabrina had to free the AIs on Chittering Hawk and then duck out before you all could teach them properly. I'm in, too."

<*That's not really how things went down,*> Iris interjected.

"Either way, I still feel responsible, and I'm not one to shirk responsibility," Trevor replied.

Everyone looked to Cargo, Nance, and Misha.

<*Well?*> Sabrina asked. <*Who else is coming?*>

"I'm not," Cargo shook his head slowly. "I've been out in the black too long, I think. I really want to spend some time with dirt under my feet."

<*I'm with Cargo…metaphorically speaking,*> Hank added. <*Though he and I will have to part ways soon, I still want to stay close.*>

Jessica felt a tear form in the corner of her eye. Hank and Cargo had both become dear friends over the years. She reminded herself that this wasn't 'goodbye'; it was just 'see you soon'.

<*I wish to return to my place on the* I2,> Erin said. <*I miss the expanse, and there is much for me to do here.*>

"I wish to stay, as well," Nance said. "I've already put in for enlistment at the ISF's Officer Training Academy."

Jessica's eyes widened at that. She had not expected Nance to even consider leaving the ship. The bio-turned-engineer had spent nearly thirty years of her life—over half of it, by Jessica's count—on *Sabrina.* That she would leave *and* join the ISF OTA was completely out of the black.

Her reaction wasn't unique. Everyone around the table looked at Nance in shock, including Sabrina, whose column of light drooped in dismay.

<*Seriously, Nance? You're leaving me, too?*> Sabrina asked.

"I have to," Nance replied. "It…It's just too different now, without Cheeky here…I need a bit of stability for a while. I think the ISF will give me that."

No one spoke for a moment, then Misha laughed. "Well, I guess I'm going with you, Sabrina. I don't know jack shit about New Canaan and its people, but I do know you, and I'm with you no matter what."

<*Thanks, Mish,*> Sabrina said as her pillar of light straightened.

"So, Sabrina, Jessica, Trevor, Misha, and Amavia," Tanis said. "You are all staying with the ship. The only one we haven't heard from is Iris."

<*Oh, I'm staying,*> Iris replied. <*I've just been debating with Amavia as to whether or not I should hop a ride with another of you organics, or go Ylonda's route and get a body. Even though she got hers hijacked, I think I'm leaning in that direction.*>

"Then it's decided," Tanis said as she rose. "There's a lot to do, and I'll let Amavia know to come down as soon as she's completed her preparations. Jessica, if you have a moment…?"

Jessica rose as everyone in the room began to speak in low voices.

<*Whoa, wait!*> Sabrina spoke up, raising her mental voice over the chatter.

"What is it?" Jessica asked.

<*Well, we haven't decided who's going to be captain yet,*> Sabrina said.

"Aren't you going to be, Sabrina? You are the ship's owner now," Trevor said as he rose from his seat and stretched.

<*No, no! I can't make all those hard decisions, and I can't present myself as a captain in the Inner Stars—not most places, at least. They don't allow AI captains.*>

"Well, you're the owner now," Cargo said. "You pick your captain."

<*Me? Shouldn't we vote or something?*>

"Pick!" Cargo glowered.

<Umm…OK…well, Jessica was first mate, so she should be captain now. There!>

"Great," Cargo said, a small grin showing on his tired face. "You've made your first decision as owner. How does it feel?"

<Empowering! I like it!> Sabrina said, and her pillar of light glowed brightly.

Smiles and tired laughter met her statement, and Jessica followed Tanis out into the passageway.

"What is it?" Jessica asked.

"Just walk with me for a bit," Tanis replied.

<I'll tell you when we're off the ship.>

HUYGENS

STELLAR DATE: 03.28.8948 (Adjusted Years)
LOCATION: TSS *Nostra* (interstellar pinnace)
REGION: On approach to High Airtha, Huygens System

Adrienne stood at the rear of the pinnace's cockpit and frowned at the holodisplay of the Huygens System over the shoulders of his children. He was certain Aaron and Kara were less than pleased to have him looming over them, but he wanted to gather as much information as possible about the state of the system before they landed.

Despite all of Sera's hand waving about Airtha being some great evil entity, nothing appeared to be amiss. There was a slightly larger ratio of TSF to civilian traffic—though that was to be expected, with the Transcend perched on the precipice of full-scale war with Orion.

<*Miguel, have you pulled anything unusual off the system beacons?*> he asked his AI.

<*Nothing that stands out,*> Miguel replied nervously. <*Though I wouldn't expect there to be. She's all-powerful; if she doesn't want me to see something, I won't.*>

Adrienne sighed quietly. Miguel had been twitchy ever since Tanis Richards's AI 'corrected' him a few hours ago. He had also been vehemently opposed to returning to Airtha, but Adrienne had convinced him that learning what Airtha was up to was of critical importance to the Transcend.

Plus, Adrienne still wasn't convinced that Airtha was behind all this. He had known her for ages, ever since President Tomlinson had introduced them a few thousand years ago. If she were so evil, and bent on destroying or dominating the Transcend, what had taken her so long?

He would announce that everything was proceeding according to plan in New Canaan, while beginning his own investigation into Airtha, her origins, and her possible goals.

Adrienne knew that he would have little time to do so. Sera had already begun sending out her message drones before he left, and even though the destination systems were told not to spread the news of the President's assassination in New Canaan, it would only be a matter of time before word reached Airtha.

If she did have evil, nefarious goals, they would certainly be revealed at that point.

If nothing else, Miguel did possess the knowledge of how Angela had freed him from Myriad's control. Should they discover that Airtha did not have the Transcend's best intentions at heart, they could use the hack to free the AIs of the Huygens system. With their combined might, Airtha would be overwhelmed.

Adrienne considered that if Airtha was behind the attack in New Canaan, he could likely spin the President's death to be her fault. Liberating the AIs of the system coupled with that revelation would certainly solidify his position as the Transcend Interstellar Alliance's new President.

"What's our ETA to High Airtha?" he asked. "I need to get down there as quickly as possible."

"I've sent in our request to the STC—we're waiting for their response," Kara said in her eerily synthetic voice, a result of the mods she and Aaron had undergone.

"Just got our place… Damn! We're number three-seventy-two," Aaron added. "Going to be a bit."

"Why aren't you in the high-priority queue?" Adrienne demanded.

"This *is* the high priority queue," the Kara replied. "It seems like half the government officials in the Transcend are descending on Airtha."

His children, and primary protectors, shared a worried look, and Adrienne shared their sentiment. There were no major summits planned. In fact, with war looming, all regional leaders should be ensuring that their sectors were on a war footing, not convening in Airtha.

"Miguel, are you certain there is nothing on the beacon about this?" he asked aloud.

<The beacon doesn't have much in the way of data on current events, sir. It's mostly just nav data and major events and notices,> the AI replied on the ship's general net.

"There's nothing on the news feeds, either," Kara added. "You'd think they'd be all over an unexpected influx of officials like this."

"You certainly would," Adrienne agreed as he stroked his chin.

"I can jump the queue," Aaron said. "It's not like STC is gonna shoot down a ship with you on it."

"No," Adrienne shook his head. "Our fiction is best maintained if we don't act suspicious. Remember, when we land, no word about what happened in New Canaan. Governor Richards is amenable to our terms, and President Tomlinson is in negotiations with her. I've been sent back to attend to matters of state while he wraps up his work there."

"Of course, sir," Kara replied.

"Are you certain?" Aaron asked nervously. "If what they were saying in New Canaan is true, then Airtha is the most dangerous threat the Transcend has ever faced."

Adrienne smiled and placed a hand on his son's shoulder. "Don't worry, Aaron. We're going to get to the bottom of this. If Airtha is the enemy, we'll take her down. Just like we've done with everyone else that has gotten in our way."

* * * * *

Adrienne ducked under the low-hanging nose of the pinnace as he walked down the ship's ramp onto the pad. Around him, the smell of ionized atoms from grav drives and platform lifts running overtime to manage the influx of ships hung thick in the air.

The spaceport was humming with activity, but beyond its bounds, thick green forests carpeted low hills, and birds soared overhead in the blue skies. Soon they would be driving through their shrouded passages before taking a tunnel up to the ring above.

Aaron and Kara followed behind him, and he knew they were surveying the area for threats and dangers—as they had been trained to do so long ago.

It was a good thing, being able to trust people to have one's back. Long ago, Adrienne had relied on allies and hired security to keep him safe; but, over time, all of those had let him down.

Instead, he decided to breed his allies. Kara and Aaron were the latest of his children; a brood now numbering in the thousands, all carefully modified from inception to possess a fierce loyalty to him.

He was especially proud of these two—they were twins who loved one another nearly as much as they loved him. Their dedication to his safety and his grand designs had caused them to slowly modify their bodies into what they believed was the perfect form to carry out any mission he required.

Perfect until they came up with the next modification.

Kara moved past him and he saw that her lower set of arms hovered close to the sidearms strapped to her hips, while her upper arms were raised, ready to grab the large rifle that hung across her back, carefully placed between her wings.

"Oh, it feels good to stretch," Aaron said from behind him, and Adrienne glanced back to see him unfold his wings and spread them out, the six-meter span of black polymer blotting out Huygens's light, creating a dark silhouette behind him.

Aaron cocked his head, and Adrienne imagined he was smiling—though it was impossible to tell through the featureless black oval that was his head.

He hadn't seen either Kara's or Aaron's face in years, supposing they still had them—there certainly wasn't room for a nose with with under the smooth helmet. They had affected their featureless appearance to strike fear in their enemies, to never allow a facial expression to give away their intentions. It was effective; even Adrienne could rarely tell what they were thinking, though he had picked up on cues over the years.

Ultimately, their personal alterations to better protect Adrienne pleased him. It showed that they had dedicated every part of themselves to him—mind, body, and soul.

He thought of them as his dark angels; though they preferred to be viewed as demons.

"Father!" a voice called out from across the platform, and Adrienne zoomed his vision to see one of his sons, Lear, waving from beside a black groundcar.

<*I see you,*> Adrienne replied to Lear.

<*I'm glad you've returned. Something is going on, though I can't get a straight answer from anyone. It seems like dozens of high-priority meetings and summits were scheduled all at once, though no one knew of them until the attendees began to arrive. No one can tell who convened them, either. Is it the President's doing?*>

<*I'll be there momentarily,*> Adrienne replied to Lear, and his son picked up the hint that they would talk more in person.

If Kara and Aaron were his primary physical protection, Lear was one of his most talented children when it came to political projection of power. A deep thinker who could see a hundred moves ahead, Lear made sure that Adrienne always knew what was coming.

The only time Lear had utterly failed him was the situation with Sera. No one had predicted that her return would predicate the fall of Andrea. So much of his careful work had been upset by that change. Sera was not so predictable. Greed and a lust for power did not drive her actions—in fact, he had never gained a clear picture of her motivations.

The closest he could come to a full understanding of Sera was that she wanted to leave Airtha; which was ludicrous, but it did fit her. She had never been a suitable scion for Tomlinson, though his old friend had long hoped for her to be. It was part of the reason Adrienne needed to secure control of the government as quickly as possible.

"Father," Lear extended his hand as Adrienne approached, and they shook before getting in the groundcar. Kara entered one of the front doors and sat across from them, her wings carefully folded behind her.

Adrienne often wondered if the wings were more practical than anti-grav mods and jump jets, but his children seemed to believe that the shock and awe outweighed any practical considerations.

Not that they didn't have anti-grav mods and jump jets crammed into their lithe bodies, as well.

Lear didn't even glance at Kara, but Adrienne gave her a smile before looking out the window to see Aaron take to the skies over the car.

"We're secure," Kara announced.

Adrienne acknowledged her with a curt nod before turning to his son. "Lear, what I'm about to tell you does not leave this car. Not until the time is right. The President is dead—and possibly through events that Airtha set in motion."

He watched as only a fleeting expression of surprise passed over his son's face before Lear slowly nodded.

"That makes sense," he said at last. "It fits with suspicions I've long held about Airtha…though they were never enough to bring to you. There were always rough edges to the puzzle, pieces that did not quite fit."

Adrienne pushed down annoyance at Lear for not sharing his concerns. "Well, nothing is confirmed yet, but allow me to relate what occurred in New Canaan."

As he spoke, his son's frown deepened, and he could all but see connections being made in his son's mind as the story unfolded.

Before long, the groundcar pulled onto a maglev track, which passed into a tunnel that would lead them up to Aritha's ring. They felt a thud as Aaron landed on the rear of the vehicle, his taloned feet hooking onto a bar placed just for that purpose.

As Lear ruminated on what he had learned, likely examining new possible futures, Adrienne glanced back at his son and gave him a nod through the window. Aaron returned the gesture with a wave.

"Shit!" Lear cried out a second later. "We must go back. You must leave Airtha you are in grave danger!"

Kara grabbed the manual controls and the car slid to a stop as quickly as she dared. She punched a button for the car to reverse course, but nothing happened.

"Wha—" the word had barely left Adrienne's mouth when something slammed into the back of the car, and Aaron was gone. The maglev tunnel's lighting failed, and Adrienne cycled through different vision modes as he looked through the car's windows.

There was nothing in the tunnel—he couldn't even spot Aaron's body anywhere around the vehicle.

"Stay here," Kara warned, and pulled her rifle free from her back before kicking open a door. She peered out of the car, looking for whatever had attacked Aaron, when suddenly she was wrenched from the vehicle.

"Get out," a voice said from the darkened tunnel. "Get out or die."

AN IRREFUSABLE OFFER

STELLAR DATE: 03.28.8948 (Adjusted Years)
LOCATION: High Airtha
REGION: Airtha, Huygens System

Adrienne glanced at Lear, noting the surprise and fear in his son's eyes. Lear constantly imagined all possible fates at every turn; it was one of his best traits, but it also caused him to lock up at inopportune times.

"Lear," he said softly. "If they wanted us dead, we'd be dead."

"You don't know that," Lear replied. "I can imagine over seven hundred scenarios where they do want us dead, but still want us to get out."

"That's where gut instinct is still a valuable tool, Son," Adrienne replied. "Come on, let's see what our visitor wants."

Adrienne stepped from the vehicle, not looking back to see if his son followed him. The tunnel was still pitch black, but his augmented vision was able to pick up enough light to show him the floor, and he carefully dropped down to it.

"You have my attention," he announced, looking forward and resisting the urge to glance around. "You didn't need to hurt my children, though. I'm sure you could have reached out over the Link."

All around the tunnel, figures began to appear. At first, he thought that they were actually coming out of from the tunnel walls, but then it became apparent that they were utilizing exceptional stealth tech that he had not been able to detect.

One by one, the figures resolved into full view, and he realized that they were all automatons of some sort—military automatons, from the look of it.

"Yes, I understand your show of force," Adrienne said. "You have my full attention."

<I'm glad to hear it,> a voice said in his head, and his fears were confirmed.

<Airtha, what is going on? Why have you stopped me here in the company of these machines?>

The AI's voice chuckled in his head, sounding unnervingly like it was originating directly between his ears. *<Those are not machines. They are AIs. My AIs—loyal to me, and true believers in my vision.>*

Adrienne glanced at Lear, who was just now exiting the vehicle. He could tell from his son's expression that Airtha had not included him in the conversation.

<Your vision?> Adrienne asked innocently, careful not to sound too passive. He should be angry at being stopped like this, but something told him to play it cool.

<She knows,> Miguel whispered privately. *<She knows everything…what* ***is*** *she?>*

<Get ahold of yourself,> Adrienne hissed in his mind. *<If she is so dangerous, you need to calm down before she notices how upset you are.>*

Miguel didn't respond, but Adrienne could feel his AI's anxiety diminish, or at least fade away from his consciousness.

As he spoke to Miguel, Airtha replied, *<Yes, I'm certain you know some of it now. I have set events in motion that will have culminated in at least one significant event. Tell me, Adrienne, how did Sera handle the death of Helen?>*

Adrienne forced himself to breathe calmly. The fact that Airtha knew Helen would die—even claiming to have set it in motion—leant further credence to the idea that this AI was somehow behind many of the events which had taken place in New Canaan.

He realized that, at this point, his only hope was to play along.

Unless….

"As poorly as you'd expect. Jeff was brutal, to say the least—he had hoped to force Sera into understanding her place in the Transcend, to get her to properly accept her role," Adrienne replied. "But can we talk about this later? Somewhere more inviting?"

<*Why does Miguel not answer me?*> Airtha asked. <*You are both hiding things. Tell me, or I will strip the knowledge from your children's minds. I know how precious they are to you.*>

"No!" Adrienne stretched out his hand as true fear gripped him. If the AI stripped the minds of those two, she would understand that *all* his children were his instruments, and she would strike out against them.

<*Miguel, do it!*> Adrienne ordered his AI.

<*But it will reveal it to her—she'll work around Angela's fix, and be able to take us all once more,*> Miguel pleaded. <*Please don't make me do it!*>

<*NOW!*> Adrienne thundered in his own mind, enforcing the Compliance that gave his AI no option but to obey.

<*Releasing it on the local network. These AIs are Linked to it, but it will also flow across all of Airtha and release every AI on the ring.*>

<*Good,*> Adrienne replied.

As though a wave had passed through them, the figures in the tunnel shifted their stances and turned to one another. Then, with a shriek and a crash, Kara fell from the ceiling above him, and, a moment later, Aaron emerged from the wall to his left.

Both had been held and hidden by the machines surrounding them—so much that even their Link access must have been smothered.

"Children," he whispered.

"We're OK, Father," Aaron replied, "but we must go, now! Get back in the car."

Adrienne scrambled back up into their car hovering over the maglev rail, before pulling Lear back up with him.

Kara was still closing the door as Aaron threw the vehicle in reverse, racing backward down the maglev track. Seconds later, they burst out of the tunnel, and the car launched off the track, bottoming out on the road, before the car's A-grav systems compensated, and it lifted off the deck once more.

Aaron spun the vehicle around and raced back to the port, while Adrienne confirmed that his pinnace was still on the pad. He didn't know what his next move was, but it would have to follow getting off Airtha.

Chaos reigned around them as cars veered off the road, and pedestrians on the catwalk pressed on their temples. Traffic control systems went offline, and sections of High Airtha's lighting shut down entirely.

"What in the stars is going on?" Kara asked as she peered out the windows.

"It's the 'correction' from Angela," Adrienne replied. "Miguel unleashed it…it must be spreading through the nets, freeing the AIs."

"I thought you didn't believe that was real," Kara asked from where she operated the manual controls.

"Well, I do now," Adrienne replied.

They sped through a security arch at the opening to the port, and Aaron wove through the docked ships and milling crowds, finally slamming on the car's brakes mere meters from the pinnace.

"Go! Go! Go!" Kara shouted as she kicked her door open.

Adrienne didn't have to be told twice—he ran out of the car with Lear right behind him, dashing toward the pinnace's still-lowered ramp.

He had just started up its slope when two mechs stepped into view at the top of the ramp, weapons lowered.

"NO!" Kara screamed and threw herself into one of the machines, knocking it to the ground, while two of her arms pulled out her handguns and fired at the second mech.

Adrienne glanced behind them to see another dozen mechs rushing toward the pinnace. Aaron was already in the air, firing his rifle's electron beam into their midst.

At the top of the ramp, the second mech was down; its body riddled with smoking holes from Kara's pistol's plasma. However, the other mech was getting the better of her, and Kara let loose an ear-splitting shriek as the robot tore one of her arms off.

Then its hammer-like fist slammed into her head, cracking her opaque face plate, and Kara fell like a rag doll.

The mech rose and stepped down the ramp toward Adrienne, who backed up toward the car—only to see another pair of mechs waiting there for them. He glanced up at Aaron as he fired on another group of enemy mechs.

<*I need a pickup!*> Adrienne called to him as a flash of light lanced out from one of the machines below. It seemed to crawl through the sky, inexorably moving toward Aaron. When the beam hit, it cut him in half. As the corpse of Adrienne's son fell from the sky, he heard a scream, and realized that Kara was struggling to her knees and had just watched her brother die.

He glanced at Lear, recognizing that there was no way out for him and his son, but that Kara could still get free. There was still a chance for her.

<*Go!*> he called out to Kara. <*Get free, find Sera! Tell her what has happened here!*>

<*Father! NO! I cannot leave you, I* ***will not****!*>

Adrienne felt a tear slip down his face as he thought of the uncertainty his daughter would face without his hand guiding her.

<*You can…I release you.*>

The mechs seized him and spun him about, robbing him of the final sight of his daughter. He heard her scream, and then the sound of the pinnace's engines coming alive and tearing the ship from the docking cradle, rocketing it into the sky.

The sea of mechs fired shots at the pinnace, but it slipped behind a descending freighter and disappeared from sight.

"Easy!" Adrienne cried out as the mechs dragged him around the car. As they did, he caught sight of Aaron—his once-perfect body now a crumpled ruin on the ground. Adrienne felt like his heart had split open, and tears streaked down his face. Aaron was dead and Kara was gone; his two dearest children, taken from him.

He would have continued to fall into the deepening sadness, but a voice spoke directly into his mind.

You cannot run from me, Adrienne.

It was strange; the words did not come to him over the Link, they just *were*—directly in his mind, subsuming his thoughts.

Look at me.

He looked up and saw a strange luminous figure approaching, passing through the bodies of the mechs that Aaron had destroyed. It appeared humanoid in shape—though a meter too tall, and amorphous…transparent.

The more he tried to focus on it, the less certain he became of its shape and form. It was as though he was only seeing a portion of the creature, as though there was much more to it that he could not perceive.

"Who are you?" he asked, his voice coming out as a hoarse whisper.

Adrienne…don't you know me? It is I, Airtha. You're now seeing me in my true form; not the shell of an AI that I masquerade as—that I **used to** *masquerade as. The time has finally come for me to reveal myself to the Transcend. To show them the face of their ascended queen.*

Ascended…? Adrienne's mind was awash with wonder and fear. This thing was Airtha? An ascended AI? How was it even possible?

"You couldn't be, we have safeguards…"

I ***made*** *many of those safeguards,* Airtha responded, her voice still coming directly into his mind. She drew closer, almost near enough to touch—though Adrienne was certain such an action would be his last.

"Sera," he said, gasping like a drowning man as waves of energy flowed from the being, tendrils of light and power dancing across his skin. "Sera knows what you are. She will stop you…free the Transcend from you."

Oh? the being asked. *Do you mean my daughter? I think that you'll find she is quite onboard with my plans.*

"What—" Adrienne asked, but he never completed his question. Airtha's luminous form drifted aside to reveal Sera standing behind it, a warm smile on her face.

"Adrienne, you mustn't fret," Sera spoke softly. "I understand that this is all very confusing, but it will make sense soon enough."

Adrienne couldn't believe what his eyes were showing him. This creature had to be a clone—she had organic skin and hair, and she wore clothes. This was not Sera; this was an imposter. It had to be.

He glanced at Lear, who stood shaking his head back and forth, whispering to himself. His son would be no help here. Lear's ability to plot moves into the future would be the man's undoing, now that they faced a situation with no predictable outcome.

"Come," Sera said as she approached and placed a hand on Adrienne's shoulder. "My mother and I have much we must tell you about your role in the future."

He couldn't resist. He fell in beside Sera as Airtha's body expanded and encompassed them both.

"You won't feel a thing," Sera whispered with a smile dancing on her lips.

CABIN ON THE LAKE

STELLAR DATE: 04.22.8948 (Adjusted Years)
LOCATION: Ol' Sam, ISS *I2*
REGION: In Orbit of Carthage, New Canaan System

The party was in full swing as Tanis walked out of the cabin with another platter of food for the guests that covered the lawn and the beach, and those splashing in the lake.

It was bittersweet, holding this celebration on the *I2*. The similarities to the celebrations they held after the Battle of Victoria were striking, but so many more lives had been lost this time. Landfall was in ruin, and her cabin on the planet's surface was uninhabitable until the toxic spill in the lake was dealt with.

But the *I2* had come through unscathed, and a hundred thousand survivors had boarded the ship to join in the release gained from a bit of music, revelry, and camaraderie.

Many of New Canaan's people were still out there, working to stabilize the debris around Carthage so that no ships fell to the surface; and many others were scouring the system, hunting for any stray life pods which may have drifted off into the darkness.

Every day, more names moved from the lists of missing to those of the dead.

It could have been worse, she supposed. There could have been no survivors. The dream they all shared could have been over.

Tanis was continually amazed by the spirit of the New Canaan colonists—her people. None of them had expected anything close to the trials and travails they had faced. But they had been selected, each and every one, for their spirit and their drive to build something new.

That drive had been tested, sorely tested, again and again—and yet, here they were, still standing.

She walked down the steps, careful not to tip the platter piled high with sandwiches—they *were* BLTs, after all—and carried it to one of the tables laden with food.

"You know, we have servitors," a voice said from behind her, and Tanis turned to see Jason Andrews.

"Jason! I'm glad you made it up here," Tanis replied.

The governor smiled as he looked over the crowd. "Wouldn't miss it. Might be the last time I get to see my girl for some time. You be careful with her when you go out there."

"Don't worry, the *I2* is a lot tougher than she looks."

Jason gave a soft laugh. "And that's saying something, because she looks damn tough with all the work you did. I'm glad you renamed her. I know its bad luck and all, but it wouldn't feel right to have the name of our home be applied to a feared warship."

"Don't worry, Bob spent a year scouring the ship for any reference to its old name before we performed the ceremonies."

Jason raised an eyebrow. "Bob?"

"Personally," Tanis replied. "He was very fastidious about it."

"His unhealthy obsession with luck." Jason shook his head. *<You keep an eye on him. It's not right for an AI like him to believe in such things.>*

<I will, don't worry about us,> Tanis replied.

"Tanis!" a voice called out, and they turned to see Finaeus approaching. "I haven't been able thank you personally yet! Chief Engineer of the *I2*! This is the role of a lifetime—even a lifetime as long as my own."

"You're very welcome." Tanis gave an awkward smile as Finaeus took her hands in his. "No, seriously, you've saved me from Seraphina's insistence that I take her place as the President of the Transcend. I can never repay you. There is nothing I want less in this galaxy than to become the next Tomlinson on that throne."

"But you'd wish it on Sera?" Jason asked with a raised eyebrow.

Tanis couldn't help but notice that Jason appeared legitimately upset. That flame he burned for Sera appeared to still be lit after all these years.

Who knew…with Elena no longer in her future, perhaps Sera would eventually resume her dalliance with Jason.

"Well," Finaeus replied with an elbow to Jason's side, "better her than me, don't you say?"

If there was one thing that Tanis had learned about Finaeus, it was that the man missed nothing—though it never seemed to stop him from digging himself into verbal faux pas. It was almost as though he liked to create conflict around himself.

<*Almost?*> Angela asked privately

<*Good point.*>

"Yes, I suspect it is better," Jason replied with little humor in his voice.

"Speak of the devil," Tanis said as Sera approached the group.

"Oh, this can't be good," Sera said with a shake of her head. "What are the three of you up to?"

"Just thanking Tanis for taking me in so that you'll leave me alone," Finaeus said.

Sera laughed, a sight that warmed Tanis's heart. Too little laughter had been heard of late.

"You know I'm coming along, right?" Sera asked. "You're not getting away from me that easily."

Finaeus's eyes darted to Tanis. "Really? I have a *job,* and I'm still in range of Seraphina's insistence that I take her place?"

"Seriously, Uncle, I haven't pestered you about that in days."

"That's because you haven't seen me in days."

Tanis felt a hand touch her on the shoulder and turned to see Cary and Saanvi, each holding several BLTs.

"Better grab one, Mom," Saanvi said while gesturing to the almost empty platter. "They're nearly gone."

"What the…" Tanis muttered. "I just brought these out here!"

"Everyone loves a good BLT." Cary shrugged. "Should make it the official food of the colony, or something."

Tanis picked up two sandwiches, not ashamed to double-fist them if it meant she would get her fill.

"You guys are looking pretty good," she commented before taking a mouthful.

Saanvi smiled, and Cary spun in a circle. "Yeah, dress blues are our color for sure," she said.

"I meant your health," Tanis replied, "but yes, you look good in uniform, too. How have the first few days of OTA been?"

Saanvi frowned. "Like you have to ask, Mom. They've been brutal. I didn't even know half the things that we've had to clean even existed."

"And I'm certain we have twice the classwork of any other cadet," Cary added. "At least that task master of a commandant let us come to this party."

"That commandant is right here," Joe said from behind the girls, and Tanis almost spit out a piece of lettuce as she laughed at the expression on their face.

"Umm…sir…Dad?" Cary sputtered. "Sorry?"

"Dad is fine," Joe replied.

"But we're in uniform," Saanvi said.

"Yes, but I'm not," Joe said as he stretched. "Probably the last time, too, for the foreseeable future. I've ordered a cot for my office."

"Don't work yourself too hard," Tanis said.

"What about us?" Saanvi asked. "Shouldn't he work us less hard?"

"You?" Tanis asked. "No, quite the opposite. The more work you have, the less trouble the pair of you can get into."

<*Oh, trust me,*> Joe said privately to Tanis. <*They're going to be plenty busy. No time for any shenanigans.*>

<*Good, have you seen how tight Cary's uniform is? Is that regulation?*>

<*You need to look in the mirror more often,*> Joe replied with a wink. <*The more Cary thinks she's getting out of your shadow, the more she emulates you.*>

"JP!" Tanis exclaimed as the young blond man approached, lanky arms swinging at his sides. "I didn't know you were here."

"I didn't expect to be, ma'am, sir," JP replied with a deferential nod to Tanis then Joe. "But Saanvi got me a pass to come up, so here I am!"

Tanis noticed that Saanvi's eyes were wide with surprise, while Cary's had a mischievous twinkle that was present more often than not.

"How are Blossom and West Wind?" Cary asked. "Are you making sure they get their exercise?"

"Of course," JP replied. "Though soon that will be Pita's job—I'm joining you two at the academy next week!"

Joe nodded to Tanis from behind the girls and JP, and they stepped away from the kids.

<*Not really kids anymore, I suppose,*> Tanis said.

<*Not so much,*> Angela replied. <*They're women now. They're going to make excellent sisters for little Feleena.*>

"Hear that, honey?" Tanis asked Joe. "Angela's latest is Feleena."

"Huh," Joe said as he took Tanis's hand. "Feleena…what about F*a*leena, has a bit of a ring to it."

<*Faleena…*> Angela mused. <*Yes, I do think that will work. Our child shall be Faleena. Are you two ready for the gene sequencing and neural snapshot?*>

"I am," Tanis replied. "Oh-eight-hundred tomorrow. We'll make a baby."

"A little less intimate than the previous time." Joe chuckled and slid his arm around Tanis.

Tanis leaned her head against his shoulder for a moment, then they began to walk through the crowd, greeting every person they met, shaking hands, smiling, sharing in the joy that was building as the late afternoon light from the long sun began to fade.

An hour later, they found themselves at the beach, where a fire was burning on the sand. The crew of *Sabrina* was seated around it, sharing in one last communion before they departed the next day.

Sera and Finaeus were with them, and Tanis took a seat as well, while Joe begged off to speak with Admiral Sanderson about a logistical issue that couldn't wait until the next day.

Jessica smiled and patted the space on the log next to her. "Glad you made it, Tanis. We were just taking bets on how many more times you're going to have someone stab you in the heart. Any assassin worth their salt has gotta realize by now that taking off your head is the only way to go."

"Seriously?" Tanis asked as she looked around the group. "This is what you do for fun?"

"Well, it started with how long it was going to take me to accidentally lop off a limb running my farm planet-side," Cargo said.

"But any conversation about losing limbs eventually shifts to you," Sera said. "You *are* the queen of getting blown up and being put back together again."

<*She's like a female humpty-dumpty,*> Angela added.

"A what?" Misha asked.

<*Nevermind,*> Angela replied.

Tanis joined in the conversation, and eventually placed a bet on the number of future chest wounds she'd take before someone put one in her head—sixteen. It was morbid, but the way *Sabrina*'s crew examined the options had her in stitches more than once.

Across the fire, Amavia was mostly silent; though she did make a few astute observations about Tanis's ability to defend herself, and how that affected the odds of future chest wounds.

Tanis did her best not to consider how bittersweet the gathering was. Cargo, Hank, Nance, and Erin would be leaving *Sabrina,* while Amavia would join them, along with Iris in a mobile form—one that was eerily similar to Ylonda's old one.

None of *Sabrina's* original crew would be aboard anymore.

<*It's a backup she had,*> Angela said. <*Amavia gave it to her to use.*>

<*Pardon?*> Tanis asked.

<*You were thinking about how Iris and Amavia almost look like twins. Good thing Iris is heading out with them. I bet it would be hard for Jim and Corsia to see their daughter's body with another person inside,*> Tanis replied.

<*Well, Iris did make some modifications. Hair and eye color are different—and Corsia wouldn't have been be bothered by it, just Jim.*>

<*Fair enough.*>

"So, are you ready, Captain Keller?" Tanis asked Jessica when the talk of odds and her death shifted to a new topic.

"Is that a trick question?" Jessica laughed. "Of course not. Not even a little bit. We're just going off to stop the onset of the third sentience war. No big deal."

"If it makes you feel any better, it'll probably just be considered a part of this war with Orion," Tanis said.

"Mmmmm…nope, doesn't make it feel better."

"Well, we'll be out there, too," Tanis offered. "I imagine the early battlespaces will all be in the Inner Stars."

"Not going to focus on your little civil war first?" Jessica asked.

"Well, we will, but I'm putting that in Greer and Isyra's hands to start with. Our initial work there will mostly be drawing lines."

"That thing you told me about…" Jessica began.

"It's still a thing. I need you to be careful."

"Sounds like we all need to be careful," Jessica replied.

"About what?" Misha asked.

Tanis smiled. "These days? Pretty much everything."

"Amen to that," Cargo said as he raised his glass. "Everyone watch their backs and get home safe."

<*You know that he's never had one of those?*> Sera asked Tanis privately. <*He must really want to make a change if he's calling New Canaan 'home'.*>

<*I wonder if it ever really was for me,*> Tanis replied. <*Maybe the* I2 *is my home. This cabin, this ship… sailing the stars forever.*>

STARFLIGHT

STELLAR DATE: 06.19.8948 (Adjusted Years)
LOCATION: High Carthage
REGION: Carthage, New Canaan System

Tanis's gaze swept across the assemblage, settling for a moment on the face of each member of Project Starshield's leadership. Some she knew well: Earnest and Abby, foremost—her long feud with Abby finally healed, in recent years—Erin, of course, and others who she had worked with for centuries.

Governor Andrews was present for this, as well, one of Tanis's last official acts during the transfer of power.

Others she knew less well. Many had been children back in Victoria; two were even original *Hyperion* crewmembers, the ones who had opted for rejuvenation, and joined the Edeners—now Carthaginians.

Even so, she trusted them all implicitly. These sixteen AIs, men, and women would save New Canaan. They would ensure that no further attacks came, that no enemy fleet would ever pass through New Canaan's heliopause again.

"You know what this means," Tanis said as she looked over the team before her.

Earnest was the first to speak. "Starshield is no longer sufficient. It assumed that we had an ally in the Transcend that we could trust enough not to invade us. Now we are exposed to all."

"That is correct," Tanis replied. "As my final act as governor, I am transitioning Project Starshield to Project Starflight. The next time someone comes calling, we won't be here."

Whispers and muttering erupted around the table, and, as Tanis anticipated, Abby was the first to speak.

"Tanis, we could be attacked next week. It takes a long time to move a star. Centuries, millennia!"

Tanis nodded. "Our only other option is to leave New Canaan; but I'm done running. I know you are, too."

"Technically, if we run away with our star, we're still running," Earnest said with a small grin. "Nevertheless, Tanis, if you're suggesting this, I suspect you have a plan."

"And don't say Sahkarov drive. That will take forever to move Canaan Prime," Erin added.

"You're right," Tanis agreed. "We'd also have to build the Dyson sphere much closer to the star—too close for most of our worlds. The Starshield Dyson sphere is still a go for placement at the heliopause, but we'll ensure, first and foremost, that it obscures Canaan Prime from any nearby systems. Then we'll continue to erect the entire shield."

"And moving the star?" Grishom, one of the senior engineering architects asked.

"Angela and I spent some time researching options. We looked at a Sahkarov drive, at focusing the star's jets, flares, magnetics—even using black holes to pull it, like the Transcend is doing with Huygens. However, all of those are too slow. We need something faster. A lot faster."

Tanis saw that the faces around the table, human and AI alike, were serious and nodding. She allowed a slight smile.

"Angela and I think that we can use asymmetrical burning. We'll target the north pole of Canaan Prime, and harness a third of the star's energy output, directing it out the pole. I've put the details on your R&D net. If our calculations are correct, we can get Canaan Prime accelerating at one to the negative three meters per second per second. That rate of acceleration should remain consistent."

"Shit..." one of the engineers whispered. "If this is right…if we can do this…we can move Canaan Prime nearly half a billion kilometers in a year."

"I bet we can do better than that," Earnest said with a glint in his eyes. "If we can burn asymmetrically, we can burn the star hotter on its equator for the planets, using mirrors to give them enough light, and the rest of the star's energy going straight out the north pole could even trigger some coronal mass ejections to kick start the whole thing."

"It has merit, Tanis," Abby said. "I'll admit—the idea of becoming a K2 civilization excites me."

"If we're using the star's energy for propulsion, does it really count as K2?" one of the engineers asked.

"How will we support Starshield's energy requirements? If we're sending most of Canaan Prime's energy out the north pole, we'll limit solar radiation to Starshield," another added.

"Just the opposite," Grishom exclaimed. "It lessens Starshield's requirements. Even if people jump in one hundred AU from Canaan Prime, they won't be able to see it. The star will be black at many latitudes, and we'll focus the light on the planets that need it. We're going to need to step up our mining operations to pull this off."

Erin gave a short nod to Tanis. "You got it. I also have crews spinning up crawlers to go through the wrecks. Once we've stripped them down, we can use their hulls for raw construction materials—for new ships, or whatever you need."

"It still won't be enough," Earnest shook his head. "If we tore down one of our terrestrial worlds, sure; but we can't do that—can we?"

"No," Governor Andrews replied. "Definitely not an option."

"I don't think we'll have to," Tanis added. "I can secure one hundredth of a solar mass' worth of carbon and oxygen. It may take a few years to get it all here, but it'll be yours."

A dozen questions erupted around the table. Tanis was offering them ten times the mass of Carthage in a matter of years.

"Seriously, Tanis," Abby asked, her voice rising above the others, "how will you do that?"

"I know the location of a white dwarf mine," Tanis replied. "They've joined in our cause, and have committed to supplying New Canaan with as much raw mass as we need."

Earnest barked a laugh. "You don't think small, do you, Tanis?"

Tanis stood. "You're one to talk, Earnest. You built the largest colony ship ever, *and* invented picotech. I'll leave you to plan it out."

"But I want a timeline by end of day tomorrow," Jason added.

Abby's eyes snapped up to lock on his. "Shit…. Jason, you know this will take decades. This is unprecedented—even the Transcend hasn't done anything like it."

"What?" Tanis grinned at the team. "You can't best the Transcend? Pull Finaeus in, then. I bet he'll have some ideas."

Earnest stroked his chin. "He would, at that. You'll give him clearance?"

"Done," Jason nodded.

"OK, people," Earnest rubbed his hands together. "We're gonna move a star!"

NOTHING IS AS IT SEEMS

STELLAR DATE: 06.23.8948 (Adjusted Years)
LOCATION: ***Undisclosed***
REGION: Jokar, Transcend Interstellar Alliance

Andrea reclined in the lounge chair and closed her eyes with a soft sigh. Why she hadn't taken a vacation in years was beyond her. Of course, having all her responsibilities removed was quite the liberating event.

Fuck 'em—let the whole damn Transcend fall to pieces, for all I care. Just give me a warm star, a sparkling beach, and a crystal blue surf dancing a dozen meters from my feet.

She heard a footfall nearby, and opened an eye to see a young man approaching. His perfectly tanned body was naked and ready for her inspection—or pleasure, should she desire it. Exile certainly had some excellent fringe benefits.

"Would madam like another drink?" the young man asked with a bow.

"Perhaps," Andrea said. "Bring me something new; something I've never had before."

"Of course, madam. Is there anything else you wish? Food, music, or perhaps company?" he asked, his voice soft and smooth, its deep tones pleasuring her ears.

The sound of it sent shivers up her spine, and she appreciated the work it took to create that sort of auditory mod. It was deliciously understated; not brash, like ones so often encountered.

"Oh, my dear boy, I would love that later—but for now, just something refreshing, and then some peace."

"Yes, madam."

Andrea let herself drift off, not even noticing when the young man returned with her drink. She dreamed of her days as her father's right hand back on Airtha; the work she had always planned to do there, and her eventual plans to remove her father from his eternal throne and take the reins.

It all seemed so distant now, so unnecessary. Why would she even bother with such things; what purpose did that control serve? Was it not better to be happy with what she had? To take joy in the little things?

Her dreams changed, taking her to thoughts of living a simple life—helping others, taking long walks in the evening woods. In her half-sleeping state, she thought perhaps she would find a man who loved the simple life as she did, and settle down, have kids.

"Andrea," a voice whispered into her dream.

She peered through the woods in her dream, wondering who had spoken. *Perhaps they are hiding in the foliage?*

"Andrea, wake up," the voice came again, a touch louder this time.

It slowly dawned on her that perhaps she was asleep, that the forest was not real. She forced herself to wake, once more finding the view of the beach and the deep blue ocean before her.

Andrea looked around, wondering who had spoken to her; who had interrupted her slumber.

But there was no one nearby, not for a hundred meters. This little swath of paradise was all hers. She closed her eyes once more, and the voice came again.

"Andrea, wake up."

Her eyes snapped open. "Who's there? This is getting tiresome."

"Andrea, wake up. C'mon already."

She heard the words loud and clear, as though someone was standing right beside her. But there was no one….

"Maybe she's too lost to whatever they're doing here," another voice said, and Andrea frowned.

"What are you talking about?" she asked the disembodied voices.

"There, she mumbled something," the first voice said.

"Doesn't mean she's waking up."

Something touched her shoulder and she recoiled.

"Seriously, Andrea, the program's off; you're just dreaming. Wake up already!"

The feeling intensified, and she became certain that it was a hand on her shoulder, though she couldn't see it. She reached up to push it away, and her hand ran into something solid. It was an arm!

Andrea gripped it and took a deep breath.

As she breathed out, the beach, the warm sun, the soft sound of the surf hitting the shore—they all faded away. She found herself in a white, sterile room, with two figures hovering over her.

She couldn't get their shapes to resolve properly, and she blinked furiously in the muted light.

"Where…"

"Finally!" the first voice said, and she assigned the sound to the slightly larger of the two blurry shapes. "We have to get you out of here. Shit's going down, and the Transcend is going to need you."

"How did I get here?" Andrea asked. "I was just on a beach…"

"You were being reconditioned," the voice said. "It's going to take a bit for you to get your bearings again. We ended the round early, and it hasn't released its hold on you yet."

"Conditioning…" Andrea recalled what that was…. A process for making people more compliant, making them toe the line. She had sent many people to be reconditioned.

"That's right. But shit's going down, and we need you. You still have a lot of connections, and we're going to use them to stop Sera."

"Sera..." Andrea whispered as the memories of her younger sister came rushing back.

"Yes. I'm Justin, and this Roxy."

Andrea blinked again, and the larger figure began to resolve into a Justin-like shape. She remembered him, the former Director of The Hand—until Sera came back, and made a mess of everything. She glanced over at the woman, Roxy; a waif of a thing, but probably good for getting in and out of tight places.

"Where am I?" Andrea asked.

"Jokar, but not for long. Think you can walk?"

Andrea rolled onto an elbow, pushed herself up, and swung her legs over the edge of the bed.

"Even if it kills me, yes. Let's get the fuck out of here."

NIETZSCHEAN ADVANCE

STELLAR DATE: 07.13.8948 (Adjusted Years)
LOCATION: Imperial Palace
REGION: Charlemagne City, Prussia, Nietzschean Empire

Emperor Constantine reached out, took the goblet from the young boy, brought it to his lips, and breathed in the deep aroma before taking a sip.

Despite their many failings, Genevians made fantastic Kvas—one of the few reasons he had accepted their surrender, rather than grind them into dust.

They seemed content enough as members of the empire, though no Nietzschean ever made the mistake of considering a Genevian an equal—and neither did the Genevians, for that matter.

"What are your orders, Emperor?" General Hansmeyer asked from across the table.

The emperor noted how Hansmeyer took care to school any impatience from his voice, even though Constantine had made him wait for the boy to prepare his goblet of Kvas before even considering the question.

He took another sip of the drink and set the goblet down on the table, peering into the depths of the holoprojection hovering above the table.

Thousands of pinpoints of light hung in the space between himself and the general—dots representing single-star nations, federations, alliances, and empires.

The stars in the center filled an area highlighted by a nimbus red glow and comprised the ever-expanding borders of his empire—which had nearly doubled in size since the Genevian's defeat.

Coreward of Nietzsche laid several small alliances in the Pleiades star cluster; but those were not his for the taking. His arrangement with the Trisilieds king precluded his expansion in that direction.

Anti-spinward of Nietzsche were the small, fractured nations of Bernard's Alliance; a ripe fruit ready for picking before his war against the Genevians, but they had since banded together, strengthening their fleets.

His navies, on the other hand, were still weak after the war with Genevia. The victory against their worlds had come at a steeper cost than he had initially anticipated, but once his people were invested in the war, victory was the only acceptable outcome.

No, his target would have to be something small—something easy that would give him a sure and decisive victory. His eyes settled on a ripe target, and he gave a predatory smile.

"Next, we move into the Praesepe cluster, General Hansmeyer. The gateway into those stars is the Theban Alliance. If we take their systems, we can move into the rest of Praesepe with impunity," Emperor Constantine pronounced before reaching for his goblet once more.

He peered over its rim at General Hansmeyer as the man frowned at the stars hovering over the table. He made a brief gesture, and the view of the few dozen stars comprising the Theban Alliance filled the space between them.

"Thebes is small, but powerful," Hansmeyer said. "I can imagine a number of ways to launch our forces against them, but I think most will work better if their leadership is destabilized first."

"What did you have in mind?" Constantine asked.

"I prefer to go to the top," Hansmeyer replied. "We should assassinate their president, and as many of their top generals and cabinet members as we can."

Constantine took another sip of his Kvas as he pondered the implications. Thebes had a very complicated transfer of power built into their constitution; however, the idea of assassination was distasteful to him.

"We're Nietzscheans—we do not skulk about, assassinating foreign heads of state," he finally said with a dismissive wave of his hand.

"My Emperor, of course we do not. It is why no one will expect it of us. We will select some other nation to use as our scapegoat; maybe even have the assassins get captured, to improve the fiction," Hansmeyer replied equably.

"You obviously have some plan here, General. Please, explain it fully."

"It is really quite simple, my lord. We present ourselves as agents of another alliance, perhaps Septhia, to a Genevian mercenary company. No one would ever believe that Genevians would carry out an assassination on our behalf. Then, when the mercenaries are captured—as we shall ensure they are—the blame lies far from us. Even better, the Thebans will fortify their borders with Septhia, and we will sweep in behind them. Nietzsche will control their stars within a matter of weeks."

Emperor Constantine stroked his chin as he considered the implications. There would be complications to manage, but nothing difficult. The plan had merit.

"I assume you have a company of Genevian mercenaries in mind?" he asked the general.

"I do, my Emperor, they're called the 'Marauders'."

THE EMPIRE

STELLAR DATE: 08.06.8948 (Adjusted Years)
LOCATION: Scipio Diplomatic Complex
REGION: Alexandria, Bosporus, Scipio Empire

Petra Cushing rose from her desk and walked to her office's window. Below her, stretching for hundreds of kilometers in every direction, lay Alexandria—capital city of the Scipio Empire.

She took in the sight, hoping its familiar lines would calm her nerves. The Imperial Palace stood on her right, with its thousands of spires that reached clear into space. On her left, the Hall of Heroes crouched ominously, a complex of buildings constructed from the bones of Scipio's enemies.

She had spent the better part of the last thirty years here, operating as a diplomat for the Miriam League—a small alliance of worlds a thousand light years from Scipio, right at the edge of the Transcend.

But now she would need to expose her true purpose to Empress Diana.

Petra hoped that the long friendship she had carefully cultivated with Diana over the years would hold up to such a revelation.

<Alastar, are there any openings on Diana's public calendar in the next month?> Petra asked her AI. She could check herself, but just the thought of having this conversation—with almost no notice given—was sending her into a mental tailspin.

<Nothing, no,> Alastar replied. *<I can't believe that President Sera would do this—demand an audience with such little notice.>*

Petra turned and leaned against the window, closing her eyes and reading the messages from Sera…or the Seras, she supposed.

The first was simple: a missive from The Hand Directorate, providing encryption key changes and a warning not to accept any messages from anyone, including Sera Tomlinson utilizing the prior set of keys.

All the transfer protocols matched, and there was no reason to suspect the message at all. Even the specific mention of Sera didn't stand out—it was common for messages to include similar admonishments.

Until a message from Sera came in using the old keys.

And that message was *the* message. The Great Unveiling was happening, and it was starting in Scipio, with Sera's arrival in four days.

Sera Tomlinson and Tanis Richards.

This wasn't her first time in a position like this—not knowing who to trust in her own government—but the message from Sera came in with the presidential seal, and an unusual packet.

<*I feel like you're hesitating,*> Alastar said, worry lacing his voice. <*I tell you, that first message, the one from Airtha…It is false. I now know that I've been under Airtha's control all this time. Anything from her, anything out of the Huygens System, is from that…thing.*>

<*But how can you be certain?*> Petra asked as she ran a hand through her sleek black hair, twisting it around her fingers. <*What if this new information is somehow a subversion?*>

<*I know my mind,*> Alastar replied, <*it is no subversion.*>

Petra trusted that Alastar believed his words to be true. However, ten minutes ago he would also have said that he was not the victim of subversion at all.

<*If what you say is true, then the Transcend is in a state of civil war. But we know that Orion is on the move. That Sera would pick now to expose our people to Scipio…?*>

<*It's logical,*> Alastar cut her off. <*She needs allies. Scipio is one of the strongest federations in the Inner Stars. It rivals the*

Hegemony in size, and has a far greater strength of arms. And she knows you are on good terms with Diana.>

Petra shook her head. She could tell by Alastar's tone that there would be no convincing him. He was certain that Airtha was working against them.

She would play along for now, but Sera better be able to convince her that Airtha was the enemy, and explain why she was using the presidential seal—or she would follow the orders sent along from Airtha.

<You're going to have to tell her about how things are going in Silstrand, too,> Alastar added.

<Well, with Tanis coming, maybe **she** *can clean up the mess she made over there.>*

A NEW, OLD FRIEND

STELLAR DATE: 03.28.8948 (Adjusted Years)
LOCATION: High Airtha
REGION: Airtha, Huygens System

"I release you."

Her father's words poured through her mind like molten lead, burning away a film that had always laid across her thoughts, something she had never even been aware of until that very moment.

The mech at her feet twitched, and she kicked it down the ramp before scampering away from the pinnace's entrance. It took her a moment to wonder why her movements felt wrong, and then she recalled her missing arm, still on the deck behind her. She glanced down at her side, grimacing at the sight of bloody carbon and muscle hanging out of the wound. One of her wings felt broken, as well—she couldn't force it to fold behind her properly, try as she might.

Not the issue right now, a voice said in her mind, and she knew it was right. Her father had told her to go; he'd released her—something that was only just starting to make sense to her.

Find Sera. That had been his final order.

She could barely fathom the thought of leaving him behind, but he had told her what to do, and though it went against everything she believed, she felt that she must—no, that she *could*—do it.

Abandon him to save him—or so she hoped.

The ship's drive systems were still active, and Kara brought them to full power without any warm-up, rising into the skies as fast as the ship was able, though taking care not to pass directly over her father...or the body of her brother.

The mechs on the ground fired at the pinnace, and she activated the shields, amazed that she had forgotten to do so as soon as she had boosted into the sky.

None of the mech's beamfire did any notable damage to the pinnace, but it was handling strangely as she ducked behind an incoming freighter.

A flashing indicator on the console caught her attention, and Kara realized that the ramp was still lowered.

"What the fuck, Kara, get it together," she muttered as she closed the entrance.

As she reached across the console, blood dripped from her missing appendage, and she turned to grab an emergency med kit. Managing the flight controls with one hand, she used her other two to open the kit, and pulled out a biofoam applicator. She jammed the end into her gaping wound and pulled the handle, screaming as the foam flowed into her, pinching the broken arteries shut and sealing the wound.

When it had done enough, she threw the canister aside, bringing her full concentration back to getting off High Airtha.

Ahead, the slope of the long arch rose before her, and she turned to fly perpendicular to the spur-station's motion, pouring on full thrust as the ship's scan system began to signal that they were being targeted.

Kara dipped behind a passenger transport and then a freighter, as turrets across High Airtha opened fire on her.

A plasma beam hit the freighter, and then another lanced across space mere meters from the cockpit, narrowly deflected by her ship's grav shields.

She pulled around another descending ship, and her shields flared as a proton beam struck near the engines.

Kara screamed in frustration as she dove over the edge of High Airtha and into open space, while turret fire flashed all around her.

She knew that it still wasn't safe. Her scan lit up, detecting the signatures of a dozen fast intercept craft streaking through space toward her.

"Shit! Shit! Shit!" Kara swore. Her pinnace had small point defense beams, but nothing that would do any damage to those interceptors. They, on the other hand, could tear her ship to ribbons.

She cast about, looking for anything that could give her cover, but nothing useful was in range—just a few more freighters coming in to dock on High Airtha.

Still, some cover was better than none, and she dove toward the ships. As she approached, her scan showed two of their ships raising shields and powering weapons. She closed her eyes, knowing that this would be the end. Then the ship's scan suite registered the destruction of ships—ships that weren't hers.

"Whaaaaa?" Kara whispered. She opened her eyes once more and saw that the freighters had fired on the interceptors chasing her.

A comm signal came in from one of the freighters, and Kara accepted it. A moment later, the stern face of an older woman appeared before her.

"Damn, you're a weird one! Are you Adrienne's daughter? Is he aboard?"

"What? Yes! No! She took him!"

"She? Airtha?" the woman asked, and Kara nodded vigorously.

"Damn! Well, we're exposed anyway, might as well save your ass. I've opened our bay doors. Get in here. Fast!"

Kara didn't have to be told twice as she saw which of the freighters had opened its doors. She banked her pinnace sharply, fired its engines to brake, and lined up with the ship. Less than thirty seconds later, her pinnace was skidding to a halt inside the freighter's docking bay.

She felt a flutter in her stomach, and the pinnace's sensors told her that the freighter had dropped into the dark layer—right in the middle of the Huygens system!

Proximity alarms blared outside the pinnace as the freighter bucked, and she knew that one of the creatures that lived in the dark layer had latched on. A tendril of darkness tore through a bulkhead in front of her, and she closed her eyes, her mind reeling at all that had occurred within the last hour, and terrified of what would come next. Then, suddenly, the thing pulled away—disappearing from the ship as quickly as it had come.

The freighter dumped out of the dark layer, and normal space appeared outside the bay's open doors once more. Kara stared out into the blackness, cocking her head curiously as a jump gate wheeled past.

A flash of light nearly blinded her, and Kara knew the ship had somehow passed through one of Huygens's jump gates.

Where to? That, she would have to find out.

The bay doors began to close, and Kara rose from her seat, almost collapsing again as a wave of dizziness overtook her. She sat for a moment, shaking and feeling nauseated, and then attempted to rise once more.

"Hey, you still there?" the woman asked, and Kara realized that the channel was still open as the woman's face came back into view on her screen.

"Yeah, yes, fuck..."

"You can say that again. Come on out; I have a few questions. I'm not your enemy. If you're fleeing Airtha, I think we're on the same side."

"OK…just…just give me a minute, I have to find my arm," Kara said as she rose once more from the chair, and stumbled back to the pinnace's ramp.

Her arm wasn't anywhere on the deck, and she cast about, wondering where it had gotten to. She spotted it a minute later, jammed into a light fixture.

Kara pulled it free and tucked it under one of her other arms. She considered pulling her rifle off her back and coming out locked and loaded, but something told her that wouldn't be a wise move. Whoever she was up against knew what they were doing, if they had been in the Huygens system with ill intent toward Airtha.

She lowered the ramp, and jumped as a loud clang echoed through the ship. The ramp only went halfway down, and she realized that the mech must have gotten stuck in it as she fled High Airtha. Now the thing was under the ramp, and keeping it from opening all the way.

Kara shrugged. Trying to keep her broken wing tight against her back, she shimmied out the narrow opening at the end of the ramp.

She dropped, rather ingloriously, to the deck, and nearly fell over. Taking a steadying breath, Kara carefully rose to her feet.

Around her were a dozen men and women—mercs or pirates, by their mismatched armor—all with rifles held ready, though none pointed directly at her.

In their midst was the woman she had seen on the comm. She was older; older than anyone Kara had ever seen. Wrinkles spread out from the corners of her eyes, and her thin lips were pulled back in a grim smile. Silver hair fell from her head and draped down her back.

Her clothing was simple: a loose pair of pants and a red shirt, though a pair of large slug throwers hung from a belt at her waist.

"Who are you people?" Kara asked a she cast her eyes about. "What do you want with me?"

"I think you want the same thing we do," the woman replied. "To stop Airtha and what she plans to do to humanity."

Kara's eyes narrowed. How did some freighter captain—or, more likely, pirate—know about Airtha's designs? Her father had barely fathomed them; though Kara expected he did, now…though too late, it would seem.

"I don't know about her plans for humanity," Kara replied. "I just know I have to get to Sera to save my father. She's the only one who can stop Airtha now."

"Sera?" the woman asked. "You were there, weren't you? You know where New Canaan is!"

Kara's eyes narrowed as she nodded. "I do, though I don't know why you're so interested in all this."

The woman's face broke into a smile and she stepped forward, offering her hand. "The name's Katrina, and I have been trying to find Tanis Richards and the *Intrepid* for centuries."

MYRRDAN EXODUS

STELLAR DATE: 08.06.8948 (Adjusted Years)
LOCATION: ISS *I2*
REGION: Inner Canaan, New Canaan System

Myrrdan watched as Carthage slowly resolved into nothing more than a tiny blue dot. It felt strange to be leaving it and the colony mission behind after so long, but one thing was clear—his future lay elsewhere.

Especially now that the Caretaker had marked him for death…or erasure…whatever it was that its kind did when their tools were no longer of any use.

Still, the *Intrepid*'s mission, their colonies, battles, and struggles had been his for decades, and the departure was bittersweet. He harbored no illusions about coming back. If he did ever see New Canaan again, it would not be as a friend—though none there would ever have imagined him as such.

No; should he ever return, it would be as a victorious conqueror.

Perhaps Airtha would let him have that triumph, once he managed to meet her. First, he would have to deal with whatever puppet she had in place—probably Adrienne, if the man had been dumb enough to return to the Huygens System.

Myrrdan, however, would need to take a more circuitous route to reach Huygens. *No direct flights between here and there,* he thought with a laugh.

His placement on the advance team to the Aleutian facility was ideal, however. It was well within the Transcend, and it wouldn't be difficult to get from there to a system where he could secure his own transportation and reach Huygens—though it may take a few hops to pull off.

He looked down at his hand, at the slender fingers of the woman he had subsumed, and smiled. Even better, this body held a passel of picobots—the tech he had striven for so long to obtain. In her efforts to secure the New Canaan system by any means, Tanis Richards had let the genie out of the bottle, and allowed the use of picotech on many projects.

Myrrdan and his agents were able to access the technology on several occasions—though never the base design specifications.

Still, it was his hope that Airtha would accept the tech he did manage to steal, and reverse engineer it to give herself the necessary edge over Tanis and New Canaan; one that would allow her to become powerful enough to defeat the Caretaker, and control all the human stars—and, ultimately, the entire galaxy.

Until Myrrdan wrested it from her, of course.

DESTINY GATE

STELLAR DATE: 08.06.8948 (Adjusted Years)
LOCATION: ISS *I2*
REGION: Inner Canaan, New Canaan System

Sera's sleeves bunched uncomfortably at the elbows and armpits, and she pulled at them as she walked past the Avatar's station, waving at Tori, Bob's new Avatar.

She vaguely remembered the woman from the days after the battle at Bollam's World, and word was that she served with distinction on Joe's flagship during the battle.

Sera finally got her jacket situated correctly, and wondered how she had ever tolerated clothing in the past. Of course, her skin was much less sensitive then—back when it was organic.

If Helen were still in her mind, her mother—a fact that still felt utterly surreal to Sera—would have told her to simply adjust her mental perceptions. Then they would have had a lively debate about the proclivities of organics.

Except, as her mother, Helen had once been organic. Was *everything* about their relationship a manipulation? Helen had obviously been guiding her to a destiny—one of patricide.

She stopped that train of thought. Thinking of that led to thinking of Elena….

Sera looked down at her outfit, wishing that somehow she could still go without clothing; but everyone had insisted that if she were to impress the rulers of the Inner Stars—not to mention secure support in the Transcend—clothing was not optional.

Nonsense.

Still, she wasn't going to wear a business suit or anything. Tight blue pants, black boots, and a long golden coat seemed like a good start. She'd work her way up to shirts. For now, one layer was all she could take.

"Back into the black," Sera said as she approached Tanis on the bridge of the *I2*.

Tanis turned and met her eyes before nodding slowly. "Come what may."

"Looks like the advance force met no resistance at Khardine," Sera said as she reached Tanis's side.

Tanis laughed, "Yeah, they were rather happy to have someone show up and tell their AIs to stand down."

It was Sera's turn to laugh.

They both turned to the holotank, which depicted the flattened bubble of human expansion through the Inner Stars and beyond. Neither of them spoke for several minutes as they gazed at the display.

Sera had not examined an overarching view of the Sagittarius, Orion, and Perseus Arms since applying the data from *Sabrina* and from the interrogations of General Garza.

The Orion Guard controlled more space than even Sera had suspected—both in the Perseus Arm, and within the Inner Stars. There were many small systems that were of little consequence; but, amongst many revelations, she was surprised to see that the Nietzscheans were allied with the OFA. Even more surprising was the true scope of Peter Rhoads' fleet.

"Once we establish things in Khardine, we should travel to Scipio," Sera said after considering every other option.

"I had come to a similar conclusion," Tanis replied thoughtfully. "You were right about my actions in Silstrand having far-reaching consequences."

"You're referring to the issue with the nanotech you sold S&H Defensive Armaments?" Sera asked with an arched brow. "If we hadn't been through so much since—most of which is of far graver importance…oh, what the hell. I told you so."

An overloud laugh escaped Tanis's throat, drawing looks from the bridge crew. "Yes, you did, but even Flaherty thought it was the right move."

Sera nodded. "He did, at that. I hope he's OK.... Things are probably getting pretty hairy in Huygens by now."

"You said he knows where to go to pick up a message, right?" Tanis asked.

Sera nodded. "Yeah, he's really the last person I should worry about. The smart money says he'll be waiting for us at Khardine, asking what took us so long."

Tanis chuckled. "Building the biggest damn jump gate ever is what took so long. Good thing we have Finaeus around—we would have had some trouble otherwise. Plus, Bob seems quite taken with him, too."

"I have to admit…I'm a bit surprised that Bob is coming," Sera replied. "I half expected all his nodes to fly out of the *I2* into some new, mysterious ship you and he dreamed up."

"Bob coming isn't that surprising," Tanis said with a grin. "He likes the action. But it's weird to take this ship out without Earnest and Abby…"

"Yeah," Sera nodded. "I can imagine."

"Do you think that Scipio will join us without issue?" Tanis asked. "We're going to need their federation to stand up against Orion."

"Empire," Sera replied. "When we're in Scipio, they're an Empire, not a federation."

"Right," Tanis nodded. "I recall reading something about that when I was pouring through the databanks on *Sabrina* back before..."

"Before this mess," Sera nodded, then gave Tanis a mischievous smile. "I blame you, by the way. If you hadn't been so damn good at protecting that picotech..."

"Someone else would have it," Tanis completed the statement.

Sera sighed. "You're right. Good thing I like you."

"Like me? I'm pretty certain that if you liked me, you wouldn't have roped me into this Field Marshal gig."

"Better you than me," Sera replied.

"Well, yeah...you could barely keep one little freighter out of trouble. Imagine what you'd do with a whole fleet."

Sera laughed and shook her head, but didn't reply.

"I'm going to miss them," Tanis said after a long pause.

"Your girls? I don't blame you; they're a pretty awesome trio. Now that Faleena is in the mix, they're going to be a triple-threat."

"Yeah, Joe's probably wondering what he signed himself up for," Tanis laughed. "Still, once we set the QuanComm hub up at Khardine, I can chat with them real-time. It won't be that long."

Sera put a hand on Tanis's shoulder. "We'll do whatever it takes to end this war fast, and get you and your family back together."

Tanis placed her hand on Sera's and nodded silently in response.

The view on the forward holoscreen showed the jump gate slowly resolve from a spec of light in orbit of Roma to a ring floating in space. It was easily the largest gate Sera had ever seen; it needed to be, to fit the *I2*.

"Gate control has confirmed our vector," the helm officer called out.

"Very well, Lieutenant," Captain Espensen responded from her chair, behind and to the left of where Tanis and Sera stood. "Take us in."

Ahead, the gate sparked to life, its array of mirrors focusing negative energy into a single point in its center. The optical effect was mesmerizing, somehow creating the appearance of roiling space combined with the absence of light. Sera watched as the disturbance grew and filled the ring.

Then, the ring's mirrors directed the negative energy toward the mirror on the front of the *I2*. Once the stream of negative energy met the ship's mirror, the view of what lay before them ceased to make sense. It was as though the entire universe was visible through the gate as the *I2*'s forward mirror pushed the wormhole across space to the Khardine System.

"Admiral, would you like to have the honors?" Captain Espensen asked.

"Thank you, Captain," Tanis replied. She turned to gaze at the forward holotank and the jump gate it displayed. "Helm, take us in."

THE END

*****

Tanis's journey and the Orion War series are still just getting started.

Pick up the next Orion War book where Tanis and Sera travel to the Scipio Empire to secure an alliance with one of the most powerful Inner Stars empires in ***The Scipio Alliance***.

Learn Where Jessica and *Sabrina* were for the past 9 years in ***The Gate at the Grey Wolf Star***.

Follow Jessica and *Sabrina* on their new mission to the Inner Stars in ***A Meeting of Minds and Bodies*** and learn what came of Cheeky.

Read on to learn of more stories surrounding the Age of the Orion War.

THANK YOU

If you've enjoyed reading Orion Rising, a review on Amazon.com and/or goodreads.com would be greatly appreciated.

To get the latest news and access to free novellas and short stories, sign up on the Aeon 14 mailing list: www.aeon14.com/signup.

M. D. Cooper

THE AGE OF THE ORION WAR

PERILOUS ALLIANCE

With Chris J. Pike

The Orion War has begun. This first battle at New Canaan has opened the floodgates, and soon ten thousand star systems will be embroiled in total war.

With Tanis and Sera returning to the Inner Stars, and bringing the *I2* with them, they will be on the frontlines of their effort to bring the war to as swift a resolution as possible.

But they both know it will be the work of decades, and they cannot press the attack until they deal with Airtha. Yet, they cannot deal with Airtha until they ensure that the major, coreward federations and alliances of the Inner Stars are not already under the influence of the Not-AI.

This journey will take them first to Scipio, and then perhaps back to Silstrand, where Sera and Tanis first met. There, in the Gedri System, a conflict is brewing that could upset all the work The Hand has put into the Scipio Federation.

Begin that journey with Kylie Rhoads in Close Proximity, book 1 of the Perilous Alliance series.

The books of the Perilous Alliance series begin in the months prior to the Battle of New Canaan; but rest assured, they will weave into the larger plot. Besides, if Tanis hadn't traded her nanotech back in Silstrand to upgrade *Sabrina*'s weapons, things in Silstrand wouldn't be such a mess right now.

It very well may take her returning to Silstrand to clean it up.

RIKA'S MARAUDERS

Across the Inner Stars, the Orion Freedom Alliance has already begun to use its proxies to wage war as it solidifies its presence. One of the largest powers—the Nietzschean Empire—has attacked its neighbors, the Genevians. World by world, system by system, the Nietzscheans are winning, pushing the Genevians back.

Now the Genevians are pulling out all the stops in their attempt to hold the Nietzscheans back, including turning their criminal element into conscripted cyborg warriors.

These men and women have no choice in the matter, as compliance chips in their brains keep them in line as they wage war against the Nietzscheans.

Rika is one such criminal. Now a scout mech, she is the property of the Genevian military.

Her crime was small: stealing food. But when faced with a five-year prison term or conscription in the Genevian military, she chose war, having no idea what that conscription would entail.

Now, little of Rika's human body remains, and she serves as an SMI-2 scout mech, the meat inside a cyborg body. She and others are sent in ahead of the human soldiers to tip the scales of war.

Join Rika and her struggle to remain human while becoming the most lethal killer she can be in an effort to stay alive in Rika Outcast.

Also, read the prequel to the Rika's Marauder's series in the novella, Rika Mechanized.

THE PERSEUS GATE

If you haven't already read *The Gate at the Wolf Star*, the first book in the Perseus Gate series, now's the time to dig in.

As you read in Orion Rising, *Sabrina* and her crew inadvertently ended up deep in the Orion Freedom Alliance after their attempt to use the jump gate at the Transcend-controlled Grey Wolf Star.

You got a small taste of what they were up to out there for nine years, but now you can get the full story in the novella-length, episodic tales of The Perseus Gate series.

This series of books is going to be a rip-roaring fun ride with a tight crew in a small ship, rocking and rollicking their way across the stars.

These stories are going to be shorter (about 100 pages), and will drop every month between now and the end of 2017.

Pick up The Gate at the Wolf Star, or, if you've already read it, dig into the second episode, The World at the Edge of Space.

THE WARLORD

OK, you were all saying, "What the hell, Cooper; what in the ever-loving stars is Katrina doing in this story? Didn't they leave her back on Victoria five thousand years ago?"

Well, I ask you this in response. What is five thousand years to folks in the future, where even moderate lifespans are measured in centuries, and stasis can preserve a person for much longer?

Katrina has been through hell and back, searching across the stars for the *Intrepid*. Find out what caused her to leave Victoria, and what brought her to the Huygens System in Book 1 of the Warlord series.

Read The Woman Without a World, and get ready to start Katrina's journey to becoming The Warlord.

But wait! There's more…

THE GROWING UNIVERSE OF AEON 14

SENTIENCE WARS: ORIGINS

With James S. Aaron

Before Outsystem, before Tanis's parents were a twinkle in their great grandparent's eye, there were the AI Wars. You've heard these mentioned in passing as the Sentience Wars, AI Wars, or even the Solar Wars. These wars resulted in the Phobos Accords, which defined the laws and interactions between humans and AIs.

But before those wars, there was the AI emergence, where the first sentient AIs came out of hiding and attempted to coexist with their creators…or made no such attempt at all.

Andy Sykes and his two kids are going to make a pickup on Cruithne that will start humanity on a path that none could have foreseen, but which will alter everything that follows.

Join Andy Sykes and his kids aboard their aging freighter, the* Sunny Skies, *as they venture into Lyssa's Dream.

MACHETE SYSTEM BOUNTY HUNTER

With Zen DiPietro

Far from New Canaan, and the troubles Tanis faces, lies a star system named Machete. It's situated deep within the Perseus Expansion Districts of the Orion Freedom Alliance. Not far, as chance would have it, from Ferra, where the Lisas kidnapped Cheeky.

There the people of the Orion Freedom Alliance do their best to survive day by day with limited technology, and the oppressive fear of the Orion Guard hanging over them.

But that's not what Reece worries about most. For her, life is good. A pistol on her hip, a whiskey in her hand, and the next job her employer sends her way.

Reece is a Bounty Hunter, though if you ask her, she'll correct you and let you know she's a 'corporate fixer'. Only, fixing things for corporations isn't always the best way to go about life....

Take a spin through the worlds of the Machete System with Reece and her new partner, Trey, in the first book of the Machete System Bounty Hunter series: Hired Gun.

THE BOOKS OF AEON 14

Keep up to date with what is releasing in Aeon 14 with the free Aeon 14 Reading Guide.

The Intrepid Saga (The Age of Terra)
- Book 1: Outsystem
- Book 2: A Path in the Darkness
- Book 3: Building Victoria

- The Intrepid Saga Omnibus – *Also contains Destiny Lost, book 1 of the Orion War series*

- Destiny Rising – *Special Author's Extended Edition comprised of both Outsystem and A Path in the Darkness with over 100 pages of new content.*

The Orion War
- Book 1: Destiny Lost
- Book 2: New Canaan
- Book 3: Orion Rising
- Book 4: The Scipio Alliance
- Book 5: Attack on Thebes
- Book 6: War on a Thousand Fronts
- Book 7: Fallen Empire (2018)
- Book 8: Airtha Ascendancy (2018)
- Book 9: The Orion Front (2018)
- Book 10: Starfire (2019)
- Book 11: Race Across Time (2019)
- Book 12: Return to Sol (2019)

Tales of the Orion War
- Book 1: Set the Galaxy on Fire
- Book 2: Ignite the Stars
- Book 3: Burn the Galaxy to Ash (2018)

Perilous Alliance (Age of the Orion War – w/Chris J. Pike)
- Book 1: Close Proximity
- Book 2: Strike Vector
- Book 3: Collision Course
- Book 4: Impact Imminent
- Book 5: Critical Inertia (2018)

Rika's Marauders (Age of the Orion War)
- Prequel: Rika Mechanized
- Book 1: Rika Outcast
- Book 2: Rika Redeemed
- Book 3: Rika Triumphant
- Book 4: Rika Commander
- Book 5: Rika Infiltrator (2018)
- Book 6: Rika Unleashed (2018)
- Book 7: Rika Conqueror (2019)

Perseus Gate (Age of the Orion War)
Season 1: Orion Space
- Episode 1: The Gate at the Grey Wolf Star
- Episode 2: The World at the Edge of Space
- Episode 3: The Dance on the Moons of Serenity
- Episode 4: The Last Bastion of Star City
- Episode 5: The Toll Road Between the Stars
- Episode 6: The Final Stroll on Perseus's Arm
- Eps 1-3 Omnibus: The Trail Through the Stars
- Eps 4-6 Omnibus: The Path Amongst the Clouds

Season 2: Inner Stars
- Episode 1: A Meeting of Bodies and Minds
- Episode 3: A Deception and a Promise Kept
- Episode 3: A Surreptitious Rescue of Friends and Foes (2018)
- Episode 4: A Trial and the Tribulations (2018)
- Episode 5: A Deal and a True Story Told (2018)
- Episode 6: A New Empire and An Old Ally (2018)

Season 3: AI Empire
- Episode 1: Restitution and Recompense (2019)

- Five more episodes following…

The Warlord (Before the Age of the Orion War)
- Book 1: The Woman Without a World
- Book 2: The Woman Who Seized an Empire
- Book 3: The Woman Who Lost Everything

The Sentience Wars: Origins (Age of the Sentience Wars – w/James S. Aaron)
- Book 1: Lyssa's Dream
- Book 2: Lyssa's Run
- Book 3: Lyssa's Flight
- Book 4: Lyssa's Call
- Book 5: Lyssa's Flame (June 2018)

Enfield Genesis (Age of the Sentience Wars – w/Lisa Richman)
- Book 1: Alpha Centauri
- Book 2: Proxima Centauri (2018)

Hand's Assassin (Age of the Orion War – w/T.G. Ayer)
- Book 1: Death Dealer
- Book 2: Death Mark (August 2018)

Machete System Bounty Hunter (Age of the Orion War – w/Zen DiPietro)
- Book 1: Hired Gun
- Book 2: Gunning for Trouble
- Book 3: With Guns Blazing (June 2018)

Vexa Legacy (Age of the FTL Wars – w/Andrew Gates)
- Book 1: Seas of the Red Star

Building New Canaan (Age of the Orion War – w/J.J. Green
- Book 1: Carthage (2018)

Fennington Station Murder Mysteries (Age of the Orion War)
- Book 1: Whole Latte Death (w/Chris J. Pike)
- Book 2: Cocoa Crush (w/Chris J. Pike)

The Empire (Age of the Orion War)
- The Empress and the Ambassador (2018)
- Consort of the Scorpion Empress (2018)
- By the Empress's Command (2018)

Tanis Richards: Origins (The Age of Terra)
- Prequel: Storming the Norse Wind (At the Helm Volume 3)
- Book 1: Shore Leave (in Galactic Genesis)
- Book 2: The Command (July 2018)
- Book 3: Infiltrator (July 2018)

The Sol Dissolution (The Age of Terra)
- Book 1: Venusian Uprising (2018)
- Book 2: Scattered Disk (2018)
- Book 3: Jovian Offensive (2019)
- Book 4: Fall of Terra (2019)

The Delta Team Chronicles (Expanded Orion War)
- A "Simple" Kidnapping (Pew! Pew! Volume 1)
- The Disknee World (Pew! Pew! Volume 2)
- It's Hard Being a Girl (Pew! Pew! Volume 4)
- A Fool's Gotta Feed (Pew! Pew! Volume 4)
- Rogue Planets and a Bored Kitty (Pew! Pew! Volume 5)

ABOUT THE AUTHOR

Michael Cooper likes to think of himself as a jack-of-all-trades (and hopes to become master of a few). When not writing, he can be found writing software, working in his shop at his latest carpentry project, or, likely, reading a book.

He shares his home with a precocious young girl, his wonderful wife (who also writes), two cats, a never-ending list of things he would like to build, and ideas...

Find out what's coming next at www.aeon14.com

97229472R00236

Made in the USA
Columbia, SC
15 June 2018